INTO THE WHIRLWIND

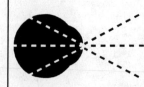

This Large Print Book carries the
Seal of Approval of N.A.V.H.

A BOSS, INC. NOVEL

INTO THE WHIRLWIND

KAT MARTIN

THORNDIKE PRESS
A part of Gale, Cengage Learning

GALE
CENGAGE Learning

...ngton H... Mich... ...Franc...o • N...... • ...ille, Maine
Merid..., Conn • M...n, O...o • ...ic...o

GALE
CENGAGE Learning®

Copyright © 2016 by Kat Martin.
A BOSS, Inc. Novel.
Thorndike Press, a part of Gale, Cengage Learning.

LIBRARY OF CONGRESS CATALOGING-IN-PUBLICATION DATA

Names: Martin, Kat, author.
Title: Into the whirlwind / by Kat Martin.
Description: Large print edition. | Waterville, Maine : Thorndike Press, 2016. |
  Series: Thorndike Press large print core | Series: A Boss, Inc. novel
Identifiers: LCCN 2016015580| ISBN 9781410491244 (hardcover) | ISBN 1410491242
  (hardcover)
Subjects: LCSH: Kidnapping—Fiction. | Missing children—Investigation—Fiction. |
  Large type books. | GSAFD: Romantic suspense fiction.
Classification: LCC PS3563.A7246 I584 2016 | DDC 813/.54—dc23
LC record available at https://lccn.loc.gov/2016015580

Published in 2016 by arrangement with Zebra Books, an imprint of
Kensington Publishing Corp.

Printed in Mexico
1 2 3 4 5 6 7 20 19 18 17 16

INTO THE WHIRLWIND

CHAPTER ONE

"Ms. Megan, thank God you're home! It's . . . it's Charlie. I can't find little Charlie."

Meg's heart took a leap as she stepped into the house, nearly colliding with her housekeeper, Rose Wills.

"He probably woke up and wandered off somewhere. He has to be here someplace." But even as she said the words, worry jolted through her. Telling herself not to panic, Meg hurried toward the stairs.

"I put him down for a nap an hour ago," Rose said, hurrying along behind her. "When I went back to check on him, he was gone."

"You know how he likes to hide. He's just found a new place." But fear had her pulse kicking up, and her stomach started to churn. At the top of the landing, she turned and ran down the hall to her three-year-old's bedroom, the housekeeper close behind her.

Charlie wasn't in his small, white youth bed. "Charlie! Mama's home. Charlie! Where are you, sweetheart?" Meg ran to the closet and pulled open the door, searched through the stuffed toys and games on the closet floor, but found no sign of her son.

Her heart was hammering now, her stomach balled into a fist. Meg told herself to stay calm. There were dozens of places a little boy could hide in a two-story house.

"Charlie! Charlie, where are you, sweetie?"

Rose's higher-pitched, worried voice chimed in. "Charlie! Come out now. Your mommy wants you."

They searched upstairs, but he was nowhere to be seen, went downstairs and searched the floor below.

"God, Rose, where could he be? You don't think he went outside?"

"I always keep the doors locked and the chain on. There's no way he could have gotten out."

They checked all the doors, but Rose was right. No way could her little boy have gotten out of the house.

Meg ran back upstairs. She returned to his room, walked over to the bed to see if the covers still held a trace of warmth. Reaching down, she touched the soft blue blanket with the sailboats on it, but none of Charlie's heat remained.

Instead, she spotted an envelope protruding from the folds, her name in ink on the front.

"What did you find?" Rose came up beside her.

"It's a letter." Her hands shook as she tore the envelope open.

"I didn't see it before," Rose said. "Oh, dear Lord." She started to tremble, her breasts heaving as the implication sank in. She was a big woman, nearly as tall as Meg's five-foot ten-inch frame. "What . . . what does it say?"

Meg read the note and her heart clutched, then turned to stone. " 'We have your son. He'll cost you ten million in cash. You've got three days or he's . . . he's dead. No police.' "

Meg swayed on her feet. She gripped the headboard, afraid she might faint. *Dear God, my baby!* She turned, let Rose pull her into a hug, and her eyes welled with tears. They clung to each other, both of them crying.

The housekeeper straightened away. "We have to call the police. They'll know what to do. They'll get Charlie back."

Meg shook her head. "No police. If we call them, they'll kill him."

Rose crossed herself. "What are you going to do, Ms. Meg?"

Meg closed her eyes and prayed for strength. Her dad was extremely wealthy. He loved his grandson. Her father could get the ten million dollars they needed to pay the ransom.

But her dad was also extremely controlling. And he believed money was the solution to everything. What if the kidnappers took the money and still killed her baby?

She thought of Charlie's father, Jonathan Hollander, the man she had married to please her dad. Yes, he was handsome. She couldn't deny she'd been attracted to his dark good looks and charming smile. Her father hadn't been able to see past Jonathan's impressive Harvard education and his family's lofty position in society.

Meg thought what a no-good, lying cheat he had turned out to be.

She couldn't go to Jonathan.

Another man's image came to mind. Smart. Loyal to a fault. Strong. Tough. Reliable. The one man she would trust with her precious son's life.

"I know someone." Strength seeped through her as determination set in. "I know a man who can bring Charlie home."

■ ■ ■ ■

Megan O'Brien parked at the end of the gravel driveway and quietly got out of her white BMW compact SUV. Through the trees, she could hear the roar of a chain saw, hear hammers banging away, see two-by-fours going up to form the sides of the house under construction.

The garage was already finished, undoubtedly full of Dirk's toys, including a Harley and a custom Dodge Viper. In the summer, he kept a boat docked on the lake below the house.

Though two other men were hard at work, her gaze went straight to Dirk. Hammer in hand, carpenter's belt dangling low on his waist, he was shirtless, though the January air was chill.

Hard muscle flexed across his back and shoulders as he pounded in a nail with an ease that said how many times he had done it. Long, sinewy muscles outlined by the soft fabric of his jeans stretched and moved as he worked on his house.

Meg's gaze went over the familiar dragon tattoo that wound over one shoulder and inched up the side of his neck. The colored ink seemed right with the sexy, short-cropped horseshoe mustache that framed his mouth and curved down to his jaw, making him look like the hard, tough man he was.

Even her terrible fear for her son couldn't block the memories of how it had felt to lie with him. Couldn't lessen the yearning that burned through her body just at the sight of him.

Meg had met Dirk Reynolds five months before when she had been preparing for the La Belle fashion show tour. Meg, one of their top models, worked for the chain of expensive lingerie stores.

She glanced back at Dirk. He and his friend, Ethan Brodie, did private investigation and personal security for Brodie Operations Security Services, Inc., the company that had been hired to protect the models after one of them was murdered.

Dirk had been her bodyguard, and though every instinct had warned her not to get involved with him, the fierce attraction between them had been impossible to resist.

Once the models returned home, Meg had ended the affair. She and Dirk weren't right for each other. Dirk lived fast and hard. He rode a motorcycle, drove a car that could go two hundred miles an hour. Dirk Reynolds was wild and fierce, while she was a

12

single mother with a son to raise.

She couldn't have Dirk Reynolds. She had a responsibility to her little boy. With a failed marriage behind her, she couldn't risk failing again.

But she had never gotten over Dirk.

Meg steeled herself and headed along the gravel driveway toward the house Dirk was rebuilding after the fire that had nearly killed him five months ago. One thing she knew, Dirk Reynolds was a hard man to kill.

Which was the reason she had swallowed her pride and her heartache and come to him. She needed him, trusted him as she never had any other man. Her little boy's life depended on gaining this man's help. This man she had loved and rejected.

She stepped out of the foliage-covered driveway into the open area around the house he was rebuilding. She had called his office looking for him. Nick Brodie, one of the other PIs at BOSS, Inc., had reluctantly told her where to find him. Maybe it was the tears he heard in her voice when she had said how important it was. That it was a matter of life or death.

With Dirk's usual keen senses, he turned, alert that someone was there, though the buzz of the saw had hid the sound of her footsteps.

For several long moments, he just stared, watching as she walked toward him. He was six-two, his body lean and sculpted. Wavy, dark brown hair curled at the nape of his neck. She forced herself to keep walking, even as his jaw locked and a fierce scowl darkened his face.

Dirk grabbed a faded blue work shirt and shrugged it on, covering most of his amazing chest. He didn't bother fastening the buttons, just strode toward her, blocking her view of the house.

He stopped right in front of her. "What are you doing here, Meg?"

"I need to talk to you. It's . . . it's urgent."

"You're trespassing. What do you want?"

She swallowed, fought to stay strong. He didn't want her there. She had known he wouldn't. Known he thought of her only with contempt. She wished he would hold her the way he used to when she was afraid. "I . . . I want to hire you."

The corner of his mouth edged into a ruthless half smile. "What for? Stud service?"

She wanted to cry. She wanted to beg his forgiveness. Tell him she had never forgotten him. That she never would. She knew it wouldn't matter to Dirk. Not anymore.

All that mattered now was saving her son.

She looked into those hard hazel eyes and for the first time wondered if she'd been wrong to think he would help her. Dear God, what would she do if Dirk refused?

A sob wedged in her throat. She fought desperately to hold on to her courage. "It's Charlie. He's been kidnapped. They left a note. It says they'll . . . they'll kill him if I go to the police."

Something shifted in those hard, condemning eyes. For a moment, the old Dirk appeared. Concerned for her, determined to protect her at any cost, even his life.

"I'll take you down to the office. Ethan's out of town with Val. I'll get Nick to work with you. Or Luke. They'll help you find your boy. They'll help you get him back."

They were all private investigators and they were the best. But they weren't Dirk Reynolds. Meg started shaking her head, couldn't stop the tears that leaked onto her cheeks. "It has to be you. I know in my heart you can save Charlie. Only you."

His jaw went iron hard. "Jesus, Meg."

"Please, Dirk. Please help me."

"Do you know what you're asking?"

She knew. There was a time he had loved her. He had begged her to stay with him, give them a chance. Meg had refused.

"He's just a little boy. I know you can save

him. You won't give up until you do."

"Jesus." He raked a hand through his heavy, dark hair. She remembered the exact silky feel of the strands between her fingers.

"The note says they want ten million dollars," she said. "They'll kill him if they don't get it."

He took a deep breath, released it slowly. "How much time did they give you?"

"Three days."

"Ten million. That's a helluva lot of money."

"My father can get it."

His gaze remained on her face. "But you don't trust him to get your boy back. That's smart, Meg, because money doesn't always work."

She swiped at her tears with the back of her hand. "Will you help me?"

His eyes went dark. "You knew I would when you came here."

"I prayed you would. I wasn't sure anymore."

He gazed over her shoulder through the trees, spotted her small white SUV. "You okay to drive?"

"I'm all right."

"I'll follow you back to your house." His mouth barely curved. "I think I can remember where it is."

16

Meg turned away from him. *Three days.* In three days Charlie would be safely returned. Dirk would go on with his life and she would go on with hers.

Three days.

The pain didn't matter. Charlie was all that mattered. Meg had no other choice.

CHAPTER TWO

Dirk pulled his metallic-orange Viper to a stop in front of Megan O'Brien's gray, two-story house. Five months ago he had walked out her front door and never looked back.

Meg had meant everything to him. He'd meant nothing to her.

She needed him now. She trusted him. But Dirk didn't trust her.

Still, he knew how much she loved her son and he would do everything in his power to see her little boy safely returned to her.

She parked in the garage as he grabbed his Browning nine mil out of the center console and clipped the holster beneath his shirt at the back of his jeans. Climbing out of the car, he walked up on her front porch. Just standing there made his chest feel tight.

The door opened. "Come on in." Meg stepped back so he could walk past, then turned toward a stout, heavyset older

18

woman with iron-gray hair. "This is Rose Wills. She's my housekeeper and Charlie's nanny. She discovered Charlie missing just a few minutes before I got back from grocery shopping."

He could see the fear in the older woman's round, lined face, the same fear Meg tried and failed to hide. "I'm Dirk Reynolds, Mrs. Wills. What time did you last see Charlie?"

"I looked in on him about two o'clock. He was napping. I went up again at three to check on him and he was . . ." She covered her mouth with trembling fingers, dragged in a steadying breath. "Charlie was gone."

"I thought maybe he had just . . . you know . . . climbed out of his bed and . . . and wandered off," Meg said. "We looked all over, but . . ." Her voice broke. Meg was hanging on hard. Dirk crushed the urge to comfort her. "We couldn't find him. The doors were locked so we knew he couldn't have gone outside. I went back upstairs and that's when I found . . . I found the note."

"Where is it?"

Meg turned, hurried off to get it. She was just as beautiful as the last time he'd seen her. She was one of La Belle's top models, a blue-eyed redhead he'd been drawn to the moment he'd spotted her standing next to her best friend, Valentine Hart, the model

19

Ethan was engaged to marry.

Dirk wasn't the type to fall for a woman, but he had fallen hard for Meg.

She returned downstairs with the note, holding it by one corner. "I touched it when I took it out of the envelope. After I realized what it was, I tried to be careful. I thought there might be fingerprints or something."

"There might be. We can always hope." He motioned for her to set it and the envelope on the dining table, looked down and scanned the words on the single sheet of paper.

We have your son. He'll cost you ten million in cash. You've got three days or he's dead. No police.

"I need to look at Charlie's bedroom."

Meg nodded, led him up the stairs. Though a La Belle model made plenty of money, the house wasn't extravagant; just a four-bedroom family home with comfortable, overstuffed, easy-to-care-for furniture in the living and family rooms. Her home's Madison Park address, however, put the house over the million-dollar mark.

They walked into a room decorated with pale blue walls, one of them papered in miniature sailboats. The blanket on the bed had a similar design. Meg walked over to the youth bed, stared down at the blanket, and her eyes filled with tears.

Dirk remembered how the blue always seemed brighter when she talked about her son. The little boy was her world. There was no room for Dirk anywhere in it. Meg had refused even to allow Dirk to meet him. The memory sliced open the old wound in his chest.

His resolve strengthened. He wasn't going there. Not now. Not ever again.

He ignored the way the light gleamed on the fine strands of her long, fiery red hair and turned to examine the room. There were pictures of the boy on the dresser. Dirk walked over and picked one of them up, a fairly recent photo of mother and son. The boy had the same red hair and blue eyes as his mother, the same wide, exuberant smile. Meg wasn't smiling now.

"At least now I know what he looks like," Dirk said.

Her head came up. She knew what he meant. In Meg's eyes, he hadn't even been good enough to be in the same room with her son.

"I was afraid if he got to know you, he would get attached to you. I didn't want him to be hurt."

"Right." He held up the three-by-five photo. "I need this for identification."

21

"Of course. Take it."

He slid the picture out of the frame and tucked it into his shirt pocket. He wished seeing the little boy's face didn't make things even more personal. He continued to survey the room. The kid had only been alone in the bedroom for an hour. How had the bastard gotten in and out without being seen?

"What about your alarm system?" Dirk asked, turning back to Meg. "How did they get past the system without setting it off?"

"We don't keep it on in the daytime. It's a very secure neighborhood. Good for a family. That's why I picked this house in the first place."

Made sense. "All right. What about security cameras? You got them, right? After I mentioned you needed to get some?"

She glanced away. "Once the tour was over and the police caught Delilah's killer, it didn't seem important. I wasn't in danger anymore." She looked up at him, guilt sliding into her pretty blue eyes. "I should have gotten them like you said. They could help us find Charlie now. I should have gotten them, but I didn't."

He caught her shoulders, wished he hadn't as soon as he felt the zip of awareness roll through him. "Nothing about this is your

22

fault. We'll use what we've got, okay? We're just getting started, yeah?"

She swallowed, nodded. "Okay."

He left her and walked over to the window. The screen was missing. He spotted it lying on the grass in the yard below. The paned sash window had been raised and not completely pushed back down. A trace of cold air whispered past the pale blue curtains. Beyond it, the hip roof was easily accessed by a latticework trellis climbing up from the back of the house.

Damn. He should have taken a better look at the security in the home when he'd been there. Would have insisted she make changes if he'd been around longer. As it was, he'd only been here a couple of days after the tour ended before Meg punted him out.

"Looks like they came in from the backyard. I need to know who's been out there. I need a list of people, anyone with access to the house. Repairmen, the guys who mow your lawn, cleaning people. Everyone."

"Okay."

"Get Mrs. Wills to help. She might think of someone you miss."

"All right."

He walked back to the little boy's bed, bent down toward the boy's pillow, recognized the pungent sweet smell. "Chloroform. That's how they got Charlie out without him making any noise."

"Oh, God. It won't hurt him, will it?"

"He'll be okay. Odds are he'll sleep a couple of hours before he wakes up." He didn't mention the possibility of an overdose or the headache the kid was going to have when he regained consciousness. She had enough to worry about already.

"I've got a fingerprint kit in my car. I'll grab it and be right back. Don't touch anything."

"I won't," Meg promised.

"I need to take a look outside, see if I can find some footprints or any other trace of these guys."

"You think it was more than one person?"

"As Rose said, it seems to have been well planned, so yeah. I think several people are involved."

Meg said nothing. The fear in her eyes said it all.

"I need to move my car," he said. "You got room in your garage?"

"You think they might be watching the house?"

"Might be, might not. Might just be doing an occasional drive-by. I'd rather play it safe. They're going to call eventually. Give you instructions. If they know I'm here, we tell them I'm the one who's going to negotiate the deal."

"There's room for your car. I'll open the garage door."

Dirk nodded, turned, and headed downstairs. He needed facts, information. Once he had a lead, he'd bring Sadie in to help. Sadie Gunderson worked as a computer expert at BOSS, Inc., where he was a private investigator/bodyguard/pretty much jack-of-all-trades.

He was ex-military, Special Forces, a former Ranger. He had extensive weapons training. Working as a PI with Ethan Brodie, once a Dallas homicide detective, Ethan's brother, Luke, a bounty hunter, and their cousins, Ian and Nick, both ex-cops, had given Dirk invaluable experience.

Along with the training he'd had in the army, he seemed to have a natural knack for sniffing out clues. He'd find the bastards who had taken Meg's boy. She was right about that.

And he would see they got exactly what they deserved.

It felt strange having Dirk in the house. Like having something wild and untamed prowling the hallways. He had always seemed out of place, like an animal that needed to be released from its cage.

He'd only been in her home a few days after one of the La Belle models had been murdered. Dirk had accompanied her to the funeral as her bodyguard. Then she and the other girls had flown to Texas to begin the fashion show tour. Dirk Reynolds and Ethan Brodie had been part of the security team. Charlie had stayed in Seattle with her parents.

Throughout the tour, Dirk had stuck by her side, determined to protect her. She could feel that same determination now, directed toward the safe return of her son. Somehow it soothed her.

Just watching him stalking through the house searching for clues seemed to steady her. Dirk would bring Charlie home. No matter what it took.

She found Rose Wills at the dining table, a box of Kleenex on top, a tissue clutched in her pudgy hand. She dabbed it beneath her eyes.

"It's going to be okay, Rose." Meg sat down beside her, not completely sure if she was saying the words for Rose or for herself. "Dirk's going to help us find Charlie."

"Mr. Reynolds . . . he isn't what I expected."

Under different circumstances, Meg might

have smiled. "No, he isn't. But he knows what he's doing."

"It was him, wasn't it? He was your bodyguard on the tour."

"Yes."

"I heard you and your friend Val talking about him once. You said he was an amazing man." Valerie Hartman was one of Meg's best friends, also a former model. She was engaged to Dirk's best friend. Val had been brave enough to risk loving Ethan Brodie.

"Dirk *is* amazing."

"I think he has a tattoo."

"There's a dragon on his shoulder." A very sexy dragon, but now wasn't the time to remember that. "The dragon's head climbs up to the base of his neck. Sometimes when he moves, part of it shows above the collar of his shirt."

"I see."

She wondered what Rose Wills did see when she looked at Dirk. The same thing her father would have seen: a man who would never fit in at the country club or among her dad's high-society friends. One of the reasons she had ended their brief affair.

"We need to make a list of anyone who has or had access to the house in the last

27

few weeks." She pointed to the notepad she had retrieved from the downstairs study she used as an office. "I've written down the gardener, the cleaning lady, the part-time babysitter." A young woman who filled in on weekends if she was needed, or when Rose had time off. "Oh, and the window washers."

"The carpet-cleaning people were in last week."

She wrote it down. "Anyone else?"

Rose pressed a hand to her forehead, rubbed a spot in the middle. "It's hard to concentrate. All I can think of is little Charlie. Is he okay? Is he scared or hungry?"

Meg's chest clamped down.

Rose plucked a fresh Kleenex out of the box and dabbed her eyes. "I'm sorry. I just . . . I feel so responsible."

Meg swallowed against the tightness in her throat. She had to be strong for Charlie. For all of them. "This was well planned. There's no way you could have known something like this would happen." She reached over and gripped the older woman's hand. "We have to stay calm. We have to help Dirk."

"Yes, yes, you're right." Rose took a deep breath. "It does seem to have been well planned. Maybe whoever took Charlie knew your schedule. Knew you would be gone this afternoon. On Wednesday you always go to the gym, then do your grocery shopping after. Who would have known that?"

Meg looked up as Dirk walked down the stairs and strode toward her. "No prints. The room was wiped clean." He paused in front of her, hands on his narrow hips, looking like a woman's erotic fantasy. Meg knew firsthand, Dirk was exactly that.

"Rose is right about them knowing your schedule. Like I said, maybe they've been watching the house. Or maybe —"

He drilled her with a glare. "Are you seeing someone, Meg? Dating someone you've only recently met?" The edge in his voice hadn't been there before. "Has he been to the house? Maybe the two of you are sleeping together?"

"No! I'm not seeing anyone! I'm not interested in dating." She didn't add she hadn't been remotely interested in any other man since she had met Dirk.

"You sure?" he pressed.

"I'm not a liar. You know me better than that. Do you really think I'd keep something important from you when you're trying to save my son?"

His hard look softened. "You're not a liar. And I know how much you love your boy."

She glanced away from the unanswered question in his eyes. *So why hasn't there been anyone else?*

He pulled out a dining room chair and sat down next to her. She forced herself to ignore the heat radiating off his hard body.

"All right, who knows your schedule? Your trainer, maybe? Write down his name and where I can find him."

She wrote it down.

"Who else? Rose said you go grocery shopping every Wednesday. Anyone there you talk to? A clerk? Someone who seems to have more than a passing interest in you?"

"No. I'm always in a hurry when I'm there. I bring my list, buy what I need, and get back home."

"Have either of you noticed anyone hanging around the house? A car, maybe, you only noticed just lately?"

Rose just shook her head.

"Not that I can think of," Meg said.

"Let's talk about your ex-husband, Charlie's father. Hollander, right? You mentioned him once on the tour."

"Jonathan Hollander. I went back to my maiden name after we divorced. Charlie uses my name, too."

"He have visitation, partial custody of his son? How did the divorce end up?"

"Jonathan didn't want anything to do with Charlie. I was thinking about divorcing him when I got pregnant. It was one of the last times we were together. Shortly after I filed, I found out he'd been cheating on me with several different women. He wasn't happy when he found out I was going to have a baby. He was hardly interested in being a father."

"What about now? He been calling, asking to see his kid?"

"No. He never wanted children. As far as I know, that hasn't changed."

"What about money? He in financial trouble, anything like that?"

"Jonathan is the president of Seattle State Bank. The Hollanders are a very influential family in Seattle. That was the reason my father was so determined I should marry him."

"Okay, we'll leave it for now. We can always look at him later. In the meantime, I need the names, addresses, and phone numbers of all the people you've put on your list, and anyone else you can think of who knows your schedule, anyone who knew you'd be out of the house at least part of the day."

"Okay."

"I'm going to call the office, see if one of

31

the guys can do a little reconnaissance, see if anyone's out there watching the house."

"That sounds like a good idea."

"You need to call your father, Meg. Unless something breaks, we're going to need that money. If we do, your dad's going to need time to get it together. I doubt he's got ten mil sitting in his checking account."

She looked up at him, wondered what he was going to say when she told him about her dad. "Have you ever heard of Burton-Reasoner Industries?"

"I've heard of them. I follow the market. I know they're a publicly traded company. Aside from that, I don't know much about them."

For a moment she was stuck on the fact Dirk Reynolds followed the stock market. "Burton-Reasoner owns insurance firms, soft drink producers, credit card companies, even utilities. For the past twenty years, the company has averaged 14.9 percent annual growth in book value. My dad holds the controlling interest in the company."

Dirk frowned. "So he's what? A billionaire or something?"

"Or something. He doesn't like being in the spotlight so he tends to fly under the radar. But I'd say he's worth at least half a billion."

A muscle ticked in Dirk's lean cheek. "So I guess now I know the reason you didn't want me to meet him."

Surprise jolted through her. "You think it was the money? It wasn't about money!" It was so many things. Too many. None of which seemed important now and none of which she could mention in front of Mrs. Wills.

Dirk took a deep breath. "So ten million doesn't mean piss to your dad, and these guys know it."

Meg straightened. "What? I thought . . . I figured they knew I could get the money. As a model, I earned a big salary. I own a home in Madison Park. I hadn't thought much further than that." She looked up at him. "So this is really about my dad?"

"It's not his fault any more than it's yours. It's time to call him. Past time. He may have some idea who these guys are. He may even have gotten a note himself."

"Oh, God, I didn't think of that. Maybe I should have called him sooner. I was afraid he'd try to take over, but maybe I should have —"

Dirk caught her arm. "You came to me. That was the smartest thing you could have done. Your dad might be rich, but he doesn't hold the power here — you do. Whatever

33

went wrong between us, I won't let him fuck this up for you, Meg."

She looked down at his big, suntanned hand, dark against her pale complexion. "I want you to handle it. I'll do whatever you say."

Dirk just nodded. Her skin felt chilled when he let her go.

CHAPTER THREE

Meg called her father on the private line in his home office. At fifty-four, Edwin O'Brien was semiretired, though he was still deeply involved in Burton-Reasoner, still had an office in the building, still held a seat on the board of directors. He played golf a couple of times a week, but he was a businessman, first, last, and always. Her mom kept busy with charity work.

The phone was picked up on the second ring. "Dad, it's me."

"Hi, sweetheart. It's nice to hear from you."

Her eyes welled. Her father loved Charlie so much. "Dad, something's happened. Someone's . . . someone's taken Charlie."

Silence fell on the line. "He's been kidnapped?"

"Yes."

His tone shifted, hardened. "Did they ask for a ransom?"

"Yes."

"How much is it?"

"They . . . they want ten million in cash. They left a note. They gave me three days to get the money." Her voice broke. "They came in the house, Dad. Charlie was down for his nap. We think they had it all planned out."

"You said *we*. Who's with you? The house-keeper?"

"Yes. And the man I hired, Dirk Reynolds. He was my bodyguard on the fashion show tour. He's also a private investigator."

"Why is he there, Meg? You don't need a private investigator. You just need to do what the kidnappers tell you."

"He's here because I trust him. You don't know these people, Dad. There's no way you can know what they're planning to do."

"They want money, sweetheart. We give them what they want, they'll let Charlie go."

Her hand tightened around her cell phone. "What if they don't, Dad? I'm not willing to take the risk. Charlie's my son. Dirk's a professional. I'm going to do exactly what he says."

She could feel the tension mounting on the other end of the line. "Charlie's my grandson, my only male heir. I'll set things in motion, line up the money. I'll be there as soon as I can. We'll talk about this when I get there." The line went dead.

Meg looked up at Dirk, saw the hardness in his features and knew he understood what was going on. "My father's stubborn. He'll want to take control."

Dirk just shook his head. "Not gonna happen, Meg. Not unless you want it to."

She bit her lip. She trusted Dirk. She wanted her son back alive. "I meant what I said. I want you to handle it."

He nodded. "Then that's what I'll do."

Dirk retrieved a recording device he kept with his PI gear in the back of his car and installed it on Meg's home phone. If the kidnappers called, he might be able to get a trace. If they called on her cell phone instead, Sadie might be able to locate where the call had come from.

While he worked, Meg used her smartphone to collect the addresses of the people on her list. According to Meg, Mrs. Wills had most of the phone numbers because she was the one who hired household staff or made necessary maintenance appointments, like carpet cleaning or plumbing repairs.

Meg filled in the name and address of her trainer and the part-time babysitter she had hired. As soon as the list was complete, Dirk phoned Sadie. Since she only worked a half day on Wednesdays and Fridays, she was at home, not in the office. He glanced out the dining room window. It was the middle of January so darkness had already fallen outside.

Sadie answered on the second ring. She was a big woman, fifty years old, with silver-blond hair and pale blue eyes. With grown kids and grandkids, she was the most unlikely computer expert he could imagine.

"Hi, sweetness, it's Dirk. I'm really sorry to bother you. I know you're not working today, but I really need your help."

Sadie chuckled. "And you think your sweet talk is going to get me to do whatever it is you want?"

"I'm hoping. It's really important, Sadie. A little boy's life is at stake."

She sobered. "What can I do?"

"His name is Charlie. He's not quite three and he's been kidnapped. Whoever took him came right into his bedroom. I've got a list of people with access. I need you to run them, see what you can find out. I want to know if they've got any priors, any financial problems, anything that would give them a motive for kidnapping."

"They ask for money?"

"Ten million bucks."

Sadie whistled. "His parents have it?"

"Granddad's got it."

"I'd say ten million is plenty of motive."

"You got that right. These guys are smooth operators, Sadie, not amateurs. I need to find out who they are. I need to know if the money is going to be enough to get the boy back home in one piece."

"You figure there's more than one?"

"Like I said, they're smooth. In and out, slick and quiet. They had inside information. They knew Meg's schedule. Maybe even knew when the boy would be upstairs for his nap. I'm thinking at least two people involved, probably three, maybe more."

"You said Meg. Charlie's mother isn't that model, is she? The one who gave you so much grief?"

"It's her boy. He's just a baby. This isn't personal. I won't let that happen."

"Be smart, hot stuff. Don't get sucked in again."

"I told you, I won't let that happen. I need your help, Sadie. Charlie needs your help."

"All right, I'll head down to the office. I may need some of that high-dollar equipment Ian paid for. E-mail whatever information you've got."

"Will do. Thanks, Sadie." Dirk ended the

call. Even before he turned, he felt Meg's eyes on him. Mrs. Wills was in the family room, knitting in front of the TV, just to have something to do.

Meg walked up to him. "It wasn't the money," she said softly. "I have plenty of money. Not ten million in cash, but enough to be comfortable now that I've quit modeling."

"You quit?"

She nodded. "After everything that happened, I just . . . I wanted to be a mother for a while. I've got enough saved to start my own business. I'm not quite ready for that yet."

Dirk didn't want to know more about Meg than he already did. He needed to keep his head on straight. Being around her was bad enough.

"I need to call the office, get someone out here to do some legwork."

Meg just nodded, turned, and walked away.

Dirk sighed with relief. He wished he could lock her away somewhere so he didn't have to look at her. Where he didn't have to remember how good it was when they were together.

He phoned his boss. "I got a problem, Ian. I could really use some help."

"It's an off week here," Ian said. The blond, blue-eyed, ex-Seattle cop was the owner of BOSS, Inc. "Ethan and Valerie are off at some fancy resort in the San Juan Islands. Nick's taking a little time with Samantha and the baby." A little boy named Travis, born not quite two months ago. "Luke's here, though, and restless as usual. Whatever you've got for him, he'll probably jump at the chance to get out of the office."

"Thanks, Ian. I'll call him on his cell."

Luke picked up on the second ring. He was tall, like all the Brodie males, with a lean-muscled build similar to Dirk's and the same blue eyes as Ian and Nick. "Hey, man, what's up?" Luke asked.

"I got a problem, buddy. I'm hoping you can help."

"I'm sitting here playing with my dick, bored out of my skull. Lay it on me."

Dirk smiled. Luke was his own man, a bounty hunter, one of the best in the country. Like Dirk, he was former Army Special Forces. But Luke was Delta, the best of the best, one of the most capable men on the planet. Luke knew Megan O'Brien was a La Belle lingerie model, knew Dirk had taken their breakup hard, but he didn't really know her.

Dirk planned to keep it that way. Meg

41

might not be interested in him, but he sure as hell didn't want her getting interested in Luke Brodie.

Dirk quickly filled him in, explained about the kidnapping of Meg's little boy.

"Not good," Luke said with the faint Southern drawl that showed up on occasion. Unlike Ethan, Luke had never quite escaped his Texas roots. "So what have you got so far?"

"Not much. Little boy disappeared between two and three this afternoon. Took him out an upstairs bedroom window. I found some footprints leading out through the alley. Meg's dad's on his way over. I need to talk to him, see if he knows anything that might help."

"If he's got ten mil in ready cash, he's the target."

"I'll be working that angle. In the meantime, I need you to take a look, see if the house is being watched. If it's clear, we'll knock on some doors, ask a few questions. See if somebody saw a vehicle out of place in the neighborhood or someone loading something into the back of a car. We need to figure out who took the boy and where they have him now."

"Give me the address."

Dirk rattled off Meg's address. "If they've

got a man out there, I don't want him to know we're doing anything but gearing up to pay the ransom."

"If he's out there, he won't see me, but you can bet I'll see him. I'll keep you posted."

"Thanks, Luke."

"Stay on the straight and narrow with the babe, yeah?"

"I hear you. I'm not going down that road again."

Luke ended the call at the same time Mrs. Wills appeared, coming back in from the family room.

"Any news?" she asked.

"We're working on it," Dirk said. "Why don't you go home and get some sleep? You won't do Meg or Charlie any good if you're exhausted."

The woman glanced toward the stairs. "I'd rather stay here. Maybe I could just sleep in one of the guest rooms. Do you think that would be okay?"

Dirk looked over at Meg. Tears were back in her eyes. Damn, he hated seeing her this way.

"Of course you can stay." She wiped away a drop of wetness. "I'll wake you up if anything happens, okay?"

Rose nodded, turned, and lumbered toward the stairs. He'd considered asking Meg how much she trusted the older woman, but unless Rose Wills was the best actress on the planet, she was grieving for the boy nearly as much as Meg.

A firm knock sounded at the door.

"That'll be my dad." Meg took a deep, steadying breath and started for the entry.

Dirk stepped in front of her, blocking her way. "Let's make sure." He strode to the door and looked through the peephole, saw a tall man on the porch with powerful shoulders, once-red hair turning gray, a firm jaw, probably early fifties, looked younger, obviously kept himself in shape.

Dirk stepped back out of the way. "It's him."

Meg unlocked the door. She looked up at her father and burst into tears. "Daddy . . ." She went into his arms and they closed firmly around her. Maybe her father's money hadn't been the problem between her and Dirk, but clearly this man was an important part of Meg's life.

O'Brien's laser-blue eyes zeroed in on him, took in his slightly too long hair, the faded blue work shirt and muddy jeans he hadn't taken time to change out of. The look of contempt the man sliced his way said Edwin O'Brien was at least part of the reason Meg had refused to give their relationship a chance.

"It's all right, sweetheart," her father said. "We're going to do whatever it takes to get our boy back."

Meg sniffed and wiped her eyes. She forced the semblance of a smile as she turned to Dirk. "Dad, this is Dirk Reynolds, the private investigator I told you about."

Instead of extending a hand, her father gave a faint nod of his head. "Reynolds."

Dirk was forced to respond in kind. "Mr. O'Brien."

Meg didn't miss the insult. She was tall, and as she pinned her father with a glare, seemed to grow even taller. "Dirk's here because I asked him to come, Dad. He was working on the house he's rebuilding after it burned down last year. He came because he knows how much Charlie means to me. Now I'm telling you, Dad, Dirk means a lot to me, too. I trust him and I respect him. I expect you to do the same."

Her father's silver-red eyebrows shot up. Dirk figured it was rare that Megan stood up to him.

O'Brien sucked it up, stuck out a strong, freckled hand. "Good to meet you. Thank you for coming."

Dirk shook, still reeling from the words

45

Meg had said. *He meant a lot to her?* What the hell did that mean? *She trusted and respected him?* If those things were true, why was she sleeping alone when he had stupidly wanted to be the man in her bed?

"I've set the wheels in motion," her father said to both of them. "I'll have the cash ready, maybe as soon as tomorrow."

"So far these guys have been smart," Dirk said. "We're looking for a way to track them, figure out who they are, but it's going to take some time."

O'Brien's heavy eyebrows slammed together. "What are you talking about? We're going to wait for their phone call, pay the money, and get my grandson back. We aren't doing anything that might get him killed."

Dirk's patience began to unravel. "You give them the money, we have no leverage. They do whatever they want with the boy. We need to know what we're up against. If possible, we need to figure out who's behind the abduction and find them before the deadline is up."

"It's too risky. I won't have you interfering in this."

Dirk cast a questioning glance at Meg. If she told him to stand down, he would. Or at least he would pretend to. Might be better if he left her out of this. Did what needed to be done without fighting to keep his emotions in check.

Meg read the message loud and clear. She looked from him to her father. "I need your money, Dad. I know how much you love Charlie so I know I can count on you for that. But I need Dirk's experience, his professionalism. I've seen the way he handles himself in dangerous situations. He knows what he's doing. I trust him to bring Charlie home."

O'Brien cast him a forbidding glance. "You're him, aren't you? Her mother and I, we knew there was someone. Someone she met on the tour."

"I was her bodyguard," he said carefully, not looking at Meg. "We got to know each other fairly well." Now that was an understatement. They hadn't spent a lot of time in bed — they'd both had jobs to do and there was a killer on the loose. But if he closed his eyes, he could still see the tiny birthmark on the inside of her thigh, remember the way it tasted beneath his tongue.

"It was more than that," her father said with an all-too-knowing glance. "I saw the way she was after you left. But I won't press the issue. As much as I'd rather do this my way, Charlie is Meg's boy. If she trusts you that much, I have to trust you, too."

Dirk made no reply. The more Meg talked about him, the less he understood why she had broken things off. Clearly, she had cared for him more than he had believed.

"Have you done this kind of thing before?" O'Brien asked. "Handled kidnapping cases, I mean."

"Yes. I've worked several ransom cases."

"And you brought the person safely home?"

He wasn't going to lie. "The first two, yes. The third time the woman who'd been abducted was killed before the ransom call was ever made."

Meg made a sound in her throat.

"That isn't going to happen this time — is it?" O'Brien said. It wasn't a question.

Dirk glanced at Meg. Her face had gone pale, making the row of nearly invisible freckles across her forehead stand out.

"No, sir, it isn't. I'm not going to let it. I'm going to make sure Charlie comes home to his mother."

O'Brien's thick shoulders relaxed and he nodded.

Dirk prayed it was the truth.

CHAPTER FOUR

Meg sat next to her father on the living room sofa. "Have you told Mom yet?"

"No, and I don't intend to. You know how she worries. She would be gravely upset and there isn't a damn thing she could do."

Her dad had always been protective of her mother. Patsy O'Brien was a frail sort of woman, though not nearly as weak as her father believed. Still, he was right. Her mother would be inconsolable. If she were there, she would only make the situation more difficult for all of them.

Meg looked up to see Dirk walking into the living room. She had always loved the way he moved, the long, impatient strides tempered by a sort of sauntering grace. She liked the way he wore his jeans, low on his hips, the faded fabric washed to a softness that outlined the muscles in his legs.

He walked up in front of her father, who slowly rose from the sofa. Her dad was over six feet, but Dirk was taller.

"I've given you some time with your daughter, time to sort all this out in your head. Now I've got some questions you need to answer. Questions I hope will get us closer to bringing your grandson home."

"All right."

Both men sat down, her dad returning to his place beside her on the sea-green, pillow-backed sofa, while Dirk sat down in a matching overstuffed chair.

Dirk leaned forward. "Let me start by saying revenge is sometimes a motive in kidnapping cases. Is there anyone you can think of, Mr. O'Brien, who might have taken Charlie to get payback for some kind of wrong he believes you've done?"

"No, of course not."

"You might want to give yourself a moment to think about that, sir. Your grandson's life depends on your honesty."

Her dad released a slow breath. "I'm a businessman, Reynolds. I'm worth a good deal of money. Have I made enemies along the way? Yes. Is there someone among them who would go after my grandson for revenge — I don't know. I don't think so, but there's no way to be completely sure."

"Fair enough. Let me ask you this: Is there anyone who might be trying to recover his money from a loss he feels you're responsible for?"

Her father frowned, pursed his lips, then started nodding. "Yes, I see what you mean. Most of the companies Burton-Reasoner owns have been profitable, but there have been a few that failed. If the doors were closed and someone lost his job — his paycheck — perhaps he would feel the ransom money was simply what's owed him."

Dirk nodded. "His lost wages plus all the pain and suffering he'd endured."

"I suppose it's possible."

"Any of those failed companies in this area?"

Her father started to shake his head.

"What about Solar-Renew?" Meg reminded him. "They closed down two years ago. I remember there was a lot of grumbling among the employees when it happened."

"Yes, yes, you're right. A couple of the top execs lost their jobs. Marcus Dunham and Bob Algreen were older, close to retirement age. I don't know if they were ever rehired anywhere else."

"I need their contact info. And a list of all the employees who lost their jobs when the plant closed down."

51

"I can do that," her father said. "Tomorrow, I'll call —"

"Tonight, sir. If it's possible. Time is of the essence in a case like this. It's going to take a while to process the information."

Her dad flashed him a look she could have sworn held a hint of respect, rose from the sofa and pulled out his cell.

"My secretary makes a small fortune," he said. "A few evening hours won't hurt her." As her father walked out of the living room to make the call, Meg went over to where Dirk stood beside his chair, staring toward the window. The drapes had been closed throughout the house, yet he looked as if he wished he could be on the outside looking in.

"I know you don't want to be here," Meg said softly. "But I'm really glad you are. Watching you work, knowing you're helping us, is the only thing that's keeping me from falling apart."

He turned, his gaze searching her face. Their eyes held for a moment, then Dirk glanced away. "We're moving ahead. As soon as we get the info from your dad, I'll call Sadie again. She'll be running the names I already e-mailed, looking for something that might click. I'll have her go to work on your dad's list, too."

She nodded.

"Look, why don't you go upstairs and get some rest like Mrs. Wills? If the kidnappers were going to call tonight, they would have done it by now."

Meg's eyes burned. "There's no way I can sleep. If I close my eyes, I'll just imagine what might be happening to Charlie. I can't stand to think of him hungry or crying. I can't stand to think of him missing his mom." Her throat closed up. "Oh, God, Dirk, I can't bear the thought of losing him."

He took a step toward her, stopped himself before he reached her. "Nothing's going to happen to your son. You can't think that way. It isn't fair to Charlie. All right?"

She swallowed, tried not to wish Dirk had kept walking, that he had pulled her into his arms. She tried not to wish she could lose herself in his hard-muscled body.

She tried to remember why she had so brutally ended their affair. But all she could see was the look on Dirk's face when she had sent him away.

Dirk's cell phone started playing Jason Aldean's "Burnin' It Down," a rock country song that was currently his favorite. He pulled the phone out of his jeans pocket, saw Luke's name, and took the call.

"I'm coming in through the back," Luke said. "Don't shoot me."

Dirk's mouth edged up. "I'll open the door." The line went dead. Dirk made his way to the door leading into the backyard off the laundry room. He glanced through the window, turned the dead bolt, and opened the door.

Luke appeared like a specter out of the darkness, dressed completely in black: cargo pants and a turtleneck sweater, a black knit cap pulled low on his forehead, streaks of greasepaint smeared across his cheeks.

When he stepped inside, Dirk closed and locked the door. As they walked into the kitchen, a little *screech* came from across the room. Dirk looked up to see Meg standing with a hand at her throat.

"Who's that?"

Meg knew Ethan and Nick, but she had never met Luke Brodie. "Meg, meet Ethan's brother, Luke. I told you I was going to call for backup."

"Yes, of course. I'm sorry. My nerves are kind of on edge."

"Understandable," Luke said. "Considering the circumstances." He dragged his cap off, dislodging his sun-streaked, short-on-the-sides, longer-on-top, brown hair. Raking his fingers through the ends, he smoothed the strands back in place.

"I feel like I already know you," Meg said. "Dirk spoke of you highly. It's good to finally meet you."

Dirk didn't miss the wariness in Luke's blue eyes as he sized Meg up. Earlier, she had changed into gray sweatpants and a loose-fitting T-shirt. Dirk was damned glad.

A La Belle model had to be tall and perfectly proportioned. Not stick thin like a high-fashion model, but toned and fit and lushly curved in all the right places. Dirk knew from personal experience why the company had chosen Megan O'Brien as one of their top ten.

Luke's intense gaze swung to Dirk. "Nobody out there. I been watching awhile. If the house was being surveilled, I would have known."

Dirk just nodded. Luke was Delta. If Luke said it was clear, it was clear.

"So no one's watching what we do," Dirk said. "They're confident. Overconfident and arrogant would be my guess. They know the family dynamics. Know her dad's got the bucks, know how he feels about his grandson. They're sure he's going to pay."

"Yeah, and they're dead certain he won't risk bringing in the cops. Got to be multiple people, just like you figured, each member of the group contributing information."

"Which gives them the whole picture," Dirk finished. He glanced over to see Luke watching Meg, giving her the fish-eye, studying her as if she were floundering on dry land, needing his help to get back in the water.

Luke was a good friend. He didn't like the way Meg had jerked him around. Dirk didn't much like it either.

But this was business, nothing more. There was a little boy to bring home. Luke was a bounty hunter. He found people for a living. Dirk was grateful for his help.

Dirk looked at Meg. "So name a person or persons who would know your schedule on Wednesdays."

"Mrs. Wills, of course," Meg said, "but Rose would never hurt —"

"Someone else. Your trainer, right?"

"Yes, but I don't think David —"

"You put his contact info on your list, yes? So Sadie already has it."

"That's right."

"Who else had the kind of info they needed? Your trainer wouldn't know what time the baby goes down for his nap, but the babysitter would. You mentioned her before."

Her eyes flashed to his. "Yes, Pamela

would know. Charlie goes down for his nap at the same time every day. Pam works weekends whenever I need her. She also subs for Rose if she gets sick or takes time off to visit her grandkids."

"She on your list?"

"Yes."

"You know where she lives?"

"She has a small apartment a few miles away. She also works part-time at a little boutique, but it would be closed by now."

"The kidnappers need someone to take care of your son. A woman who already knows him, has a rapport with him, would be the obvious choice."

Hope infused her face. "You think Pamela has Charlie at her apartment?"

Dirk shook his head, smothering the hope. "I doubt he's there. Too risky. But I'm thinking Pamela may not be there either. If that's so, she may be taking care of Charlie somewhere else."

"Why don't I pay the lady a visit?" Luke shoved away from the kitchen counter. "If she's home, she'll never know I was there. If she isn't, we need to find her."

Edwin O'Brien walked into the kitchen just then. His clothes, a navy blue V-neck sweater over a starched white shirt, were beginning to look rumpled. One glance at

Luke, dressed head to foot in black, face covered in greasepaint, and O'Brien's eyebrows shot up.

"What the devil . . . ?"

"Edwin O'Brien, meet Luke Brodie. Luke works with me at Brodie Operations. He's checked the area, found no surveillance. That's good, gives us a chance to move around."

O'Brien started nodding. "Yes, I can see where that's a good thing to know."

"Luke's going to pay a visit to the babysitter. There's a chance she's one of the people involved."

"Good God." He turned a sharp look on Meg. "Didn't you vet her? Surely you didn't just hand your son over to some woman off the street."

"Take it easy, Mr. O'Brien," Dirk warned. "None of this is Meg's fault. So far, there's no proof the babysitter had anything to do with this."

"She had references, Dad. Very good ones. I'm still not convinced she'd do anything to hurt Charlie."

"I need her address," Luke said. Meg wrote it on the notepad next to the telephone on the wall, ripped off the page, and handed it to Luke.

"I'll be back," he said as he walked out of

the kitchen, back through the laundry room door, and disappeared into the darkness.

"You got that info on Solar-Renew?" Dirk asked O'Brien.

"I had my assistant send it to my iPhone and also to Meg's e-mail address. I figured that would be the best place to retrieve it."

They'd set up her laptop on the dining room table. Dirk walked back to the dining area in the living room, leaned down, and pulled up the attachment. There was a list of thirty names, former employees. There were asterisks next to two of them, employees who'd made threats against Edwin O'Brien personally.

But the info was two years old. He needed to know what those employees had been doing since their layoff from Solar-Renew. And he needed to know what Marcus Dunham and Bob Algreen, the corporate execs, had been up to.

"I need to get this to Sadie." He sat down in front of the laptop and forwarded the names, including Dunham and Algreen, to Sadie's e-mail address.

His cell rang a few minutes after Sadie got the info. Dirk saw her name on the screen and pressed the phone against his ear. "Hey, sweetness."

"Don't you sweetness me. In case you

haven't noticed, it's after midnight. That's way past my bedtime and I'm still at the office."

"It's way past Charlie's bedtime, too. You can sleep late in the morning. What have you got for me?"

The humor was gone from her voice. "Checked out the housekeeper just in case. Rose Wills has two kids, four grandkids, and a comfortable savings account. No reason to think she's involved."

"I don't think so either. What else?"

"Went through all the maintenance folks. Gardener — illegal, barely speaks English. Does good work, according to the reviews he gets on Angie's List. I don't think he's got the juice to pull off something this complicated."

"So not the gardener. Who else?"

"Not the carpet-cleaning guys, either — father and son, own their own business. No priors, nothing that looks suspicious. Took a look at the guy at the gym, Meg's trainer, David Wilkerson. College grad, works as a senior lab tech at the hospital in the evenings. Does physical training part-time. No connections to anything shady. Tidy little savings account."

"So he doesn't need the money."

Sadie scoffed. "Everyone needs ten million bucks."

"Good point. What about the babysitter?"

"Pamela Vardon. Now she's more interesting. Her record's clean. No priors, nothing like that. But she comes from a broken home. Dad was abusive. Mom was a drunk. Pamela works two jobs just to stay afloat."

"She knew Charlie's nap time," he said. "That was crucial to making this whole scheme work. Luke's on his way over to her apartment. I have a feeling she isn't going to be there."

"You think she took the boy?"

"No. It took some strength to get up on that roof and into the kid's bedroom, then get back down carrying the boy. She didn't take him, but my gut says she's in it up to her eyeballs."

"Pretty eyeballs," Sadie corrected. "I'll send you her picture."

The computer signaled incoming mail. He brought it up and looked down at the dark-haired girl staring back at him. If she looked anything like her photo, Pamela Vardon was more than pretty, she was beautiful.

"I sent you something else before you called," Dirk said. "You get it?"

"I got it. Haven't had time to look at it yet."

Dirk went on to tell Sadie about Edwin

O'Brien and Burton-Reasoner Industries. He told her about Solar-Renew and how the company had failed, told her about the layoffs and disgruntled employees, including the names of the two men O'Brien's assistant had said made threatening remarks.

"I'm also interested in Marcus Dunham and Bob Algreen. They had big jobs, Sadie, a lot to lose. See if either or both have been rehired someplace else."

"I'm on it," Sadie said and hung up the phone.

Dirk looked over at Meg. Her face was pale, the stress beginning to take its toll. It wasn't supposed to bother him, not anymore. But he had known from the moment he had spotted her walking toward him at his house that what happened to her was going to take a toll on him, too.

CHAPTER FIVE

Meg glanced at the clock. It was after one in the morning. The coffeepot was empty again. She needed to brew another pot. She glanced at the sienna granite countertop in her all-stainless kitchen. A shiny black coffeemaker, a top-of-the-line Krups, sat on the counter above the dishwasher, but she couldn't find the energy to move in that direction.

Meg raked back her hair, stylishly cut into layers that usually floated around her face. At the moment the long, red strands hung as limp and lifeless as the rest of her felt.

She didn't need more caffeine. She was already shaky and exhausted to the bone. At the same time restless energy poured through her. Worry and fear for her son numbed her mind yet kept her nerves strung to the breaking point.

Her head jerked up at the sound of a cell phone ringing. She realized it was her dad's, saw him stand up from the breakfast table where he sat and pull it out of the pocket of his slacks. He said something she couldn't hear, hung up, and walked toward her across the kitchen.

"Who was it?" Meg asked, terrified the kidnappers had finally made a ransom call to her father.

"It was your mother. I called her before I left the office, told her I had a meeting that might run late in the evening. She figured I should have been home by now. She was worried something had happened to me on the freeway."

"You need to go home, Dad. Either that or you have to tell Mom what's going on."

Her father shook his head. "I won't do that. Once Charlie's safe, I'll tell her everything that's happened. Not now. Not when I know the awful distress it will cause her."

In a way he was right. When the pressure of Edwin O'Brien's job as president of Burton-Reasoner had become too much for his wife to handle, Patsy O'Brien had come close to a nervous breakdown.

Her father had been frantic. He had stepped down immediately and her mother had recovered, but her dad had never forgotten the lesson. Since then, for him, family came first. That hadn't changed.

"Meg's right," Dirk said as he strode into the kitchen. "If you're worried about your wife, you need to go to her, make sure she's okay. You know, there's always a chance these guys may try to contact you directly. It's not likely they'll call in the middle of the night, but we can't be completely sure."

Tension seeped into her dad's thick shoulders. "I hadn't thought of that."

"You need to be home if that happens. I'll be here with Meg, and so will Mrs. Wills. I'll be working on the computer, doing more digging. In the morning, if it looks clear, I'll talk to the neighbors, see if they noticed anything out of the ordinary in the last couple of days. I'll stay on this, Mr. O'Brien. I won't let up until Charlie comes home."

Her dad released a slow breath. "All right. I'll go home. I'll make sure your mother is okay and be there in case these men call." He looked over at Dirk. "But I expect you to keep me apprised of everything that happens."

"You're an essential part of this, sir. Without your help, nothing is going to happen."

"You were Meg's bodyguard. I expect you to protect her the way you did before."

"You can count on that, sir."

Meg's gaze swung to Dirk. He would be

there for her, the way he was before. She had known she could count on Dirk. He was solid as a rock. Why hadn't she understood how important that was?

Meg walked her father to the door. He looked as haggard as she felt. She watched him all the way to his black Mercedes sedan, parked at the curb, watched him climb in and drive away.

As she closed the front door, she felt Dirk's presence behind her, turned to look into his hard, handsome face. Dear God, she had missed him. Until she'd seen him today, she hadn't realized just how much.

"You okay?" he asked.

She took a shaky breath. "I'm all right. What can I do to help?"

"Not much either of us can do till Luke gets back or we hear from Sadie. If you won't go upstairs, at least lie down on the sofa and get some rest. You won't do anyone any good if you're too exhausted to function."

Meg thought of her son, forced herself to stay positive. "You really think it's Pam?"

"We'll know more when we hear from Luke."

As if the mention of his name had brought his return, Luke walked silently into the living room. She hadn't heard a sound as he'd returned through the kitchen. She wondered how he could have gotten inside with the doors locked, then remembered the way Dirk had managed to get into her hotel suite unnoticed on the tour.

"The girl, Pamela, wasn't there," Luke said. "I looked around inside. Looks like she packed up before she left."

Meg made a sound in her throat. "You think she has Charlie?"

Luke shook his head. "I didn't see any sign of a kid. She didn't take everything, but some photos were gone from the wall, a few spaces looked empty on the dresser in the bedroom. I figure she's planning to take her share of the money and split, start over somewhere else."

She could almost see Dirk's mind working. "They're sure they'll get away clean," he said. "I don't like it. It's like they know something we don't."

"Whatever it is, sooner or later, we'll figure it out." Luke ambled over to the computer on the dining table, looked down, saw the photo of Pamela Vardon Dirk had pulled up on the screen.

"Beautiful girl. Too bad about the wrong turn she's made. She's gonna look real sweet to those big bull dykes down at the state correctional facility."

Meg felt the blood drain from her face. Pam had always seemed like such a nice girl. She felt sick to her stomach.

Dirk must have noticed. He flashed Luke a look of warning and for the first time that night actually touched her. She felt the heat of his hand at her waist as he drew her against him. It was all Meg could do not to slide her arms around his neck, lean into him, and start to weep.

Dirk caught her chin and tipped it up, forcing her to look at him. "Hey. Pamela Vardon isn't your problem, okay? If she's involved, she'll get what she deserves. Right now the only person you need to worry about is your son."

She bit her lip. "I liked her. I paid her more than I should have. I knew she worked two jobs. I wanted to help her."

"Maybe she'll remember that. Maybe she'll take extra good care of Charlie, yeah?"

Meg swallowed, nodded. "Maybe it's good that Pamela is the one who's with him."

"We can't be sure of that," Luke reminded her. "But at this point it's a better than good possibility."

"If we could find her," Meg said, "maybe we could find Charlie."

Dirk's head snapped up. "Christ, yes. Maybe we damned well could."

■ ■ ■ ■

Dirk turned away from Meg and strode over to where Luke stood next to the computer. "Dammit, I should have done this as soon as you got back." Would have if he had kept his head on straight and wasn't worrying about Meg.

As he slid into the chair in front of the laptop, he looked over his shoulder at Luke, whose raised eyebrows said he was thinking the same thing. He needed to forget about Meg and do the job. He and Luke weren't brothers by blood, but they were just as close. Every time Luke glanced between him and Meg, his friend worried Dirk would let her back into his life, let her fuck with his head again.

She moved up beside him and his groin tightened as he recognized the faint floral scent of her perfume.

"What are you doing?" she asked.

He forced himself to concentrate. "You've got Pam's phone number, right?"

"I've called often enough to know it by heart."

"Good, what is it?"

"It's 555-761-4359."

Dirk phoned Sadie. "The babysitter's on

the move. I need you to ping a number, give me a location." Dirk rattled off the number.

"Hang on, hot stuff. Let's see if we can find your girl."

Dirk waited tensely, looked up to see the color back in Meg's face. He could read the tension in Luke's wide shoulders. It matched his own.

"Got her," Sadie said into the phone. "House in Kirkland." She gave him a number on 105th Avenue NE.

"That's the other side of the lake," Dirk said. "I'm on my way. Listen, Sadie, it's getting late. Why don't you go home and get some sleep? This doesn't work out, we'll start again in the morning."

"I think I'll just catch a nap here," Sadie said. There was a sofa in the employee lounge the guys used when they were working a case and got in too late to head home. "Good luck tonight."

"Thanks, sweetness; you're the best. I'll get back to you in the morning."

"Sooner if you find the boy."

"Will do." The call ended and Dirk shoved up from the chair. "We've got her." He repeated the street number on 105th Avenue in Kirkland. "That's nearly a thirty-minute drive from here." Pulling his Browning nine mil out of the holster clipped beneath his work shirt, he dropped the magazine to check the load, then shoved it back in and reholstered the weapon. He glanced up at the sound of Luke's M9 Beretta sliding back into his shoulder holster.

"If she's with the boy, the kidnappers could be there," Luke said. "You're going to need some backup."

"Someone needs to stay with Meg."

Meg shot him a look. "Luke doesn't need to stay with me because I'm not going to be here. I'm going with you."

"Bullshit. It's too dangerous. You're staying right here in the house."

"If my son is there, he might need me. I'm going, Dirk. I heard the address. If you won't take me, I'll go by myself. I'm going to be there — one way or another."

Dirk started to argue, saw Luke's mouth edging up. His friend cast Meg a different sort of glance, one Dirk thought held a trace of respect.

"She's the boy's mother" was all Luke said.

"Fine. She can come, but she stays in the car." He turned. "You don't get out no matter what happens. I don't care if you look up and see the goddamn sky falling down. You stay in the car till we come back. If Charlie's there, we'll bring him out to you."

71

Her chin went up. "Fine."

"No arguments. You do exactly what I tell you. Got it?"

"Yes. I've got it. I haven't forgotten how stubborn and overbearing you can be."

"Oh, yeah?" Why that irritated him, Dirk couldn't say. "Is that what happened, Meg? I forced you into my bed?"

She flushed. "No. I didn't mean it that way. You know that isn't what happened."

"You're right. It wasn't my bed we were in — it was yours."

"Okay, you two," Luke drawled. "You can punch it out later. We need to go."

"Go get your jacket," Dirk said to Meg. As she hurried toward the stairs, he caught the jar of greasepaint Luke tossed him and streaked black lines over his face. "I drove over in the Viper. Your car okay?"

"Sure. It's parked down the block. I'll pick you up."

By the time Meg returned downstairs in a pair of black jeans, a puffy dark blue jacket over her sweatshirt, Dirk had left a note for Rose in case she woke up, snagged his black leather jacket out of the Viper, and strapped on the ankle gun he kept beneath the passenger seat.

Meg's eyes ran over his face, taking in the streaks of paint. "You really think they might be there?"

"They could be."

"I don't want anything to happen to you. Maybe we should just call the police."

He took hold of her hands. They felt icy cold. "We have no idea what we're going to find when we get to the house. Once you call the police, it can't be undone."

She took a deep breath and squared her shoulders. "You're right. Let's go get Charlie."

Dirk nodded and led her toward the front door. When he opened it, Luke's battered, two-toned, black-and-tan Bronco idled at the curb, the engine growling like a predator.

"You sure we'll make it in that thing?" Meg asked as she hurried in front of him down the brick walk toward the curb.

For the first time in hours, Dirk grinned. "Luke's a bounty hunter. He does a lot of undercover work. Beat-up old Bronco blends in, goes unnoticed. But there's a Racing five-liter Aluminator XS Coyote engine under the hood. That's five hundred horses, honey. Got a Cobra Jet intake manifold and fully ported aluminum heads. She's a real beast. Luke calls her Lucky Lady."

She tossed him a look. "I hope she's lucky

tonight."

Dirk's grin slid away as he jerked open the backseat door and Meg climbed into the SUV. "So do I, honey." He slammed the door. "So do I."

Meg sat stick straight in the backseat of Luke's high-powered Bronco. Besides the fancy engine, the car had a GPS navigation system built in below the dash. He had already punched in the Kirkland address where they hoped to find Charlie. Meg's heart squeezed at the thought.

"Buckle up," Dirk commanded, riding shotgun next to Luke. Meg clicked her belt into place, heard two more buckles click, and leaned back to look out the window.

It was ink dark, only the pale light of a fingernail moon casting faint shadows over the landscape. At this hour the roads were mostly empty. She could hear the roar of the Bronco's powerful engine, feel its vibration. Thinking of the junk heap it looked like made her want to smile.

She didn't. Smiling would be a betrayal of Charlie.

Instead, she thought about the men she never would have met if it weren't for the murder of one of La Belle's top models. These tough, amazing men who were going after her son.

She was glad her father had gone home. Her dad would go ballistic if he knew what they were planning to do. But Meg trusted these men. She hadn't met Luke before tonight, but Dirk had spoken of him often and highly. She knew he was ex-military, like Dirk, part of some Special Forces unit. She knew Dirk respected him greatly. She believed the men would do their best to bring her baby home.

She caught Dirk's strong, handsome profile as the Bronco rolled along. He ran a hand over the short-cropped mustache around his mouth, down to his hard jaw. The first time she'd seen him she'd thought it made him look like a badass. A very hot, very sexy badass.

And she had been exactly right.

A badass when it came to protecting her. A sweet, affectionate man when it came to the way he treated her, a total hunk in bed. She had given him up for Charlie, for the steady, predictable, stable sort of life she was determined to give her son. But she had never met a man who could come close to replacing Dirk.

An ache throbbed beneath her breastbone. After she'd quit modeling, her father had encouraged her to start dating. He'd invited her to lunches at the country club, where the son of a friend would conveniently appear and be invited to join them. Her dad seemed to have forgotten what a failure his first choice of husband had been.

Vaguely, she wondered if she should call Jonathan, let him know his son had been abducted. But the hard truth was Jonathan didn't give a damn about Charlie and never had.

"This is it," Dirk said, jarring her out of her thoughts, making her heart jerk, then thump against the inside of her chest. "Circle the block," he said to Luke. "Let's see if we get any movement inside, anyone moving around in the area."

Gripping the edge of her seat, Meg leaned toward the window to stare into the darkness. As they drove past a row of older homes, she could just make out the numbers they were looking for beside the front door of a single-story house with a one-car garage.

No lights were on. The house looked empty except for a wisp of smoke floating out of the chimney. Luke kept driving and turned at the corner.

"Looks like there's an alley," Dirk said. "Let's check it out on foot."

Luke drove a little farther, pulled over in

front of a house with a "For Sale" sign in the yard. The home appeared to be vacant.

Dirk swiveled in his seat, pinned her with a look of warning. "Remember what I said. Stay down and out of sight." Soundlessly, the men cracked open their doors. The dome light didn't come on.

"Good luck," she said softly.

Dirk made no reply, just turned and slipped off out of sight. Meg ducked down into the floor well. Closing her eyes, she said a silent prayer for Charlie. A prayer for Luke. And a prayer for Dirk, the man she still loved.

CHAPTER SIX

"You called her honey," Luke said darkly as they moved through the night toward the mouth of the alley that ran behind the house. "I can't believe you called her honey."

"It just slipped out, okay? I was just trying to be, you know, nice."

"Bullshit. You've still got a thing for her. I can see it in your face every time you look at her."

"I don't have a thing for her. Not anymore. She's beautiful, is all. You've got to admit Meg's really hot."

"Okay, so she's hot. So what?"

"A guy can appreciate a beautiful woman, can't he?"

"Not if he's thinking with his dick instead of his brain. Meg's bad news, bro. You know it. I know it. The only person who doesn't know it is her."

Dirk made no reply. Luke was right. Seeing Meg again made him ache for her the way he had before.

"So what about that girl you've been dating?" Luke pressed, determined to keep badgering him. "What's her name . . . Stella? She's beautiful, too. She's fucking gorgeous."

"She is, yeah. She's just not . . . I don't know, she's just not . . ."

"She's just not Meg, right? Be careful, bro. That's all I'm saying."

"If you're interested in Stella, I haven't called her in a couple of weeks. We were never exclusive anyway."

Luke just shook his head.

Both of them fell silent. The mouth of the pitch-dark alley closed around them. The time for talking was over.

They headed down the narrow passage lined with trash cans, papers, and miscellaneous garbage, and began slipping quietly along in the shadows. Dirk recognized the grape-stake fence that ran along the sides of the house, pointed it out to Luke, then pointed to the house.

They split up, Dirk circling left, Luke right. The house was a simple rectangular design with a chimney on one side, a garage on the other, and porches off the front and rear. All the shades were drawn, no light, nothing moving behind the windows on his side of the house. The garage was locked. He couldn't see anything through the dirty window.

Turning, he headed back to the rear, caught up with Luke at the bottom of the steps leading up to the back porch.

"Anything?" Luke asked.

"Not a thing. You?"

Luke shook his head.

"We need to go in." Dirk was already pulling his lock picks out of his jacket pocket as he silently climbed the back steps, opened the screen door, and slipped inside out of sight. Luke was right behind him, gun drawn and pointing downward.

The lock wasn't much. In seconds, Dirk had it open. He pulled his weapon, turned the knob, and eased the door open a couple of inches. Staying to the side, out of the line of fire, he nudged the door farther open with his boot, saw only a dark, empty kitchen, and stepped inside. Luke followed him in.

They began clearing the house, first Dirk in front, then Luke, then Dirk, then Luke, moving with the military precision that still came as naturally to them as breathing.

"House is empty," Dirk said, holstering his weapon, flipping on the lights to examine the interior. A living room, two bedrooms, and a bath. A furnished rental: basic brown sofa and chairs, twin beds in one room, a queen in the other. By now, Sadie would have the owner's name and address.

"They're gone," Luke said, walking over to the still-smoldering fire. "But someone was definitely here and they haven't been gone that long."

Dirk's gaze went to the fireplace. A small, smoke-blackened piece of a pizza box and the last burned remnants of a paper Coke cup lay in the coals at the bottom of the fireplace.

Softly, he cursed. Whatever evidence might have been in the house was little more than ashes. Whoever they were, these guys weren't dumb. They'd wiped their prints at Meg's house and gotten rid of anything here that might have prints or DNA.

He and Luke made a sweep of the interior, looking for something they might have missed, found nothing, and returned to the kitchen.

"What's that?" Luke pointed to a piece of paper spread open on the kitchen counter.

"Looks like they left us a message." Dirk walked to the counter, reached for the note, and saw the lock of fine red hair lying on top. If he'd had any doubt the kidnappers had been there, that doubt was gone.

Anger rippled through him. Carefully pocketing the little boy's silky red hair, he picked the paper up by one corner and began to read the words scratched in blue ink.

" 'This is your first mistake. Make it your last or the boy is dead. You've got forty-eight hours left.' "

Luke hissed out a breath. "Son of a bitch!"

Dirk's jaw clenched so hard it hurt. He glanced back at the smoldering fireplace. "They haven't been gone that long. Twenty minutes max."

"Just long enough to pack up, get rid of evidence, and hit the road. How the hell did they know we were coming?"

Dirk's gaze swung to Luke's, the truth crashing in on both of them at the same time.

"Damn! Meg's house is bugged." Luke slammed out the back door, Dirk right behind him, both of them racing toward the Bronco. As Dirk opened the passenger door, Meg popped up in the backseat.

"Where is he? Where's my baby?"

"He wasn't there, Meg." Dirk could have sworn he personally felt the sharp stab of her pain. "They knew we were coming."

Meg made a sound in her throat as the

engine of the SUV roared to life and Luke hit the gas. "How could they possibly know?"

"They planted surveillance equipment in your house," Luke said.

Dirk leaned over and grabbed Luke's gym bag off the backseat, pulled out a towel, and wiped the paint off his face. "Which means they know we pinged Pamela's cell and that's how we found them." By now they had undoubtedly ditched the phone, making it impossible to track them.

Meg looked up at Dirk. "Surely you don't think Pamela had the knowledge to install that kind of equipment?"

Dirk handed the towel to Luke. "If it's just a listening device, it can be really small, easy to hide. Anyone who came into the house could have done it. If it's cameras, placing them would be harder."

"Cameras? Oh my God."

"Take it easy. No use jumping to conclusions." They were flying down the freeway, passing the few cars on the road, going too fast and hoping they didn't get stopped by the police. The kidnappers had cut the drop time to forty-eight hours. Dirk didn't tell that to Meg.

Instead, just before they reached the house, he turned in his seat to face her.

"We're going to do a sweep of the interior, find whatever devices they're using and disable them. I don't want them knowing any more than they do already."

Which was every damn thing they'd done so far.

"Luke and I both have the type of scanners it takes to find whatever they've put up. It shouldn't take us too long."

Meg fell silent. She didn't say more until they stepped into the entry. When she started to speak, Dirk held a finger against his lips to silence her, then pointed to the sofa, asking her to wait until they were done.

As he went out to the garage to retrieve his scanner, he reached into the pocket of his shirt.

The soft red strands of Charlie's hair seemed to burn his fingers.

"You take the upstairs," Dirk said to Luke. "I'll work down here."

"What about Rose?" he asked.

"I'm right here," Rose said as she came down the stairs. "What's happened?"

"Go over there with Meg, Rose. We'll talk in a minute."

"Did something happen? Did —"

Dirk held up a hand to silence her, then pointed to the sofa. Meg motioned her over and Rose sat down next to her.

While Luke worked the upstairs bed-rooms, Dirk moved through the rooms downstairs. His scanner was only slightly bigger than his cell phone, looked a lot like one. The device could detect wireless, hard-wired, and self-contained cameras. It could also find wireless audio bugs, telephone taps, and laser microphones.

In his line of work, it was a handy little gadget to have.

Twenty minutes later, Dirk looked up to see Luke coming down the stairs with six tiny bugs in his palm. Dirk had found six more. He took them out to the garage, crushed them with his boot, then tossed them into a baggie in case they needed them for evidence.

The women were still sitting in silence when he walked back into the living room.

"Will someone please tell me what's going on?" Rose apparently had waited long enough.

"Someone bugged the house," Dirk replied.

"What does that mean? Bugged?"

Keeping it simple, he said, "A bug is a listening device, Rose. The kidnappers wanted information."

"You mean they've been . . . they've been

listening to us?"

"You're lucky they didn't put up cameras." The thought of the bastards watching Meg undress made Dirk's stomach burn. Invading her privacy was bad enough.

"You don't think it was me?" Rose said, her face suddenly ashen.

Meg flashed Dirk a look, reached over and squeezed Rose's hand. "We don't think it was you, Rose. We know how much you love Charlie."

We? Surely she wasn't including him. Dirk didn't think Meg had ever thought of them as a *we.* That was the problem.

Rose suddenly jumped up from the sofa, her plump body snapping to attention. "The PG&E men! Oh, dear Lord, I forgot all about them!"

Dirk strode toward her. "Take a deep breath, Rose." He waited for her to pull in some air and settle. "Now, what PG&E men are you talking about?"

"Two men. They came to the house a week ago. They were wearing those blue coveralls, you know? The ones that say PG&E on the front?"

"All right, go on."

"They said they had received a report of a gas leak in the neighborhood. They wanted to check, make sure everything in the house was working properly, make sure the house was safe. They seemed like nice men just doing their jobs. So I let them in." She turned away and her eyes filled. "Are they . . . are they the ones who took Charlie?"

"We don't know yet who took Charlie. And you didn't do anything wrong. They did."

Meg cornered Dirk in the kitchen. The sun was coming up, just cresting the horizon, thin beams of light sifting through the stark branches of the leafless trees in her big backyard. She hadn't had a moment of sleep, but then, neither had Dirk.

Half an hour ago, Luke had left. He planned to go home and shower, then head down to the office. "Call me if you need me," he'd said to Dirk as he'd headed out the door.

Rose had left for home to change into fresh clothes. Meg had gone upstairs, hadn't had the energy to shower, but had managed to change clothes. Dressed in jeans, sneakers, and a sweatshirt, she was back downstairs, ready to make coffee and face the grim day ahead.

The rich aroma of French roast said Dirk had already brewed a pot. She crossed the ceramic tile floor, a warm buttercream, to where he stood, lounging back against the granite counter, his hazel eyes watching her as he sipped from a thick ceramic mug with bright yellow daisies on the side.

He had always seemed so out of place in her house, too wild to be fenced in. If he'd stayed, it would have been like trying to turn a panther into a house cat. Watching him now, she felt his restless energy, reluctantly admitting that nothing had changed.

Still, she was drawn to him. Pulled by an invisible cord that made her yearn for him just as strongly as she had almost from the moment she had first seen him. She stopped in front of him, wanted to reach out and touch him so badly her hands trembled.

She clutched them together behind her back. "You haven't slept all night. I know you're at least as tired as I am. Why don't you go home for a while? At least take the time to shower and change."

"I'll clean up here. Luke's stopping by my apartment to pick up some clothes. He'll drop them by before he heads into the office."

She just nodded, tried not to imagine Dirk stripping and climbing naked into her shower. Tried not to remember she had fantasized about joining him there, but they'd never had time to make it happen. Never really had time to explore the fierce sexual attraction that even now made her heart beat too fast.

"You doing okay?"

The words jerked her sharply back to reality. Charlie was missing. That was no fantasy. Her eyes started to burn. How could she have forgotten Charlie even for a second? Dear God, was her little boy all right? She prayed they hadn't hurt him.

She felt Dirk's big hands settle on her shoulders. "Don't go there, Meg. Charlie's okay. That's what you keep telling yourself. He'll be back home soon. That's how you get through this, yeah?"

She couldn't stop herself. She stepped forward and moved into his space, so close they were touching full length. For an instant, his hard arms came around her. Meg closed her eyes and rested her head against his shoulder.

The next thing she knew, he was moving away from her, distancing himself as he had from the moment he had seen her walking toward him at his Lakehurst house.

"I'm sorry," she said. "I didn't mean to do that."

A muscle ticked in his cheek. "You're just tired. We both are. Maybe you should try to get some sleep."

She just shook her head. "I need to call my dad. Tell him what's going on."

"I'll call him, bring him up to speed. I'll tell him about the bugs."

"Will you tell him about last night? About going to the kidnapper's house?"

"Do you want me to?"

"No. He'll pressure us both to do this his way, and I'm not willing to do that."

"Then I won't tell him. I won't lie to him, but I won't say more than I have to."

She nodded. She felt the same way. "So what do we do now? Do we just wait for the kidnappers to call? Wait till they tell us where to take the money?"

"We aren't waiting for anyone. I talked to Sadie while you were upstairs. She's digging deeper into Pamela Vardon, looking for connections to anyone who might be involved."

"Yes, that's good."

"You mentioned the references she gave you. Were they people you knew?"

"One of the mothers she worked for lives in the neighborhood. She had also worked at the day-care center and they gave her a glowing review."

"So not likely the people she's involved with now."

"Not likely."

"Sadie located the owner of the rental, but he wasn't much help. Lives in California, made a deal for a two-week rental. Renter paid cash through the mail. Used a phony name."

Another dead end. Meg walked over and poured herself a mug of coffee, wrapped both hands around it to keep it steady. "I didn't ask you last night. Maybe I was afraid to hear the answer. Now I need to know."

Dirk took a drink of his coffee. "What's the question?"

"Are you sure Charlie was in the house last night? Before we got there, I mean."

Dirk lifted the flap on the pocket of his blue chambray work shirt, reached in and drew something out. "Put out your hand."

She extended her hand. Dirk turned it over and carefully rested something in her palm. A sob broke loose as she recognized the shiny red lock of her little boy's hair.

She didn't hear Dirk move, just felt his arms around her again. "Take it easy, honey. They left it so we'd know he was okay." He lifted her chin. "Remember what I said. He'll be home soon. You just keep thinking that, okay?"

She swallowed, managed to nod. When he let her go, a chill took the place of his warmth.

"I'll call your father. I put his number in my contacts before he left last night." Pulling his phone out of his pocket, he walked past her out of the kitchen.

CHAPTER SEVEN

Dammit, what the hell was wrong with him? Luke would still be chewing his ass if knew he'd held Meg the way he had. Jeez, and he'd called her honey again. Stupid, stupid, stupid.

But damn, he felt sorry for her. He knew she was suffering. He knew the way she felt about her little boy, knew the kid meant everything to her. It was the elephant in the room, the main reason she had ended things between them. She couldn't see Dirk as a father.

Hell, maybe she was right. He'd come from a broken home, never had a real family, didn't know jack about being a dad. His own father had left when he was eight years old, abandoned him to a single mom who scrubbed toilets in a seedy motel just to keep a roof over their heads and food on the table.

His mom had died the day he'd turned

eighteen. The next day, he'd enlisted in the army. He'd gone to junior college on the GI Bill after he'd left the Rangers, then gone into private security, which fit his talents perfectly.

Meg wanted someone stable to help her raise Charlie, and maybe she was right. With his background, he had no idea how to be a family man.

He didn't know how to be a dad, and yet at that moment, the mere thought of Meg's innocent little boy in the hands of those thugs made him sick to his stomach. He had to clamp down on the rage boiling through him to stay in control when he wanted to tighten his hand into a fist and punch something.

He stayed calm for Meg. She needed him now in a way she hadn't before, even when her life was in danger. It didn't matter that he didn't come up to whatever standards she expected in a man. No way was he going to let her down.

When the clock hit eight a.m., he phoned the Pacific Gas and Electric Company. After being jerked around for a couple of minutes, he got through to a supervisor, who checked the records and told him what he'd already guessed.

No leak in the gas line had been reported

in the Madison Park area. The men who'd come into the house hadn't worked for PG&E.

At least he had a description. Rose had described one of the men as tall and skinny, with a crooked nose and very curly brown hair. The other man was shorter, stocky build, balding, with a fringe of sandy hair.

"The tall, skinny man was very polite," Rose had said. "Both of them were."

"Anything else about them you recall?"

"Well, I heard the shorter man call the taller man Cliff. I don't think he realized I was close enough to hear."

"How old were they?"

"In their late thirties, I guess. After that I went into the family room and I didn't see them again until they left. They said everything was okay, then went out to their truck and drove away."

"I don't suppose you can remember the license plate number."

Rose shook her head. "I never even thought to look." She sighed. "I wish I could think of something else, but I'm afraid that's it."

It wasn't much, but it was better than nothing. Cliff was a common name, but if it tied in with something else, it might prove a useful bit of information.

Next Dirk phoned Meg's father.

"Just a minute," Edwin O'Brien said. "Let me put you on hold while I go into the library so we can talk."

Edwin picked up the conversation a few minutes later. "Sorry about that. Meg's mother is already suspicious that something is wrong. After all these years, I guess she knows me too well."

Must be nice, Dirk couldn't help thinking, to have a wife a man loved enough to want to protect her the way O'Brien did his.

"So where do we stand?" the man asked.

"A couple of things you should know. Two men dressed like PG&E workers came into the house last week and installed a dozen listening devices throughout the house. We found them, disabled them. But they're aware we've been trying to find them. They've moved up the deadline."

"They called?"

"They left a note. Also, it looks like the babysitter's definitely involved. I've got someone looking into her background, her friends, anyone who might be part of this."

Silence fell. "I don't like this. If these people know you've been digging around, trying to find them, they might kill Charlie."

"They've heard enough to guess we haven't found anything. By now they probably know Luke and I are both PIs. They'll know I won't let you give them the money without proof of life. Which means they won't kill the boy before they get their hands on the cash."

"I still don't like it. You could be wrong about all of this. I say we give them what they want and bring my grandson home."

"If we could be sure the money would be enough to buy his release, we'd do that. Unfortunately at this point there's no way to know for sure. That's why we need more information."

A long pause ensued. Then O'Brien sighed into the phone. "You aren't leaving me any choice."

"No, sir."

"We still need to have the funds available. I'm in the process of converting the sum into cash, mostly twenties, nothing larger than hundred dollar bills. It's taking more time than I thought, but I assume that's the way they'll want it."

"Oh, yeah. You'll make them very happy with that." Assuming the greedy bastards actually got their hands on the money, which Dirk was fervently hoping they wouldn't. "I'll keep you updated if anything

97

new turns up, or if we get a ransom call."

"All right. Tell Meg I'll be over in a couple of hours. I told Patsy I had a golf game this afternoon."

"I'll tell Meg." Dirk hung up the phone.

Meg needed someone to talk to, someone besides Rose Wills or her father. Someone other than Dirk or Luke. She needed a friend, someone she trusted. Her best friend, Valerie Hartman, soon to be Val Brodie, was off somewhere with Ethan. No way would Meg intrude.

She thought about calling Isabel Rafaeli, another La Belle model, but what was happening felt too personal to share with any but her closest friends.

She glanced away from where Dirk sat at the computer, working on leads, she presumed. Determined to control her fear for Charlie and ignore her ache for Dirk, she wearily climbed the stairs. She hadn't showered yet, just dragged on clean clothes and headed back downstairs. Maybe a few minutes under the hot spray would revive her spirits a little.

Rose was just coming down the hall with an armload of towels as Meg walked toward her bedroom.

"I freshened the guest room bath." Rose

managed a weary smile. "Your friend Dirk was in there washing up. He wasn't as messy as most of the men I know. He wiped up the sink after he was finished and hung up his facecloth."

Meg nodded. "He was in the army. A Ranger. I guess that stayed with him."

"A Ranger. My daughter's husband was a Ranger. He's very good to her and he loves their two boys."

Meg felt a pang in her chest. "I guess some men settle down after they leave the service."

Rose's silver eyebrows drew together. "I don't think Mike has changed very much. He was a good man then. He's a good man now."

Meg thought of Dirk, thought of his two-hundred-mile-an-hour Viper, his flashy speedboat, his Harley. "Dirk's not the kind of man to settle down."

Rose glanced toward the stairs as if she could see him sitting at the dining room table, his head bent over the laptop. "He isn't what I expected."

Meg's lips thinned. She was tired of people making assumptions about Dirk. "Yes, you already said that."

"He isn't what I expected, but I don't think having a tattoo is such a bad thing, do you? It doesn't have anything to do with the person he is inside."

Her throat tightened. She could still remember running her hands over the beautiful colors imbedded in his skin, the feel of his muscles bunching as she traced the outline of the ferocious dragon that wound seductively over his shoulder and crept up his neck. "No, it doesn't have anything to do with who he is inside."

"The way that man looks at you." Rose shook her head. "He has very strong feelings for you, dear."

Meg stared into the woman's round face and read the concern stamped into her features. She couldn't believe she was having this conversation with her housekeeper, and yet she couldn't stop the words from pouring out.

"I loved him. I've never felt that way about anyone. Not the man I married. Not anyone. I loved him, but I knew it would never work."

"Why not? You don't think he would have been a good husband, a good father to Charlie?"

"I don't know."

"If you loved him, dear, maybe you should have taken the time to find out."

The words stung. But maybe she needed

to hear them. She was grateful Rose was strong enough to say them. "Dirk isn't like other men. He deserves to be free, to live his life to the fullest. He shouldn't be tied down to a woman with a child to raise. A little boy who isn't even his son."

There was pity in Rose's expression. "Perhaps that wasn't your decision to make. Perhaps you should have let Dirk decide the answer to that."

Pain sliced through her. She watched the heavyset woman continue on down the hall with her armload of towels. She had always kept Rose at a distance. It was the way she'd been taught to deal with people who worked for her.

But the truth was, Rose was a friend. She was as distraught over Charlie as Meg was, barely hanging on by a thread.

Meg realized she valued the woman's opinion, had for quite a long time.

Her mind went back to Dirk. Surely the decision she'd made had been the right one. Charlie had to come first. The danger he was in only made the truth more clear.

No matter what Rose said, she had done the right thing. Once her baby was home, she would make the same choice again.

Meg went into her bedroom and closed the door. She didn't want anyone to hear her crying.

Dirk sat in front of Meg's laptop, his cell phone on the table beside it. He was on speakerphone with Sadie, still at work in the office this morning, back on her computer and hard at it.

"I've looked over the employee list for Solar-Renew," she said. "A guy named Pedro Martinez wrote a letter that appeared in the editorial section of the Seattle *Times,* but nothing seems to have come of it. There was general bitching and complaining on the local media. Martinez was pretty vocal, but he's working now, got hired shortly after all the brouhaha settled down."

"What about Dunham and Algreen? Anything show up there?"

"They were highly paid executives. Dunham was CEO and president of the company. Algreen was CFO. Algreen was laid off for nearly two years before he got rehired at a company called North Pacific Wind and Solar as head of the accounting department. A couple months later, Dunham went to work for Blue Ridge Energy in Tennessee. Moved there to take the job."

"So Algreen's still in Seattle?"

"That's right."

"How much was he being paid at Solar-

Renew?"

"Three million a year plus bonuses."

Dirk whistled. "And now?"

"Eight hundred thousand. Plus he gets expenses and stock options."

"So getting the ax from Solar-Renew cost him millions and he still isn't back to where he was before. Might make him believe he deserves to recoup his losses."

"Could be."

"If it's him, he probably hired someone to handle the dirty work. Can't see a corporate exec changing diapers and trying to manage a crying kid."

At a sound behind him, Dirk turned to see Meg looking over his shoulder at the computer screen. Her eyes were puffy, as if she'd been crying again. They were still the prettiest shade of blue he'd ever seen.

The soft curve of her breasts beneath her fuzzy yellow sweater drew his attention. He remembered their exact shape and size, the weight of them in his hands, the taste of her nipples on his tongue. He forced the images out of his head and wished he had good news.

"Charlie doesn't wear diapers," Meg said with a hint of defiance Dirk was glad to see. "He's very bright. Rose and I potty trained him about six months ago, before I left on the tour."

"Good to know," Dirk said. The way she was looking at him down her nose, ready to go toe-to-toe, reminded him of the old Meg, the woman he had fallen so hard for.

He didn't want to remember that so he returned his attention to the lady on the other end of the phone.

"Make another pass at Algreen, Sadie. Look for any sign of him slumming, connecting with an ex-con, someone not in his usual social circles. Check his e-mail if you can get in. See if anything jumps out."

"Will do."

"Where are we with Pamela Vardon?"

"Might have something for you there. I located her mother in Portland, gave her a friendly phone call. I pretended I was a friend of Pam's, looking to get in touch with her. Mom was about half sloshed when she answered. Lamented how her daughter never called anymore, not since she's been running around with some joker named Vincent Sandoval. Mom said he was a gambler, a con man, and a real no-good." Sadie scoffed. "Takes one to know one, I guess."

"Impressive. Maybe you should think of going for your PI license."

"No, thanks. More trouble is the last thing

I need. The bad news is, Vincent Sandoval's an alias. Nothing pops up under that name."

"Keep at it. Thanks, Sadie." Dirk ended the call, picked up his cell, and shoved it back into his pocket.

"So Pamela was seeing someone," Meg said. "You think her boyfriend might be one of the men who took Charlie?"

"I don't know. She ever mention him?"

Meg fell silent, trying to remember, then shook her head. "I don't think so. But we didn't talk much. I was either going out or tired after coming home from work."

"Luke was in her apartment, but he didn't really get a chance to look around. I'm going back. Maybe I can get a fingerprint, something to identify this guy. You talk to Rose, see if she's heard the name."

Meg nodded and headed off to speak to the housekeeper.

Luke had left a couple of hours ago. Now the familiar, two-and-one rap at the door said he was back.

Dirk scrubbed a hand over his face. He was bone-tired. With any luck, Luke had brought him something clean to wear. Maybe a shower and fresh clothes would help bring him back to life.

Meg must have heard the knock. Dirk glanced over as she walked up to the door, checked the peephole, then unlocked the dead bolt. "Come on in," she said to Luke. A gust of wind blew in behind him.

"Have you heard anything?" Meg asked him.

"Not yet. Sadie may have caught a lead." In a long-sleeve, faded army T-shirt and jeans tucked into soft, rough-out, knee-high moccasins, footwear Luke favored, he sauntered over to Dirk, tossed a yellow canvas satchel at his feet. "You talked to her, right? You know about Sandoval?"

"I know."

"I asked Mrs. Wills," Meg said. "Pamela never mentioned him."

Dirk leaned down and grabbed the satchel, shoved back the dining chair, and stood up. "I'm going upstairs to shower and change. Then I'm heading back to Pam's apartment, taking a fingerprint kit. Maybe we can find out who this guy Sandoval really is."

"I'll catch a few z's on the sofa while you're upstairs." Luke could sleep anywhere; they both could. It was part of their military training. Just a couple of minutes could make all the difference in a guy's reactions. Maybe when he got back, he'd crash for an hour himself, try to recoup a little.

Dirk took off for the guest bedroom he had slept in when he was there protecting Meg. There was a queen bed and a bath with a shower. He'd rather be climbing into either one of them with Meg, but he wasn't a masochist so that wasn't going to happen.

Dirk stayed in the shower a little longer than he'd intended, wound up cranking the temperature down to cold when an image of Meg popped into his head. Meg on the tour, lying naked on top of him in the big bed in her plush hotel suite. Remembering the way her fiery hair fanned over his chest, he started getting hard.

Since he didn't have time for fantasies about a woman he could never have and could no longer risk wanting, he turned off the water and climbed out of the shower, determined to focus on bringing her little boy home.

Dressed in clean, faded jeans and a forest-green Henley, back in his comfortable low-topped leather work boots, he headed downstairs. Asleep on the sofa, Luke woke up as Dirk's foot hit the last stair, sat up wide awake and completely alert. "You ready?"

"I'm ready. If there's no sign of anyone watching the house when we get back, we'll stop and knock on some doors, see if someone saw something that might prove useful."

Luke nodded. His intense blue gaze swung to Meg. "You okay here by yourself?"

Meg started shaking her head, shifting layers of silky hair across her shoulders. Dirk's groin tightened. He itched to grab a fistful, wrap the soft strands around his hand, and drag her mouth up to his for a deep, burning kiss.

Christ alive, the shower hadn't helped. Instead, the hunger was getting worse, the craving he had felt for her the first time he had seen her. Somehow he had to make it end.

"I want to go with you," she said.

Pamela was off with the kidnappers. It would probably be safe enough to bring her along, but he desperately needed some time away from her.

"You need to stay here in case the kidnappers call. If they do, just remember it'll be recorded. Try to keep them talking long enough to get a trace."

"You think they'll call?"

"No. I think they'll stick to the schedule, but there's no way to be sure. Rose is here and your dad's on his way. You'll be okay."

He turned to Luke. "They already know who we are, and Pam isn't there anyway.

Let's take my car."

A broad grin spread over Luke's face. He loved the Viper. "Good idea" was all he said.

CHAPTER EIGHT

Meg nibbled a piece of the melba toast she kept in the house for Charlie. Her stomach felt shaky from lack of food and not being able to sleep. Her eyes felt gritty from too much crying.

She had to get hold of herself, had to be strong for her son. *What would Valentine do?*

It was a joke. Sort of. Valentine Hart, her best friend's stage name, was one of the models whose life had been threatened when they were on tour. Val had once saved Isabel Rafaeli by cracking Izzy's attacker over the head with a curling iron. Val was softly feminine, with enough self-confidence to lean on a man when she needed him. But she was tough as nails when she had to be.

Meg thought of her friend, and the things that had happened to her on the tour, and resolve settled deep in her bones. She had cried enough. She had to eat, had to sleep, had to regain her strength. Charlie needed her. She intended to be as strong as Val had been.

She finished the melba toast, walked over, and opened the pantry. Tears threatened when she looked at the box of Cocoa Puffs Charlie so dearly loved.

Ruthlessly, she forced the memory away, though her hand shook as she took the box down from the shelf. Walking over to the cupboard, she grabbed a bowl, filled it with cereal, and added milk.

Seating herself at the kitchen table, she forced herself to eat every bite.

Mrs. Wills walked in just as she finished. "Good girl. You're taking care of yourself. That's important. Now you need to get some sleep."

"I'm going to try. I need to sleep, but I don't know if I can."

"Just do your best. You'll need your strength when Charlie comes home."

Meg ignored the tightness that suddenly rose in her throat. Carrying her dishes to the sink, she rinsed them and put them in the dishwasher, then headed for the stairs. The Cocoa Puffs had settled her stomach and given her a little strength. She curled up on top of the mattress and closed her eyes, but sleep still wouldn't come.

She stared at the ceiling for long, endless

moments, finally deciding she'd stay in bed till Dirk got back.

Dirk. She had known the instant she had seen him, seen the hard, compelling planes of his face, how difficult having him in the house was going to be. He was tough and strong, his beautiful, amazing body honed to flesh-covered steel. Everything about him appealed to her on a physical level. Add to that, he was smart and loyal and caring.

It would be so easy to fall back into the trap of loving him. In truth, she had never stopped. But nothing had changed. He was still wild and untamed and she was still a mother with a child to raise.

She tried not to think what it would be like to lie with him again, to feel that hard body pressing her down in the mattress as he took her with wild abandon, giving her pleasure unlike any she'd ever known.

Having him make love to her would ease some of the pain, free her mind for a few precious moments from the terror, the fear for her baby, the uncertainty of what lay ahead.

Meg bit her lip. Even if she went to him and begged him to take her, Dirk would refuse. She had cut him out of her life with knife-sharp precision. One day they were laughing together. The next she had sent him away without a hint of warning.

Meg closed her eyes against the images rolling around in her head. She and Dirk in bed, her snuggling against his shoulder. Then Meg and little Charlie, his small hand in hers as they hurried along the path at the zoo, Charlie bubbling with excitement at seeing the zebra, the black-and-white horsey, he called it.

Sadness threatened to swamp her. She thought of Val and how strong she was, and refused to let it happen again.

Weariness settled over her, invading every muscle and joint. She tried to turn her mind into a flat black canvas, tried not to think at all.

But she still couldn't fall asleep.

"How you holding up?" Luke was driving.

In a moment of stupidity, Dirk had weakened and let him get behind the wheel. They were going too fast, the engine revved to whining. Luke slammed on the brakes and took a corner, hit the gas, shifted, and revved the engine again. Luke Brodie never went slow.

"I could use a couple of hours' sleep, give my brain a chance to catch up."

"That's not what I meant, bro, and you know it."

He knew it, wished he didn't have to answer. But Luke would just dog him until he did. "Truth is, it's hard to think when I'm around her. It's probably that perfume she wears, you know? It smells like flowers. Gets into my head."

"It doesn't get in my head, and therein lies the problem. It's not Meg's perfume that's driving you crazy. It's Meg. She's still got you by the balls, bro, and I think you know it."

Dirk ignored a shot of irritation. "What do you want me to do? Throw her to the wolves? Leave her little boy in the hands of those frigging gangsters?"

"No. I'm just saying . . . you need to keep your head in the game, put your feelings for Meg on a back burner. You can do it. We've both been trained to compartmentalize. Call what's her name when this is over. Stella. Get a little — hell, get a lot. Get your brain unclogged and you'll feel a whole lot better."

Screwing some babe he wouldn't remember the next day was definitely what Luke would do. Then again, Luke had never had it this bad for a woman.

"What is it about her, anyway? I get she's beautiful. She's a lingerie model. Got the perfect body and all that, but still. There's gotta be something special about her. Right?"

Dirk sighed, resigned to finishing the discussion. "I can't explain it exactly. Maybe it's just pheromones or something. I wanted her the first time I saw her. The more I got to know her, the more I liked her. She's sweet and she can be funny. She was good at her job and I could tell she was a really great mom. She was all bottled up when I met her. In bed, I mean. I don't think her ex was much into sex. Or at least not into sex with his wife. With me . . . well, once I got her going, it was like I'd unleashed a tiger."

Luke chuckled. "Way better than Stella, I guess."

There was no need to answer that. "And there's this thing when she looks at me. Like I'm some kind of hero. That's what she thinks. That's the reason she came to me to rescue her son. Christ, I don't want to let her down."

"You're not gonna let her down. We're gonna catch those pricks and bring her kid home." Luke sliced Dirk a look. "You do that, maybe she'll take you back."

Dirk started shaking his head. "No way. I'm not taking a risk like that again. And you're right about getting my head straight.

From now on, Meg's just a piece of furniture I have to walk past when I'm in the house."

Luke grinned, a tiny dimple showing in his left cheek. It drove women crazy. "Just a few more days, bro, this'll all be over."

Luke was right. Just a few more days. Dirk prayed all the promises he'd made to Meg about bringing her son home safe wouldn't be just hot air he'd spouted to try to ease her fear.

Luke rounded another corner and slammed on the brakes, jarring him out of his thoughts. The Viper slid to a stop on a side street next to Pamela's apartment building. "Let's go see what Charlie's babysitter can tell us."

Dirk grabbed his fingerprint kit from behind the seat and they headed around the building, a four-unit, two-story structure that had recently been painted a slightly too bright shade of blue.

They slipped into the tiny, nothing back-yard and went in through the rear door, the way Luke had entered the night before. After clearing the house, confirming no one was home, they set to work.

The apartment wasn't much. Off-white walls and unimaginative brown carpet. But Pamela had made the place her own with bright floral posters and colorful throw pillows on the beige sofa and chair. No photos sitting around. She definitely wasn't coming back.

While Luke searched for anything that might have DNA, Dirk dusted for fingerprints in the bedroom, figuring the only prints there would likely be Pam's or Sandoval's.

Luke ambled in through the open bedroom door. "Find anything?"

"I got a nice print off the clock on the bedside table. There's a box of Kleenex and some K-Y Jelly in the drawer on the left, some rubbers on the right. I'm thinking Sandoval slept on the right. If so, the print could be his."

Luke held up a brown paper evidence bag. "Starbucks coffee cup. Found it in the trash. It was buried pretty deep. I figure a couple of days old."

"There's a coffee machine on the kitchen counter so it's probably not Pam's."

Luke grinned. "Prints and DNA. This could be our lucky day."

"Could be. But if this guy's involved, I'm thinking he's not a major player. Not smart enough. So far the kidnappers have been very careful. Sandoval is a wild card. My guess, he's in for a share of whatever Pam's getting. Those guys may not even know he exists."

"If you're right, he's probably expendable."

"Yeah, and likely Pamela, too. No loose ends."

"Let's find this guy. Maybe he'll lead us to Pam and the kid."

Dirk and Luke left the apartment the way they'd come in. One thing Dirk knew: He was driving the Viper back to Meg's.

CHAPTER NINE

Both men were sleeping, Luke sprawled on the sofa in Meg's living room, Dirk asleep on the couch in the family room.

Before he'd come back from Pamela's apartment, Dirk had called to tell her about the fingerprint and the Starbucks cup he and Luke had found. They were stopping at BOSS, Inc., leaving the print with Sadie to run through AFIS, the national fingerprint database, then dropping the paper cup at a place called Bellevue DNA Testing. A lab tech named Carrie — a lady friend of Luke's, according to Dirk — was making a special rush effort to find a match.

When they got back to the house, Meg had summoned enough energy to scramble them some eggs, fry some bacon, toast some twelve-grain bread, and brew a fresh pot of coffee — about the extent of her cooking skills, aside from an occasional batch of spaghetti made with bottled sauce or baking brownies for Charlie.

Still, the guys seemed to enjoy the meal. They ate like lumberjacks starved for a week.

Afterward, while they waited for word from Sadie and results from the lab, Dirk had done his best to convince her to go upstairs to get some sleep. But she had tried and failed before. Maybe if she were cuddled up next to him —

Meg cut off the thought. That wasn't going to happen. Not now, not ever.

She looked across the breakfast counter into the family room, caught a glimpse of Dirk's wide shoulder, all that showed above the back of the sofa in front of the fireplace, where he slept on his side.

If Charlie were home, he would be stretched out on the carpet, propped on his elbows in front of the TV watching cartoons, laughing at whatever it was an almost-three-year-old thought was funny.

A fresh round of tears collected in her throat. Meg sucked in a determined breath and forced away the urge to cry.

She couldn't afford to give in to her tears, couldn't afford to think of the terrible things that might be happening to her son. Pamela was with him, she reminded herself. She had always been good with Charlie. The

120

kidnappers just wanted money. Pam would keep Charlie safe.

She glanced at the kitchen clock. Dirk and Luke had been sleeping for almost two hours. The afternoon was dragging, moving with agonizing slowness. A few minutes ago, her dad had called her cell and told her he was on his way over, that he was only a few blocks away.

Meg told him about the fingerprint and possible DNA they had found, said that everything was on hold until the test results came back.

"Where are the men now?" her dad had asked.

"Taking a power nap." That's what Dirk had called it. "They were awake all night. They're trying to keep their focus." She asked him to come in through the back door so he wouldn't disturb them.

She heard him outside just then, caught his wave through the kitchen window as he walked past, and went to let him in through the laundry room. He stepped through the door, pulled her into his arms, and gave her a badly needed hug.

He kissed her forehead, caught her shoulders, and stepped back to survey her pale, weary face. "You look exhausted, sweetheart. Have you had any sleep at all?"

121

Meg smoothed flyaway loose strands of the ponytail she had haphazardly fashioned that morning. "I've tried. I didn't have much luck."

"You can't go on like this. You have to get some rest. You won't be any good to anyone if you're dead on your feet."

"I know. Maybe I'll try again later."

Her father nodded, both of them knowing how useless the effort would be. "So we're waiting for something to break?" he asked.

"Either that or a ransom call. Dirk doesn't think the kidnappers will phone before the deadline."

"Good. Getting that much money in cash on such short notice wasn't as easy as I imagined."

Meg looked into his beloved face, finger-combed his fading red hair back into place, wished she could smooth the worry lines from his forehead. "I know you'll get the money. I know you'll do whatever it takes to bring Charlie home."

He caught her hand, wrapped his fingers around it, and squeezed. "I wish this hadn't happened to you. You don't deserve it. In a way, I'm the one who's responsible. The money I've made — that's what they're after. Doesn't matter to them that I've worked hard all my life and earned every penny."

She glanced up at the sound of footsteps, felt a little rush of awareness as she watched Dirk approach in that restless stride of his.

"People like these," he said, "they don't care where the money comes from or who it belongs to. They want it. They're willing to do whatever it takes to get it."

Her gaze ran over him, the dark-blue thermal that hugged his wide shoulders and impressive chest, the jeans riding low on his hips. He'd had less than two hours' sleep and yet he looked alert and rested, looked as good as he had when she had first seen him hammering away on his house.

It didn't seem fair.

"How long before we hear anything?" her father asked.

"Hard to say." Dirk walked over to the coffeepot and poured himself a cup of the French roast she had brewed. "Sadie's still digging into Bob Algreen. Might be something there, but it wouldn't be him personally. He'd hire the players, people who know how to get something like this done. She's looking into his e-mail, seeing if there's anything suspicious. She'll be checking his credit card records, trying to see if he's visited the kinds of places he could make the necessary contacts."

Her dad studied Dirk with renewed interest. "You really think there's a chance Bob Algreen is the man behind this?"

"What do you think? You know him, right? You think he'd go this far to get payback for losing his job?"

Her father ran a finger over one of his thick, red eyebrows. "I don't know. I did a little digging myself. Stopped by the country club on my way over here, talked to a few of my golf buddies. I dropped Algreen's and Dunham's names, asked what they were up to lately. Both were members of the club when they worked for Solar-Renew."

"And . . . ?"

"And one of the guys told me Bob's wife has lung cancer. She was a smoker for years."

"He'd have insurance, right? With the company he works for now? North Pacific?"

"She was diagnosed while he was laid off. He's covered now, but apparently he incurred a boatload of bills."

Dirk took a sip of his coffee. "We'll stay on him. Nice work, by the way."

Her dad seemed pleased by the words. He wanted to help. He wanted to bring Charlie home.

Her father turned his attention to her. "I

came by to make sure you're okay. If you need me to stay, I will. If not, I've got a little more legwork to do to get the funds lined up."

"Dirk and Luke are here, and Rose will be coming back. I'm okay."

Her dad bent and kissed her cheek, looked over at Dirk. "Keep an eye on her, will you?"

"I'll take care of her."

"And keep me posted."

Dirk nodded. "Same goes."

At the words, Meg thought her dad stood up a little straighter. She appreciated the way Dirk was handling him, making him an important part of what they were doing, more than just the man with the money. She had never imagined her dad and Dirk would get along. Now she wondered. . . .

Luke was still sleeping when her father slipped out the back door, leaving Dirk in the kitchen, coffee mug in hand.

He headed for the dining room. "Let's see if Sadie's sent any mail."

Meg followed him, heard his cell start playing, and her pulse kicked up.

Dirk dragged out his phone, spoke into the receiver, listened, then mouthed, "It's the lab." The call went on for a couple of minutes. "That's great, Carrie. Thanks for the extra work. I really appreciate it, and I know Luke does, too."

As the call came to an end, Luke wandered into the dining room. "What's up?" he asked, raking his fingers through his sun-streaked brown hair.

"That was your girlfriend," Dirk said. "Or should I say one of your girlfriends, specifically the one who works at the lab. Carrie came up with a DNA match on the coffee cup. Guy named Vincent 'Vinnie' Santini."

Luke smiled. "Vinnie Santini, alias Vincent Sandoval."

"Exactly."

"Last known whereabouts?"

"Portland, Oregon."

"Same as Pam's mother," Luke said.

"Yup. Vinnie did two years at the Columbia River Correctional Institution for a string of burglaries in the Portland area. He just got out six months ago."

"Pam lived in Portland before she moved here," Meg said. "I remember she mentioned it."

Dirk's gaze swung to her. "How long's she lived in Seattle?"

"At least a couple of years. She's worked for me for more than a year. She was working at the day-care center before that."

"So a couple years back, Pam meets Santini in Portland," Luke said. "He catches up with her again in Seattle when he gets out of jail."

Dirk sat down in front of the laptop, set his coffee mug down on a coaster on the dining table, and brought up his e-mail. "Carrie sent us a photo."

Meg and Luke both leaned in to look over Dirk's shoulder.

"Guy's real pretty," Luke said. "Except for the nose. Black hair, strong features, Italian-looking."

"He's handsome," Meg said. "His nose just gives him character."

"Yeah, all of it low," Luke said.

Dirk reached for his coffee mug and took a sip. "If he's in touch with Pam, he knows we tracked her to the kidnappers' safe house."

"Which means," Luke said, "by now he's gone to ground."

"So how are we going to find him?" Meg asked.

Luke rubbed his unshaven cheek. Neither of the men had shaved in the last two days. Amazingly, they looked even hotter with beard shadows along their jaws.

"Let's see what Sadie can tell us." Dirk e-mailed Santini's name to his office, along with the rest of the info the woman named Carrie had given him.

A minute or two later, the computer dinged with an e-mail reply. "Sadie took a look at the court docs," Dirk said. "Santini claimed he had a gambling addiction. He committed the burglaries to get money to support his habit. Threw himself on the judge's mercy."

"Did it work?" Meg asked.

"Santini agreed to join Gamblers Anonymous. In return, he got a lesser sentence and a year's probation." Dirk looked up from the screen. "I know this guy Santini's probation officer. Allen Whitlow. Good guy. He works out of the Seattle Justice Center. Might be able to give us Santini's address."

Dirk phoned his friend, but by the time the call was over, he was shaking his head. "Santini was using Pam's address as his place of residence." Dirk pushed back his chair and stood up. "Add to that, he hasn't shown up for his last two appointments."

Meg's shoulders sagged. It seemed like they had hit another dead end.

"I might know someone who can help," Luke said, rubbing the back of his neck.

"You always know someone," said Dirk.

Luke flicked him an amused glance but made no reply.

"Okay, so let's talk to this guy you know," Dirk said. "See if he knows where to find

Santini."

"Unfortunately the two of us aren't exactly chummy. Quan Feng's his name. Runs an illegal gambling parlor in the International District. Mid- to higher-level play, manages to stay off the grid." Luke's gaze shifted to Meg. She could feel the power of those intense, laser-blue eyes as if they had reached out and grabbed her.

"Santini's a gambler," Luke continued, his eyes still on her face. "Odds are that hasn't changed. Feng knows everything that goes on in the gambling world. Everything and everybody. He caters to the kind of people who prefer to keep their personal business on the down low. The ones who like to move around in the shadows. The bad news is, if we want to talk to Feng, we'll need a way in."

Luke was sending her a message, Meg realized. A little chill ran up her spine. She understood where he was going. "You think a woman will help you get in."

"No way." Dirk moved between her and Luke. "That isn't going to happen. Meg's a mother, for chrissake. Her boy's been kidnapped. No way are we involving her in this."

"I'm already involved," Meg said.

"You might be recognized," Dirk said,

scowling.

"I don't work for La Belle anymore and I'll change my appearance. I won't be recognized."

"The boy's her son," Luke said. "Should be her decision."

Meg's gaze went to Dirk. The muscles in his jaw were tight. He looked ready to plow a fist into his best friend's face.

"We need to find Santini," Meg said before the tension in the room could escalate any further. "I'll do whatever that takes."

Dirk stared at Luke. "You sure this is the only way?"

"There're other ways. We just don't have time to dick around and figure them out."

Dirk must have read the resolve in Meg's face. "How rough is this joint?" he asked Luke. "Doesn't sound like a safe place for a woman."

"She'll be fine. There'll be other women there, and we'll be right beside her. We just get in, find Feng, get him to answer our questions, then get the hell out."

Dirk released a frustrated breath. His hazel eyes returned to Meg. "Okay, you're in. But you do what I tell you. *Exactly* what I tell you."

For some crazy reason his macho, overprotective attitude made her feel better. He was worried about her, taking care of her the way he had before. If it weren't for Charlie, she would have smiled. "I'll do whatever you say."

The tension in Dirk's shoulders relaxed. He reached out and touched her cheek. Meg fought not to close her eyes and lean into him.

"Okay" was all he said.

Chapter Ten

"Wear something sexy," Luke said to Meg. "Not too classy, a little on the trashy side."

"Christ," Dirk swore.

"Feng loves women. Especially beautiful women. He thinks having them around is good for business."

"I thought you didn't know him that well," Dirk grumbled, thinking the last thing he needed was to see Meg dressed in something that showed off her perfect body. He'd been hard half the day just watching her walk around in jeans and a loose yellow sweater. Wrong time, wrong place, definitely the wrong woman, but there it was.

"It's common knowledge on the street," Luke said. "Feng's a little kinky. Show up with a hot lady and you're in."

"Kinky? Son of a bitch."

"You and Luke will both be with me," Meg reminded him. "I know you'll keep me safe. I just need a little time to get ready."

Dirk sighed. "We won't be leaving for a while. Take all the time you need."

Turning, Meg disappeared up the stairs.

Dirk's gaze slid to the window. It was dark outside, clouds drifting over a waning moon, a sharp wind blowing in off Puget Sound, whistling through the naked branches of the trees in Meg's yard.

They'd been waiting for night to fall. Luke insisted they had one chance to get to Feng, and that meant they had to be sure he was there when they got to his bar, the Golden Lily. He'd be there, Luke was fairly certain, because he came in around midnight most nights.

Waiting for the hours to pass, they'd spent the rest of the afternoon and early evening following up on the leads they were still working, Dirk praying the entire time they'd find something that would give them a break in the case so they wouldn't have to go to kinky Quan Feng's bar.

By the time darkness had settled in, they knew the fingerprint he had found on Pam's nightstand belonged to Pam. No help there, but along with the DNA on the paper cup, at least they knew for certain she and Santini were connected.

Luke had knocked on a few doors in the neighborhood and spoken to an elderly lady who remembered the PG&E van. It was white with the company logo on the side. She hadn't noticed the license plate number. The two repairmen the neighbor had seen, one tall and skinny, one stocky and balding, had confirmed Rose's description. Nothing new there either.

Sadie was still digging into Bob Algreen. That iron was still in the fire, but so far she'd found zip. They were down to the short strokes on this. At the moment, Santini was all they had. Finding him through Feng was a long shot, but with time running out, there was no other option.

Rose had come to the house and stayed with Meg all afternoon, fixed a meat loaf dinner for all of them, then returned home for the night. Edwin O'Brien had phoned several times, stopped by again, then went home to his wife, thank God.

Dirk didn't want to imagine the tirade O'Brien would launch into if he knew the plans Dirk had for his daughter tonight.

A noise overhead, footfalls in the bedroom upstairs, drew Dirk's attention. He glanced up at the ceiling as if he could will Meg to come down, started pacing at the bottom of the stairs.

"Take it easy." Luke sauntered up beside him. "She's a woman. Doesn't matter how pretty she is, she's got to go through the routine. She has to do her makeup, fix her hair, find exactly the right outfit. It's like planning the invasion of Normandy."

Dirk just grunted and wished the evening was already over.

Seated at the dressing table in her bathroom, Meg stared at the woman in the mirror. When she'd been modeling for La Belle, her appearance had been everything. It was the reason she'd had the expensive lighted dressing table installed in her big marble bathroom off the master bedroom.

She studied her tear-ravaged face. Always fair-skinned, she looked pale to the point of sickly tonight. Every freckle stood out, her eyelids were puffy, worry lines marred her forehead. Her lips were dry and chaffed and a little too pale.

Feeling suddenly overwhelmed, she rested her head on the table and closed her eyes. She didn't want to look pretty. Not when her son was out there somewhere crying for his mommy. Not when he might be hurt, when terrible things might be happening to him. Not when she wasn't there to protect him.

She dragged in a steadying breath. Now wasn't the time for self-pity. She had to find her son and bring him home. Meg sat up and faced herself in the mirror. Dirk and Luke were doing their best to find Charlie. She had to do whatever it took to help them.

She glanced at the clock. Nine p.m. She could do this. She just needed a little time to pull herself together.

Turning on the water in the shower, she stepped under the steamy spray. She stayed a minute or two longer than she needed, letting the heat of the water revive her a little. As she blew her freshly washed hair dry, she could see the red highlights returning. For the next few minutes, she creamed her face and body, then began carefully applying her makeup. It was going to take a lot of work to make herself look presentable, but a model knew all the tricks.

It seemed to take forever and what felt like a gallon of makeup, but eventually she finished her face and went on to style her hair, plumping it up, giving herself a big-hair look that completely changed her face. Satisfied she looked good enough to pass inspection, she moved to the closet and began her search for just the right thing to wear.

Discarding one outfit after another, she finally chose a slinky, tight-fitting silver dress with a ridiculously short skirt and low-cut top that she had worn in a La Belle ad a couple of years before.

Strappy silver high heels, a little silver bag, and she was ready.

Turning toward the full-length mirror on the bathroom door, she took a long, assessing look at herself and barely recognized the woman she had become.

Meg thought of Charlie, felt a tight knot rising in her throat, and fought the urge to cry.

Not tonight. Tonight she wasn't a mother. She was another woman completely — a lady of the evening. She was Candy, she decided on a whim. Molten hot and sexy, Candy. She almost smiled at the absurdity. She didn't feel the least bit hot, more like something the dog dragged in.

You can do this, she told herself. Grabbing her little silver handbag, she walked out the bathroom door.

Dirk was still pacing. Luke had gone out to his car, his home away from home, and now wore black jeans, a black wool blazer, and a pair of orange-and-black sneakers. He'd used his electric razor to give himself an almost-shaved appearance, and moussed his short hair up on top. He looked like an overpaid software techie.

Dirk grinned. A bounty hunter was a man of many disguises. Dirk had seen him dressed as everything from a pizza delivery boy to a priest. Tonight Luke looked as if he had money to burn. He would definitely have to park the Bronco down the street.

The Viper — now that was the way to travel. Dirk would be driving Meg to the Golden Lily in style. Upstairs above the bar was a gaming parlor. An expensive sports car and a beautiful woman said he could afford to be there.

He'd added his black leather jacket to the jeans and long-sleeve navy thermal he was wearing. Unfortunately his Browning nine mil would have to stay in the car under the driver's seat. If they were lucky enough to get into the gaming room, there was a good chance they'd be searched. The weapons could get them ousted before they ever got to Feng.

At the last minute, he decided to risk the palm-size .22, five-shot revolver he kept in his glove box. It might go unnoticed in the spot he liked to carry it, the front pocket of his jeans. No big deal if they made him leave it at the door. At least they wouldn't take him for a cop.

Luke was carrying a four-inch switch-blade, a finely honed, custom-crafted knife.

Luke particularly fancied knives.

Dirk had started pacing again, checking his heavy steel wristwatch every few minutes, when Meg appeared at the top of the stairs. He squeezed his eyes shut, then opened them again to be sure he was actually seeing what he was seeing, part of him praying he wasn't.

Sweet holy God.

In a dress so short it barely covered her sexy heart-shaped ass, Meg started down the stairs. Silver spangles shook every time she moved. The bodice was cut way too low, her pretty breasts shoved up and barely contained by the stretchy sequined fabric.

Blue shadow highlighted her eyes, which were rimmed with black liner. She'd blackened her long, thick lashes and painted her mouth a ripe cherry red. Fiery red hair swung loose down her back. She had pulled some up on the sides but left a few flyaway ends next to her cheeks.

She looked like a tart, the most delicious, desirable, pretty little tart he'd ever seen.

Dirk wanted to kill Luke Brodie.

She swung the strap of her silver purse over her shoulder as she reached the bottom of the stairs.

"I'm ready," Meg said.

Luke's brilliant blue eyes ran over her

from head to foot. "Well, you certainly are, sweet cakes," he drawled.

A muscle clenched in Dirk's jaw. Forcing the hands fisted at his sides to relax, he reached out and caught Meg's shoulders, turning her to face him. "You remember what I said? You do what I tell you."

"I remember."

Dirk let her go. "You need a name, something besides Meg or Megan."

"I'm Candy," she said without hesitation. "For tonight, I'm Candy Molten. That's who I am."

His mouth edged up. *Oh, yeah, baby.* He almost said the words as his gaze slid down to the plump mounds of her breasts, barely concealed by the dress.

Instead, he turned to Luke. "We'll meet you there." Setting a hand at Meg's waist, he urged her toward the Viper parked in her garage.

"Why aren't we all going together?" Meg asked.

"The Viper's part of our cover," Dirk said. "Only two of us can fit inside."

"Plus it's always smart to have a second way out if the plan goes south," Luke said, which Dirk wouldn't have, since he didn't want to worry Meg any more than he had to.

"Okay," she said.

He guided her out to his car and settled her in the passenger seat, fought to ignore the faint scent of flowers that always drove him crazy.

They clicked their seat belts into place and they were off, the low-slung sports car racing along through the darkened streets.

"This car is really beautiful," she said, running a manicured hand over the dash, which had more lighted gauges than an airplane cockpit. "It fits you perfectly."

Why that irritated him he couldn't say. "You must think I'm pretty superficial."

She sat up a little straighter. "No, that isn't what I meant."

He gunned the engine and zipped around a corner, still about half-pissed and not quite sure why.

"I used to love cars. I bought myself a Shelby Mustang when I first started modeling. I never really liked college, barely made it through. There was a time I wanted to be a female race-car driver."

He tried to picture Meg behind the wheel of a high-powered Indy car, couldn't make it happen. "You still like to drive?"

She shrugged. "These days, all I drive is my little SUV. I think that's one of the reasons my dad pushed me so hard to get married. He figured it would settle me down. Which it did."

He flicked her a glance. "So you were a wild child back in the day?"

She smiled for the first time since her son had disappeared. "A little wild, I guess. No drugs, nothing like that. Though I used to like drinking tequila. I think Jonathan was attracted to that side of me. Meg, the party girl. As soon as we were married, he insisted I change."

"But you like being a mom, right?" The minute the words were out of his mouth, he regretted them. He didn't want her worrying about Charlie. She needed to stay focused, same as he did.

Meg seemed to feel the same. She was playing a role, determined to remain immersed in it. *Candy Molten.* His lips twitched in amusement.

"I love being a mother," Meg said. "Having a child of your own is the best feeling in the world. I wouldn't mind having more kids someday."

He used to want kids. Over the years, somehow the idea had faded. For a while when he'd been with Meg —

"I'm sorry about your house," she said as the Viper prowled the darkness. "Val told me what happened the night it burned down. There were pictures of the fire on the news."

He'd loaned the place to Val and Ethan as a safe house. Turned out not to be safe for any of them.

Dirk shrugged. "I really liked that house. It was crazy. The place was outdated, still had the previous owner's furniture in it, an old lady who died without any heirs. I kept it longer than I usually do. Once I get them remodeled, I usually turn them over."

"You remodel houses?"

"On the side, yeah. I buy houses, fix 'em up, and sell them. I've been doing it for years, Meg. I told you before, I wasn't some loser off the street."

Meg fell silent as Dirk wove the Viper in and out of traffic. He slanted her a look, found himself staring at the long, sexy leg showing beneath her skirt, cursed, and returned his gaze to the street.

He needed to keep his head in the game, not be thinking about how sexy Meg looked dressed like a hooker.

"I wasn't fair to you, Dirk," she said, completely out of the blue. "I assumed things about you I shouldn't have."

He shot her a glance. "You're right, you did. Doesn't matter now. All that matters is getting your boy back."

Meg made no reply. Dirk stepped on the gas.

Chapter Eleven

In Seattle's International District, Chinese, Filipino, Japanese, Vietnamese, and Southeast Asians all lived together side by side. The bar Feng owned, the Golden Lily, was on Maynard near Weller, a narrow establishment on the street level of a four-story brick building. The bar sat next to a martial arts school, Ling's Noodle House, the Tea Gallery, and a Vietnamese restaurant called Tips'.

A bulky Asian, legs splayed, hands crossed in front of him, stood next to the front door as they drove up. Dirk spotted Luke walking toward them, got out, and went around to help Meg out of the car.

"Thank you," she said as she stepped up onto the curb. Noticing the goose bumps rising on her arms in the damp, chilly air, Dirk peeled off his leather jacket and draped it around her shoulders. Luke joined them. The bulky Asian gave them a once-over and they walked into the bar without a problem.

The interior was a mix of American and Chinese: a long black granite bar lined with black-and-chrome bar stools, Formica-topped tables, and black vinyl chairs spread haphazardly around the room. A shuffleboard table rested along an exposed-brick wall while a digital jukebox played rock music from the opposite wall.

"Evanescence," Dirk said, recognizing the band as they strolled through the dimly lit bar with Luke right behind them. Three Asian men, early twenties, lean and athletic, black leather jackets and motorcycle boots, sat at the bar.

A young Asian couple was making out in the corner.

Two men sat at another table, the lights of their smartphones glowing, more interested in sending text messages than talking to the woman sitting across from them.

"This way," Luke said, urging them to keep walking. The guys at the bar had spotted them. Meg returned Dirk's jacket, settling into her role, and Dirk drew her a little closer, just to make sure the men knew she belonged to him. At least for the night.

The lighting was dim, neon pink tubes running behind the back bar, green and red Tsingtao beer signs on the walls. A hanging lamp on the end of a chain shed a cone of light over the shuffleboard table, but no one was playing.

There were pool tables in the back. A loud *clack* drew their attention as a cue ball slammed into a ten, which knocked the twelve and thirteen into side pockets.

They kept walking, stopped next to an elevator with a stainless-steel door. A big Asian stood beside it, arms bulging with muscle. But the tight buttons on his shiny gray suit said he was a little overweight.

Like the guy out front, he was more show than go, Dirk figured, not in great shape but a menacing appearance that kept the customers in line.

Luke stopped directly in front of him. "We're friends of Lee Cullen's. Lee said this was a place we could find a little action."

Meg's eyes widened as Dirk pulled out a roll of hundreds, peeled one off, and tucked it into the Asian's thick-fingered hand.

The man pocketed the bill, looked them over, spent a little too long sizing up Meg. "I will tell Quan Feng you are here." The man walked away. The sound of his heavy footfalls rang, then faded as he reached the top of a set of back stairs. Apparently the elevator was only for guests.

Dirk knew Lee Cullen through Luke. He

was half Chinese, half Irish. He'd invented an ultraviolent military computer game called Iron Warrior and made a boatload of money, but he liked to keep a low profile. Luke had worked for him a couple of times, digging up info on his competition.

Dirk hadn't known Cullen liked to gamble. He hoped the guy's name would be enough to get them through the door, that and bringing Meg to tantalize Quan Feng.

He looked over at the woman beside him. "You okay?"

Meg just nodded. He could feel her nerves humming and eased her a little closer. "You're doing great. Everything's gonna be fine."

She relaxed a little, managed to smile, and laced her arm through his, as if they were a couple. He wished it didn't feel so good.

He thought about what she'd said. That she had underestimated him. He figured it was true, though it didn't really make any difference. It was over between them. Nothing could change that. Meg had burned that bridge as surely as his house had burned down.

The big Asian returned, pushed the button next to the elevator, then stepped back as the door slid open.

Meg walked in first. Dirk and Luke followed her inside. This time the big Asian joined them. The elevator went up two floors before it came to a stop and the door reopened.

A man in a black suit stood outside the entry to the casino, tall and slim, with coarse, black hair and a greasy smile. "I am Louis Chan, the manager. The man with you is Fu Han. You understand we have certain rules. You won't mind if Mr. Han makes certain you are following them."

Easing Meg a little behind him, Dirk raised his arms, allowing the big Asian to do a search. Han patted him down but didn't make contact with the little .22 in his pocket. Han found Luke's knife, which didn't please him.

The Asian held up the knife. "You will get this back when you leave."

"Long as you remember where you got it," Luke warned.

Han made no reply, just slipped silently back into the shadows. Meg accepted a glass of champagne off a passing waiter's tray and they wandered toward the tables. While Luke casually circled the room, looking for Feng, Dirk set a possessive hand at Meg's waist, guided her over to one of the blackjack tables, and took a seat.

Playing her part, Meg eased up close

behind him. The soft scent of her floral perfume wrapped around him and Dirk silently cursed.

To distract himself and play the role he was there to play, he pulled out a roll of hundreds, money he kept in a hidey-hole in his car. In his business, it was always better to be prepared.

He bought in with five hundred, stacked the chips in front of him, and eased into the play with a twenty-five-dollar bet. This wasn't a high-roller joint, but it wasn't a dive joint either.

A sexy little black-haired waitress appeared. Dirk ordered a Jack and Coke while Meg sipped her champagne. Across the room, he caught a glimpse of Luke sauntering toward an obese, bald-headed Chinese man who had to be kinky Quan Feng. Even from a distance, Dirk could see Feng's beady black eyes fix on Meg.

Dirk's jaw went tight. Unfortunately their plan was working.

"Okay, baby," he said, placing a fifty-dollar bet. "Time to bring your sugar daddy some luck."

Meg's cheeks flushed. Then, to his complete surprise, she leaned down and very softly kissed him. Full lips that tasted like cherries sent a rush of heat straight to his groin.

"Good luck," Meg whispered in a low, throaty voice. Not Meg, he realized as she gave him a wicked smile. Sexy hot Candy Molten. Didn't matter which woman she was. That kiss had made him hard.

Luke ordered a scotch rocks at the bar, then carried his glass over to the fat man seated at a table near the far end. A guy drinking Red Bull and vodka sat alone at another table, his tie askew, eyelids drooping, on the verge of being shit-faced drunk.

The room wasn't big by casino standards. He counted five card tables where they played three and four card poker. Other patrons, both male and female, most of them Caucasian, played blackjack, Spanish 21, or pai gow.

In the outskirts of the city, minicasinos like this were legal. Not in Seattle proper. How Feng managed to escape being shut down, Luke had no idea.

"Mind if I join you?" he asked, then sat down before Feng could object.

The huge Chinese shifted his excessive bulk, his head swiveling on a body with no neck at all. "You are new to our venerable establishment," Feng said. "A friend of Lee

Cullen, I am told."

"Lee and I are friends." Luke took a drink of scotch. "I know he comes here once in a while so I used his name. I need to talk to you."

Feng sipped through the straw in his drink, club soda from what Luke could tell. The guy was no fool.

"Many people wish to speak to me," Feng said. "Most are not so bold."

"I'm looking for someone. Your reputation says you're a man who might help me find him."

Feng shrugged his enormous shoulders. "I'm a businessman. It pays to be aware."

"The guy's name is Vinnie Santini. Might call himself Vincent Sandoval. Vinnie likes to gamble. Got the bug. I'm hoping you know him, maybe know where I can find him."

Feng stirred the soda with his straw. "You are here for information. Information is a very valuable commodity."

"That's true," Luke said.

"If I give you Santini, I will want something in return." Feng's gaze moved across the room to Meg. Even with too much makeup, a too-tight dress, and big hair, she was the most beautiful woman in the room. "If I help you find him, what is in it for me?"

Luke sat up a little straighter. "I'll tell you what's in it for you if you *don't* help me find him. Trouble with a capital *T.* Santini's involved in something very big and very illegal. He's going down hard, and anyone in his way is going down with him. The cops'll be digging into every nook and cranny of his life. Gambling is part of it. Tell me where he is and I'll do whatever I can to keep your name and business out of it."

"You are police, then?"

"No. Just an interested party."

Feng's small, black eyes returned to Meg. "I want the woman. She stays when you leave. I'll tell you where to find Santini. In exchange, the woman stays with me."

Not good. Luke's gaze traveled across the room. Dirk hadn't missed Feng's interest in Meg. He'd lose it if Luke even pretended they were leaving her behind.

"The woman belongs to my friend. He doesn't like to share."

"You knew I would want her when you brought her here."

Luke didn't deny it. "I'd heard rumors. I knew you liked beautiful women. Who doesn't?"

The slash that was Feng's mouth curved faintly. "I would enjoy tying her up. A woman with hair like flames . . . no doubt she needs discipline."

Luke clamped down on a curse. Thank Jesus Dirk couldn't hear. "I can't give you my friend's woman, but I'll give you this." Luke pulled out a business card and handed it to Feng. "Tell me where to find Santini and I'll owe you."

Feng smirked. "You will owe me." He looked down at the plain white card, studied the simple black letters. "Luke Brodie." Those little pig eyes came back to Luke's face. The smirk was gone. "I have heard the name. It is said you are a good man to know."

"I can be. Or I can be a very bad man to know."

Feng pocketed the card. "During the day, Santini gambles at a place called the Mayfair. A bowling alley out in Kenmore. It opens at ten a.m. Vinnie likes to play there in the mornings. If he gambles tomorrow, that is where he will be."

Quan Feng tapped the card in his pocket. "You owe me, Luke Brodie. Do not forget."

"I won't forget." Luke took a drink of his scotch. The ice rattled as he set the glass down on the table, then stood up and walked away.

Owing a man like Quan Feng was the last thing he wanted. But as he strode toward

Meg and saw the desperate, hopeful look on her face, he knew that no matter what it took, if it helped find her boy, repaying the debt would be worth it.

CHAPTER TWELVE

As Luke approached, Meg unconsciously reached for Dirk, caught his arm, and hung on. There was something in Luke's face, something that told her he had found Vinnie Santini. Or at least knew where to look for him.

"Let's go," Luke said.

Dirk scooped up his chips. "I'll be right back." He flashed her a look. "Stay close to Luke." While he went to retrieve his money — she had a feeling he had lost a little on purpose — Luke urged her toward the door.

"Did you find him?" she asked. "Did you find Santini?"

"I know a place he might be in the morning. That's more than we had before."

"Yes . . . yes, it is." She blinked to keep her eyes from filling. Tomorrow they would find Santini. Then they would find her little boy.

The big Asian, Fu Han, appeared, reminding her of the role she was playing. He handed Luke the knife he had taken.

"Thanks," Luke said. "It's one of my favorites."

Meg shuddered to think how many knives Luke might own. He and Dirk both seemed to have plenty of weapons.

She turned to see Dirk walking toward them. She loved the way he moved, the confident energy, the way his eyes always seemed to find her, the way, once they did, she couldn't look away.

The elevator rattled up and the door slid open. Instead of the car being empty, five men walked out. The two in front held big black pistols pointed toward Dirk and Luke. They were in their early thirties, one in skinny jeans and a slim-fitting blazer with the sleeves pushed up, with the words Lone Wolf tattooed on his forearm.

The second man wore a Henley with jeans and expensive, black-and-silver designer sneakers. They looked more like metrosexuals than hoodlums.

The other three men were younger, knit caps pulled low, T-shirts and low-riding jeans. Street punks, Dirk would call them. None were Asian.

"Get back inside," the guy with the tattoo demanded, apparently the leader.

Luke said the f word under his breath, and Dirk eased Meg a little behind him. She started to tremble.

"We're just leaving," Dirk said. "We don't want any trouble."

"You *were* leaving." The guy in the expensive sneakers waved his gun toward the casino. "Now you aren't."

Dirk had her easing backward toward the casino exit when Feng's two security guards and the manager arrived, which put them in the middle of a circle of hostile men.

All of them froze. She felt Dirk's hand ease something out of his pocket, heard the faint, muffled *click* of Luke's knife sliding open and locking into place.

"Where's Feng?" the guy with the tattoo asked. He was good-looking in a designer suit sort of way, with high cheekbones and perfectly arched dark brown eyebrows. She wondered vaguely if he paid to have them plucked.

"Mr. Feng is busy," said Fu Han. The big Asian stood with his legs splayed, but his size wouldn't help him against a gun. "I would advise you to leave."

"Tell him Rick Bledsoe is here. Tell him we need to talk."

Feng waddled up just then, his heavy body swaying from side to side as he moved. "You are disturbing my guests, Ricky. What do you want?" People were beginning to stir, heads turning their way.

"You call me Ricky again, fat man, and it won't matter what I want. You'll be too dead to care."

"You're behaving very badly — Rick. Your father will not be pleased when he hears you are poaching on his territory."

"My father is old and worn out. I'm taking over. Now pay me what you owe and we'll leave." Some kind of protection money, Meg guessed.

"I do not think so," Feng said. "I have been paying long enough. Those days are over."

Rick turned to his sneaker-clad friend. "Tell him, Jimmy, what's going to happen if he tries to stiff me."

"You don't pay," Jimmy warned, "there won't be a stick of furniture left in this place in one piece."

Luke shifted beside her. "I don't think that's a good idea. How about you, Mr. Feng?"

"Not a good idea at all," Feng said.

Rick turned a hard look on Luke. "Who are you?"

Luke shrugged. "Just a guy who owes Mr. Feng a favor."

Feng smiled.

"Well, I don't care who you are." Rick waved the barrel of the pistol. "Feng pays or the place goes down."

Meg didn't see Luke move, but suddenly Rick's gun hit the ground and slid across the floor. Luke stood behind him, an arm locked around Rick's neck, the point of his knife nudging the artery pumping wildly in Rick's throat.

Dirk had moved, too, a long leg kicking out, hitting Jimmy's hand and knocking his gun in the air. Dirk's tiny revolver flashed, then the barrel dug into the flesh beneath Jimmy's chin.

"If you two don't want your blood running all over the floor —" Luke said.

"Or your brains splattered all over the ceiling —" Dirk added, nudging the revolver a little deeper.

"I'd suggest you call off your wannabe thugs and leave Mr. Feng alone," Luke finished.

Rick's fingers curled around the arm wedged beneath his chin. "Who are you kidding? You won't hurt me. My father's on the city council. You touch me and you'll spend the next ten years in prison."

Luke spun the man around so quickly it was more a blur than a movement. The knife blade was gone, the hilt in his palm. A fist drove into Rick's stomach, doubling him over, then Luke punched him hard in the face.

Rick went sprawling. When Luke took a menacing step in the guy's direction, Rick curled into a protective ball and started to whimper.

Beginning to panic, Jimmy whirled away from Dirk, threw a wild punch that Dirk blocked, then another he ducked. The revolver disappeared into Dirk's pocket and his mouth curved into a hard-edged smile.

Dear God, Meg thought, *he's enjoying this!* A single hard punch to Jimmy's stomach sent him to his knees. Bending over, he began making retching noises, fought to suck in a breath of air.

The tiny revolver was back in Dirk's hand, pointed at the three younger men, who seemed frozen in shock where they stood. They raised their arms above their heads and backed toward the elevator. "We just came along for the ride, man," one of them said.

"Yeah, well, ride the hell out of here," Dirk said. "Take your two loser buddies with you."

"Show your face in here again," Luke added as Feng's men retrieved the discarded weapons, "and Mr. Feng calls me." He flicked a glance at Dirk. "And him."

Dirk's hard smile returned. "That's right. If you're smart, you'll put the word out that Quan Feng has friends who take care of him."

All three younger men nodded. Rick and Jimmy staggered to their feet, wove their way into the elevator along with the others, and the door slid closed.

Luke pinned Feng with a look. "We good?" he asked.

Feng's gaze slid over Meg like something slimy out of the gutter. "I would have preferred the woman, but yes, your debt is paid."

Meg started shaking. The elevator dinged its return and they all walked inside for the ride down to the bar. Meg felt Dirk's hand settle at her waist.

"It's all over, honey. Everything's okay."

Luke shot him a look, and they rode the rest of the way in silence.

Dirk checked to be sure Rick and his gang were gone, checked again outside, then they headed for their cars.

Meg leaned back in the passenger seat of the Viper. Though the adrenaline rush was over, tremors still shook her. Every bone in her body ached from lack of sleep, but knowing tomorrow they would talk to Vinnie Santini, find out where Pam and the others were holding Charlie, a fresh shot of nerves rolled through her.

She wearily closed her eyes, but the last thing on her mind was sleep.

Dear Lord, she prayed, *let Vinnie Santini know where to find my son. Please keep my little boy safe until we can bring him home.*

CHAPTER THIRTEEN

When they reached Meg's house, Luke peeled off, heading for his Bellevue apartment for some badly needed downtime. He'd be back in the morning for the trip to the Mayfair Bowling Alley, where there was a good chance Vinnie Santini would show up to gamble.

Dirk's hand fisted. He was more than ready for the meet. In the meantime, as tired as he was, he wouldn't have much trouble falling asleep.

Parking the Viper in Meg's garage, he guided her into the house, watched as she kicked off her high heels, then pulled the clips out of her long, red hair and shook it free. With a tired sigh, she wearily lifted the fine strands up off her shoulders, then let them fall back again. She was exhausted, he knew. She hadn't slept at all since her little boy had been abducted.

Dirk felt a pang in his chest. He'd been

proud of her tonight, proud of how strong she'd been. She wanted her baby returned and she was doing everything in her power to make that happen.

They paused at the bottom of the stairs. "Tomorrow's a big day," he said. "We both need to get some sleep."

"I know. There's a blanket and pillow on the sofa in the family room."

"What about you? You need some rest, too."

She sighed. "I wish I could. I'm just . . . I'm too keyed up to sleep." She swallowed and shook her head. "I can't eat. I can't sleep. I just lie there counting every heartbeat, every breath of air going in and out of my lungs. Whenever I close my eyes I think of Charlie and it's like . . . it's like if I sleep, I'm failing him."

Dirk caught her shoulders. "You aren't failing him. You're trying to keep it together so you *won't* fail him."

Big, teary blue eyes centered on his face. She was standing barefoot on the bottom stair, bringing her height level with his.

"I'm so tired," she said. "You could make me sleep. We could make love and then I could sleep." Before he could move, she leaned in to him, her full breasts sinking into his chest, her soft lips coming down over his.

Heat and need hit him like a punch in the stomach. Hot desire clawed at his insides. This was Meg and he wanted her. Ached for her, just as he had before.

For a moment he kissed her back, just sank in and took what he wanted, let the softness of her lips stir the fire in his blood. When she opened, inviting him in, his tongue slid over hers and he went iron hard.

He'd wanted Megan O'Brien since the moment he had seen her strutting down the runway in a pair of strappy high heels, a tiny silver thong, and angelic white-feathered wings.

That feeling was nothing compared to the all-consuming lust he felt for her now, after five long months without her.

"Dirk . . ." Her arms slid up around his neck. "I need you." She kissed him wildly and he kissed her back, tasting, remembering, yearning. It took every ounce of his will to finally pull himself free and step away.

"We can't do this, Meg. I'm not going there with you again."

Her eyes filled, making them look even bigger and bluer. "I can't take any more, Dirk. I'm going to break; I can feel it. I'm begging you. Just this once. Just for tonight. Please, Dirk."

He clamped down on his raging need. "Maybe you could take a sleeping pill. You must have something around here."

"I don't want a sleeping pill! My son is missing! I can't bear to think of what might be happening to him! I want someone to hold me. I want someone to touch me. I want to forget for a while. Make me forget, Dirk. Please."

He was a strong man, but he was no saint. When a woman who looked like Meg begged a man to take her, when that man wanted her the way he'd never wanted another woman, there was only one choice.

Pulling her back into his arms, he claimed her mouth in a deep, thorough kiss. Sliding the silver skirt up to her waist, he cupped her perfect heart-shaped ass and dragged her against him, let her feel the hard ridge beneath the fly of his jeans.

Meg moaned into his mouth and pressed herself more fully against him. The kiss went wild and fierce. He liked to kiss and he loved kissing Meg. He loved the way she tasted, loved the full lips that melded so perfectly with his.

He unzipped the stretchy silver dress down to her waist, then slid the straps off her shoulders, exposing the white lace demi bra that shoved her breasts up like a feast.

Bending his head, he tongued her nipple through the sheer fabric, then unfastened the front hook, dragged the bra off, and tossed it away.

Smooth, plump breasts filled his hands. He knew the exact size and shape, knew the weight of them, knew how good they felt nestled in his palms.

He bent and took the fullness into his mouth, heard Meg moan. Arching her back, she urged him to take more of her, and he didn't disappoint. While his mouth worked her breasts, his hand moved down her body, slid over the tiny strip of satin between her legs.

He was hard as granite, pulsing with the beat of the blood pumping through his veins.

"Take me," Meg whispered, "I don't want to wait." He didn't want to wait either. He wanted to be inside her so bad his hands clenched into fists.

"Please, I need you so much. Make love to me, Dirk."

Make love to me. The words hit him like a blow. He couldn't do this, refused to feel that kind of heartache again.

"Dirk, please." Her slender fingers cupped him through his jeans, and arousal burned through him. His resolve weakened. Jesus, he wanted her.

He gripped her shoulders, commanding her attention. "If we do this, it's just sex, Meg. You understand? Just sex, nothing more. We do this, it doesn't change a thing."

A little sob came from her throat. "I don't care, I don't care. I need you. I can't take any more."

He knew what asking him was costing her. Knew she had pushed herself to the ragged edge. He tried not to think that any other man could do the job as well as he, wanted to believe this meant something to Meg, no matter what he'd said.

Sliding an arm beneath her knees, he scooped her against his chest and strode up the stairs, carried her down the hall to her bedroom, set her on her feet next to the bed.

Meg framed his face between her hands and kissed him. "I want you inside me." Another soft kiss. "Your condoms are still in the drawer."

His lust-fogged brain hadn't thought of protection so that was a big problem solved.

Meg worked his belt buckle and buzzed down the zipper on his jeans. *It's just sex,* he reminded himself. Just a way to help Meg escape her nightmare, at least for tonight.

Dirk opened the drawer and pulled out a condom, tore it open, and slid it on as he backed her up against the wall. The dress bunched around her waist. Her pretty breasts bobbed free. She was the sexiest thing he'd ever seen.

Easing her little white satin panties down over her hips, he let them fall to her ankles, and Meg stepped out of them. Dirk kissed her, felt the heat of her fingers around him, guiding him inside her. Lust hit him hard and he fought not to come.

Lifting her up, he wrapped her long legs around his waist, buried himself deep and began to move, taking her with hard, heavy strokes that sent fresh heat burning through him.

Meg moaned.

"Easy, baby." He wouldn't come until she did, not if it killed him. He was doing this for her, giving her what she needed. Giving them both what they needed.

And it wasn't going to be over anytime soon.

Beneath his thermal, he felt her nails digging into his shoulders as he drove into her. His belt buckle clanked, her head tipped back, and she cried out his name. Meg came hard, but he didn't stop. Not until he had driven her up over the peak again.

His climax was explosive, drawing his insides into a hot, tight knot and making him groan. For long seconds, he just held her, her arms around his neck, her head resting on his shoulder. Then he felt the wetness of her tears.

"Oh, God, Dirk." She started to cry as he set her on her feet next to the bed.

"Easy, baby." Gently, he stripped off the rest of her clothes. "It's all right, honey. We're going to bring Charlie home. Everything's gonna be okay." For long seconds he just held her, let her cry out some of her grief.

Then he lifted her into his arms and settled her on the mattress. "You think you can sleep now?"

Meg wiped away her tears. "I can if you lie down beside me."

He reached down and touched her cheek. "If I do, I'll want you again."

Fresh tears spilled over. "Yes, please."

Meg didn't care what Dirk said — it wasn't just sex, at least not for her. Dirk wasn't just a man she was using to help her get through the worst days of her life. He was the lover she had missed every night since she had sent him away.

She watched as he pulled his long-sleeve

thermal off over his head and tossed it away. Removed his work boots and slid out of his jeans. She loved his lean, magnificent body, the sculpted muscles, the six-pack ridges across his flat stomach, the trail of dark hair that arrowed from his navel down into his jeans.

She thought she saw a new tattoo on his shoulder, but in the darkness she couldn't make out what it was. Then he was kissing her and she was kissing him back and the thought slid away.

He was gentle with her this time, kissing her breasts, then moving lower, using his talented hands and mouth to drive her to the peak, then gently nudging her over.

He took his own pleasure, but she knew hers came first. He was taking care of her, the way he always had. She loved that about him. The way he watched out for her. She loved so much about Dirk.

Her eyes burned in the darkness. What she felt for Dirk didn't matter. Dirk wasn't the kind of man to repeat a mistake, and to him that was all she was. He'd been convinced they had a future. She had known all along they didn't. She had thrown his care of her back in his face, and aside from the sex she had offered him tonight, the sex she'd so badly needed, she'd given him nothing. They were over.

She knew it and so did Dirk.

It was late in the night. With Dirk lying spoon fashion behind her, a hard arm draped over her ribs, she fell asleep for a while, a few minutes of blessed slumber after days without it.

Sometime in the night, she'd started to dream, sweet dreams of Dirk that turned into sadness and loss, then terrifying nightmares about Charlie.

She was awake now, her mind spinning with thoughts of her son. Charlie's darling little-boy face, the freckles on his nose, his red hair sticking up near the cowlick at the back of his head.

Fear for him clogged her throat. Had sleeping with Dirk been a betrayal? Had those few moments of escape been moments she should have spent praying for her son?

Her eyes filled. Where was her baby now? What was happening to him?

"You aren't asleep," Dirk said, a gentle rebuke.

Meg wiped tears from her eyes and rolled onto her back to stare up at the ceiling. "I slept for a while. Thank you for that."

He leaned over and kissed the side of her neck, traced a finger between her breasts, slid his hand down between her legs. In minutes she was ready for him again, welcoming him inside her, seeking the few desperate moments of peace he so easily gave her.

By the time he was finished, every part of her body felt limp and sated, her mind little more than a hazy blur. As her eyes slid closed, a deep sleep enveloped her.

This time she didn't dream.

CHAPTER FOURTEEN

It was early, a weak sun graying the horizon through a sky heavy with clouds. Dirk left Meg asleep in her bedroom, went into the guest room and took a shower. Dressed in khaki cargo pants, a dark brown long-sleeve T-shirt, and his low-topped leather work boots, he headed downstairs, in desperate need of a cup of coffee.

When he reached the kitchen doorway, the rich aroma hit him. A pot had already been brewed.

Luke sat in a chair at the kitchen table, a ceramic mug resting next to his iPad.

"Come on in," Dirk said sarcastically, wandering over to the counter to pour himself a cup. "Make yourself right at home." The doors were all locked. He hadn't heard Luke come in. The man moved like a freaking ghost.

"Sleep well?" Luke asked with a disapproving glare and the lift of a single dark eyebrow, clearly guessing where Dirk had spent the night.

"I could use a few more hours."

"I'll bet you could."

"If it's any of your business — which it isn't — last night wasn't about me, it was about Meg. She's barely holding it together, Luke. She's a friend. She needed me last night. I gave her what she needed."

Luke's disgruntlement faded. "Maybe you did, but at what cost to you, bro?"

Dirk didn't answer. His head was still too full of Meg. Even after a long, hot shower, the smell of her perfume teased his senses. He could still taste her on his tongue.

It had taken him months to get over her. Now he was right back where he'd been before.

"We need to get her boy back before you fuck yourself up completely," Luke said.

Dirk sighed. "You're right. We bring Charlie home and I'm out of here." He glanced down at Luke's iPad. "Anything new from Sadie?"

"She ran the Bob Algreen lead into the ground. Nothing there. It definitely isn't him."

"Someone's behind this and it's not Santini or the babysitter." The girl was too young, Santini not smart enough.

Luke nodded. "Maybe good ol' Vinnie will enlighten us."

Dirk glanced at the clock. It was eight in the morning. Soon they'd be leaving for the Mayfair, which opened at ten.

"If Vinnie doesn't show or doesn't have the answers we need," Luke said, "we'll have to pull back and wait for the ransom call. We won't have any other choice."

"I don't like it. Puts the kidnappers in charge."

"I don't like it either. With any luck, Santini's itch will get him to the Mayfair and he'll give us a location."

Dirk's jaw hardened. "If he knows where they are, he'll tell us. We won't need any luck."

The faintest edge of a hard smile appeared on Luke's mouth. Dirk downed his coffee, and the men headed off to collect their gear. Together they had a pair of tactical vests, flash grenades, Dirk's Browning, an AR-15, and a .45 S&W, Luke's M9 Beretta, his short-barreled tactical shotgun, and various and sundry weaponry they both had stashed away. They also carried earbuds for communication.

There was more out in the Bronco. Luke carried enough artillery to supply an army, plus he'd loaded Dirk's extra weapons into the back when he'd retrieved Dirk's clothes.

If Santini gave them the kidnappers' location, they'd be ready to head straight there.

Dirk clipped his holster onto his belt, pulled out his Browning nine mil and checked the load while Luke checked his Beretta. They were both wearing ankle guns, Dirk a .38 snub-nosed revolver, Luke a Glock 27, subcompact .40 cal.

Dirk shoved his little .22 revolver back into his jean's pocket. The switchblade was probably in a pocket of Luke's desert camos or stuffed down one of his heavy leather army boots.

Dirk glanced out the window. It was a dark, ominous morning, but the thick gray overcast would help them blend in, make them less noticeable as they waited for Santini at the bowling alley.

"You better leave a note for Meg," Luke said, and Dirk nodded.

He had just scratched out a message and set it on the dining room table when a knock sounded at the front door.

Luke went to check. "It's O'Brien." He pulled open the door.

"I got the money." Edwin O'Brien strode into the entry. "It's mostly hundreds, banded in thousands, a few stacks of tens and twenties, all stashed in twelve twenty-pound canvas bags locked in my trunk."

"Jesus," Dirk said. "I hope to hell you trust the people who helped you put it there."

"They're good people. They know how much Charlie means to me."

"I'm glad you came," Luke said. "You can stay with Meg. We've got a lead. We're just getting ready to leave."

"Mrs. Wills said she'd be over this morning," Dirk added, "but it'd be good for you to be with Meg if the kidnappers call."

"You think they will?"

"Like I said, I think they'll stick to the plan. That means no call till this afternoon. They've thought this through. They've got an exit strategy. They have contingencies in place in case something goes wrong." Like they had when Pam's phone had been pinged, giving away their location. "They don't want any more hiccups."

"We need to leave," Luke said.

"Where are you going?" O'Brien asked.

"We've got a possible location for the babysitter's boyfriend. We need to talk to him."

"If you've found something, maybe it's time to bring in the police."

Dirk turned at the sound of feminine footfalls, felt a tightening in his chest when he spotted Meg.

"We aren't doing that, Dad. If we do, they might kill Charlie." She looked better this morning, a faint trace of color in her cheeks, the smudges gone from beneath her blue eyes. He'd done that for her. It was impossible to regret what had happened between them last night.

"We've got to go," Luke said.

Meg straightened to her impressive five-foot-ten-inch height and looked Dirk straight in the face. "Yes, we do, and I'm going with you. If Santini tells us where to find Charlie, we can go get him."

Dirk's gaze ran over her clothes: dark blue jeans and a black turtleneck sweater, her feet in a pair of hiking boots, her hair pulled tightly back at the nape of her neck. She'd thought this through. It was going to be hell trying to talk her out of it.

He reached out and caught her shoulders. "You can't go this time, hon— Meg. Today's the big payoff. These guys are bound to be nervous. Anything could set them off. If we go after Charlie, I need to be able to concentrate on keeping him safe and not worry about what might be happening to you."

"He might need me, Dirk. I'm his mother. I have to be there. I promise I'll stay out of your way."

O'Brien spoke to his daughter. "You're

being ridiculous, Meg. These men are professionals. You're a woman."

"She's a woman all right," Luke drawled, sticking his two cents in again where it wasn't wanted. "No doubt about that. But I think she's proved herself. She deserves to be there if that's what she wants."

That was totally true, but it didn't change anything. "Jesus, Luke. We can't take her with us. It's too dangerous."

Luke's laser-blue eyes zeroed in on Dirk's face. "Santini may not even show. If he does and we get a location, Meg can stay in the car. If we find the boy, he's going to need his mother."

"I'm going," Meg said. "Charlie's my son. I have to be there, Dirk."

He looked up at the ceiling, fighting for control. Much as he didn't want to take her, part of him admired her courage. Add to that, there was no way he'd stay home and wait if the boy were his son.

A sigh of resignation whispered through him. "You'll do what I tell you, right? Just like before?"

"I will, I promise."

"We need to go now," Luke said.

"Say a prayer for us, Daddy." Meg leaned over and kissed her father's cheek, then turned and started walking toward the door.

"You've got my cell number," Dirk said to O'Brien. "Call if you hear from them." Then they were out the front door and heading for the Bronco.

The Mayfair Bowling Alley in Kenmore sat in the crotch of a strip mall on NE Bothell Way, a nothing, single-story, out-of-the-way place with a cluster of cars parked out front. It was ten after ten, the bowling alley/minicasino already open for business. Her father's arrival, Meg's argument with Dirk, and a traffic snarl had cost them a few precious minutes.

Meg sat tensely in the backseat while Dirk phoned Sadie and read off the plate numbers of the cars in the lot, hoping to find a vehicle registered to Sandoval, Santini, or Pamela Vardon.

Nothing came up.

They waited a few more minutes, watching from inside the Bronco, parked near the back of the lot. There was no sign of Santini.

"We're going in to take a look," Dirk said to Meg, cracking open his door. "Keep your eyes open. You've got your cell. Pull up my number. If you spot Santini, give me a heads-up. Whatever happens, in no case do you get out of the car. Understood?"

She lifted her chin. "I'm not an idiot. Of course I understand."

His mouth edged up, lifting one side of his sexy mustache. "Stay out of trouble."

The men split up, Dirk heading for the front door, Luke detouring around back in case Santini was already inside and tried to run. Meg watched Dirk's tall, lean, V-shaped body as he strode toward the entrance and tried not to think of what had happened last night.

For five long months she had tried to forget how good they were together. Tried to forget the way he knew exactly where to touch her. Exactly how to please her. How to make her forget everything but him.

She should be embarrassed by the way she'd begged him to take her, but she wasn't. She'd needed him last night and Dirk had been there for her.

She needed him now, needed him to help her find her son.

Meg stayed low in the seat but remained vigilant, hoping to spot Santini's arrival. Minutes slipped past, but still no sign of the man whose photo she had memorized.

Her nerves hiked up when an older-model brown Chevy Malibu pulled into the lot. The driver parked in a space close to the front door, got out, clicked the locks, and headed for the bowling alley.

Medium height, olive complexion, perfectly styled glossy black hair. A handsome, well-dressed man in his early thirties. *Santini.* Meg's pulse leaped. Grabbing her cell phone off the seat, she hit the Send button, heard Dirk pick up on the other end of the line.

"He's here. He's almost at the front door."

"Good girl." The line went dead.

The next thing she saw was Dirk appearing in the entrance to the bowling alley, standing in the door frame, blocking Santini's way, then pushing him back out the door.

Dirk said something she couldn't hear, whirled Santini around, and jammed him up against the wall so fast it was almost a blur.

He dragged Santini's arm up in back and pulled a plastic tie out of his pocket. Santini struggled, but Dirk held him easily, jerked his other arm behind him, and bound the man's wrists.

From the corner of her eye, she spotted Luke racing around the building to join them. Meg watched with a mixture of nervousness and hope as Dirk and Luke marched Santini across the parking lot toward the Bronco.

Luke opened the tailgate and shoved the man into the back, and Dirk followed him into the space behind the backseat. Until that moment, she hadn't noticed the metal rings welded into the side of the cargo area. Now, as Dirk secured the prisoner to the rings, it occurred to her that a bounty hunter would need a way to transport his prisoners.

"This is kidnapping," Santini sputtered, tugging on the restraints.

"Yeah, you'd know all about that, wouldn't you, Vinnie?" Dirk climbed out and slammed the tailgate, locking Santini inside, walked around, and slid into the backseat next to Meg.

Santini's handsome face looked pale as Luke fired up the powerful engine and the SUV shot out of the parking lot and roared off down the street.

"Who are you? Where are you taking me?"

"Depends on how fast you tell us what we want to know," Dirk said.

"I don't know what you're talking about. I don't know anything."

"My ass," Dirk said. "And you can be sure whatever it is you say you don't know is exactly what you're going to tell us."

"You're crazy."

"Is Pamela with my son?" Meg asked over

185

the backseat. "Where have they taken my boy?"

Santini started trembling, though secured as he was, he could barely move. "I told you, I don't . . . don't know anything."

Dirk's smile could have cut nails. "You know how we don't do waterboarding anymore because it's considered torture? Well, waterboarding is going to look like a fun day at the beach when we're through with you."

The rest of the blood drained out of Santini's face. He tugged on the restraints, rattling the metal rings, must have realized the men had come well prepared.

"I don't know anything," he said again, but the words came out in barely a whisper.

Meg didn't know what Dirk and Luke had planned and she didn't care. She wanted her little boy safely home.

And there was every reason to believe Vinnie Santini knew where to find him.

CHAPTER FIFTEEN

Dirk sat next to Meg on the brown vinyl sofa in the living room of Luke's rustic one-bedroom cabin. Perched on twenty rural acres on the side of a mountain, looking down on the tiny town of Gold Bar, the place was a fortress, with perimeter alarms, security cameras, and chain-link fencing.

There wasn't much inside: a galley kitchen with an old, freestanding white stove, a propane fridge, and a counter with a sink. There was a bedroom and a tiny bathroom. A living room with a cast-iron stove that was the only heat in the house. A windmill and a propane generator provided electricity, which ran the lights and the well pump.

When Luke was in Seattle, he usually stayed in his Bellevue apartment, but when he wanted a little peace, he could get way off the grid.

Or bring a suspect in for questioning with no worries about being disturbed.

"Be a good time for you to take a walk," Dirk said to Meg. "This shouldn't take long."

She didn't argue. "All right." She wanted her little boy safely returned. As the door opened, a gust of cold wind blew loose strands of bright hair against her cheeks. Meg flicked a glance at Santini that held very little sympathy and made her way out the door.

They pressed Santini for answers. In less than ten minutes, he broke. He was sitting on the floor, hands bound behind him, his back against the wall. The instant Luke pulled out his eight-inch KA-BAR knife and started wiping down the gruesome, serrated blade, Santini started whining.

"I told you I don't know anything."

Dirk scoffed. "So you said about a hundred times. I guess we'll see. Drop your pants."

"What?"

"You heard me. We're gonna make sure you don't spawn any more lying little Santinis."

Santini started shaking.

Luke tested the sharpness of the blade with the end of his finger, drawing a thin line, just enough for blood to well on the tip. "I hear it doesn't hurt all that much.

Not if the knife is sharp, and I guarantee this one is."

Dirk walked closer to where Santini huddled against the wall. "Just a quick little slice and it's over."

Luke held up the blade, a demonic expression of anticipation on his face. Dirk was beginning to wonder how much of it was faked. "Your pants," Luke said. "Or we take them down for you."

A sob broke from Santini's throat. "All right, all right — I'll tell you! Just stay away from me with that god-awful knife!"

"Start talking," Dirk said.

"There was a man. He . . . he came to see Pamela."

"What's his name?"

"I don't know his name." Santini's black eyes darted toward Luke. "You have to believe me — I don't know his name!"

"Go on," Dirk urged.

"The . . . the man said if Pam would help him kidnap the little boy she took care of, she would get a share of the ransom money. Her share was a lot — half a million dollars. He promised they wouldn't hurt the boy. The man said they'd let the boy go as soon as they got the money. She'd have enough to start a new life somewhere else."

Dirk grunted. "A new life with you, right?"

189

"Pamela loves me. She wants us to get married."

"Somehow you don't look like the marrying kind," Luke said.

"But it helps if the lady has half a mil in cash in her purse," Dirk added.

Before Santini could reply, the front door swung open, letting in a fresh gust of wind. Apparently Meg had been standing out on the porch, listening to the conversation.

She stormed toward Santini like a whirlwind, leaned down, and got right in his face. "Where is my son? Where have they taken my boy?"

When Vinnie hesitated, Luke held up the knife, turned it so the wicked blade glinted in the light.

Santini swallowed. "There's . . . a little lake on a piece of private land. There's a small house there with a dock on the water. That's where they've got the boy."

"How many men?" Dirk asked.

"I don't know. Pam never said exactly. I know there was more than just the one Pam talked to."

"So two at least and also Pam."

"That's right."

"How do you know about this place?"

"Pam called me from the safe house where they first took the boy. She was getting scared of the men. She heard them mention something they called their 'bug-out spot.' She wanted me to know where it was in case she didn't show up at the place we were supposed to meet after she got her money."

"What's the location?" Dirk asked.

"Pam said it was down Highway 203 south of Duvall. It's at the end of a dirt road beside an old house on Big Rock Road."

The knife made an ominous sound as Luke slid it into the scabbard strapped to his thigh. "We need the address," he said.

"Will you let me go if I tell you?"

Dirk forced himself not to reach for Santini's throat. "We'll let you go as soon as we get the boy out safely." They'd let him go all right. Straight into police custody.

Santini made a sound of resignation and spit out the property address.

"Duvall isn't that far away," Luke said. "Maybe twenty-five miles from here. Big Rock Road isn't much farther."

Dirk felt a rush of adrenaline. "We're on a roll. Let's hope it continues." He looked up to see Meg walking toward him, hands planted on her hips, drawing his attention to her perfect curves and reminding him of the amazing sex they'd had the night before. He shook his head. He had a little boy to rescue. Now wasn't the time for a walk down forbidden-memory lane.

Meg went into a stare down. "Don't even think of telling me I can't go with you. I've been in this from the start. I'm going to finish it."

Dirk knew better than to look at Luke, couldn't tamp down a thread of hope that his friend would help him convince her. One glance and he knew he was screwed.

Luke shrugged. "It's her kid" was all he said.

There was no point in arguing when he couldn't possibly win, and he didn't have time to try. "Fine, you can come, but —"

"But I'd better do what you tell me," Meg finished.

Dirk's lips twitched. Damn, she was amazing. "That's right, you'd better."

Luke left them for a moment, disappeared into the bedroom, then strode back out and handed Meg a .38 revolver. "If things go sideways, you can use this for protection. Keep it with you in the car."

"She doesn't know how to shoot a frigging gun," Dirk said.

"She can aim and pull the trigger, can't she?"

"Yes, she can," Meg said. Reaching out, she carefully took the holstered weapon from Luke's hand.

"Fuck," Dirk grumbled. While Luke began to check his gear, Dirk unloaded the revolver and showed Meg the basics of how to use it.

"It's like Luke said. You just point it and pull the trigger. It's easier if you cock it first." Walking around behind her, trying to ignore the sweet ass nestled against his groin, he showed her how to pull back the hammer, how to aim, then firmly squeeze the trigger. "Just remember to keep your eyes open when you fire."

She held up the revolver, pointed it toward the window, cocked it, and squeezed, a loud click on the empty chamber.

"The trick is to hit your target. If you do, he's in trouble." He reloaded the five bullets he'd taken out, then returned the gun to Meg. "Just make sure you don't shoot one of us."

Meg didn't see the humor; she just nodded.

They left Santini tied up and secured to an iron bar, not surprisingly mounted on a wall in Luke's living room, and returned to the Bronco. In minutes they were outside the chain-link fence, weaving their way down the mountain toward the house on the lake off Big Rock Road.

■ ■ ■ ■

The half-hour ride to the lake gave Dirk time to go over the plan. He and Luke had both done extractions in the army. They knew how to get it done, how to get in and out, fast and clean. This was different, though.

This was Meg's son, the most important person in her life. Add to that, Charlie was only a baby. He couldn't help them in any way. Dirk could only pray the little boy was alive and unharmed.

As usual, Luke drove faster than he should have, slowing only when he was forced to, and not all that much, until they were south of Duvall and rolling along Big Rock Road.

The vacant, falling-down, single-story blue-gray residence had the address in rusted metal numbers on the badly listing mailbox out front. Next to the dilapidated wooden structure, a muddy, rutted road disappeared into the woods at the back of the property.

Luke turned down the dirt lane but didn't go far, just rounded a slight bend in the road and pulled the Bronco into a copse of trees where it couldn't easily be seen.

Dirk turned and spoke to Meg over the

back of the seat. "We need to recon the area," he explained as Luke turned off the engine and climbed out of the SUV. "You've got a gun. If you have to, don't be afraid to use it."

Meg touched the holstered .38 lying on the seat beside her. "I won't need it. You'll be back soon with Charlie."

Wishing he could make her that promise, he reached over and gently cupped her cheek. Then he turned, cracked open his door, and stepped out of the vehicle.

They headed up the muddy road, he and Luke both wearing tactical vests, flash grenades attached, armed with a pair of semiautos, extra clips, and ankle guns. Strapped to his leg, Luke carried his favorite knife, and there was more weaponry in the box in the cargo area of the Bronco.

As they walked up the lane, both of them shoved in their earbuds, gave a quick test, and found them working. Dirk thought of Meg but didn't look back as they rounded a corner and the Bronco disappeared from view.

A quarter mile in, they split up and slipped into the leafy foliage lining both sides of the road. Another quarter mile and Dirk spotted the dark, glassy surface of a small lake surrounded by heavy foliage.

Maybe a half mile long, he figured, probably great fishing, secluded, except for what appeared to be a small home at the opposite end.

Up ahead, a run-down wood-frame house with a screened-in front porch sat at the edge of the water, not far from a wooden dock that protruded into the lake. A couple of aluminum fishing boats bobbed alongside the dock. A pair of fishing poles stuck into the air from the boat on the right.

A familiar voice spoke softly through his earbud. "I'm on your left," Luke said.

Dirk turned and spotted him in the foliage twenty yards away. "I'll take the far side," Dirk said as he pulled his weapon, which left Luke the near.

"Copy that." Luke moved silently toward the house, both of them on the lookout for a guard who might be posted somewhere in the area.

Walking silently, gun in hand, taking one measured step after another, Dirk eased toward the open space behind the house, dropped down behind a heavy thicket of evergreen shrubs in the shadow of a low-branched pine to survey the area.

Though the dirt road continued around the lake, a pair of vehicles sat beneath the naked branches of a sycamore tree at the back of the house.

According to Santini, the Chevy he had been driving belonged to Pamela. Dirk made his way toward an older white Buick and rested a hand on the hood. The engine was cold. The Buick had been parked for a while. The hood of the Ford pickup next to it was also cold.

"Two vehicles," Dirk said into the mic attached to his earbud. "They've been there a while."

"We need to get a look inside, see if the boy's really here."

"I see a partly open window in what looks like the living room," Dirk said.

"Roger. I'll check this side."

Moving quietly, Dirk eased closer. One of the sash windows was shoved up a couple of inches to let in fresh air and the curtain was cracked just enough that he might be able to see inside. He moved in, flattened himself against the wall next to the window.

"I'm goin' crazy with all this waitin'," a man's voice said. Through the parting in the curtains, Dirk could see a short, stocky guy with a ring of sandy hair around his balding head. "The old man's bound to have the money by now. Why can't we just make the goddamn call?"

"We aren't calling because it isn't time,

you moron. We have a plane to catch — unless you want to hitchhike out of the state. And it won't be ready till the designated time."

The second man was tall, skeleton thin, with a wide nose that looked like it had been broken, and very curly brown hair. "Just take it easy, okay? The deadline's only a few hours away." The two of them perfectly fit Rose's description of the phony PG&E men.

"I guess you're right," the stout moron grumbled. "In the meantime, why don't we take care of the girl and the kid?"

The tall, skinny man — had to be the one Rose had heard called Cliff — blew out a breath. "Sometimes, Mickey, you're just flat stupid. The boss says they won't give us the money without proof of life. That means we have to keep the kid alive till we pick up the dough."

Dirk felt the words like a kick in the stomach. The kidnappers never planned to give Charlie back to Meg. Too many things could give them away. DNA on the little boy's clothes, fingerprints on his body; there were a million ways to catch criminals these days.

"We'll get rid of them when the time comes," Cliff said. "The lake is deep enough no one will ever find the bodies."

Dirk clenched his teeth so hard pain shot into his head. Thank God Meg had called him. He scanned the room but saw no sign of the little boy or Pam. Dropping lower, he eased back toward the rear of the house, found Luke there, waiting behind the row of shrubs.

Dirk holstered his weapon. "Two men inside," he said. "No sign of the kid or the girl. They're still alive, though. They're planning to kill them once they get the money, dump the bodies in the lake."

"Motherfuckers."

"Yeah."

"Charlie and the girl are in the bedroom," Luke said. "Her blouse is torn and she's got a black eye, but otherwise she looks okay. She's curled up on the bed. Little boy's curled up against her."

Dirk's chest tightened. "I'll phone Sadie, give her our location, tell her to call the cops in what? Twenty minutes?"

"Sounds about right. Cops get here too soon, this turns into a hostage situation."

"Or a shoot-out," Dirk said grimly. "We need to get them out of there."

Luke grinned. "Two against two? Piece of cake."

Chapter Sixteen

Meg sat in the Bronco, her fingers curled into the backseat, eyes trained on the empty dirt road stretching in front of her. She itched to get out of the car, follow Dirk and Luke to the house by the lake, find her son and bring him home.

She wouldn't, of course. She wouldn't do anything that might cause the men trouble. She had promised not to get in their way.

Straining for any sound of their return, she heard nothing but the rush of the wind through the trees, the rustle of leafless branches. A storm was moving in, a drizzle beginning to fall.

If she'd had the windows rolled down, she might have heard the approaching footsteps. Instead, she jerked at the light *tap-tap* against the window glass beside her, and turned to see the barrel of a pistol pointing directly at her head.

Adrenaline surged through her and yet she

felt frozen in the seat.

"Reach for the pistol and you're dead," the man said. Well-dressed in a pair of dark slacks and expensive Italian leather dress shoes — Prada, she figured, if she knew her designers, which she did. He was medium height, late thirties or early forties, athletic build. Though his dark hair was slightly receding, he was still an attractive man. "Open the door."

Meg swallowed, fighting for calm, knowing how important it was to make the right moves. She flicked a glance at the gun on the seat and saw a second man on the other side of the Bronco, his pistol pointed at her from the opposite direction. He was bigger, muscular. She couldn't see his face.

"The door," the first man said. "Open it now."

Her heart beat wildly. Dear God, what about Charlie? What about Dirk and Luke? She should have listened, shouldn't have come. She had put them all in danger.

She cracked open the door, her mind spinning with ways to alert the men, her hiking boots sinking into the mud as she stepped out of Luke's battered SUV. "Who are you?"

The man in the designer shoes gave her a polite, hard-edged smile. "You may call me Thomas. It isn't my name, but it will do for

201

now. And you're Megan. Little Charlie's mother."

Her stomach roiled with nausea. She clamped down on a shot of fear. "What have you done with my son?"

"Why don't I take you to him? I assume your detective friends are somewhere about. Quite clever, they are, finding us here. I don't think they'll be pleased to see you, however." He nudged her with the barrel of his gun, urging her to walk back down the road the way Luke had driven in.

Around the first bend, a silver Honda Accord sat off to one side, a Hertz rental plate frame on the front. The men were from out of town. The one who called himself Thomas spoke well, seemed intelligent, and dressed well. Probably the man behind the kidnapping. She wondered how he'd come up with the scheme.

Thomas opened the rear passenger door and motioned for her to slide onto the seat, then slid in beside her, his gun pressing into her ribs. The other man climbed in behind the wheel of the Accord, filling the seat completely.

As he started the engine, Meg took a deep breath and fought for control, desperate to think of a way to warn Dirk. At the moment all she could think to do was get them to

shoot her and hope Dirk heard the sound
— not the greatest plan.

A shiver slid through her. She might not
have any other choice.

"We've got surprise on our side," Dirk said,
his attention fixed on the house.

"Smash and grab?" Luke asked.

"Affirmative. You want the front or the
back?"

Luke's expression hardened. "You take the
back, bring out the kid and the girl. I'll go
in the front."

"You sure?"

Luke's features turned to granite. "Oh,
yeah, I'm sure."

At the steely glint in Luke's blue eyes,
Dirk wondered if his friend might cut off
the kidnappers' balls for real this time.

"Give me two minutes to get in place,"
Luke said.

Dirk looked down at his watch, started to
give a nod, then heard the sound of tires
churning up the road. "Someone's coming."

Luke's gaze shot down the lane. Dirk's
pistol was already in hand, his grip on the
big semiauto reassuring. Luke palmed his
weapon, they split up, and slid quietly off
into the woods surrounding the clearing.

Standing in the shadows out of sight

behind the thick trunk of a tree, Dirk watched a silver Honda Accord roll toward the house. Rental car. Three people inside.

His stomach cramped at the sight of Meg sitting next to a man in the backseat of the car. The guy lifted his hand, showing off the gun he pressed solidly against her head.

Jesus God, Meg. He shouldn't have caved to her wishes, should have left her home. Should have tied her up if he'd had to.

The car pulled up and stopped next to the other two. The engine fell silent and the doors cracked open. A man wearing black slacks and a button-down sport shirt, oddly stylish attire for a kidnapper, hauled Meg out of the vehicle and positioned her in front of him. He was clean-shaven with a receding hairline, his dark hair perfectly groomed. Most likely the brains of the operation.

The man in charge pressed his big semiauto firmly against Meg's temple. "Mr. Reynolds, I know you're out there, you and your friend, Mr. Brodie. As you can see, the situation has changed, and not in your favor."

Dirk silently cursed. Not only had they spotted the Bronco, the bugs the men had planted in Meg's house had given them their names. Two minutes on Google and the bastards knew all about them, knew they were PIs, knew they were former military, which meant they knew he and Luke were armed.

"I need you to come out from wherever you are," the man said mildly. "If you don't, I shall pull the trigger on my weapon, firing a bullet into Ms. O'Brien's very lovely head."

"Don't do it, Dirk!" Meg shouted. "They'll kill you!"

They'd try. That was for sure.

He heard running footsteps. The men from inside had heard the commotion and rushed out to join the fray. They rounded the corner, weapons drawn, and raced toward their friends.

Dirk settled a little lower in the bushes. "Looks like we're having a party," he whispered into his mic.

"The more, the merrier," Luke replied.

They both held positions that gave them clear shots at the men. There were four of them now, with plenty of firepower, and Meg in the middle.

Things couldn't get any worse.

Scratch that. Pam had just run out of the house, carrying Meg's little red-haired boy.

"Charlie!" Meg shouted. Dirk could hardly believe his eyes when Meg jerked out of her captor's arms and started running. Dirk started firing.

Thank you, Jesus, there is a God. Dirk laid down a line of cover, bullets flying, scattering the men, keeping their attention off Meg. He hit curly-haired Cliff in the chest, taking him down and out. Luke double-tapped the short, balding guy, and he went down flat on his back, blood oozing out of a wound in his chest.

Meg kept running, moving in a zigzag pattern she must have seen on some cop show on TV, dodging bullets, and amazing him yet again.

She scooped Charlie out of Pam's arms, swung a punch that knocked the babysitter flat on her ass, and started running again, ducking out of sight around the corner of the house.

Dirk concentrated on the firefight going on in front of him, pulled off a couple of rounds but couldn't wipe the grin off his face.

The two men in the Accord had taken cover behind the car; one of them was as big as a house and, the way he was firing, clearly had some military training.

Dirk spotted Luke moving around behind them and laid down a stream of bullets, keeping the men pinned down. Slugs pinged around him, sending wood chips into the air beside his head. They were zeroing in on his location. He had to move.

Luke blasted away, drawing their fire, but the men stayed low and out of sight, pinned behind the car. From a fresh position, Dirk squeezed off a couple of shots. So did Luke. Luke was moving again, silently making his way through the heavy grass and foliage, closing in on the men from behind.

Return fire came from the other side of the Accord, but only from a single pistol. Each shot was placed with precision. The big guy, he thought, and unease filtered through him. Where was the second man? And where were Meg and Charlie?

From the corner of his eye, he saw them coming out from around the house, Meg with her hands bound behind her, the guy in charge holding little Charlie, the gun pointed straight at his head. The little boy reached out to his mother as the kidnapper ran toward the dock with the boy in his arms.

Dirk stayed hidden but moved toward them through the foliage, watching as the man jumped into one of the aluminum fishing boats. Meg jumped in behind him. The kidnapper pulled the starter rope on the outboard engine; it caught and a plume of smoke fluttered into the air.

Dirk steadied his aim, his pistol pointed at the kidnapper, his finger itching to squeeze the trigger, but Charlie and Meg were both in the way and he couldn't risk taking the shot.

The kidnapper dragged Meg down on the seat beside him, keeping her in the line of fire, settled Charlie in front of him, and the boat roared off toward the open water.

Leaving the big man to Luke, Dirk raced down the incline toward the lake, bullets kicking up dust behind and in front of him, both gunmen firing in his direction. Luke returned fire, forcing the second man to focus on him, giving Dirk a chance to reach the other aluminum boat.

He jumped in and prayed the engine would start, yanked the rope handle, then swore when nothing happened. He could hear Luke and the other man exchanging gunfire as he yanked the handle on the rope three more times and still got no response.

Sending up another silent prayer as the handle dug into his palm, he yanked again and again as he watched the kidnapper steer farther and farther out into the lake.

A string of whispered curses, a last desperate pull, and the motor fired then roared to life. Dirk grabbed the tiller and cranked the throttle, and the boat surged away from the dock. He revved the throttle full speed, racing after the kidnapper's boat, now a good long distance ahead of him. Water rushed against the hull. Fear for Meg and Charlie ate at him, making his stomach churn.

Don't let him hurt them, he silently prayed.

He could see the shore in the distance, had no idea what the man would do once he reached it. Maybe the guy had a car parked at the opposite end of the lake as a backup means of escape.

So far the kidnappers had been well prepared.

The motor was racing full speed. With less weight in the boat, Dirk was gaining, but not fast enough. Not nearly fast enough.

He was closing the distance, getting a little nearer, when the unthinkable happened. The boat ahead of him slowed, the kidnapper stood up, dragged Meg up, and pushed her into the icy water. He threw little Charlie in beside her, then shoved the throttle wide open — and left them there to drown.

CHAPTER SEVENTEEN

As the icy water surged over Meg's head, terror struck like a knife in her heart. With her arms bound behind her, she held her breath and plunged deep into the lake. For a moment she lost her bearings. Dear God, where was Charlie?

Kicking her legs, she shot herself to the surface and frantically whirled in every direction in search of her little boy. She heard him thrashing and crying for his mama, saw him go under, then spotted his bright head as he came up for a breath of air.

For an instant his terrified eyes met hers, then he went under again. Meg went after him, fear and determination driving her on. Dirk was coming. She had to keep her son alive until he could get there.

Fighting down her terror, Meg searched the murky depths but couldn't find her son, came up for another breath of air and saw him paddling frantically a few feet away. Spitting out a mouth full of water, she managed to keep her head up long enough to turn around and grab hold of his red-striped polo shirt with her bound hands as he slid under again. She dragged him to the surface but couldn't quite hold on to him.

Charlie went under. Meg ducked down and saw him, turned and grabbed him again, shoved him up but couldn't reach the surface herself. Her hiking boots weighed her down, exhausting the muscles in her legs. Her air was almost gone.

Dear God, she and her baby were going to drown before Dirk could reach them.

She knew he was coming, had spotted the fishing boat racing toward them across the lake. She just had to keep her baby alive until he could get there.

Sinking deeper, she searched madly, fear and the cord immobilizing her arms, making her movements clumsy. Her lungs ached. She couldn't hold her breath any longer. She kicked to the surface and saw Dirk's aluminum boat approaching.

She had to find Charlie. Dear God, where was Charlie? She went down again, coughed and sucked in water, shot to the surface for more air, then went down again. She spotted him, but he wasn't moving. She turned and snagged his little red polo shirt, and with her bound hands hauled him up to the surface — but couldn't reach it herself.

Her breath was gone. She was going to die here today. With a last burst of energy, she kicked to the top, saw her son's bright red hair and unconscious body floating on the water an instant before he started sinking again.

She heard the *clank* of metal as Dirk's boat reached her and he tossed the anchor into the water.

"Save . . . Charlie!" she yelled at him, the effort sucking more water into her lungs. She slid back into the water, drifted lower, down toward the bottom of the lake. Her mind felt fuzzy, her limbs no longer able to respond to her commands.

A glimpse of Dirk's powerful body diving into the water was the last thing she saw. Dirk would save Charlie. He wouldn't let her precious son die. How could she not have believed in him? How could she have sent him away? Then her mind went blank as she drifted into the reeds at the bottom of the lake and everything went black.

Save Charlie! Meg's plea echoed in Dirk's head as he dove again and again into the dark waters of the lake in search of her little boy. He couldn't save them both. She knew it and so did he. He'd be lucky to find the boy and get him out before it was too late.

A silent scream filled his head. He loved Meg. And because he did, he would do what she asked. He dove again, tried to see any sign of the boy, any sign of Meg.

In the minutes before he'd reached them, he had ripped off the bulky Kevlar vest, holstered his weapon and set it aside, and tugged off his heavy leather boots.

Powerless to help her, he had watched Meg fighting to save her son, watched as she spent herself, determined to keep her baby's head above water. The boy had been limp and unmoving the last time he had gone under.

Dirk pulled in a breath and dove again. The boy was here somewhere. He just had to find him. His hand touched something silky. He grabbed hold and pulled with all his strength. The little boy floated up. Dirk pushed him to the surface and followed him up, sucked air into his tortured lungs, then lifted the unconscious child over the side of the aluminum boat.

He couldn't save them both. Meg had known it and so had he.

His chest clamped down. *Fuck that,* he thought, turned, and dove back into the icy water. Again and again he dove, going deeper, fanning out, searching until his legs cramped and his lungs burned from lack of oxygen.

Where are you, baby? His chest ached and it wasn't from lack of air. He dove again, went deeper, stayed down longer. But he had to think of Charlie, had to surface and give the baby CPR. He had promised Meg.

Just as he started toward the top, he saw her hazy image in the water a few feet away, her hair unbound and floating around her face, making her look like a mermaid.

With a last burst of strength and only a second of air, he caught her hair, kicked, and hauled her up, exploding to the surface and dragging in great lungfuls of oxygen. Meg floated up beside him, but she wasn't breathing.

He had to get her out of the water. The aluminum boat rocked as another boat pulled up and the driver cut the motor. Bigger, a KingFisher with an outboard Merc and a blue canvas top. He had no idea where it had come from, but then he saw Luke, and a fraction of his fear lifted away.

Luke spotted the baby and jumped from the bigger boat into the smaller one to start CPR, while the gray-haired driver made his way to the side and reached down for Meg.

Working together, they brought her out of the lake into the bigger boat.

Dirk's muscles trembled with fatigue as he gripped the side and hoisted himself over the edge. Hurriedly, they positioned Meg in the bottom of the craft, cut the cord around her wrists, and Dirk started CPR.

Five rescue breaths, forcing air into her lungs, then thirty chest compressions. Two breaths, then thirty compressions. He flicked a glance at Luke, working over little Charlie, ignored the thick knot swelling in his throat, and continued to work on Meg.

"Charlie's breathing!" Luke shouted, and Dirk felt a wave of relief and a burning behind his eyes.

Come on, baby. Two more breaths, then thirty compressions. Two more breaths. Meg started to sputter and cough, music to his ears. She gasped in a lungful of air, coughed, and spat out water, and he eased her onto her side, into the recovery position.

"Easy, baby. You're okay. Charlie's safe. You're both okay. Just take it easy."

She started crying. "Charlie's okay?"

"He's breathing. He's in the other boat. We need to get you both to the hospital."

"I want to see him." She tried to rise, coughed, and he eased her back down. He hadn't missed the dark bruise on her cheek.

No way would she have let the kidnapper take her without a fight.

"Luke's with Charlie," he said. "Just hang on a little longer." He wanted to hold her, promise her he'd never let anyone hurt her again. Instead, he turned away. "You ready to head back?" he called to Luke.

"House is clear. The cops should be there by now."

Dirk glanced back toward the dock and saw distant red and blue flashing lights. Both outboard motors fired up without a hitch, thank Jesus, and they headed back across the lake.

"My name's Arnie, by the way." As he expertly steered the boat through the water, the gray-haired man reached out a hand Dirk shook. "I own the house at the other end of the lake. I heard boats on the water, motors running real hot. Took a look with my binoculars and saw you were in trouble. Your friend, Luke, came racing around the lake road and pulled his Bronco up in the yard, and so here we are."

"You got here just in time. I'll never be able to thank you enough."

"No need for thanks. Just glad I could help."

"You happen to see where the man in the other boat went?"

"Saw where he beached a ways from the house and took off into the trees. I heard the sound of an engine. Must have had a car parked somewhere down the road."

"I figured he might. Whoever he was, the guy was a pro."

"Luke told me about the kidnapping. I guess you two took care of the others."

Three down, either dead or wounded. Dirk just nodded.

"I hope you catch the bastard who got away."

"So do I." But he didn't think catching the man was going to be easy. As he'd said, the guy was a pro. Even with the FBI on his tail, which by now they would be, there was a chance the man would escape.

Dirk looked down to where Meg lay curled on her side in the bottom of the boat. He didn't know when he had reached down and caught hold of her hand, but there it was, firmly gripped in his.

She didn't seem to want to let go.

Neither did he.

A pair of ambulances were on the scene when they arrived, along with a line of police cars. EMTs wrapped Meg and Charlie in blankets, placed oxygen masks over their mouths, and loaded them onto stretchers.

Meg pulled the mask aside. "Come with me," she pleaded, still holding Dirk's hand as the gurneys reached the ambulance door.

"I can't," Dirk said. "Two men are dead. Another is barely hanging on. The cops are going to have a lot more questions."

She squeezed his hand. "You'll come, though. You won't just disappear."

He managed to smile, trying not to remember the sight of her unconscious body floating in the water. "I'll come."

One of the EMTs pulled the oxygen mask back over her face, then they were loaded into one of the ambulances. The badly shot-up Mickey was loaded into the other. With any luck the guy would live.

They needed answers. At the moment, Mickey the Moron was the only one who had them. Dirk had only that one brief moment with Meg. The cops had been waiting, guns drawn, when the boats had reached the dock.

He'd been given a moment with Meg after his identity had been confirmed, then he and Luke had both been interviewed. By the time they had their guns returned and changed into some dry clothes in the back of Luke's Bronco, they'd spoken to half a dozen uniformed police officers, two detectives, and FBI Special Agent Ronald Nolan.

Dirk knew Ron Nolan fairly well. He was a few years older than his own thirty-two, wore his sandy brown hair combed back, athletic, career-minded, and good at his job. They had met on a homicide case that crossed over state lines. Dirk had been hired by the family of the murdered wife to look into the husband as a suspect.

The police had cleared him. Dirk had found new evidence linking him to the crime, and Nolan had been key in making the arrest.

"We've got two dead guys," Nolan said as they stood a ways from the house while CSIs worked the crime scene, "another guy in critical, and another still on the loose. We've also got a young woman who is either part of the crime or one of the victims."

"Or both," Dirk said. "The babysitter was essential to the plan. She was getting half a mil to feed the kidnappers the info they needed. She's involved up to her pretty little neck. The fact that she ended up assaulted by her cohorts was an unfortunate turn of events, but I imagine she's learned a valuable lesson."

"What's that?"

"Crime doesn't pay."

"Anything else you can tell me about the man who got away? We've taken statements from your friend Brodie, including a description that confirms yours. We'll also be speaking to Ms. O'Brien and her father. Anything you can add?"

"My guess, the guy was the brains of the operation. Smooth, polished, ready for anything that might come his way. He had a safe house and a bug-out location, had an extra vehicle parked on the other side of the lake. I can give you more, but it's pure speculation."

"I'd like to hear it."

"Average-looking, nothing about him that stood out. He's the kind of guy who can blend in wherever he wants. I think he uses that to his advantage. He's a loner, doesn't work well with others, expects them to do exactly what he says. I'd say he was going to pay these guys something, nowhere near equal shares, have them get rid of the babysitter and the kid, then he was going to disappear."

"Which he did."

"Exactly. I heard one of the kidnappers mention leaving by plane. You check private airports?"

"We're working on it," Agent Nolan said.

"Could be the way he planned to escape.

Could also be he just told the others that. Could be there never was a plane. Or it was just meant for him."

Nolan nodded. "At this point, anything's possible. Since the ransom call was never made, we don't know where the kidnappers planned to pick up the money, which would have helped us narrow things down."

"A lot of things we don't know."

"I know one thing," Nolan said. "Mother and child are safe and well, and Edwin O'Brien will have ten million more in the bank tomorrow than he thought he was going to have. You did damn good, Reynolds, you and Brodie, but it could have gone the other way. Next time make the call. That's what the FBI is here for."

"With any luck, I won't have the problem again."

Nolan handed him a business card. "Call me if you think of anything else."

Dirk nodded, waved the card over his shoulder as he turned and started back to the Bronco. Luke was already there, champing at the bit to get back to Seattle.

"Where do you want me to drop you?" Luke asked as he started the engine.

"My apartment. I'm headed to the hospital to check on Meg, but I want to ride my bike, clear my head."

"I don't blame you. I'll go by to see her as soon as I get the chance." Luke drove the Ford on down the dirt lane. "So what's the deal with the two of you? You gonna start dating her again?"

"I don't know."

"I get what you see in her, bro. I didn't at first. Now I do."

A ghost of a smile touched Dirk's lips. "Meg's special. No doubt about it. Doesn't mean her opinion of me has changed. Even if it has, doesn't mean it would work any better the second time than it did the first."

"Give yourself some time, man. Just take it slow. Maybe you'll figure things out."

But Dirk had figured things out five months ago. And aside from the fact Meg had hired him to rescue her little boy, nothing had really changed.

"I can't believe this! You're telling me you didn't get the money? All you had to do was make the call!" Jonathan leaned over the sleek teakwood desk in his study. "The deadline was only a few hours away. How could you screw things up so badly?"

"I wasn't the one who screwed up, Mr. Hollander. You never bothered to mention that your wife's very close friend was a private investigator. You never hinted that she might hire the man to help her find her son."

"I don't know what you're talking about." Jonathan sat back down in the expensive brown leather chair behind his desk, which matched the sofa in front of the fireplace. The study was large, the entire house professionally decorated with contemporary furniture and dark wood accents throughout.

The bookshelves were filled with valuable first editions, at least those he hadn't yet sold. There was a view out over manicured lawns. In the mirror, he caught a glimpse of his black hair and the hot color in his cheeks.

"I'm talking about Dirk Reynolds," Moore said mildly. "The man is ex-military and extremely capable. He and his friend Luke Brodie were on to us almost from the start."

After receiving a phone call from the man seated across from him, Jonathan had left the bank early and driven home to meet him. His name was Thomas Moore, or at least that was what he'd called himself the last time they had spoken.

Today, instead of having thick, dark hair and a receding hairline, his hair was white-blond and cropped very short. Instead of the expensive slacks he'd been wearing before, he was dressed in a pair of khaki pants and a yellow Ralph Lauren pullover. Casual clothes, though he still wore designer shoes: loafers today, Ferragamo perhaps.

Moore looked completely different, even carried himself in a slightly different manner. Yet every man had his foibles. Fashion seemed to be his.

"If you were worried about Reynolds, you should have shortened the time line. You should have done something!"

"Perhaps. But then, I'm not the one with the problem, am I? My employer sent me to you as a courtesy. I came to help you raise the money you needed to pay off your loan. You are the one who came up with the plan to kidnap your son."

"It should have worked, dammit! All you had to do —"

"All *you* had to do was give us the correct information. That you did not do."

Unease filtered through him. Moore was completely unreadable. Not a trace of emotion showed in his features. Yet an air of menace clung to him like a layer of perspiration.

"I don't know anything about this man Reynolds," Jonathan said. "Meg never mentioned him. Neither did her father."

"He was her bodyguard on the fashion

show tour last summer. And her lover —
according to the babysitter."

Jonathan grunted. "Meg does what she
pleases. She was always headstrong. I never
could control her."

"Clearly that is true."

His nerves began to hum. Whoever he
was, Moore was a dangerous man. "How
much does the babysitter know?"

"Nothing that can help the police. My as-
sociate is dead, a man who also knew nothing. One of the men Pamela was working
with is dead. The police can track their
identities, but it won't lead them to you or
to me. The other man is in the hospital in
critical condition."

Panic tore through him. "Mickey Degan. I
spoke to him when all this started. He
knows who I am."

"Yes, I believe you mentioned that. I as-
sure you, he won't be alive much longer."

The hair rose at the back of Jonathan's
neck. "You'll . . . you'll make sure of that?"

"Tying up loose ends is part of my service.
Unfortunately for you, you still owe my
employer a great deal of money. I spoke to
him a few hours ago. He is extremely
unhappy and rapidly losing patience. You
know what will happen when he does."

Jonathan felt sick to his stomach.

Sitting in a low-backed brown chair, one of the two in front of the desk, Moore examined his manicured nails. "He won't just kill you, I'm afraid. He likes to make an example of people who don't keep their word."

Jonathan moistened his lips, which suddenly felt dry and tight. "I'll get the money. You have to tell him that. You need to convince him."

"And how do you propose to make that happen?"

"I don't know. . . . Perhaps . . . perhaps we could take the boy again, go directly to Edwin with the ransom note this time. We should have done that in the first place."

Thomas looked at him as if he were mentally deficient. "They'll be watching the boy much closer now. Perhaps your wife's bodyguard friend will take the job himself."

Jonathan raked an unsteady hand through his thick, black hair. He rested his elbows on the top of his desk in an attempt to look at ease. "If Reynolds hadn't stuck his nose in, everything would have gone according to plan. The boy would be home with Meg and Gertsman would have his money."

When Thomas made no reply, Jonathan felt a chill. For the first time he wondered if Moore would have stuck to the plan, wondered if Charlie would have been safely returned. No matter how desperate he was for money, he wouldn't have allowed the men to harm his son.

"Without Reynolds's interference, Mr. Gertsman would have his money," Moore said with maddening politeness. "Plus a few million for you as well."

"It was just seed money, a way for me to get things rolling again and get back on my feet."

As Moore stood up from his chair, Jonathan stared into his inscrutable features and felt a wave of fear.

"Ask Mr. Gertsman what I can do to repay him," Jonathan said, also rising. "Anything he wants. I'll do anything."

One of Moore's bleached eyebrows went up. "Anything?"

Jonathan nodded, hoping his chin didn't tremble. "I'm in banking. I have powerful connections. Surely there's something he wants. I'll do whatever it takes to make things right between us."

"I'll relay the message," Moore said. Turning, he walked out of the study. Jonathan's heart was still racing when the door closed with an ominous click behind him.

CHAPTER EIGHTEEN

Meg sat propped up in her hospital bed in a private room in the Bellevue Medical Center. Charlie slept curled beside her. Ever since Dirk had lifted him out of the fishing boat and carried him to a waiting ambulance, he had been clinging to her like a monkey.

EMTs had treated them both for hypothermia, though the cold lake water had actually helped save their lives by slowing down the drowning process. They'd been given warmed oxygen to help clear their lungs, been checked and rechecked, pronounced on the road to recovery. With any luck, they would be released in the morning. Meg couldn't wait to get home.

Special circumstances — the kidnapping little Charlie had suffered — had convinced the doctors to allow them to stay together overnight for observation.

Meg tugged down the hospital gown she

was wearing instead of her wet clothes. It was evening. She wasn't alone, hadn't been since a few minutes after her arrival at the hospital. She felt her mother's hand against her cheek, looked up, and smiled at the woman with the silver-blond hair and, at fifty-five, a still-lovely face. Meg glanced from her mother's worried features across the room to where her dad slept in a chair.

Her parents had been there all evening. Though visiting hours were over, her dad had managed to sweet-talk the nurse into letting them stay.

"I'm okay, Mom. Really."

"You should have told me what was going on, dear heart. You and your father both think of me as this fragile little flower and I'm just not that person anymore."

Meg took hold of her mother's fine-boned hand. "I know that, Mom. But you know how Dad worries about you. Besides, there wasn't anything you could do." She smiled. "At least, not until now. Now I have you to keep me and Charlie company while we recover."

"Your father said your friend Dirk Reynolds saved Charlie's life. He said those men would have killed him. Dirk saved your life, too, of course, when you were foolish enough to go along with him to the kidnappers' house."

"I had to go, Mom. But you're right. He saved us both."

"He hasn't been by to see you."

Her heart squeezed. "He had to talk to the police."

Her mother gave her a pitying glance. He would have been finished hours ago.

"He said he'd stop by," Meg said. "Dirk always keeps his word."

"Well, then, I hope I get a chance to meet him."

Meg just nodded. In the past few days, her father had come to respect Dirk. Her mother saw him as some kind of hero — which was exactly the way Meg thought of him.

She never would have believed her parents might approve of him. It was one of the reasons she had ended their relationship. If only she could go back in time, handle things differently.

But that wasn't the way things worked.

"You and Daddy need to go home," she said, releasing her mother's hand. "Charlie and I will be fine. I'll call you in the morning. If the doctor says we can leave, we'll need a ride home."

Her mother leaned down and kissed her forehead, pressed a soft kiss on Charlie's cheek. He didn't even stir. Meg planned to call a good child psychologist, a doctor who could help her baby get through the trauma of the kidnapping.

Aside from clinging to her more than he usually did, so far he seemed okay. The doctors said he hadn't been physically injured, and being as young as he was, it wouldn't take him long to forget the incident.

Meg hoped they were right. But she didn't think he would forget nearly drowning anytime soon.

A soft knock sounded at the door, then it slowly eased open. Dirk stood in the doorway. He was wearing clean jeans and a dark green Henley. His shoulders looked amazingly wide, and she could see the outline of the lean, powerful muscles beneath his snug-fitting, long-sleeve shirt. His horseshoe mustache was trimmed very short, his slightly too-long hair neatly combed. It still curled softly at the nape of his neck.

A little tug of awareness warred with her emotions and tightened her chest. "Mom, I'd like you to meet Dirk Reynolds."

Dirk stepped in and quietly closed the door. His hazel eyes went straight to Charlie and a look of relief washed over his features.

He turned his attention to her mother.

"It's nice to meet you, Mrs. O'Brien."

"You as well, Dirk. I want to thank you for what you did for my daughter and my grandson."

He just shrugged. "Meg asked for my help. Helping people is what I do for a living."

"Perhaps," her mother said, which was her mom's way of saying she understood how much more it was than just a job.

"I asked you to save my son," Meg said, tears filling her eyes, "and that's exactly what you did."

"Luke gave him CPR."

"You saved him. I knew you would." She blinked and the tears in her eyes began to roll down her cheeks.

Dirk looked uncomfortable. "Please don't cry. I didn't come here to make you cry."

She sniffed, accepted the Kleenex her mother handed her, and blotted her eyes. "You're right. I'm sorry. Thank you for coming."

Was it only last night he had been in bed with her, his hard body pressing her into the mattress? Only last night, and already they were back to polite conversation. Her heart broke all over again.

Across the room, her father stirred to life and sat up in the chair, spotted Dirk, and came to his feet. "Reynolds. About time you showed up."

"Yes, sir. I went for a ride first on my Harley. I needed to clear my head."

"I imagine you did." Her father walked over and shook Dirk's hand. "You have my eternal gratitude, son, as I'm sure you know. I've spoken to the police. I know all the details. Whatever fee you charge — you earned every dollar."

Dirk shook his head. "No fee. Not this time. You can pay Luke. I did this for Meg."

Her heart stumbled, squeezed hard inside her chest. She needed to talk to him, and not in a room full of people.

"I think we've stayed long enough," her mother said, gently steering her father toward the door. "Meg and Charlie need to rest." She turned to Meg. "We'll be back to get you in the morning." Her mother looked at Dirk. "You're welcome in our home anytime, Dirk. Thank you again for saving our family."

Her dad squeezed Dirk's shoulder as he walked out of the hospital room. Charlie shifted against her in the bed and she realized he was awake and staring at Dirk.

"Charlie, this is a friend," Meg said. "His name is Dirk."

"Hey, Charlie."

The little boy started trembling. He turned his head into Meg's shoulder and started crying softly.

Meg tightened her arms around him. "It's okay, sweetheart. You don't have to be afraid. Dirk's our friend."

"Make him go away! He's a bad man!" Charlie let out a shriek and started crying louder, kicking his feet and trying to burrow into her.

"I'm scaring him," Dirk said. "He remembers me from the lake."

Meg spoke to the little boy gently. "It's all right, sweetie. Dirk is the man who pulled you out of the water. He saved us, sweetheart."

Charlie just kept crying.

"I better go. Seeing me is making him remember what happened. I don't think that's a good idea right now."

A lump rose in Meg's throat. It was like déjà vu, the replay of a nightmare. Sending Dirk away because of Charlie.

She smoothed the silky red hair on her little boy's head and he began to quiet. He still wouldn't look at Dirk. "I'll be home tomorrow," she said. "I'd really like for us to talk. Could you . . . do you think you could come over?"

Dirk glanced away. "I've got a lot of

follow-up to do. I may not have time."

He was leaving, just like before. She couldn't let it happen. "We . . . umm . . . still need to find the man who got away. My father mentioned hiring you to look for him. We need to talk about it." Her dad had suggested it. But at the moment it was just an excuse for her to see Dirk.

"The police can handle it." He looked at Charlie, who was sniffling, his head buried in her lap. "Might be better if you worked with someone else."

"I don't want someone else!" When Charlie jerked, she forced herself to calm down, bent, and kissed the top of his head. "If I had gone to someone else, there's a good chance my son would not be . . . wouldn't be here with me now." She swallowed. "Please come over tomorrow, Dirk. I really need to see you."

Something moved across his features. She might have called it yearning. Or maybe she'd just imagined it.

"I'll stop by late in the afternoon. Your folks are taking you home tomorrow, right?"

"Yes, as soon as the doctor releases us."

"All right, I'll see you then." Pulling open the door, he stepped out into the hall. The door whooshed closed behind him.

Her eyes burned. She stroked her son's

head and he looked up at her.

"He's a bad man," Charlie said.

"No, sweetheart, he isn't. Dirk is one of the good men. He's like a policeman. You know what policemen do? They save people. When the bad man took us in the boat, Dirk came after him. When the bad man threw us in the water, Dirk dove in and pulled us out. He's mama's friend, Charlie. He saved us."

Charlie sniffed. "I wanna go home."

"I know you do. So do I. We're going home in the morning. Grandma and Grandpa are coming to pick us up." She rubbed gently between his small shoulders. "Right now, we need to sleep. Mama's really tired. How about you?"

Charlie yawned. "Me too."

She clicked the button and turned off the light, snuggled down next to her son. In the last three days, she had only slept a few hours, only been able to sleep at all because Dirk had been in her bed.

She closed her eyes. As tired as she was, there were so many images in her mind, she wasn't sure she could fall asleep. She remembered the barrel of the gun pressed against the window of the Bronco, then the feel of cold metal against the side of her head. She remembered the awful moment

236

she had heard Charlie's small body hit the water and knew he was going to drown.

As if the nurse knew her thoughts, a wide-hipped woman named Emma walked in. She handed Meg a paper cup with a pill in the bottom, then a small cup of water.

Emma waited until Meg swallowed it. "It's only a light sedative," she said. "The doctor gave your son something earlier. He'll go back to sleep as soon as you do. You need to rest and so does he."

She nodded. The nurse tidied up and left the room. Charlie settled down, then drifted back to sleep.

Meg closed her eyes. When she opened them again, it was morning.

CHAPTER NINETEEN

Sitting at his desk at BOSS, Inc. the following day, Dirk looked up to see Sadie coming down the stairs, curly, white-blond hair flying as she hurried toward him, a mother wolf racing to protect her pup.

He had phoned the office yesterday afternoon, wanting to bring them up to speed before the kidnapping and dramatic rescue of a mother and her son broke on the evening news. He'd spoken to Sadie and Ian, reported what had happened at the lake, and let everyone know he and Luke, Meg and Charlie were safe.

But this was the first time he had been in the office.

Sadie stopped beside his desk and planted her hands on her hips. "Well, you look none the worse for wear, considering you damn near killed yourself trying to save your ex-girlfriend from drowning."

"I'm fine. So's Luke. I told you that

yesterday. I stopped by to see Meg and Charlie at the hospital last night. They're both doing okay. They're being released this morning."

"Well, that's good news." Her voice softened. "I'm glad you and Luke were there to save them."

His chest tightened. He didn't want to think what might have happened if he had refused Meg when she had come to him for help. "Yeah, so am I."

"Where are you on the case? On the news it said the man who escaped still hasn't been apprehended."

He shook his head. "As far as I know, they haven't caught him. I'm working with the FBI, Special Agent Ron Nolan. You might remember him from a couple of years back."

"I remember Nolan. Nice fella. Seemed to know what he was doing."

"Soon as you're finished playing mother hen, I'm going to call him, see what the feds have come up with."

Sadie grunted. "Fine. Next time I won't worry about your sorry ass — or Luke's either, for that matter — neither of you appreciate my concern."

Dirk grinned. "You know I love your mothering, sweetness." Since he didn't have a mother of his own. "I'm sorry I worried you."

"That's better." The stout woman turned and headed for the stairs. "Let me know if you need any more help," she called over her shoulder.

Dirk chuckled. He loved that woman. She really was the mother he'd never had, a far better lady than the one who had left when he was so young he couldn't remember her face.

Leaning back in the black leather chair behind his desk, he picked up his cell phone. The office was modern, done in black and chrome. Ian Brodie, the company's owner, worked upstairs, which was also Sadie's domain. There was a room down the hall from her office where the guys could crash if they got in too late to drive home.

The downstairs was open, no cubicles. The guys weren't the type to be boxed in. A waiting area up front was furnished with a black, butter-soft leather sofa and chairs and a black granite coffee table that matched the rest of the modern decor. In the main area, rows of black-topped desks were provided, one for each of the guys who worked with the company.

Dirk brought up Ron Nolan's number and

hit the Send button. "It's Reynolds," he said when the FBI man answered.

"Tell me you busted the a-hole who tried to kill Meg and her boy."

"I wish to hell I could," Nolan said. "He's still out there somewhere."

"I was afraid you'd say that. You gotta have something. What have your guys come up with so far?"

"Not enough, I can tell you. The car was rented under the name Thomas Moore. The O'Brien woman said the kidnapper called himself Thomas, so that fits. Forty years old, born in Upstate New York, went to Columbia University. Yada yada yada. The bad news is, nothing checks out. Thomas Moore is an alias."

"What about fingerprints? There must have been some in the car or in the boat he drove across the lake."

"We got prints. The guy isn't in the system."

"Not AFIS or anywhere else?" There were a number of print recognition systems besides IAFIS, which held the info on seventy million subjects and seventy-three thousand terrorists.

"Nothing so far."

"DNA?"

"The CSIs might find a hair or something

in the car, but it looked pretty clean."

"What about the security cams at Hertz? Maybe they got a shot of the guy you can run through facial recognition."

"We're working on it. In case nothing usable turns up, we've asked the O'Brien woman to come in and give us a composite sketch. We'd like you to corroborate, since you both got a good look at the guy."

"Not a problem." Not for him. He didn't like Meg being dragged back into this mess. "What about Vincent Santini? The cops have him in custody, right? Picked him up at Luke's place?"

"Santini's in custody. Says he doesn't know squat, and I believe him."

"What about Pamela Vardon? She must know something."

"Turns out the skinny dead guy hired her. He also raped her out at the lake. Name's Clifford Sykes. Only been out of jail a couple of months. Pamela's pretty shook up. She never saw Thomas Moore until that morning, and she only got a glimpse of him before he took off in the boat."

"Who was the big guy? The one in the car with Moore?"

"Maxwell Bremmer. Paramilitary. Called himself Mad Max. Only been here a couple of years. Before that he was somewhere in

South America. We don't know where. Haven't been able to figure out how he's connected to this."

"He was working with Moore. That means you could have a foreign connection of some kind. You're checking Moore's fingerprints with Interpol, right? The guy's a smooth operator. I can see him moving around Europe easy enough. South America wouldn't be a stretch."

"Running his prints right now, just waiting for the call."

"So at the moment what you've got is a big fat zero."

"We got a guy out of surgery at Bellevue Medical Center who knows plenty. We're just waiting for him to wake up."

"Good ol' Mickey."

"Michael 'Mickey' Degan. Two-bit criminal. Got a rap sheet ten pages long."

Dirk ran his fingers down his mustache. "You said you were bringing Meg in to do a sketch?"

"That's right."

"What time?"

"She's supposed to call, come in some time this afternoon."

"I'll have her there at three. Will that work?"

"Sounds good."

"Thanks for keeping me in the loop, Ron. I run across anything, I'll let you know."

"I owe you from before. I'll keep you posted as much as I can." Nolan ended the call.

Dirk had promised to talk to Meg that afternoon. He'd take her down to FBI headquarters. Keeping her busy with the case would be a whole lot easier than talking about what had happened between them.

A helluva lot easier than sifting through the embers of an affair that had died five months ago.

It was amazing how fast little kids recovered. Or at least that was how it seemed. Meg and Charlie had both been pronounced physically fit and released from the hospital that morning.

Meg's parents had brought them to her house, fussed over them, then finally returned to their own home. Rose had come over, cried, and hugged them, then started cleaning and picking up the house as if it were just another day. Putting things back on an even keel somehow made Meg feel better.

Even Jonathan paid a surprise visit. He'd heard the story on the morning news. He'd been worried sick, he said. He stayed long enough to check on Charlie, talk to him for a couple of minutes, then he headed down to his office. Meg had been surprised to see him at all.

She glanced up at the clock on the wall in the kitchen. It was almost one p.m. Charlie was playing with his toys in the corner of the family room while Meg sat at the kitchen counter, trying not to keep checking the time, wishing Dirk would appear on her porch.

The doorbell rang and her heart jumped. She smoothed the dark blue skinny jeans she was wearing with a pair of open-toed, low-heeled sandals and a silky, off-the-shoulder turquoise blouse, clothes she hoped looked casual yet sexy, and hurried to the door.

Feeling only a niggle of disappointment when she checked the peephole and spotted her best friend, Valerie Hartman, and Val's fiancé, Luke's brother, Ethan, Meg pulled open the door.

Val swept her into a hug. "Oh my God, we just heard! Are you okay? Is Charlie okay? I can't believe you didn't call me!"

Former La Belle model Valentine Hart stood five-foot-nine — an inch shorter than Meg — had honey-blond hair, blue eyes, and an amazing set of dimples. She loved animals, had quit modeling to complete her degree in veterinary medicine.

"We're both okay," Meg said. "Thanks to Dirk and Luke."

"You should have called us." Ethan followed Val into the entry. "I would have come home to help. I hope you know that."

He was a big man, six-three, two hundred plus pounds of solid muscle, with short black hair and a face that could make a woman swoon. Val had fallen in love with him during the fashion show tour, when he and Dirk had traveled with the show as bodyguards.

"I didn't call because I wanted you to enjoy your time together. You deserved it. I had Dirk's help, and your brother's."

"Sadie brought me up to speed this morning," Ethan said. "I called Val and told her."

"We wanted to make sure you were okay," Val said. Meg noticed Ethan's big hand resting possessively at her waist as they walked farther into the house.

Val was marrying Ethan. Meg hadn't been strong enough to risk her heart with Dirk. Instead, she had stupidly sent him away.

Charlie looked up and spotted them, dropped his big toy dump truck, grinned, and ran to Val, who bent and scooped him up in her arms.

"Hey, Charlie!"

"Hey, Valentine!" Charlie always called her that. Dirk often did, too. Val never seemed to mind, though it was just a stage name. "Will you play trucks with me?"

"Why don't I play trucks with you?" Ethan suggested. "We'll let your mommy talk to Val, okay?"

"Yes!" Charlie shot his small fist into the air. He was growing up so fast. He loved playing games with Ethan, who had plenty of kid experience since he had a daughter two years older.

Ethan chuckled as Charlie raced him back to his green John Deere tractor, bright red fire engine, and big yellow Caterpillar earth mover in the corner.

"I could use a cup of coffee," Val said.

"Good idea. I just brewed a pot."

Val linked arms with her and they headed over to the breakfast counter that opened into the family room. The house had a separate living room that Meg kept nice and neat, but this room was where they mostly lived. A flat-screen TV that usually had a cartoon show playing, toys, and stuffed animals scattered around.

There were plenty of educational books, and Meg had just bought Charlie a Kindle

Fire Kid's Edition tablet.

While Meg headed for the coffeepot, Val settled on a stool at the breakfast bar and surveyed the printed sheets scattered on the granite top. "So you're finally looking at real estate listings."

Rental spaces, possible locations for the boutique she wanted to open. Meg poured a mug of coffee for Val and set it on the counter, then filled one for herself and sat down on the tall wooden stool on the opposite side.

"I would have done it sooner," Meg said, "but I couldn't decide what kind of store I wanted to open. After what's happened, I think I know."

Val took a sip of her coffee. "You ready to talk about it?" *It* being the kidnapping that had nearly gotten her and her baby killed.

Meg sighed. "I've tried not to think too much about it, but it's probably good to get it out in the open."

For the next few minutes, Meg filled Val in on the abduction, how Dirk and Luke had tracked the kidnappers to the house at the lake, and how Dirk had saved her and Charlie from drowning.

"Dirk's a good man," Val said.

"I know that. I've always known that." The story continued, finished with Meg admitting she'd slept with him. She ended with a simple, "I made a mistake, Val. I want him back."

"Wow. I didn't see that one coming. You've always been so sure it would never work."

"I thought it would work for me. I wasn't sure about Charlie. I didn't think it would work for Dirk. I didn't think Dirk was the type for a ready-made family."

Meg sipped her coffee. "I also figured my parents would never approve, and they're very important to me. Now I realize I should have taken the chance. I should have chosen Dirk over my parents' approval. I should have given us time to figure things out."

"Okay." Val looked down at the sheets of paper scattered all over the counter. "So how does the kidnapping and sleeping with Dirk have anything to do with opening a boutique?"

Meg took a sip of her coffee. "I quit modeling because I wanted to be a mom and spend time with my son. It didn't take long to figure out baking cookies for Charlie, playing tennis at Dad's country club, and gabbing on the phone with Mom weren't enough to keep me happy."

"We talked about that. It was the reason you've been wanting to go back to work."

"I knew I wanted to open a shop. I knew it had to be about fashion, right? That's what I understand. But not just the latest in sexy lingerie."

"No, I wouldn't want that either."

Meg flashed her a look. "Especially after the job nearly got you killed."

"There is that."

"Before I married Jonathan, I was athletic, competitive, even daring. I loved to ski and scuba dive. I loved fast cars and even riding motorcycles."

"Don't tell me you want to be a race-car driver again."

Meg laughed. "I'm not the least bit interested in returning to my wilder days, but when I was with Dirk and Luke, I found that part of myself again. Opening a boutique that caters to women who love sports and want to look stylish while they're participating — I think that's what I want to do."

Mulling the idea over, Val sipped her coffee, then set her mug back down on the counter. "I like it — I totally do. It's an interesting concept. Seems to me the possibilities are almost unlimited."

"I've still got to think of a name, something catchy, but I'm going for it."

"And Dirk?"

"When I was drowning in that lake and I thought I'd never see my baby again — never see Dirk — I realized you have to grab on to what you want out of life. You have to take risks. I'm going to tell Dirk I made a mistake. I'm going to ask him to forgive me and give us another chance."

"You think he will?"

Her shoulders slumped. "I don't know. Maybe not at first. But I'm not going to give up until I know for sure I'm not what he really wants. I'm going to find a way to convince him to trust me again."

"He was really upset when you ended things. I think he's determined not to get hurt that way again."

"I know."

"I've got an idea. Tell him you want to go for a ride on his Harley. That'll throw him off balance enough you might get him to listen to you."

Meg grinned. "Funny thing is, I'd really like to go."

Val grinned back, so wide she dimpled.

CHAPTER TWENTY

Dirk knocked on Meg's door that afternoon. He'd phoned earlier, told her he'd take her to FBI headquarters to do the composite sketch, and she had agreed. As he stood on her porch, he could hear her soft, feminine footfalls padding toward him across the carpet, and a memory arose of her long, pretty legs wrapped around him as he moved deep inside her.

His groin tightened and his pulse kicked up. Then she pulled open the door and smiled at him as if she hadn't seen him in weeks instead of just last night, and his chest clamped down.

Damn, she was beautiful.

She took a step back. "Come on in."

He shoved his lust down deep, forced his emotions under control, and glanced toward the family room. "How's Charlie doing?"

"He seems fine. Which worries me a little. I've got an appointment next week with a child psychologist. She's supposed to be really good. I want her to see him, tell me what she thinks."

"Sounds like a good idea. Give him a chance to open up about what happened." He looked down at his heavy wristwatch. "We need to get going. The feds will be expecting us."

"Rose is here. Charlie's down for his nap. I was hoping we'd have a few minutes to talk."

"No time. We can talk in the car on the way."

Her warm smile faded. She guessed he was stonewalling, which he was. They were over. There was nothing to talk about except the case, and they could do that on the road.

"All right, fine, let's go." She grabbed her purse and snagged her sweater off the back of the sofa but didn't put it on.

They headed out to his Viper, parked in front of the house. Dirk settled Meg in the passenger seat, then rounded the hood and slid in behind the wheel. He cranked the engine, which roared to life and crooned its familiar purr.

As he pulled the powerful car out onto the street, his gaze cut to Meg, and he tried not to notice the way her loose turquoise blouse had slipped off one shoulder. It reminded him how soft her skin felt beneath his hands, how much she loved it when he cupped her breasts.

"Have you talked to the police?" she asked, dousing the hunger burning through him, thank Jesus.

He concentrated on the road. "Spoke to the FBI this morning. Agent Nolan says they haven't got much so far. They're waiting to see if the rental car security cams picked up any usable images. If they get something, they'll run it through facial recognition, see if anything turns up."

"That sounds promising."

"They're also waiting to hear from Interpol on a print they got off the boat the kidnapper abandoned across the lake. They're hoping it belongs to Moore."

"Moore? He's the man who got away?"

"Thomas Moore. Like the poet. That's the name he was using." He clicked on his blinker and changed lanes. "Unfortunately it's an alias."

"Moore would have needed a fake ID and credit cards to rent a car," Meg said. "He really had the kidnapping well planned out."

"The guy was a pro. He won't be easy to find."

"What about the other three men?"

"Clifford Sykes, deceased, was the tall,

254

skinny guy. The one in the hospital is Michael 'Mickey' Degan. Both two-bit criminals. Nothing that links them to Moore. The big guy in the car was a merc." He caught her uncertain glance. "Mercenary. Paramilitary. Last known location somewhere in South America. The feds are following up on that, hoping it'll lead to something." The car moved easily through traffic, cutting around an old blue beater in the slow lane.

"Degan's still at Bellevue Medical?" Meg asked.

"That's right. I called to check on him this morning. He had surgery to repair the damage from the slug I planted in his chest. The feds'll be talking to him as soon as he's out of the ICU." His jaw tightened. "So will I."

"I want to be there."

As he spotted his exit up ahead and pulled off on the ramp, Dirk flicked her a sideways glance. She'd been in it from the start. Part of him felt guilty for her close call with death. Another part was glad she'd been there. If she hadn't, there was a good chance her boy would be dead.

At least she wouldn't be in any danger this time.

"All right," he said. "Nurse Ratched

promised to call and let me know when he's awake."

"Nurse Ratched?" Meg's throaty laughter slid right through him. He had really missed that laugh.

"She must be some nurse," Meg said. "She's a friend of yours?"

He nodded. "I took a bullet a couple years back. Abigail Rathburn was my nurse. I called her Nurse Ratched. She was bulldog mean, but she had a heart of gold. She's helped me a few times since then."

"I remember seeing the scar on your lower back. I thought it happened in the Rangers."

He shook his head. "Street gang. I'd just gotten my PI's license. Guy hired me to help him get his son into rehab. Kid's buddies didn't like the idea. The good news was, seeing his friends shoot a man in the back straightened the kid's ass right up. Went home to his folks and been walking the straight and narrow ever since."

Meg cast him a soft smile of approval. It shouldn't matter, but it did.

As the Viper rounded a corner, FBI headquarters appeared up ahead, a glass highrise on 3rd Avenue in downtown Seattle. Dirk parked the car in an underground garage half a block away and they both got out of the vehicle.

At least she hadn't mentioned their *talk* again.

Dirk tried to convince himself he was glad.

Meg pulled her sweater on against the late January chill, Dirk slid into his leather jacket, and they started toward the entrance to the tall, cement-and-glass building that was FBI headquarters.

Stopping for a moment at the corner, Meg waited next to Dirk for one of Seattle's electrical trolleys to drive past, then they continued on to the glass front door.

Special Agent Ron Nolan had visitor badges waiting for them at the reception desk. As Meg pinned hers on, one of the security guards, a curvy little blonde, looked Dirk up and down, assessing his tall, broad-shouldered build and the sexy way he wore his black leather jacket, worn jeans, and work boots. Her hot look said she would like to eat him up, and Meg suffered a twinge of jealousy she had no right to feel.

Didn't matter. She sliced the girl a hands-off glance and the girl looked away.

Dirk didn't seem to notice as he clipped on his badge and they headed upstairs.

Agent Nolan was waiting when they stepped off the elevator. He was medium height, an average-looking man whose eyes reflected his intelligence and an intensity that said his job was important to him.

"Thanks for coming in," he said. "I've got news. I would have saved you a trip, but the info just came in. Let's go into the conference room where we can talk."

Agent Nolan led them down a busy hallway, past men in dark suits and women in modest skirts or slacks wearing comfortable shoes. They stepped into a room behind a glass wall and Meg sat next to Dirk at a long mahogany table.

Agent Nolan set up his laptop and opened the screen. "The fingerprint we got off the aluminum boat popped up on Interpol. It belongs to a guy named Raymond Neville. Forty years old, born in England. Both parents deceased. No siblings. Before they died, his folks spent every pound of their savings trying to get their son through medical school. Raymond decided there were a lot easier ways to make money than being a doctor, and the pay was a whole lot better."

"Professional hit man?"

"In the beginning. He's branched out since then. Now they call him The Fixer. Someone wants something done, he's the go-to guy, the man who can make it happen. Neville's wanted in half a dozen coun-

258

tries in Europe and the Baltics. Rumor is for the past few months he's been working for someone in South America."

"South America. Same as Mad Max Bremmer. Interesting."

Nolan turned the computer around so they could see the screen. "That's the only known photo of The Fixer in the system." A fuzzy image of a man with thick, brown hair and horn-rimmed glasses. There was nothing about him that made him stand out and nothing that looked familiar to Meg.

"The guy's a real chameleon," Agent Nolan said. "According to Interpol, people have described him as bald with a big nose, an older man with thinning gray hair, and a young guy with a crew cut. And he's got a drawer full of identities to match his many appearances."

"I gather there was nothing on the Hertz cams," Dirk said.

"Nothing usable. He kept his head down. What little we could see matches the description you and Ms. O'Brien gave us."

"So you don't need us to do a sketch," Meg said.

"Not much point in it. Thomas Moore, or whatever name he's using now, won't look anything like the man you saw at the lake."

"So someone hired The Fixer to help him

set up a kidnapping that would have paid ten million dollars," Dirk said. "Less, of course, what it cost to get the job done."

"That's about it. It's rare that one of his schemes ever fails."

Dirk glanced at Meg but spoke to Nolan. "You don't think The Fixer will go after the boy again?"

Nolan shook his head. "It took weeks, maybe months of planning to get to Charlie the first time. I don't see it happening again any time soon. But the guy has a reputation for accomplishing his mission, so there's no way to know exactly what he'll do. After a job, he usually just disappears."

"I don't like it," Dirk said.

"The man's no fool. No way he's going to make another attempt without being prepared."

"Maybe not, but as you said, there's no way to know for sure."

The door of the conference room opened and one of the agents leaned in. "Sorry to bother you, Ron, but there's a call you need to take. Shall I have it patched in?"

"I'll take it in my office. We're almost through here."

The agent nodded, slipped back out into the hall, and closed the door with a soft click.

"Sorry, where were we?" Nolan asked.

Dirk went back to the conversation. "I was saying there's no way to know for sure what Neville will do, which is a roundabout way of saying the boy might need protection."

Nolan shook his head. "No way the cops or the FBI is going to spring for security when there's nothing to indicate the child is in any kind of danger."

Meg figured Agent Nolan was right. The police couldn't afford to protect everyone. Still, she didn't like the little thread of uncertainty that slipped down her spine.

"All right, I'll take care of it," Dirk said. "Anything else you need from us?"

"If there is, we'll let you know." The agent rose from his chair while Meg and Dirk rose from theirs. He walked out the door. "Keep me posted," Dirk said.

"Same goes," said Nolan.

They left the office and walked back to the car. They were pulling out of the parking garage when Dirk's cell phone started playing a rock country song. He hit the Hands Free button on the steering wheel as the car rolled into the street.

"Reynolds."

"Dirk, it's Abigail. The man you asked about — Michael Degan? They just moved him out of the ICU into a private room."

"He's awake?"

"Off and on."

"Thanks, Abby. I owe you."

The nurse laughed. "That's what you always say. One of these days I'm going to collect." The line went dead and Dirk pressed the End button on the Hands Free.

"I have a feeling Nurse Ratched isn't some sixty-year-old woman," Meg said.

"Actually, she's a single mother, same as you. Only she's in her late forties. Two kids and a grandkid on the way."

"So you and she never —"

"No. She's just a friend."

Meg hated feeling such a wave of relief. "So we're on our way to the hospital?" she asked as Dirk stopped at a red light.

"Unless you want me to take you home."

"No, I want to be there when you talk to Degan. Maybe he knows something that'll help us find The Fixer." She leaned back as Dirk stepped on the gas and continued through the downtown traffic. "What about Charlie? You don't really think Neville might come after him again?"

"I think Nolan's right. No way the guy's working without some kind of plan. The thing is, he doesn't need Charlie. He could go after you or your mom and still get your dad to pay the ransom."

"I never thought of that."

"Even if he wanted to try, putting a plan together takes time. Plus he'd need a new crew, people he can count on. He'd need a way to transport you, a place to keep you till the money was paid."

"So at least for now we're safe."

"Yeah. On the other hand, I'd rather err on the side of caution. I'll bring in one of the guys from BOSS, Inc., park him in front of your house for a while. Ethan's good with kids. If it looks like there might actually be a threat, I can ask him to help."

Meg didn't argue. Now wasn't the time. Maybe after they talked, he would reconsider and handle the job himself.

Or maybe not.

When they reached the hospital parking lot and Dirk turned off the car, he reached beneath the seat and pulled out his pistol.

A chill slid through her. "You're taking your gun?"

"Like I said, I'd rather err on the side of caution."

Meg didn't argue. She trusted Dirk. Now more than ever. Cracking open the door, she climbed out of the car as Dirk clipped the pistol on to his belt, out of sight beneath his black leather jacket.

Together they headed for the entrance to the hospital.

CHAPTER TWENTY-ONE

Bellevue Medical Center hummed with activity as Dirk shoved through the revolving glass doors and waited for Meg to walk past him into the foyer. The acrid hospital smell of alcohol and cleaning products hit him as he urged her toward the front desk.

People shuffled out of their way, fanning out in different directions. Doctors and nurses in scrubs moved purposefully down the hall.

"We're looking for a patient named Michael Degan," Dirk said. "He's just been released from the ICU."

The plump, dark-haired receptionist behind the front desk shoved on a pair of reading glasses and checked her computer screen. "Mr. Degan has just been placed in a private room on the seventeenth floor." She pulled off the glasses. "Elevators on your left. Check in at the nurses' station when you get out on your floor."

"Thanks."

They rode upstairs with a couple of older women, white hair, polyester pants, and flowered tops. The women got out on sixteen and the elevator rose again.

When the doors dinged open, Dirk spotted the nurses' desk across the hall and started toward it; Meg stayed close beside him. He had a hunch being there to see the man who had kidnapped her son sparked memories she would just as soon forget.

A little brunette in scrubs stood up from her chair behind the counter and gave him an inviting smile. He wished he were more interested.

"We're looking for Michael Degan," he said. "Can you give me his room number?"

"You're family?"

"Oh, yeah. We're brothers. You couldn't tell?"

Next to him, Meg hid a smile.

The brunette seemed to believe him. He decided to overlook the insult.

"Mr. Degan is in room ten. You can see him for a few minutes, but he's still recovering from surgery so you can't stay long."

Dirk turned to Meg. She looked paler than she had a minute ago. Maybe he shouldn't have brought her. "Why don't you wait for me here?" he gently suggested. "I'll talk to Degan, see if he knows anything. Okay?"

"I want to be there."

He sighed. She'd always been stubborn. That hadn't changed. Taking her hand, he started down the hall, walked past a man in a hospital gown rolling an IV pole along beside him. As they passed room eight, a gray-haired doctor in scrubs came out of Degan's room, his attention fixed on the clipboard in his hand, half-glasses riding low on his nose.

Worried the doctor might try to keep him from talking to Degan, Dirk waited as the man strode off down the hall in the opposite direction and disappeared around the corner.

Dirk's attention swung back to Degan's room. No cop posted outside the door? It bothered him, but as Nolan had said, the city's budget was tight. Degan would be handcuffed to the bed and he wouldn't be in any shape to attempt an escape.

On the other hand, what if the man knew something about The Fixer? Something that could give the police his current location? It wasn't like Ron Nolan to leave a valuable asset at risk.

Dirk glanced toward the end of the hall,

his instincts kicking in, his senses suddenly alert.

"Stay here till I make sure everything's okay," he said to Meg.

"What's going on?"

"Just stay here." Pulling his pistol, he shoved the door open with his boot and did a quick scan. Degan's eyes were open and staring. Blood everywhere, the sheets scarlet, pools of red all over the floor. Gun in a two-handed grip, he went in, spotted a uniformed police officer slumped in a chair, ran over, and checked the side of his neck. A pulse throbbed. Dirk bolted for the door.

"Officer down! Degan's dead! Call security! Tell them to seal off this floor!" He tossed his cell phone to Meg. "Call Nolan! I'm going after him!"

Turning, he raced down the hall after the gray-haired doctor who had just left Mickey Degan dead in his room.

Neville had less than a minute head start. He would be walking, blending in. Dirk pounded down the hall, slowed as he rounded the corner, caught a glimpse of a man in scrubs moving purposely toward the elevator at the end of the corridor.

He spotted Dirk, whirled and pulled off two shots. A group of nurses screamed and started running. "Get down!" Dirk fired two return shots as Neville stepped into the elevator and the doors rolled closed behind him.

Dirk raced for the stairs.

Meg's hands shook as she pressed Dirk's cell phone against her ear. "Agent Nolan — this . . . this is Megan O'Brien. I'm at the hospital with Dirk. Mickey Degan has been murdered. Dirk . . ." She swallowed. "Dirk went after the man who killed him."

"I'm on my way." Agent Nolan said something she couldn't hear. He was moving, she could tell, his footsteps pounding down the hall. "I've dispatched men to the scene. The cops will be there before we are. Are you somewhere safe?"

"I'm on the seventeenth floor, just down from Degan's room. I heard shots. I-I think Neville is shooting at Dirk." Meg's heart raced with fear for Dirk. She couldn't believe it was happening again.

"Take cover and stay out of sight until we can get there." Agent Nolan's phone went dead.

Meg ran behind the counter that enclosed the nurses' station and ducked down with two other women. She could hear pounding feet and people yelling. She caught a glimpse of a group of security guards scrambling past, heading in the direction of the gunfire. A couple of doctors ran into Mickey Degan's room to take care of the downed policeman.

Meg had no idea where Dirk was. Dear God, she prayed he was safe.

"Police!" someone shouted. "Stay down and keep out of the way!" A group of uniformed police officers ran past her down the hall. Meg stayed hidden behind the counter and so did the two nurses. Two more joined them, all of them crouching down in case more shots were fired.

It seemed like forever before she spotted Dirk's familiar tall frame striding back down the hall in her direction. Relief hit her so hard she felt dizzy. She shot up from behind the counter and ran toward him, colliding with his chest. "Thank God you're okay."

Hard arms closed around her. "I'm all right. It's over. Everybody's okay."

"Everybody but Mickey Degan."

"Yeah." He tipped his head toward Mickey's room. "How's the cop?"

"I don't know. The doctors are in with him now." She hadn't looked in Degan's room. She didn't want another ugly memory lodged in her brain. "You didn't catch Neville."

He shook his head. "We traded shots up

here. He went down in the elevator. I took the stairs down a couple of floors, then caught another elevator to the bottom. He fired a couple of rounds at me as he left the building; then he ducked around a corner and just disappeared."

"It was him, though, right?"

"Had to be. He went to medical school. He knew how to use a needle, gave the cop a shot in the neck with a syringe full of something, then dragged him inside. Disconnected the machines hooked up to Degan so the alarms wouldn't sound, then slit the guy's throat."

Meg swayed against him.

"Sorry. I shouldn't have told you."

She drew in a calming breath. "I'm in this. I can handle it. I don't need to be protected from everything that happens."

He looked down at her, must have read something in her face. "Maybe not."

Meg waited while Dirk spent the next half hour talking to the police; then Agent Nolan arrived and they told their stories again.

"How's the uniform doing?" Dirk asked.

"Had a nice little nap, thanks to Neville. Looks like he's gonna be okay."

Just as they were ready to leave, a policeman walked up to the FBI agent with a paper bag in his hand. "We found this in a trash can down the alley. Bloody scrubs the guy was wearing were in there, too."

Nolan looked into the bag. "Man's gray wig. Figures." He turned to Dirk. "Why don't you two go on home? There's nothing more you can do here."

Dirk just nodded.

Meg felt his big hand span her waist as he urged her toward the elevator. They rode down in silence, then walked out to the Viper, parked in the lot.

Dirk held the car door while Meg slid into the passenger seat. He leaned down, and for the first time that day, Dirk smiled. "I never knew you were such a trouble magnet, Ms. O'Brien."

Meg managed a faint smile in return. "There's a lot you don't know about me, Dirk. That's the reason I want us to talk."

He reached down and gently cupped her cheek. "All right. After what you've been through, I guess you deserve a chance to speak your mind." He slammed the door, walked around, and climbed in behind the wheel.

The engine roared to life and they headed back to her house. The sun was out, but the afternoon was waning. It was a warm, beautiful day, and tomorrow was supposed to be even better. A good day for what she had in mind.

"You don't think Neville will come after us the way he did Mickey Degan?" she asked as the car rolled along.

Dirk cast her a sideways glance. "Not likely. Neither of us can identify him. All the people involved are dead except for Pamela, and she never talked to him, didn't even know he existed until that day at the lake."

"So none of us are a threat to him."

"No. Odds are, now that he's eliminated the only possible connection, he'll leave the country."

She turned to look at him, appreciating his handsome profile, the capable way he handled the powerful car. "Odds are?" she repeated.

"We can't be a hundred percent certain he won't come up with another scheme to get his hands on your dad's ten mil. Which is why I'm going ahead with that surveillance we talked about. And we need to beef up your home security. I'm going to suggest your dad make arrangements at his house, too."

She sighed. "An upgrade to my alarm system is a good idea, but I hate the notion of having to be guarded all the time. I had enough of that while we were on the fashion show tour."

"Until we figure things out, you don't have much choice."

True, but instead of some nameless man sitting in a car out front, she couldn't help wishing Dirk would be the man watching out for her and little Charlie.

At least he had agreed to hear what she had to say. With any luck, no one would be abducted or murdered before she got the chance. After that, she'd know better where she stood.

They pulled up in front of the house and he walked her to the door. There was a package sitting on the porch. Meg grinned when she saw it and scooped the package up in her arms.

One of Dirk's dark eyebrows arched in silent question.

"Research," she said. "Something I bought on the Internet and had shipped to the house overnight."

She glanced over his broad shoulder to see a plain brown Buick pull up to the curb on the opposite side of the street.

"That's a guy named Diego Montoya," he said. "Good at surveillance. Got a sharp eye, and he's tough enough to deal with a problem if one comes up. He'll be rotating in with a couple of other guys so you'll be covered twenty-four/seven."

She sighed.

"It won't be for long. A guy like Neville's not about to just sit around doing nothing. Sooner or later something will break."

"I hope so."

"Listen, I've got a couple of things to do. We can talk first if you want."

But he looked like he'd rather make a run for it, get as far away as he could — not a good start.

"Why don't we talk tomorrow? It's supposed to be a beautiful day. Maybe you could . . . umm . . . take me for a ride on your Harley."

Disbelief widened his eyes. "You're kidding, right? Since when do you like motorcycles?"

She shrugged. "Since I was in high school. It's been a while since I've been on one, I admit. I think it would be fun."

He frowned. "You're a mother. You've got a little boy to think of."

"So don't take me on the freeway. We live in a beautiful place. We've got parks and streams and mountains. There has to be a dozen places you could take me."

Interest flickered in his hazel eyes, which looked greener now than brown. "You sure?"

"I'll bring lunch. We'll have a picnic."

He nodded. "Okay. If you're sure."

Meg smiled. "Late morning sound okay?"

"Fine. Say eleven?"

"Sounds good. I'll see you then."

As Dirk headed for his car, Meg walked into the house and closed the door, her package clutched against her chest. It was Vika, sold by MotoSport. Dirk was going to be very surprised when he saw it.

Worry filtered through her. Before the abduction, she hadn't seen him in months. She hadn't been in his life and he hadn't been in hers. He'd told her more than once he wasn't interested in going backward.

Meg closed her eyes and leaned against the door. She wasn't ready to give up. Not yet. Dirk was worth fighting for.

If there was one thing she'd learned about herself since the kidnapping, it was that she was a fighter.

CHAPTER TWENTY-TWO

Dirk roared up in front of Meg's Madison Park house on his custom Dyna Low Rider. He figured it was rare for the people in the expensive neighborhood to see a bike like his parked on the street.

He had purposely worn his leathers: black leather chaps over his black jeans, a black T-shirt with the sleeves cut out, and heavy motorcycle boots. Might as well let Meg see the man he really was, not the hero version she had made up in her head.

Let her see how right she'd been when she'd told him how totally unsuited they were and sent his ass packing.

Unzipping his studded leather jacket, he strode up the path to the porch and knocked on her door. She wanted to go for a ride. She had no idea how badly he wanted to give her one. Only not on the back of his bike.

He steeled himself as the ornate door

swung open. Rose Wills stood grinning in the entry. "Dirk!" The heavyset woman launched herself, knocking him a few steps backward as she enveloped him in a hug.

"You brought our baby home safe! You'll never know how grateful we all are for what you did." She gave him another warm hug. Dirk smiled down at her, and Rose let him go.

Thank-you hugs could really feel good sometimes. "I was just doing my job, Rose. We're all grateful it worked out the way it did."

"Come on in. Meg's upstairs. She'll be down in a minute."

He nodded, followed the heavyset woman into the house. As they reached the entrance to the family room, he spotted little Charlie playing on the floor in front of the coffee table with what looked like a computer tablet.

"He got a Kindle Fire Kid's Edition for Christmas," Rose said. "He can already do more stuff on it than I can."

Dirk smiled. "I don't doubt it. Seems like these days, they're born with the knack." The kid looked up and saw him, and his face went from intense concentration to uncertainty.

Damn, Dirk hadn't thought about scaring

the boy when he'd put on the leathers. He was gearing up for the kid to burst into another crying jag when Charlie stood up from the coffee table and started walking toward him.

With his red hair and freckles, tall for his age like his mom and the rest of the O'Brien family, Charlie was a really cute kid when he wasn't upset. The little boy walked right up to Dirk and just stood there staring. It made him kind of uneasy.

"Mama said you was a policeman. Is that your uniform?"

He chuckled. "I'm not exactly a policeman, but sometimes I do the kind of work a policeman does." He thought of the way he must look to a not-quite three-year-old, in his snug black leather chaps, jacket, and boots. "This is what I wear when I ride my motorcycle."

Charlie's blue eyes rounded. "You got a modor . . . cicle. Can I see it? Can I?"

"If you look out the window, you can see it parked in front of the house."

Charlie took off running, his small legs moving like pistons across the floor, making Dirk grin. Hearing light female footsteps, he turned to see Meg coming down the stairs.

For a second, he forgot to breathe.

"Jesus, Mary, and Joseph." She was a biker's wet dream, decked out in tight black leather pants and a fitted black leather jacket that nipped in and stopped at her waist. Black leather boots with a slender heel came up to her knees, shoving her up a couple more inches.

He clamped down on a vicious shot of lust. "You look . . . wow, you look great."

"The outfit was in the box on the porch. The clothes are research for the boutique I want to open, all but the boots, which I already had. I've decided I want to specialize in high-end women's sports clothes. Snow skiing outfits, motorcycle leathers, tennis clothes, stuff like that."

"Yeah, I remember you mentioned opening a boutique." He relaxed. Maybe she didn't want to talk about the two of them at all. That was good. Right?

He felt something tugging on his chaps, looked down to see Charlie staring up at him. "Can I go for a wide on your modocicle?"

"I don't think your mom would like that very much, Charlie." He turned to Meg. "I guess he . . . umm . . . likes my bike."

"He likes trucks, cars, anything with an engine." Meg crouched down beside her son. "Not today, sweetheart. When you get bigger you can go for a ride."

Dirk wondered if she was thinking he'd be around when the kid got older. It made him feel funny inside.

"We'd better get going," she said as Rose Wills walked up and handed them a bag that apparently held their lunch. "We'll be back this afternoon."

"I wanna go for a wide," Charlie whined, his face scrunching up. He was seconds from a good loud cry.

"Let's go play with your Kindle." Rose picked him up, propped him on her generous hip, and started for the family room. "We'll read *Mike Mulligan and His Steam Shovel.* You like that one."

Charlie continued to whine and struggle in her arms.

"Hey, bud!" Dirk strode over to where Mrs. Wills set the boy down on the sofa. "You aren't big enough to go for a ride on my bike yet, but someday you will be. You can't cry about it. That just won't work. But when the day comes that you're old enough, I promise I'll take you, okay?"

Charlie sniffed.

"Okay?"

He nodded. "Okay."

"Now tell your mama good-bye."

He waved toward where Meg stood next

to the door. "Bye, Mama."

"Good boy." As Dirk strode out of the family room, Meg and Rose both just stood staring.

Dirk's gaze fixed on her face. "What? I was a kid once."

Meg started grinning. "Let's get out of here before he catches his breath and starts all over again. Charlie's very persistent when he wants something."

"Kind of like his mother," Dirk mumbled. They headed out to his motorcycle, black with an orange dragon winding around the tank; it had an extended front wheel, a Sundowner seat, and 103 cubic inches of go power. The dragon on his helmet matched.

Meg paused next to the bike. "Impressive." She smiled. "I can't wait to take a ride."

"I've had it a while. I had it customized when I bought it." He stuffed their lunch into a saddlebag, grabbed the spare helmet off the seat, and tossed it to Meg, who pulled it on over her fiery hair. She'd clipped it back at the nape of her neck, but a few wispy strands fluttered next to her cheeks.

His groin tightened. He wanted to unfasten the clip and slide his fingers into the silky strands, wrap a fist around them, and drag her mouth up to his for a deep, burning kiss. He wanted a lot more than that.

Pulling his own helmet on, he swung aboard the bike, and Meg swung on behind him. He could feel the heat of her body, those long legs snug against his thighs, her soft breasts pressing into his back. He couldn't remember the last time he'd had a woman aboard. Damn, it felt good.

He told himself it wasn't because the woman was Meg.

"You ready?"

"All set." She took a firm hold on his waist and he dragged in a calming breath.

"You've ridden before, right? You know to lean with me, not in the opposite direction."

"It was way back, but yes, I remember."

"Good girl." Dirk kicked up the stand, fired the engine, gunned it, and they were off.

He knew where he wanted to take her. It was the warmest day they'd had so far this year and it hadn't rained, so it was nice and dry.

On the way over to Meg's he'd stopped by the lake house, checked in with the construction crew, still hard at work though he hadn't been there to help as much as he usually did. They were making good progress, finishing the framing, getting ready to start on the roof.

The Harley hummed along the road. He was in no hurry. He loved being out in the sunshine, loved the feel of the fresh air rushing past, the feel of the heavy machine throbbing between his legs.

He wondered if Meg felt it, too, wiped the next thought out of his head.

Winding his way up into the hills, he turned down a dirt road and continued to a favorite spot next to a stream. It was completely private, perfectly hidden away.

The ground was dry. Taking an old blanket out of the other saddlebag, he spread it open on the grass, set the lunch bag down on top of it, and took out a couple of Cokes.

He'd rather have a beer, but Meg was a mom and he wasn't taking any chances.

"This is wonderful." Meg wandered over to look at the stream. Frothy water churned and bubbled, ran over the rocks in the middle and along the banks.

"Eat first or talk first?" he asked.

"Talk — unless you're starving."

"I had breakfast; I'm okay."

She moistened her lips and he realized she was nervous. "I'll take one of those Cokes," she said.

He fished one out and handed it over. Both of them sat down on the blanket. "It's

Diet," he said. "I remember that's what you like."

She ran a finger around the rim of the unopened can. "I remember everything about you, Dirk."

His chest went tight. Then, suddenly, he was angry. "You remember everything? Then you remember that you're the one who ended things between us. You're the one who said it would never work. Nothing's changed, Meg. I'm the same man I was before and you're the same woman."

"I'm not the same. I'm different. I understand things I didn't understand before."

"Oh, yeah? Like what?"

"Like what a good man you are. I understand that I shouldn't have made assumptions about you. I shouldn't have assumed you would never fit in with my family, never be able to handle being a dad to my son."

He stared at her, his eyes hot with rage and the feelings of betrayal he'd thought he'd overcome. "You meant everything to me, Meg, and I meant nothing to you."

"That's not true!"

"It is true! You threw me away, Meg! Like I was a piece of trash. You threw me away!"

She looked stricken. "No!"

He shot up off the ground and strode over to the stream, stared into the water, fisted his hands on his hips. Dragging in deep breaths of air, he fought for control.

He felt Meg's arms slide around his waist, felt her cheek against his back. His eyes slid closed. He had loved her so much.

"Have you ever made a mistake so big it just consumed you?" she asked softly. "Have you ever made a wrong choice you wished you could undo more than anything in the world?"

He could feel her trembling. He turned, saw fat tears rolling down her cheeks.

"What are you saying, Meg?"

"I made that kind of mistake when I sent you away. I tried to get over you. I told myself giving you up was the best thing for both of us, but it wasn't. I've thought of you day and night since the moment you walked away."

"Meg, don't."

"Now I'm begging you to let me back in. I'm asking you to forgive me for being a fool, to say you'll try again."

His throat ached. He hadn't expected their talk to go this far. Hadn't expected to see the depth of her regret in those beautiful blue eyes.

"Give me another chance, Dirk. Give us another chance."

He started shaking his head. "I can't,

Meg. The feelings I had for you ran deep. I thought you felt that way, too. You didn't give me any warning, just cut me out as if I never existed. I can't deal with those kinds of feelings again."

Instead of arguing, she reached up and slid her hands into his hair, cupped the back of his head, and brought his mouth down to hers for a very tender kiss. She trailed kisses along his jaw, pressed her lips to the side of his neck, kissed the head of the dragon that crawled up from his shoulder.

"Meg . . ." Yearning burned through him. Need. And fierce, deep desire. His body tightened and he went rock hard. He wanted this woman, had always wanted her.

Meg kissed him again, deeper this time, her tongue in his mouth, her breath coming fast, her thundering heartbeat matching the speed of his own.

"I want you," she said, sliding her arms up around his neck. "I need you, Dirk. Please forgive me." She kissed him again, her leather pants rubbing erotically against the hard ridge beneath his fly surrounded by the leather chaps.

Her hand went there, cupped him, squeezed very gently, made him groan.

Meg slid the leather jacket off his shoulders, let it fall to the ground. She shoved up his black sleeveless T-shirt, silently insisting he pull it off over his head. Reaching behind his neck, he tugged it off and tossed it away.

Slender hands roamed over his bare chest, tracing the muscles, outlining the sinews, the ladder of muscle down his stomach; then she pressed her mouth over his heart.

He didn't move. It took every ounce of his will. He knew what he would be risking, knew the power he would be giving her.

She caught sight of the small tattoo on his upper left chest, reached out, and touched it. It was the tattoo of a heart cracked in two.

"This wasn't there before," she said, drawing the shape with the tip of her finger, her eyes moist and so incredibly blue.

He thought of the hurtful way they'd parted and some of his anger returned. "No, it wasn't. It's a reminder never to love a woman again. But if you think I put it there because of you, you're wrong. There was someone else, another woman."

She didn't buy it. Meg wasn't a fool. "What was her name?"

"Stella," he ground out. "Her name was Stella." He was a lousy liar. It was Luke who was the master.

He caught Meg's shoulders. "You think I didn't have other women after you were gone? I had women. Plenty of them. I would have done anything to forget you, Meg. Anything."

She reached up and gently touched his cheek. "Did it work?"

His heart was pounding. His chest ached. "No." Hauling her hard against him, he kissed her, a long, deep, saturating kiss, his tongue sweeping in to claim her, his body rigid against hers.

He kissed her and ached for her, and still he wanted more.

He took a step back, drew in a shaky breath. Braced his feet apart and crossed his arms over his chest. "You want this? Take off your clothes."

Her eyes locked with his, but she didn't hesitate. Her jacket went first. She pulled off the black scoop-neck top she wore underneath, shed her black lace bra.

His erection throbbed. God, she had the prettiest breasts, full and round, perfectly formed.

"Lose the rest," he demanded.

Meg sat down on a rock beside the blanket and pulled off her boots. The leather pants molded to her body, but there was a band of black elastic down each side, making them comfortable to wear and easy to remove.

He went hard to the point of pain as she peeled them away, leaving her naked except for a tiny scrap of black lace that disappeared between her legs.

Jesus God, it was a sin for a woman to look that good.

"Take the clip out of your hair."

She complied, then shook her head, setting the fiery mass free.

"The thong," he said, his voice gone rough. "Take it off."

She shimmied the little scrap of lace down over her hips and lay back on the blanket, propped on her elbows like a feast.

She gave him a wicked smile. "Your turn," she said.

Dirk shook his head, his return smile grim. "I'm not waiting that long." He came down beside her on the blanket, leaned over, and started kissing her. Her hands were all over him, touching, teasing his nipples, driving him crazy.

He cupped her breasts, took each one into his mouth, suckled and tasted and heard her soft moan. He stroked her, found her ready. He'd known she would be.

He felt her hands working his zipper, reaching inside to free him. He was hard as granite and ready to burst.

"Easy," he said. There was a pair of condoms in the back pocket of his jeans. He was no fool either. Dragging one out, he sheathed himself, took a moment to enjoy the feminine sight she made stretched out in front of him. He shifted between her legs, settling there, and eased himself deep inside.

Then he was moving hard, driving deep, taking her as if he had every right.

Maybe he did. She'd seduced him bold as brass. She belonged to him — at least for now.

He drove into her, felt those long legs wrapping around him, heard her little mews of pleasure as he carried her to the peak, watched her beautiful face as she climaxed, then took her to the edge again, up and over, before he joined her in release.

When they were finished, he rolled to his back and removed the condom. Just lay there spent and wishing he had more will-power. Or maybe not.

After a while he straightened his clothes, zipped his jeans, and lay back again, enjoying the warmth of the sun on his bare chest and leather-covered thighs.

"I can't make any promises," he finally said. "I don't trust anymore — not the way I used to. I don't know if I'll ever be able to again."

She leaned over him, her warm breasts

plumping on the muscles across his bare chest. "But you'll try? You'll give us the chance I was afraid to give us before?"

"I don't know."

"We're good together, Dirk. At least admit that much."

"It's just sex, Meg."

She shook her head. "I don't think so." She kissed his broken heart tattoo. "Will you have supper with us tonight?"

When he didn't answer, she kissed him, trailed kisses along his jaw and down the side of his neck. "You could stay the night and we could have more *just sex.*"

He fought a smile. "Food and sex with a beautiful woman. Hard offer to turn down."

She sat up on the blanket, her breasts swinging free and arousing him again. She reached down and cupped him through the black jeans fabric surrounded by snug black leather. "Yes, I see how hard it is."

Dirk wrapped his hands around her waist, lifted her, and settled her astride him. "I'll come to supper. In the meantime, why don't we go ahead and have a little more *just sex* right now?"

Meg laughed her throaty laugh, and the sweet sound slipped right through him. He was in deep trouble here.

Add to that, there was still a killer on the loose.

At least he'd gotten his wish. From now until it was over, he'd be the man protecting Meg and little Charlie.

CHAPTER TWENTY-THREE

Jonathan Hollander sat behind his impressive rosewood desk in the president's office at Seattle State Bank. His computer was on, the screen filled with a list of the bank's wealthiest clients. He needed money. These people had it. All he had to do was figure out a way to get it.

Hearing a light rap on the frosted glass door, he glanced up to see his secretary, Marliss Meyers, ease it open a crack and stick her head in.

"I'm sorry to bother you, Mr. Hollander, but there's a gentleman out here —"

"Use the intercom, Ms. Meyers. I've told you that before."

"But you said if it was important . . ." She was a pretty little redhead in her late twenties, not the brightest bulb on the string, but he'd always liked redheads. The girl was ambitious. He wondered what she'd do to get ahead.

"Fine, what is it?"

"There's a gentleman to see you. His name is Thomas Calvin. He says he has an appointment, but I didn't see it on your calendar. He was very insistent, but he seemed really nice. I think I must have made an error. Shall I show him in?"

A tremor of unease moved through him. He'd been expecting to hear from Moore. He had a strong suspicion Thomas Calvin was the same man who had called himself Moore only a few days ago.

"Yes, please show him in."

Marliss motioned behind her. Thomas Calvin smiled his thanks at her as he entered the office, and the secretary closed the door.

The man's pleasant smile faded. With his bald head and broad nose, he looked nothing at all like Thomas Moore, yet Jonathan had no doubt it was he.

"You shouldn't have come here." Jonathan rose from behind his wide desk. "We're supposed to meet somewhere else, somewhere private. I can't risk anyone connecting us."

Thomas Moore/Calvin scoffed. "I don't care in the least what you risk. Now sit down and pretend to do your job. That is what you mostly do so it shouldn't be much of a problem."

Jonathan's mouth went tight. He sat back

down in his chair. "What do you want?"

Thomas took a seat across from him. "It doesn't matter what I want. What Mr. Gertsman wants is what matters, and that is a check in the amount of six million dollars."

"Five million," he corrected.

"Six with interest. Are you prepared to repay that amount?"

"You know I'm not."

"Since my employer assumed as much, he has decided what he is willing to accept from you instead."

A chill trickled down his spine. Otto Gertsman was renowned in the international banking community for his ruthlessness in business. Whatever Gertsman would demand in exchange for the original three million dollars Jonathan had borrowed to recoup his stock market losses would be worth more than twice that much.

"I'm listening," Jonathan said.

"Your wife."

The words hung in the air. "My wife? Megan and I are no longer married."

"Well, then, trading her as payment for your debt shouldn't be much of a problem."

"Trading her? Otto Gertsman is willing to trade my ex-wife for three million dollars?"

"Six million."

"For God's sake, what's he planning to do with her?"

"What Mr. Gertsman does with his personal property is no concern of yours."

"But —"

"It's well known that Otto Gertsman has a penchant for objects of great beauty. He owns several Rembrandts; a Stradivarius violin crafted in 1721. That era is considered the golden age of workmanship and thus those instruments are the most valuable. He owns a 1936 Bugatti Atlantic worth over thirty million dollars, racehorses, the Bouvier Diamond, and a priceless Fabergé egg. As you can see, his collection is extensive, and money is no object."

"Megan is a person, not a piece of art."

"Your wife is an internationally famous model known for her beauty. Two years ago, she did a photo shoot in Buenos Aires, which was where Mr. Gertsman first took notice of her. The media loved her. They called her the Fire Angel because of her stunning face and flame-red hair."

Jonathan wasn't sure whether to feel relieved or wildly afraid. "If that's all he wants, I'm certain I can arrange for Meg to meet him, have supper with him at whatever place he chooses."

Thomas's bark of laughter grated on Jon-

athan's nerves. "You don't seem to understand. Mr. Gertsman likes to *possess* beautiful things. To *own* them. That includes
women. In exchange for the money you are
unable to repay, he expects you to deliver
your ex-wife into his care — where she will
remain. Indefinitely."

Jonathan swallowed past the knot of fear
in his throat. "You're . . . you're talking
about another kidnapping."

"The term is a little crass for what Mr.
Gertsman has in mind. You will deliver Ms.
O'Brien to a previously determined airport,
where Mr. Gertsman will have a luxury jet
waiting to pick her up. She will board the
plane and be whisked away to his private
compound. What happens after she arrives,
I have no way of knowing."

"My God."

"We'll need to work out a strategy, of
course, something that will not turn into
the debacle you caused before."

Jonathan started shaking his head. "We
may not be married, but the woman is the
mother of my son. I won't do it."

"You didn't mind putting the boy at risk."

"I thought it would be easy. I didn't know
her former boyfriend was going to botch
things up and get people killed." He cast a
disgusted look at Thomas. "I didn't realize

you would try to kill my son." He'd seen the news. He knew what had happened at the lake. He'd had to leave the room to go throw up.

"If I had tried to kill the boy, he would be dead."

Jonathan straightened, worked to bolster his courage. "She's my son's mother. If something happened to her, who would take care of him?"

"Her parents are quite wealthy, as we both know, and they are completely enamored of the child. The boy would never want for a thing."

Jonathan shook his head. "I'm sorry, I won't do it."

"You said you'd do anything. I believe those were your words."

"Tell Gertsman he'll have to think of something else."

Thomas's smile turned feral. "I'll tell him you refused his very generous offer. Unfortunately for you, Mr. Gertsman rarely takes no for an answer."

"I don't . . . don't understand. If he wants her so badly, why doesn't he just take her? We both know he has that kind of power."

"I'm afraid you are missing the point. You are the one who owes the debt. You must be the one to repay it. You must find a way to give him the woman."

Jonathan stood up behind his desk. "I'll get the money. I just . . . I need a little more time, is all. I can find a way if I just have a little more time."

Thomas rose from his chair. "Your time, Mr. Hollander, has run out." He walked to the door and pulled it open. "I'll be in touch."

The chill returned, sliding like cold grease down Jonathan's spine. Fighting not to call the man back, he watched the door close softly behind him.

"I seduced him."

Val's eyes widened. "What?"

"That's right. I did what you suggested — I asked him to take me for a ride on his Harley. I brought a picnic lunch and I seduced him."

Meg and Val were sitting at the breakfast counter the following afternoon while Charlie played with his trucks in the family room.

Val grinned and started laughing. In the background, the sound of hammers and drills echoed throughout the house as the men from the alarm company Dirk had insisted she call upgraded her security system.

"It was your idea," Meg reminded her.

"Yeah, and it sounds like it turned out to be a good one. So what happened after?"

"It was more like what happened before. I told him how sorry I was for the breakup. I told him I'd made a huge mistake and I asked him to give us another chance."

"And Dirk said . . . ?"

Meg took a sip of coffee from the mug in her hand. The smell of chocolate chip cookies baking in the oven filled the air. "I guess it was sort of good news/bad news. The bad news is he doesn't know if he can ever feel the same way about me again. The good news is he's coming over for supper and spending the night."

"Wow, that really is good news/bad news. The bad news is you could really get hurt. The good news is you're bound to have some really great sex."

Meg shook her head. "The thing is, this isn't just about sex, not for me. And as much as he tries to tell me that's all it is for him, I don't believe it."

"I think he was in love with you. It tore him up when you ended things. He had no idea it was coming. For him, it seemed to happen completely out of the blue."

"I thought he knew the tour was all we'd ever have. I was prepared for us to end, but Dirk wasn't. I don't think he'd believe me if

I told him losing him hurt me as much as it did him."

"You're right; I don't think he'd see it that way."

Meg sighed. "A thousand times I thought about calling him. I wanted to call him so badly. God, it took me months to get over him. The minute I saw him again, I knew I never really had."

"You put Charlie's welfare first. That's what mothers do."

"That's what I thought at the time."

"Having a child could still be a problem. He's always lived on the edge. He's got no idea how to be a dad."

"I didn't know how to be a mother before I had Charlie. Dirk was willing to take the risk before, and I should have let him. If I'd given him a chance, I would have realized he's exactly the kind of man I'd pick to be Charlie's father."

"He's got tattoos and he rides a Harley."

"He rebuilds houses and he's good enough to make a very decent living. He's honest, capable, and smart. And he's amazingly protective."

"Well, he's certainly nothing like your slick-talking ex-husband. But I only met him once. You introduced us at a charity event when we were modeling. You were already divorced by then."

Meg sipped her coffee. "Jonathan was handsome and charming. I admit I fell for him at first. Add to that, he had the pedigree my parents — mostly my dad — thought was important. Jonathan's family had lost most of their fortune, but not their place in society. He was older, sophisticated, smooth as silk. My parents both got sucked in. Now they see what a total jerk he is."

"It didn't take you long to figure it out. You were only married a couple of years."

"Actually, I'm embarrassed I didn't figure it out a lot sooner."

"Yes, but if you hadn't married him, you wouldn't have Charlie."

"True, and I could never regret my baby."

The timer went off and Meg went around the counter to take the cookies out of the oven. She set the tray down on top of the stove to let them cool.

"Those smell delicious," Val said, inhaling deeply.

Charlie came racing up just then, red hair flying, reminding Meg that she needed to take him for a haircut.

"Can I have a cookie? Can I?"

"It's *may* I have a cookie, and they need to cool a little first."

He made an unpleasant, disappointed

303

sound in his throat, and Meg laughed. "Okay, you can have one." Grabbing a paper napkin, she wrapped the cookie in it and handed it to Charlie. "But you'd better be careful. They're still really hot."

"What do you say to your mom?" Val coached.

"Thanks, Mama!" Charlie raced back to the family room, plunked himself down on the floor, and grabbed one of his trucks. The engine sounds he made were muffled by the cookie in his mouth.

Meg returned to her stool and Val took a sip of her coffee. "You realize if this doesn't work out with Dirk, it's going to break your heart even worse than before."

Meg's throat tightened. "I know. When we got back to Seattle after the tour, I thought I was doing the right thing. I thought Dirk wasn't right for me and Charlie. Now I know he's exactly the right man for us. If it doesn't work . . ." She shook her head, let the sentence trail off.

They both knew how much it was going to hurt.

Val leaned over and hugged her. "Maybe he'll figure things out."

Meg wiped a tear from the corner of her eye. "Whatever happens, I have to try."

Val set down the mug and climbed off her

stool. "The afternoon's almost gone. I'd better get going."

"You haven't forgotten you agreed to help me decide which merchandise I want for the boutique?"

"Are you kidding?" Val grinned. "I can't wait to get started. That's going to be great fun." Reaching over the counter, she grabbed a cookie off the tray. "Now I'd better go so you can get started on dinner."

Meg smiled. "Rose fixed lasagna. All I have to do is heat it up and make a salad."

Val nodded. "Good, then you'll have plenty of time to seduce him again."

Meg grinned, reached over, and grabbed a cookie. "Dirk's usually a take-charge kind of guy. I'm hoping this time he'll seduce me."

CHAPTER TWENTY-FOUR

Dirk punched the button on the elevator, rode up in silence with a couple of FBI suits, then stepped out on the fifth floor of their headquarters building. Ron Nolan was waiting, ready to lead him down the hall to his office. The FBI agent had phoned earlier to ask if Dirk could stop by.

"What's going on?" Dirk asked as he closed the office door.

Nolan pointed to the chairs on the opposite side of his desk. Dirk slid into one of them and settled against the back. The room was tidy. The only personal touches were photos of Nolan's sailboat on the wall and pictures of his wife and kids on the desk in front of him.

The agent sat back down in his chair. "We caught a break in the case. Interpol called. One of their agents got a tip from an informant that Raymond Neville is in Buenos Aires. Arrived on a flight from Jorge

Chávez Airport in Lima. He was using an alias he's used before. Thomas Calvin, a British journalist. The informant claims he's currently somewhere in the city."

"So you don't have him in custody?" Dirk said.

"Not at this time. He was spotted. By the time an arrest could be made, the guy had disappeared. The point is, the man is no longer a threat to Ms. O'Brien, her son, or anyone involved in the case. He's gone to South America to lick his wounds. If he follows his usual pattern, he'll stay off the grid until someone else requires his services."

"How sure is Interpol that their informant's information is good?"

"They're convinced the intel is correct."

He should have been relieved. He was, Dirk told himself. The O'Brien family was no longer in danger. He could stop worrying about Meg and Charlie.

Still, he couldn't get the image of Mickey Degan's bloody corpse out of his head. Neville was thorough. That kind of guy didn't just walk away.

"Neville's The Fixer," he said. "People hire him to handle their problems. Someone hired him to set up the kidnapping. We need to find out who that was."

"We're working on it. Sooner or later

something will turn up."

"Your informant says Neville's back in South America," Dirk persisted. "That was his last known location before he showed up in Seattle. Maxwell Bremmer was also connected to that part of the world. There has to be a link."

"We haven't found anything so far. We'll stay on it, of course. I just wanted you to know it looks like your clients are safe."

Clients. Meg and Charlie were far more to him than that.

"We need to find the link between Neville and Bremmer. I've got a hunch that's the key to this whole kidnapping case."

"Like I said, we'll stay on it, but this is FBI business, Dirk. You need to let us handle it from now on."

In other words, butt out.

He thought about pressing Nolan for more, but he could tell by the hard set of the man's jaw that he'd gotten all he was going to get.

"Whatever you say, Agent Nolan." He stood up from his chair. "Thanks for the heads-up."

"If something more turns up, I'll do my best to let you know."

"Thanks." With no further comment, Dirk walked out of the office, closing the door behind him. As far as he was concerned, the case wasn't over until he found Neville or reached a solid dead end.

From FBI headquarters, he drove the Viper down to BOSS, Inc. If anyone could find the connection between Mad Max Bremmer and Raymond Neville, it was Sadie. He also wanted to talk to Luke, see if he had any ideas.

Dirk found Sadie upstairs behind her bank of computers, reading glasses on the end of her nose, head down, then up, as she typed, then looked at the screen. Curly, platinum hair pitched backward and forward around her face as she worked.

She turned in his direction as he walked into her office. "There you are. What's up, hot stuff?"

"I know you're busy, sweetness, but I need you to do something for me."

She huffed. "Big surprise there."

A faint smile touched his lips.

"So what is it you're desperate for this time?" Sadie asked.

"One of the men killed in the shoot-out up at the lake was a guy named Maxwell Bremmer. Mad Max, they called him. I e-mailed you a file. There isn't much in it, but it's all I could get my hands on."

Before he'd gone to FBI headquarters,

he'd done some work on the computer in his apartment. He'd e-mailed Agent Nolan and asked him to send the info the bureau had collected on Bremmer. The FBI man had grudgingly agreed.

"According to the feds, before Bremmer came to the States, he was somewhere in South America," Dirk said as Sadie searched for, then popped open the file.

He walked around behind her and studied the screen over one plump shoulder. "He was a mercenary, paramilitary, soldier-for-hire kind of guy. I need to know who he worked for. Raymond Neville was also known to be somewhere down there. I need to know how they're connected."

"I'll take a look at what you've got on Bremmer and Neville, see if I can add anything useful."

"Thanks, Sadie."

By the time he got downstairs, Luke was behind his desk, leaning back, a pair of worn army boots kicked up on top.

"Hey, bro. Got a minute?" Dirk asked.

"Sure." Luke shifted, swung his long legs to the side, and sat up. The overhead light gleamed on the sun streaks in his short, brown hair. "How's everything with Meg? How's her kid doing?"

Dirk sat down in the chair next to the

desk. "Charlie seems good. Meg's taking him to see a kid shrink. Make sure he's handling the abduction okay."

Luke nodded. "Sounds like a good idea. Speaking of the kidnapping, anything new on the case?"

Dirk had been keeping Luke up to speed on everything that had happened and the info the feds had come up with — which wasn't all that much.

"I spoke to Ron Nolan again about an hour ago. Interpol says one of their informers tipped them that Raymond Neville just arrived in Buenos Aires."

"Have they picked him up?"

"Looks like the guy's gone to ground. No idea where he'll turn up next."

"I guess it's good he's left the States. Be better if they had the prick in jail, or better yet, in the morgue with Mickey Degan. At least Meg and Charlie are safe."

"Yeah, that's the general consensus."

"You might as well pull off the security detail."

Dirk ran a hand through his hair. "Hard to justify leaving a man out there if Neville is thousands of miles away."

Luke nodded. "I heard Pamela's out on bail." Being a bounty hunter, Luke knew every bail bondsman in the city and a good number in the other forty-nine states. "Santini's out, too. With Neville gone, I guess they aren't likely to get their throats cut."

"Neither of them can identify Neville," Dirk said.

"Too bad the guy offed Degan before you got a chance to talk to him. He knew something or he wouldn't be dead."

"The way I've got it figured, Neville is near the top of the food chain. He knew Bremmer from somewhere in South America and hired him to assemble the players. Bremmer hired Degan and Sykes. According to Pamela, Sykes was the guy who brought her into the picture. She never saw Bremmer or Neville till that day at the lake."

"So Bremmer was Neville's main man, but he's dead, like everyone else. No loose ends."

"The thing is they call Neville The Fixer for a reason," Dirk said. "He's a problem solver. He didn't come up with the idea for the kidnapping. He carried it out for someone else. Maybe it was someone with a grudge against Edwin O'Brien. That seems the most likely explanation, but Sadie dug deep and she didn't find anything."

"Doesn't mean it isn't so."

"I know. But I'm just not feelin' it." As he ran through the case in his head one more time, Dirk gazed out the window. The sun hung low on the horizon as the day slipped away. Tomorrow the weather was changing, getting colder again. He turned back to Luke. "We need to find out how Neville knew Bremmer. It has to be something to do with South America. That's where Neville is now and where both of them were at one time or another."

"Bremmer was a merc. I know some people down there. Maybe one of them can help us."

Dirk's mouth edged up. "You always know some people."

"Yeah. Makes life easier."

Though few people knew it, during his time in the military, Luke had spent months in some godforsaken jungle in South America hunting down a drug lord bent on genocide of the local indigenous people. He had a gift for languages, was fluent in Spanish, spoke better than average Farsi, Arabic, and Pashto. A handy guy to know.

Dirk checked his watch, then stood up from the chair. "Listen, I'll talk to you later. I gotta go."

"Hot date?"

The blood leaped in Dirk's groin. "The hottest."

"That has to be Meg. Watch yourself, bro."

"She . . . ahh . . . thinks we should give it another try."

Luke sat up straighter in his chair. "What do you think?"

Dirk shrugged, hoping Luke wouldn't dig any deeper. "The sex is great."

"Yeah, well, you told me Stella gave a great —"

Dirk hissed, cutting off the words.

"She might be a better choice," Luke said.

"Not the same thing, bro."

"Yeah," Luke said softly. "I know."

At the knock on her door, Meg untied the apron around her waist and pulled it off over her head. Tossing it up on the kitchen counter, she hurried to let Dirk in the house.

In the entry she paused, took a deep breath, and wiped her damp palms on the pale blue, curve-hugging cashmere sweater she wore over a pair of black leggings.

She couldn't believe she was nervous. She'd been a highly paid lingerie model admired by men all over the world. It took a lot to rattle her.

But Dirk wasn't just another man. He was the man she wanted in her life again. She didn't dare think further than that.

With a second deep breath, she opened the door. Dirk stood on the porch, taller than she was, even in her mid-heeled shoes, so incredibly male with his dark, slightly too-long hair, amazing body, and sexy biker mustache. She couldn't believe he was standing there holding a small bouquet of pink tulips in his hand.

"I thought you might like these," he said, holding out the flowers.

Her eyes stung. "I love them." She accepted the bouquet and stepped back so he could walk into the entry.

"Smells good," he said, maybe a little nervous himself. "What are you cooking?"

"I've got lasagna in the oven. I'd love to tell you I made it myself, but it was Rose. I'm just making the salad."

His mouth curved into a smile. "Lasagna sounds great."

She led him into the kitchen, where he settled himself on a stool at the breakfast bar while she found a vase and put the tulips in water. Carrying them over to the kitchen table, she put them down in the center. Surrounded by the white plates she had set out for supper, the flowers looked perfect.

She could feel Dirk watching her as she walked behind the breakfast bar and went back to work, setting out a ceramic bowl and collecting the ingredients for her salad.

"Where's Charlie?" he asked.

"He's upstairs watching TV. I don't think he heard you come in or he'd probably be down here asking you a thousand questions about your bike."

She pulled the freshly washed lettuce apart and tossed it into the bowl. "He's so inquisitive. He wants to know about everything. How, what, why, when, and where are his favorite words."

"That's good. Means he's smart, like his mom."

She smiled. "You think I'm smart?"

"Yeah, I do."

"I barely got through college."

"There are different kinds of smart, you know."

She wondered which kind of smart he thought she was but didn't ask. "You want a beer or something?"

"A beer sounds good."

She pulled a bottle of Bud out of the fridge, twisted the top, and set it on the counter in front of him.

"Thanks."

"I really enjoyed the ride, by the way. It was a lot of fun."

His hazel eyes gleamed with amusement. "I enjoyed the ride, too. Both of them."

Warm color slid into her face. She couldn't

help remembering how good it was making love with him. But it was always good with Dirk.

To distract herself from thoughts it was too early to have, she grabbed a tomato and started chopping it up, tossed it into the bowl. "So what's new on the case?"

Dirk upended his beer and took a long swallow. Just watching the way his throat moved up and down turned her on. It was ridiculous but true.

He set the beer back down on the counter. "I wish we didn't have to talk about the case tonight, but I have news. It might make you feel a little better."

"Did they catch Raymond Neville?"

"No, but according to the feds, he's left the country. Word is he showed up in Buenos Aires."

Meg felt a wave of relief. "So he's abandoned his kidnapping scheme. That's good news. Charlie and I are safe, and Dad doesn't have to worry about Mom, either."

"Nothing's one hundred percent, but that's the way it looks. Just to be sure, I'm working a couple of different angles. I'd still feel better if the bastard was in jail."

Meg turned back to her salad. "I wonder what he's doing in Argentina."

"That's the ten-million-dollar question.

With any luck, maybe we'll figure it out."

The sound of running feet ended the conversation.

"Dirk!" The little boy ran straight toward him, slid to a halt at his feet, and craned his neck to look up, up, up at Dirk's face. "Did you wide over on your modo-cicle?"

Dirk smiled. "Not tonight. I drove over in my car."

"What kinda car?"

"Oh, no," Meg said beneath her breath, knowing Charlie would go bonkers over the Viper.

Dirk grinned and flashed her a look. "It's parked out front. You can see it from the window."

Charlie took off running for the living room. For several long seconds he stood staring in total silence. Then his running feet pounded back into the kitchen. "What kinda car is that? Does it go fast? Can I have a wide in it?"

Dirk reached down and lifted the little boy up on his shoulders. "Maybe after supper. We'll have to ask your mom."

The sports car wasn't exactly kid friendly, but maybe just this once. Charlie would be thrilled.

Dirk set the boy on a stool beside him, and for the next twenty minutes, Charlie pummeled him with a jillion questions about his *Wiper.* When Dirk mentioned he also had a high-powered ski boat, the questions started all over again.

"Will you take me in it?" Charlie asked.

"It's too cold right now, bud. The boat's in storage. Maybe when it warms up we can all go out." His eyes found Meg's. There was something there. A mixture of fear and hope.

Meg understood that look completely.

CHAPTER TWENTY-FIVE

Meg stood at the sink, washing the last of the supper dishes, while Dirk stood next to her drying. They had just returned from a trip to the ice-cream parlor: a peppermint cone for her, peanut butter chocolate chip for Dirk and Charlie.

Meg had buckled her son into the front seat of the Viper on her lap. She was breaking the rules, just this once, giving Charlie a chance to ride in Dirk's amazing car.

Dino's Ice Cream was only a few blocks away. They could make the short trip by weaving through neighborhood streets so there wasn't much danger.

And Charlie had been enthralled.

He was upstairs now, tucked into bed and hopefully sleeping.

Meg rinsed the salad bowl and handed it to Dirk. "You remember that boutique I mentioned?"

He wiped the bowl dry and set it on the

counter. "You said you were trying to decide what kind of store you wanted to open."

"That's right. And I think I've figured it out."

"Yeah?"

"I want a place that sells specialized high-end women's sport clothes. Snow skiing outfits, motorcycle leathers, tennis clothes, stuff like that. The pants I was wearing on our ride were Vika — that's a brand I'm interested in carrying. They're expensive but worth it."

His lips edged up. "Whatever you paid, trust me, honey, they were worth every dime."

Thinking of the hunger in his eyes when he had seen her in the tight leather outfit, Meg felt a surge of heat she forced herself to ignore. "First I need to find a location, then Val's going to help me pick out merchandise."

"You both know clothes. She should be a big help."

"That's what I think, too." Meg picked up a sponge and started wiping off the counter. She felt the brush of Dirk's lips on the back of her neck and a little shiver went through her. He turned her into his arms.

"The kitchen looks fine." Dipping his head, he kissed her, softly at first, teasing the corners of her mouth, then coaxing her to open for him. He took the kiss deeper, hotter, drawing her in until she was pressing herself full length against him and all she could think of was getting him into bed.

"Let's go upstairs," Dirk said softly, nibbling the side of her neck.

Oh, yes.

He caught her hand, kissed the palm, and started tugging her out of the kitchen, paused to kiss her one last time as he guided her toward the stairs.

By the time they reached the bedroom, she was breathing too fast, Dirk had her sweater stripped off, and his T-shirt was gone.

They tore off the rest of each other's clothes and tumbled onto the bed. She was on fire for him as he pressed her down in the mattress and kissed her breasts, started nipping and kissing his way down her naked body. He wasn't in a hurry, just taking his time, making her burn.

A soft moan escaped. She ran her hands over his powerful back and shoulders, testing the hard planes and valleys, the way the muscles flexed and moved. She was more than ready, moving restlessly beneath him, when a sharp scream tore through the house.

Meg's whole body jerked. Dirk was off the bed in a heartbeat, grabbing his pants as he ran across the room. Meg heard the sound of running feet, the door flew open, and Charlie rushed into the bedroom.

"The bad man is here! The bad man is here! He's trying to get me!"

"Stay here!" Pants in hand, Dirk ran into the hall and raced naked toward Charlie's bedroom.

Meg snatched the little boy up on the bed and into her arms, her pulse racing wildly.

"It's okay, it's okay," she soothed, though she was as terrified as Charlie. "Don't be afraid, sweetheart. Dirk is going to take care of us."

Trembling, wishing there was something she could do to help but afraid she would just get in the way, Meg grabbed her robe off the chair in the corner, shrugged it on, then sat down on the edge of the mattress with Charlie in her lap.

She breathed a sigh of relief when Dirk padded back into the bedroom a few minutes later, bare-chested but wearing his jeans, his worried gaze going to her son.

"Did you get the bad man?" Charlie asked.

"Everything's okay, bud. You don't have to be afraid." Dirk pulled the chair over and sat down across from them. "It was only a dream, Charlie. The windows were locked. No one can get into your room. It was a bad dream, but you're okay now."

Charlie started crying, turning his head into Meg's shoulder. He was shaking all over, his face streaked with tears.

"It's okay, sweetheart." Meg smoothed a hand over his bright red hair. "You're safe here with Mama and Dirk."

"I'm scared." He looked up at her and she could see the lingering fear in his eyes. "Can I sleep in here wiff you and Dirk?"

She glanced at Dirk. He wasn't used to little kids. He didn't expect his night of hot sex to be ruined by a little boy's nightmare.

His eyes found hers. "I'll head on home. I'll call you in the morning."

Charlie started breathing too fast. "No! I want Dirk to stay! He's a policeman. He can keep the bad men away!"

"I'm not a real policeman, bud — and you don't need a policeman. There's no one here who can hurt you."

Charlie whimpered. "Please don't go."

Meg kissed the top of his head, spoke to Dirk. "I've got an appointment with the psychologist tomorrow. I should have known something so traumatic wasn't just going to go away."

Dirk reached over and caught Charlie's

shoulders. "I'll tell you what, sport. You and your mama can sleep in here. I'll stay down the hall in the guest room. That way I'll be real close by if you need me, okay?"

Charlie looked at him with big blue teary eyes. " 'Kay."

Meg met Dirk's gaze over Charlie's head. "Thank you," she whispered. "I'm sorry about . . . you know . . . tonight."

He just grinned. "There'll be another time, baby." He started walking, paused at the door. " 'Night, bud."

" 'Night, Dirk."

Dirk walked out the door.

There would be another time? He wasn't upset?

Meg felt something squeezing inside her chest and realized it was her heart.

It was late. Jonathan stirred beneath the covers, his mind climbing up from sleep. Slowly opening his eyes, he blinked himself awake, turned his head to look at the red numbers on the digital clock next to the bed. Three a.m. Jonathan concentrated, straining to hear what had awakened him. A noise, something out of the ordinary, not just the usual night sounds in the house.

As his eyes grew accustomed to the darkness, he caught movement, a shadow stepping away from the wall. He jerked upright, his hand shooting out for the phone on his bedside table, a scream lodged in his throat.

A wide palm covered his mouth, pressed him down in the mattress. "Not a word or you're dead." A second figure stood next to the bed, his gun pointed at Jonathan's head. Square jaw, buzz-cut hair, big, beefy arms. Thick lips and a flat nose. He was built like a weight lifter but looked more like a boxer.

Sweat broke out on Jonathan's forehead, though the room was cool. He managed to nod, and the man released him but kept the gun aimed straight at him.

The man he'd spotted first walked over to join them. Taller, solidly built, a craggy-faced man with weathered, smoker's features.

"Get up," the man said, his voice low and rough. The smell of stale tobacco clung to his clothes.

Jonathan carefully slid from beneath the covers, his silk pajamas slipping easily along the sheets. "What do you want?"

"We're here to deliver a message," the boxer said.

Jonathan stood up a little straighter, determined to brazen it out. "What are you talking about? What message?" He thought about screaming, but there was no one else in the house. He had help, but the house-keeper only worked three days a week and the neighbors were too far away.

"The message is from Moore," said the craggy-faced man, who seemed to be in charge. "Thomas Moore. He says you'll understand once it's delivered."

Thomas Moore — Thomas Calvin. A dark chill swept through him. The message was from Otto Gertsman.

He started to say something — he wasn't sure what — when the boxer slapped a strip of duct tape over his mouth, whirled him around, and slammed him face-first into the wall.

His arms were dragged behind him and bound with another strip of tape, then the two men dragged him over and shoved him down in a chair.

Nausea rolled through him. Gertsman wanted his six million dollars. By now it could be more. For an instant he thought he might throw up and drown in his own vomit.

"Mr. Moore says you have something that belongs to someone else," said the craggy-faced man. Jonathan battled the nausea down as the boxer knelt and bound his ankles. "He says you need to see that this particular something gets delivered."

Good God! Gertsman still wanted Meg.

The boxer spoke up. "You understand the message so far?"

He managed a nod.

"Unfortunately there's more to the message," said the craggy-faced man. "Call it insurance that the message is completely understood."

The boxer pulled something from his pocket and knelt in front of the chair. The man grabbed his bare foot, and before Jonathan realized what was happening, the cold, sharp jaws of a pair of nippers bit into his little toe. Behind the tape, Jonathan shrieked in pain as the toe snapped off.

The boxer held the bloody piece of flesh up for him to see, then dropped it into his lap. Jonathan started to whimper.

When the man reached for his other foot, Jonathan screamed, tried to kick and twist away, but his struggles were useless. The little toe snapped off, the man rose and tossed the second pale lump into his lap.

"Tape them up real good and you should be able to walk just fine," the craggy-faced man said. "You have work to do so we wouldn't want to disable you completely."

"We'll cut off more than your toes if we have to come back," the boxer warned. "Then we'll kill you."

Tears rolled down Jonathan's cheeks. He wondered how much blood was dripping onto the thick white carpet. He wondered if he'd be able to walk again without limping.

He wondered how he'd be able to explain the injury without involving Gertsman or admitting his own part in the kidnapping attempt on his son. Without confessing to the three million dollars he had embezzled from the bank and lost in the stock market.

Money he had replaced with a loan from Otto Gertsman. Money he still owed.

"One last thing." The smoker's raspy voice roused him enough to realize the men were still there. "Moore says he'll be back to help you solve the problem. When he gets here, he expects your full cooperation. Is the message understood?"

Jonathan managed a single faint bob of his head.

"Cut him loose," the smoker said.

When the boxer flipped open a four-inch pocketknife, Jonathan felt a shot of terror. The man merely sliced through the duct tape around his wrists, carefully refolded the blade, and slid the knife back into his pants. The two men walked to the door, pulled it open, and disappeared into the hall.

Jonathan just sat there, pain ripping

through him, blood soaking into the hem of his silk pajamas where they pooled on the floor at his feet. When he heard the sound of an engine starting somewhere down the block, he tore the duct tape off his mouth with shaking hands, then unwrapped his bound ankles.

Pushing himself up from the chair, he hobbled into the bathroom, rummaged around under the sink until he found gauze pads, alcohol, and adhesive tape, then sat down on the toilet and began to bandage his throbbing toes.

He had a doctor friend who owed him a favor. Doctors had to keep their mouths shut; patient confidentiality and all that. He'd have to think of a credible story, but he could manage that.

He'd have to take tomorrow off, take care of his feet, and find a pair of shoes that would fit over the bandages.

And, God forgive him, he'd have to think of a way to get Meg on a plane to South America.

CHAPTER TWENTY-SIX

Dirk left a note for Meg, saying he'd talk to her later, and left the house. He wanted to be gone before Rose Wills showed up. No use complicating things any more than they were already.

He thought of Charlie and hoped the little boy would be okay. He figured taking the kid to a shrink was probably the best approach.

After he'd left the Rangers, he'd spent a couple of weeks talking to a doc friend himself, a guy who'd served and worked with vets. He'd been lucky, never had PTSD or anything like that. But there were some things he'd needed to get off his chest and talking to the doc had helped.

From Meg's he went by his apartment to shower and change, then headed for the house he was rebuilding on Lakehurst Drive. He talked to Rollo Davis, the older man he'd hired to run the job, and was pleased with the progress the crew was making.

Then he stopped a few blocks away, at a house he'd stumbled onto after the fire and bought fairly cheap. Mostly cosmetic work to put the place in shape, and that work had been done.

As promised, the Realtor had planted a "For Sale" sign in the front yard. With any luck, he should net at least a hundred thou on the sale.

The office was his destination. He'd phoned Sadie to ask about her progress on Bremmer, but she hadn't been able to find anything useful to add to his file.

Parking the Viper in the lot, Dirk shoved through the back door. As he stepped into the building, Luke walked toward him.

"Saw you pull in, bro. I was just getting ready to call. I got something for you."

"I hope it's a lead on Raymond Neville," Dirk said.

"Not exactly. Mad Max Bremmer."

"Almost as good. Let me grab a cup of coffee and you can fill me in."

The corner of Luke's mouth edged up. "Late night?"

Dirk smiled. "Yeah, but not the way you think. Meg's little kid had a nightmare, screamed loud enough to shake the house down, and scared the piss out of me. That pretty much put my night of hot sex on hold."

Luke chuckled. "No wonder you need coffee. I could use another cup myself." Luke headed toward the employee lounge and Dirk followed.

Behind them, in the main part of the office, an area they called the bull pen, Nick Brodie, Luke's black-haired, blue-eyed cousin, sat behind his desk, his chair tipped back against the wall. Looked like he was texting someone, probably his cute little wife.

Ethan was talking to Diego Montoya, one of the guys who'd been keeping tabs on Meg's house. He was off the job now. Dirk still wasn't sure how he felt about that.

He tossed both men a wave. Nick waved back. Ethan tipped up his chin, but he and Dee were on a case, Dee's Latino features intense.

Earlier, on the drive to the office, Dirk had taken a call from a former client, a rap singer who was having stalker trouble with a fan. Normally, Dirk liked working with the guy, who called himself M-Jazz, but the job meant traveling, and he just wasn't comfortable leaving town right now.

Leaving Meg and her boy, if he were honest.

He and Luke walked into the break room. "So which hot babe kept you up late last night?" Dirk asked as Luke poured two Styrofoam cups of what smelled like fresh brew. "Jennifer or Shannon? Or did you finally break down and call Stella?"

Luke scoffed. "Not much into sharing, bro."

Dirk chuckled. "Yeah, me neither. So who was she?"

"Girl named Devon I met at Mulkey's Tavern." It was a locals' joint on the lake, not too far from the office. Tucker Mulkey was a vet and a mutual friend.

"Lady was a real bombshell," Luke said. "Problem was, when I took her back to her house, damn woman wanted to tie me up."

Dirk grinned. "Like that's gonna happen."

"Yeah, I mean I didn't even know her. So I declined and she gave me the boot. Said vanilla sex wasn't her style."

Dirk laughed. "I thought you liked it a little rough."

He shrugged. "I might not have minded tying her fine ass up, but like I said, this just didn't feel right. I think I'm getting burnout or something."

"Yeah, I guess. Hard as you hit it, it's a

definite possibility." They sat down at the round black-topped table and each took a sip of the scalding hot coffee, exactly the way Dirk liked it.

"Maybe you'll meet someone who really does it for you," Dirk said. "Someone worth more than a night."

Luke sipped his coffee. "That might be good, at least for a while. Long as there aren't any strings."

Luke was a confirmed bachelor. Then again, that's what Dirk had been until he'd met Meg. It remained to be seen how that would shake out.

"So what have you got for me?" Dirk asked, taking a drink of coffee.

"After we talked yesterday, I called an old army buddy of mine. Name's Morgan Flynn. Big Irishman from Boston. I gave him all the info we had on Bremmer, which wasn't much, and asked him to dig around, see what he could find out. He called me back at four o'clock this morning — the bloody sod. That's seven a.m. for him, with the time difference. I guess he figured I wanted the intel more than I wanted to sleep."

Dirk grinned. "Good thing you weren't with the bondage babe."

Luke grunted. "Yeah."

"So is this friend ex-military?"

Luke nodded. "We were deployed down there together. He got out before I did, went back to South America, took a job working private security in Buenos Aires."

"And?"

"Flynn made some calls, came up with a guy who knew Bremmer, knew him when he was working as a merc. According to the guy, Bremmer grew up in Argentina. He tried to join the Argentine Army, but they turned him down for mental instability. Bremmer went rogue."

Luke leaned forward. "Here's the interesting part. Turns out Bremmer's a German name. Flynn's buddy says his granddad was a Nazi. Said Mad Max was a neo-Nazi himself."

"Jeez, he really was crazy."

"I did a little research after I got to the office. Nine thousand Nazis fled to Argentina after the war. Lot of them moved into an area called the alpine region. Guess it reminded them of home. There's a town named Bariloche. Last year they had an exclusive, all-night party on April twentieth — that's Hitler's birthday, bro. You had to be on a secret list to get in."

"Man, that's sick."

"Yeah, well, Bariloche is a famous Nazi

village, and that's where Mad Max Bremmer was born."

Dirk rolled the info around in his head.
Neville had been spotted in Argentina.
Bremmer was an Argentine. That he was a
Nazi might or might not be part of the
equation. They needed more.

"What was Bremmer doing in the States?"

"Flynn says he'd only been here a couple
of years, working as an enforcer for someone
big in the international community."

"I'm guessing Flynn didn't know who."

"Unfortunately no."

"I need to talk to Meg's dad. He runs in
the big leagues. Maybe he pissed off someone way more powerful than we've been
thinking."

"Could be. In the meantime, I'll bring
Sadie up to speed."

Dirk nodded, finished his coffee, and
pushed up from his chair. "Thanks, bro.
That's good intel. I owe you, man."

"Hell yeah. Tell Meg to fix me up with
one of those sweet little honeys who model
for La Belle and we'll call it even."

Dirk grinned. "In your dreams." Without
looking back, he headed for the door.

Sitting at the dining room table in front of
her laptop, Meg filled out another sheet of

paperwork online. She had been at it for hours. Applications for a Tax ID number, resale permit, fictitious name, sales tax permit, the list went on and on.

This morning, she had gone to the bank to set up a business account for the boutique she was calling simply She.

Meg glanced up at the sound of her cell phone chiming and took a hopeful breath. She'd found the note Dirk had left on the kitchen counter, but all it said was *talk to you later.* How much later, she had no idea. Last time it had been five months.

When she saw the caller was Dirk, relief trickled through her. She purposely let it ring again, not wanting to seem overly eager, then picked up the call.

"Hey . . ." She wondered if he could hear the smile in her voice.

"How'd it go with the doc?" he asked, surprising her.

"Dr. Murphy was great. Charlie felt comfortable with her right away."

"Did he tell her what happened at the lake?"

"He told her how he woke up in this strange place and that his head hurt. He said he was really scared. Charlie . . . umm . . . talked a lot about you."

"Me?"

"Yes. He said this policeman who was his mama's friend came to the lake and saved us. He told her all about your car and your motorcycle."

Dirk chuckled. "Maybe he won't have any more nightmares."

She hoped not. "Will you be around to find out?"

Only a moment's hesitation. "Actually, I was planning to come by this afternoon. I've got a couple of questions I need to ask your dad. I'd rather do it in person. I thought maybe you'd go with me. It might be a little better if you were there."

"Of course I'll go." She wanted to know what questions Dirk planned to ask, but she'd know soon enough. "What time will you be here?"

"I phoned your dad earlier. He said any-time this afternoon was good. He's working at home today. I'm already on my way. I'll be at your front door to pick you up in about five minutes — if that works for you."

Oh, yeah, that worked just fine. "Sure. I'll see you soon."

Ending the call, she ran upstairs to change out of her loose-fitting jeans and T-shirt and into a pair of dark blue skinny jeans, a white turtleneck sweater that hugged her curves, and low-heeled, knee-high brown leather riding boots.

The weather had begun to change; a cold front had swept down from the north. Thick gray clouds boiled over the distant horizon, bringing the threat of a storm.

Meg grabbed the brown leather shoulder bag that carried her essentials and stepped out into the hall.

"I'm going out for a while," she called to Mrs. Wills. When the heavyset woman walked out of Charlie's bedroom, Meg mouthed the word *Grandpa's,* and Rose smiled.

Both of them knew if she said the word aloud, Charlie would pitch a fit to go with her.

"You won't have to stay late," Meg said. "I shouldn't be gone too long."

"Charlie wants Sloppy Joes for supper," Rose said. "If that's okay, I'll make the fixings and leave it in a pan on the stove. I'll set everything else out on the counter."

"That'd be great. Thanks, Rose. Be sure to lock the door after me and set the alarm." Better safe than sorry.

Meg descended the stairs and walked into the slate-floored entry. Grabbing a navy fleece jacket out of the closet, she pulled open the front door and went out on the porch to wait for Dirk.

She hadn't mentioned Dirk's name for the same reason as before. If Charlie knew, he'd want to come along. It didn't matter where, as long as they went with Dirk.

She frowned as she stood there waiting, spotting the sleek burnt-orange-metallic sports car, watching the Viper prowling the street toward the house.

Charlie was getting a little boy crush on Dirk. He didn't really have a dad. Dirk was a superhero to Charlie. Of course he would idolize him.

Her dad and Charlie were close, of course, but grandfathers didn't count, no matter how athletic and vital they were. Kids seemed to know the difference; she had no idea how.

It worried her to think what would happen to Charlie if things didn't work out with Dirk. It was one of the reasons she had ended their relationship before.

Shaking the unwanted thought away, she hurried down the walkway when the Viper drove up, pulled open the passenger door, and slid into the seat. The smell of leather and man and a trace of Dirk's woodsy cologne sent a tremor of awareness through her.

As she buckled her seat belt, she felt his warm fingers against her jaw, turning her to face him. Bending, he captured her lips in a welcome kiss that sent heat all the way to her toes.

"I missed you," he said, smoothing a finger down her cheek.

"I missed you, too."

Dirk kissed her again, then put the car into gear and pulled away from the curb. Sexual heat thrummed through her, pulsed out into her limbs. Their interrupted night had left her aching with need. Dirk had to be frustrated as well. Maybe tonight would change that, though he hadn't said whether he planned to stay.

"So what's going on?" she asked.

He flicked her a sideways glance as he continued down the street. "I talked to Luke this morning. He's got a friend in South America, guy named Morgan Flynn. Ex-military. Works private. Long story short, Flynn says Bremmer's a neo-Nazi from a town called Bariloche in Argentina."

"Argentina. That's the last place Neville was spotted."

"That's right. Before that, Bremmer was working in the States for somebody big in the international community. Neville's the kind of guy whose expertise doesn't come cheap. That means he was working for someone big, too. Since he dropped out of sight in Buenos Aires, I'm thinking Argentina is where we might find their employer."

"Bremmer was a Nazi?" Meg repeated, still trying to get her head wrapped around the idea.

"That's what Flynn says. Apparently thousands of them fled from Germany to Argentina after the Second World War."

"Now that you mention it, I remember seeing something on the History Channel about that. When the Nazis left the country just before the fall of the Third Reich, they took boatloads of priceless art with them. They took money, diamonds, gold, wealth stolen from the Jews and the people in the countries they occupied. Some of them became extremely rich."

"That could fit. Still not sure how the Nazi angle plays into this. Hell, maybe it doesn't."

Reading his frustration, she reached over and squeezed his amazing bicep. When the muscle flexed as he made a turn, her stomach melted. Wow, the man was definitely equipped to push her hot buttons.

"We know a lot more than we did," she said, forcing her mind back where it belonged. "We just have to keep looking."

He cast her a glance and smiled. "You're right. Maybe your dad can help."

"That's what you want to ask him about? You think he knows something about Nazis in Argentina? Because I don't think he does."

A muscle ticked in his jaw. "I want to know if he pissed off some megabucks dude bad enough to want revenge."

CHAPTER TWENTY-SEVEN

Dirk drove down the long, curved driveway that led to Edwin and Patsy O'Brien's luxury home in the exclusive Highlands area of Seattle. Some of the houses he had passed were over-the-top palatial, fifteen-thousand-plus square feet, with views out over the Puget Sound.

Dirk knew house values. Buying, remodeling, then reselling homes was a major part of his income. As he pulled up in front of the house, he figured the big white colonial on a couple of manicured acres was worth three to four million, depending on the market.

Expensive, but not over the top for a guy who could raise ten million in cash in three days. His respect for O'Brien crept up a notch.

As Dirk turned off the engine, Edwin stepped out on the porch. He was wearing comfortable khaki chinos, a forest-green sweater, and a pair of scuffed brown loafers.

Dirk and Meg both got out of the Viper. Meg waited for Dirk to round the hood and together they walked up the curving brick path to the house.

"Come on in," Edwin said warmly, reaching out to shake Dirk's hand. "I was hoping you'd bring Meg along. We don't get to see her enough."

She leaned up and kissed his cheek. "If Charlie and I were here every day it wouldn't be enough for you."

Edwin laughed and Meg smiled. Dirk thought how lucky she was to have a family who loved each other so much. As a kid he had longed for even one parent who loved him.

"Where's Mom?" Meg asked as her father led them into the house.

"She's at a committee meeting for the Heart Association. She'll be sorry she missed you. The good news is she made those coconut macaroon cookies you like."

"Yum," Meg said, grinning. "I love those."

Dirk's stomach growled as the aroma of coconut and vanilla drifted out of the kitchen, reminding him that he hadn't eaten all day.

"They smell delicious," he said.

Edwin led them through an interior that

was very traditional, with paned windows, hardwood floors, white walls, and molded ceilings.

The living room was off to one side, a cream sofa and chairs on a textured throw rug, brass lamps on the walnut side tables. A small, tidy stack of *Architectural Digest* magazines sat on the walnut coffee table.

As Edwin led them down the hall toward his study, Dirk caught a glimpse of a very modern kitchen with white cabinets and white-and-gray granite countertops.

"Beautiful home," he said.

"Thank you. It was built in nineteen twelve, but it was remodeled before we bought it. We did more work ourselves."

"Nice job. It looks brand-new."

They went into the study, which also had molded ceilings. A manteled fireplace was set into one wall. The room had an old oak desk and lots of bookshelves. On a coffee table in front of a navy blue plaid sofa and matching chair sat a silver tray stacked with cookies, a carafe of coffee, and white porcelain mugs.

"Help yourself."

Both of them dug in, Dirk grateful for something to fill his stomach, then he and Meg sat down on the sofa while Edwin took what appeared to be his favorite overstuffed chair.

"So what can I do for you, Dirk?"

Dirk set his half-empty mug down on a coaster on the table. "You're aware Raymond Neville has left the country?"

"Yes, the FBI has been keeping me informed. I presume you're still working the case."

"That's right. At the moment, I'm following a couple of leads, trying to find the man Neville worked for."

Edwin frowned. "I thought Raymond Neville was the man behind the kidnapping. You think he was working for someone else?"

"Neville was known as The Fixer. He was well paid for getting jobs done. So, yes, I think he worked for someone with enough money to afford his services."

Edwin seemed to mull that over. "Go on."

"Your company mostly does business in the United States, right?"

"That's correct."

"Neville landed in Buenos Aires and disappeared. One of the men killed in the shoot-out was born in Argentina and worked there until recently. I need to know what connection you have to that part of the world."

"Our holdings are almost wholly American. We do own a small private jet service that provides international travel between Canada, the US, and Latin America, but that's about it."

"So there's no one down there who might have a reason to want revenge? No one who might have a personal vendetta against you?"

"No." Edwin sighed. "I wish I could help you — you have no idea how much — but I'm still not convinced the kidnapping had anything to do with me, aside from the fact the kidnappers knew I had the money to pay the ransom."

Dirk smoothed his fingers over his mustache down to his jaw. "All right, forget about revenge. Do you know any big-money players in Argentina or anywhere in South America? Someone you might have met? Someone who came here and you played golf with? Had dinner with?"

Edwin started shaking his head. "I've never done business with anyone from Latin America. Aside from our interest in Fly Private Jets, I have no connection at all. And Burton-Reasoner only owns thirty percent of the stock. We're really not that involved."

Dirk sat back on the sofa. He'd been so sure there was some sort of connection.

Now it looked as if they'd reached another dead end.

He glanced over at O'Brien, saw his thick, red eyebrows draw together. "What is it?" he asked.

Edwin's gaze met his. "I don't know anyone from that area, but now that I think about it, I recall Jonathan saying something about a banking deal he was working on a few years back that involved a billionaire from South America."

"I remember that, too," Meg said. "He was really excited about it. He saw it as an opportunity to expand the bank's customer base."

"We never looked into Hollander," Dirk said darkly. "We were following leads that led us in a different direction. Could have been a big mistake."

"I don't think Jonathan ever mentioned the man's name," Edwin said, "or if he did, I've forgotten." He glanced over at Meg. "Do you remember, sweetheart? I believe at the time the two of you were still married."

Meg shifted to the edge of the sofa, her fingers curling around a navy plaid cushion. "You can't think Jonathan was involved in his own son's kidnapping? He's never been much of a father, but I can't believe he would do something that could get his son killed."

Dirk felt an unexpected shot of jealousy. "You were only married to the guy a couple of years. How can you be sure what he might or might not do?"

Meg looked crestfallen. She swallowed. "Maybe you're right," she said softly. "I never really knew him."

Feeling like a jerk, Dirk reached over and caught her hand, laced her fingers with his. "Hey . . . even if Jonathan's involved — which at this point we have no real reason to believe — it has nothing to do with you. None of what happened was your fault, baby. None of it. Okay?"

Gratitude swept over her features. She looked up at him and nodded. "Okay."

Her dad flicked him a glance that might have held approval. He turned his attention to Meg. "Sweetheart, do you remember Jonathan saying what kind of business the bank was doing for the man in South America? He talked about work sometimes. He talked about banking when we were at the golf course. I'm sure he must have done that at home, too."

"He liked to talk about his job. Being president of the bank. He thought it impressed me."

"Did he mention who he was dealing with in South America?" Dirk asked.

"I wish I could remember. I was about to file for divorce so I wasn't paying much attention. I know it had something to do with shipping. Goods coming into Seattle from out of the country."

"Perhaps it was something to do with a letter of credit," Edwin suggested. "A document from the bank guaranteeing a buyer's payment in full would be a necessary part of that sort of transaction."

"I remember him saying the man was a multibillionaire. Jonathan was always impressed by men of great wealth."

"I need to talk to him," Dirk said, standing up from the sofa.

Meg stood up, too. "I want to go with you."

Dirk ran through the scenario and nodded. "All right. Might be better if you were there. We'll talk to him together, but not yet. First I want to know everything I can find out about Jonathan Hollander."

The afternoon was slipping away. Dark clouds hovered over the city, a portent of rain. But the streets were still dry as the Viper rolled down NE 8th Street in Bellevue, where the office of Brodie Operations

Security Services, Inc., was located.

Meg had never been there, though Val had told her the office was really nice, very masculine, with lots of black leather and chrome, nothing at all like the shabby rooms in old detective movies Val had imagined.

As the car pulled into the parking lot behind a two-story, freestanding brick building and Dirk turned off the engine, Meg's thoughts turned to the reason they had come.

"You don't really think Jonathan was involved in the kidnapping, do you?"

Dirk turned in the seat to face her. "We need information. Jonathan Hollander might be able to give us something we can use."

Meg wasn't sure what Dirk really believed, but for Jonathan's sake — and her son's — she hoped her ex wasn't involved.

They crossed the lot, shoved through the back door, and Dirk led her into the office. Dark gray carpet, sleek black leather and chrome, masculine and tasteful, just as Val had said. A "No Smoking" sign rode above the door to what appeared to be an employee lounge so there were no ashtrays overflowed with cigarette butts.

Some of the desks had file folders stacked on top. Apparently Dirk's was one of them.

He walked over and checked his in-box, sorted through a couple of notes he found in the tray, then set his hand at her waist and guided her toward the stairs.

In a glass-enclosed office, a heavyset woman with very curly platinum-blond hair worked behind an array of computer screens. She rose from her chair, grabbed her purse, and was heading for the door as they walked in.

"Bad timing, hot stuff," Sadie said. "I was just leaving." She flashed Dirk an evil grin. "Don't try to stop me or I'll have to hurt you."

Dirk laughed. He tipped his head toward Meg. "Sadie Gunderson, this is Megan O'Brien."

"It's nice to meet you," Meg said.

Sadie eyed her with a trace of disdain. "The redhead. I know who you are. I'm glad your son is okay." Apparently it was the warmest greeting the woman could muster.

"Thank you for everything you did to help us find him."

Sadie just nodded, a look of warning in every glance she cast Meg's way. Clearly she was protective of Dirk. *Don't hurt my boy again,* that warning look said.

Meg wanted to tell her that she planned to do everything in her power to keep all of them from getting hurt, including herself and little Charlie. But now wasn't the time for that conversation.

"We've got a new player in the game," Dirk said. "Jonathan Hollander, Meg's ex-husband. I was hoping you'd take a look at him, see what you can find out."

"You think he's connected to the kidnapping?" Sadie asked.

"Could be. Apparently he's had business dealings with someone from South America. That could connect him to Neville and Bremmer."

"Seattle's a very international community," Meg defended, unable to stop herself. "Jonathan works with people from all over the world."

"It's a long shot, I'll admit," Dirk said. "Hollander's the president of Seattle State Bank. Not likely he'd be involved in kidnapping his own son, but —"

"But it'd be good to know his personal financial situation," Sadie finished.

"Exactly," said Dirk.

Meg flashed the woman a glance. Could Sadie really look into Jonathan's finances? Meg wanted to ask, but she wasn't that dumb.

Sadie remained standing, the strap of her purse slung over one hefty shoulder. "You should have run him before," she said to Dirk, casting Meg another dark look, as if she were the reason for the lapse. "The husband is always the first suspect in a domestic crime."

Dirk was nodding, not happy to think he might have overlooked something inportant. "You're right. We were following the leads we had. They got us to the lake, but then Neville got away. Now we're trying to figure out who hired him. South America figures in somehow. Apparently Hollander had dealings with some billionaire businessman down there. I need to talk to him, but I want to know as much as I can before that happens."

"I'm happy to help — you know that. Unfortunately I'll be out of town for the next few days. I'm going to a beautiful resort in the San Juans, completely out of cell phone range — a break I completely deserve."

"No question of that," Dirk said, though Meg could read his disappointment. "What's the occasion?"

"My daughter and her husband's tenth anniversary. The whole family's going."

"Sounds like fun," Dirk said. "Promise you'll check out Hollander as soon as you get back?"

"I'll get on it first thing. It might take a little time, but I'll stay on it till I have something."

"Thanks, Sadie. Have a great time on your trip."

Sadie nodded and headed for the door.

"Nice to meet you," Meg called after her, but only got a faint grunt in return.

They headed downstairs.

"Sadie can do that?" Meg asked as soon as they were out of earshot. "She can hack into Jonathan's bank accounts?"

"Sadie's . . . ahh . . . talented. None of us ask how she does it. I'd appreciate it if you didn't either."

Meg nodded. She didn't know how the woman could manage something like that and she didn't want to.

A couple of guys had come into the office while they were upstairs. She recognized Nick Brodie — hard to miss with his amazingly handsome dark features and brilliant blue eyes. Like Ethan and Val, Nick and his wife Samantha were also good friends.

Nick walked over and slapped Dirk on the back. "Hey, bro," he said to Dirk. He leaned over and kissed Meg's cheek. "Good to see you, Meg. How's Charlie doing?"

"He's had a few bad moments, but I think he's going to be okay. How're Samantha

357

and your little Travis?"

Nick grinned. "They're both doing great. Travis said his first word."

"Da Da, right?" she said.

"Yeah, how'd you know?"

Meg just laughed. Nick was the proudest papa she'd ever seen. She envied Samantha that. Meg couldn't help wondering whether Dirk would be the generous, loving father she imagined him to be.

"I'm on my way out," Nick said. "Samantha's cooking coq au vin for supper. Coq au vin, man. Some fancy French dish. Can you believe that? I don't want to miss it."

"I don't blame you," Meg said. Samantha was a fabulous cook. Val wasn't half bad either. Meg could barely bake a frozen pizza.

"Tell Sam to send Meg the recipe." Dirk winked at Meg as Nick headed out the door.

"Very funny." Meg didn't think she would ever be any kind of cook, but maybe after she got her boutique up and running, she'd take some lessons, surprise him with a decent meal once in a while.

She'd do it for Dirk if things worked out between them. If he could handle being a father.

If Dirk decided to stay.

A lot of ifs. Meg shoved the unwanted thoughts aside as she followed him out the back door.

Across the parking lot, Nick waved as he climbed into a big black SUV with the words BOSS, Inc. on the side.

"I use one of the company cars when I need to transport people," Dirk said. "I've got an old Buick parked in my storage unit I use for undercover work."

"I wondered," Meg said. "The Viper isn't exactly inconspicuous."

He grinned unrepentantly. "Not exactly." With a hand on her waist, he guided her across the lot. They had almost reached the car when a sleek red Corvette Stingray drove in and pulled into one of the nearby spaces.

The powerful engine went silent. The door cracked open and a gorgeous, long-legged blonde stepped out, all heavy golden curls, short, tight skirt, and a body that would match any of the models who worked for La Belle.

Next to her, Dirk's wide shoulders went tense.

"Hey, Dirk!" the blonde called out, striding toward him on a pair of platform heels that pushed her well over six feet. "I was hoping I'd catch you here." She glanced at Meg as if she had only just noticed her standing there. "I'm Stella," the blonde said with a smile.

Meg felt a surge of jealousy so strong it made her ears ring.

"Stella, this is . . . ahh . . . Meg."

Stella kept smiling. "Nice to meet you, Meg."

"You too," Meg choked out, surprised she could form the words. She was still trying to grasp the notion there really was a Stella, a woman Dirk had loved enough to tattoo a broken heart on his chest when he lost her.

Stella's big brown eyes swung back to his face. "So . . . umm . . . I guess you've been busy. I kind of thought I'd hear from you by now."

"I meant to call . . . I. . . . Look, Stella, I'm on a case. And you're right. I'm really busy. I'll give you a call when I get a chance."

"Oh. Okay." She looked over at Meg. "You must be the client. Nice meeting you." Turning, she took a couple of long, leggy strides, the round, toned cheeks of her ass moving with perfect precision, and slid back into the Stingray.

Meg had been a model. She still stayed in shape and she knew she was more than pretty. But so was Stella. She was gorgeous.

Tossing a wave out the window at Dirk, Stella shoved the Stingray into gear, gunned the engine, and drove out of the parking lot.

Meg couldn't look at Dirk. "I need to get back. It's time for Rose to go home."

"Look, Meg, I told you there were other women. I didn't lie to you."

"I know. I just . . ." She blinked, fighting to hold back tears. It was crazy. She had no claim on Dirk. Not since the day she had sent him away. "You're right, I'm sorry. I just . . . I really need to get going." She hurried to the Viper, tried to open the passenger door, but it was locked.

Dirk walked up behind her. She could feel his warm, hard body an instant before he turned her into his arms. When she tried to look away, he caught her chin, forcing her eyes to his face.

"Dammit, I lied about the heart, okay? It wasn't Stella. I don't give a fuck about Stella. It was you. It was always you." And then he kissed her.

And kissed her and kissed her. And even when it started to rain, he kept right on kissing her. Her arms slid around his neck and she was kissing him back and she didn't want to ever let him go.

She was drenched and laughing by the time Dirk released her.

He trailed a finger along her jaw. "So, are

we okay?"

She nodded, pretended the tears on her cheeks were raindrops as she dashed them away. "We're okay."

"All right, then. Now I'll take you home."

She went up on her toes and kissed him one last time, then waited for the click of the locks and slid inside the car, her skinny jeans squishing water onto the expensive leather seats.

He'd tattooed the broken heart on his chest because of her. For a moment she smiled. Then she remembered it was there to remind him never to love a woman again.

Meg's smile slipped away.

CHAPTER TWENTY-EIGHT

As Dirk drove toward Meg's house, the rain beat down hard, making the roads slick, forming puddles on the asphalt that reflected the taillights of the cars in front of him. The rhythmic slap of the wipers warred with "Burnin' It Down," the song that began to play on his cell phone.

He hit the Hands Free and heard the husky voice of M-Jazz, the rapper, scrape over the line.

"Dirk, it's M. I need you, man. I got trouble and I don't know what to do about it. Can you come over?"

"What's the problem?" Dirk asked.

"It's that crazy dude I told you 'bout, man. He tried to break into my freakin' house. He was armed, dude. I saw the gun when he ran away. I need you to find this guy, get him off my back."

"You call the cops?"

"Yeah, I did. They're putting an extra car

in the neighborhood, but that don't cut it, man."

"You're right. You're at the point you need personal protection. You need a bodyguard, M. I wish I could do it, but —"

"I know. I'm gonna hire somebody, but I got a gig tonight. I really need your help."

Dirk glanced over at Meg. After the hot kiss in the parking lot, he had plans for her this evening. But even great sex wasn't worth letting one of his clients get killed.

"I can be at your place in an hour," he said. "I'll take a look around, see if the guy left any prints, anything we can use to find him. I'll go with you tonight and set up some kind of ongoing protection starting tomorrow."

"That's great. I'll see you in an hour." M signed off and Dirk turned to Meg.

"Looks like the evening I was hoping for is going to be postponed."

"That's all right. You can come over when you're finished."

"M's got a gig. I'll have someone covering his house, but I still won't get done till late."

The smile she gave him was so full of promise his blood pumped faster and his groin tightened.

"I don't mind," she said softly.

Dirk thought of what would happen when

he joined her in bed and stifled a groan. "Okay, then. I'll come over when I'm finished."

"You have a key to the front door and you know the security code on the new alarm system, right?"

"I know it." He pulled the Viper up in front of the house a few minutes later and walked Meg into the entry. Mrs. Wills was just getting ready to leave.

"Charlie's had supper," the heavyset woman said as she shrugged on her long, beige coat and pulled her umbrella out of the brass can beside the front door. "He loved the Sloppy Joes." She glanced at Dirk and smiled. "There's enough left on the stove for both of you."

"Thanks, Rose," Meg said. "I'll see you in the morning."

The housekeeper left and Meg turned to Dirk. "Are you hungry? I could fix you a sandwich to take with you."

His stomach growled. He was starving. "That sounds great."

Meg made him a Sloppy Joe she wrapped in foil, put the sandwich and a can of Coke in a plastic grocery bag, and walked him to the door.

"Don't wait up," he said as he leaned down and brushed a kiss over her lips.

"I won't. You can wake me when you come to bed."

Oh, man, yeah. He kissed her again. "I'll see you later. Lock the door and set the alarm."

She just nodded. Dirk headed for the car, unwrapping the sandwich and digging in along the way. Messy but delicious. He climbed inside the Viper and fired up the engine. He tried to keep his mind on the business of keeping M safe, not the lust for Meg running hot in his blood.

Meg slept fitfully. Charlie had kept her company for a while, the two of them watching TV together in her big king-size bed. He'd finally gotten drowsy and she'd carried him to bed. He was used to sleeping in his own room. Until the kidnapping, he had preferred it.

Tonight he'd snuggled down in his youth bed, hugged his pillow, and fallen deeply asleep.

Meg was the one having trouble sleeping. She kept an ear cocked for the sound of Dirk's footsteps coming up the stairs. The hours crept past and he still wasn't there. He had said he'd be late, but maybe he had run into trouble. Or maybe he had just changed his mind.

Dirk still hadn't made any real commitment — not that she expected him to, at least not yet. Finally she heard his boots pounding up the stairs and relaxed enough to fall asleep, curled on her side.

She woke up when he slid into bed beside her, fit himself spoon fashion behind her. She glanced at the clock. It was almost three in the morning.

"Sorry, I'm so late. Go back to sleep, baby." He kissed the back of her neck and a little curl of heat slid into her belly.

She didn't want to sleep. Not with Dirk Reynolds in her bed. When he draped an arm over her middle, she moved his hand so it covered her breast over the short lavender silk nightie she was wearing. When she fit her bottom snugly against his groin, she felt his erection stir.

"So I guess you aren't that tired," he whispered against her ear.

"Are you?" she whispered back.

He slid up the silk nightie, leaving her bare to the waist. "No," he said softly. He slipped the straps of the nightgown off her shoulders, baring her breasts, too, then ran his thumb over her nipple.

Her stomach clenched as he caressed her, bent and kissed the side of her neck. She started to roll onto her back, but his firm grip held her in place. His talented hands found her sex, toyed with her, stroked her. She was way more than ready when he drew her up on her knees and came up behind her.

God, he felt good as he slid himself inside and slowly began to move.

Oh, she liked this. Liked the way it made her feel so feminine, liked the way he took charge, liked that he was so powerful, so male.

He caught her hips to hold her steady and began to move faster, deeper, harder. Need swept through her, pulsed out through her limbs. Her stomach muscles contracted and ripples of heat rolled through her. She started coming. Arched her back to take him deeper, felt a fresh rush of pleasure, moaned his name, and came again.

Dirk followed her to release, his muscles going rigid, his head thrown back, a growl locked low in his throat.

For several long moments they remained where they were, their bodies still joined as they spiraled back to earth. Then Dirk tumbled her down on the bed, the two of them still locked together.

"Sleepy now?" he asked, nuzzling the nape of her neck.

She gave him a drowsy smile, nodded, and

yawned. " 'Night."

Dirk chuckled and rolled out of bed to take care of the condom she'd barely realized he'd put on. Meg hadn't told him yet, but while she was in the hospital, she had gotten a birth control shot. Since she knew he wasn't the kind of man to take chances with his body, she figured in a few more days they wouldn't need any more condoms.

It was her last, very pleasant thought as she drifted off to sleep.

Two days passed. Meg had found a location for her boutique and it was perfect. The interior would have to be gutted and remodeled to fit her particular needs, but that was part of the lease agreement that was being prepared.

Dirk had been helping her with the store design in the evenings and was surprisingly good at it, but then, he had a lot of experience remodeling the houses he sold.

He spent most of his days at the office, trying to dig up information that might help them solve the kidnapping. She knew he had been looking into Jonathan's activities, but he had admitted that so far he'd come up with nothing.

The rest of the time he was working to

help his rapper friend line up security for an upcoming concert tour.

He had stayed with her every night and it had been heaven. Last night they had all gone out for pizza at Chuck E. Cheese's. Dirk and Charlie had played the arcade games until past Charlie's bedtime. As she watched the two of them together, it seemed Dirk was having as much fun as her little boy.

Meg grinned. Every woman knew men were all little boys underneath.

This morning, after a night of amazing sex, she had slept a little late. Dirk had kissed her, gone down to fix Charlie a bowl of cereal, then left when Rose arrived, heading off to work.

Now, sitting at the dining table in front of her laptop, Meg poured over Web sites filled with women's sportswear. Upscale brands like Stella McCartney, Kelly Dooley, Lucas Hugh, Bogner, and Gorsuch. She planned to carry expensive sporting apparel that was beautifully designed, as well as some more affordable brands like Adidas and Juicy Couture.

Her cell rang as she clicked up another Web site and began to scan photos of snow-skiing outfits. It made her want to get out on the slopes again. She wondered if Dirk preferred skiing or snowboarding; but then, he was probably good at both.

She picked up her cell phone, checked the caller ID, but didn't recognize the number. "Hello?"

"Megan. How are you? It's Jonathan."

He rarely called. She wondered what he wanted. "I'm doing very well." She glanced at the computer screen and couldn't hold back a smile. "I've decided to open that boutique we talked about when we first got married."

"Well, good for you."

Surprise trickled through her. He had wanted her to stay home, spend her time entertaining his clients. He had only tolerated her modeling because the pay was so good and her dad had given the job his stamp of approval. Jonathan never went against her father.

"I'm really excited about it," she told him.

"So you've found a location?"

"A tenant vacated a space in Rainier Square. It's the perfect spot for the high-end merchandise I'll be selling, and it's less than four miles from the house."

"Good choice. The Fairmont is just across the street, lots of people with money. How's Charlie? You mentioned taking him to a therapist when I saw you at the hospital."

It was amazing they were still talking. Since the divorce, their conversations had been brief to say the least, and only when absolutely necessary.

"I took him to see a doctor named Sharon Murphy. She specializes in child psychology."

"That's good. Charlie is the reason I called, Meg. I'd really like to talk to you about him. I know I haven't been a good father, but after what happened at the lake . . . well, it opened my eyes. Charlie is my son. He could have been killed and I would never really have known him. I want us to get reacquainted."

Meg couldn't believe what she was hearing. Jonathan had never shown any interest in their child. Maybe almost losing his son had changed him in some way.

"I'm listening."

"I was hoping we could get together, talk things over. I have some time later this morning."

Dirk had been digging into Jonathan's activities for days and come up with nothing. He was still waiting for Sadie to get back, but Meg didn't believe her ex-husband would purposely do anything to hurt his son.

"Why don't you come over here?" she

asked. Where Rose was cleaning upstairs and Dirk could join them.

"Mrs. Wills is there and so is Charlie. It wouldn't really be private. We could meet at Starbucks, have a cup of coffee and talk things over. Surely with all that's happened, it's not too much to ask."

Meg took a deep breath. That they were divorced didn't change the fact that Jonathan was Charlie's father. Meg knew how much her little boy yearned for a dad who loved him and wanted to be with him. If Jonathan was serious, maybe they could come up with some kind of plan.

Still, she didn't want to do anything foolish. "Starbucks sounds good." Plenty of people at Starbucks and she wouldn't have to stay long.

"I have some appointments later," Jonathan said. "We could meet in an hour, if that works for you."

She was planning to go downtown anyway. She had an appointment with the leasing agent for another look at the boutique space; then she was signing the papers her attorney had already approved. The timing would work just right. "An hour's fine."

"How about the Starbucks on East Madison? It isn't far from your house, and there's a parking lot right there, so parking shouldn't be a problem."

"That'd be great."

"I'll have a nonfat cappuccino waiting. Still your favorite, right?"

She smiled. This sounded more like the Jonathan she had known before she married him. "Yes, it is."

"I'll see you there in an hour." The line went dead. Meg set the phone back down next to her computer. She had time to get a little more work done before she left the house.

Jonathan's hand shook as he handed the disposable phone back to Thomas Moore, or whatever he was calling himself today. His eyes had changed from blue to dark brown — contacts, undoubtedly — and instead of a blond buzz cut, he had black hair, obviously a wig, but it must have been expensive because it was nearly impossible to tell.

Next to him stood the brawny man who looked like a boxer. A few feet away, the craggy-faced man he'd dubbed the smoker pulled out a cigarette and set it between his fleshy lips but didn't light up.

"Megan's agreed to meet me at Starbucks in an hour," Jonathan said, the words a little raspy, forced between his dry lips. They were standing in the middle of an empty warehouse on Harbor Island.

Jonathan was familiar with the location. He had first met Otto Gertsman when the big German had traveled from Buenos Aires to Seattle to expand his container shipping operation.

Through a friend of Jonathan's father's in the steel industry, one of Gertsman's many endeavors, the German had come to Jonathan with his banking needs. Jonathan had been more than happy to help. Bringing in a megaclient like Otto Gertsman was a real feather in his cap.

Moore gave him the smug, condescending smile Jonathan had come to hate. "Well done," he said. "You're quite a proficient liar when you put your mind to it."

"You didn't give me any choice." Moore had called him at the office, given him an address on the island, and insisted Jonathan meet him there. When he'd arrived at the empty warehouse, Moore and his two thugs had been waiting.

He glanced at the disposable phone the man had insisted he use to call Meg. "What if she tells someone she's meeting me?"

"Just tell them she never arrived. There won't be any proof."

He had made the call and set up the meeting just as Moore had demanded. He didn't want to lose any more appendages so playing the part of repentant father hadn't been as difficult as he'd thought.

"I've done what you asked," he said. "I don't want any more to do with any of this. Go do whatever evil you have planned and leave me out of it."

Moore chuckled softly. "Unfortunately for you the choice isn't yours. You're leaving here with these two gentlemen — one way or another." His gaze touched on each of his men. "I'll meet you at the airport."

Jonathan felt sick. He knew Moore's plans, knew he had a private jet waiting at Boeing Field to fly Meg out of the country. OGAR International, Gertsman's company, was based in Buenos Aires. Where the big German would be taking Meg from there, Jonathan had no idea and didn't want to know.

She'll be all right, he told himself. Otto was a businessman, not a murderer. He just wanted to spend some time with a beautiful woman he'd become somewhat obsessed with. He also wanted Jonathan to suffer in some way for the money he had borrowed and couldn't pay back.

Eventually he'd let Meg go.

Or at least that's what he told himself.

He wondered what would happen to him if Meg returned and pointed an accusing finger, but he couldn't let his mind stray that far ahead or he wouldn't make it through the morning.

"Time to go," the boxer said, shoving him toward the big metal door he'd driven in through. A white van sat next to where he'd parked his candy-apple red Cadillac just inside the warehouse entrance. The boxer gave him a shove toward the van, then opened the sliding door on the side and urged him to climb inside.

Fear pounded through him, became a roaring in his ears. What if they didn't let him go? What if they killed him instead?

"Don't piss yourself," the boxer said, following Jonathan into the van, apparently reading his mind or perhaps the bloodless color of his face. "The boss said to bring you back and let you go as soon as we deliver the package to the airport. He says you know you're a dead man if you don't keep your mouth shut."

The smoker slid into the driver's seat and lit the cigarette still dangling from his lips. He blew out a lungful of smoke, making Jonathan's nervous stomach heave. The engine started, the metal door rolled up, and the van pulled out onto the road.

For a moment Jonathan closed his eyes. The boxer was probably telling the truth. They weren't going to kill him. He was more valuable to Gertsman alive than dead. He was the president of Seattle State Bank. There were people he knew, decisions he could influence from such a powerful position.

The German had him by the balls and both of them knew it. He'd do whatever he was told from now on.

He didn't like it, but he wasn't man enough to do anything about it.

He knew it. And so did Otto Gertsman.

Chapter Twenty-Nine

The weather had improved. Dark clouds continued to hover over the city, but this late in the morning the temperature had warmed, and sometime last night it had stopped raining. There were a couple of workman's orange cones in the spaces in front of Starbucks when Meg arrived so she pulled into the parking lot next door.

There were plenty of unoccupied spaces, which made parking easier anyway. She turned off the engine, pulled her light jacket a little snugger around her, and slung her handbag over her shoulder. Climbing out of the compact BMW SUV, she started across the lot. She didn't see Jonathan's red Cadillac coupe, but a white van idled just a few feet ahead of her, blocking her view of the windows and the people at the small round tables inside.

She made her way around the side of the van, heard the rumble of the heavy panel door sliding open. The next few seconds passed in a terrifying blur as two men leaped out of the back and grabbed her. A meaty hand clamped a rag over her mouth as she tried to scream and the men dragged her the few feet backward toward the yawning dark cavern that was the inside of the van.

She tried to kick, tried to fight, but the man's big hand kept the rag over her mouth and only a muffled squeak escaped. She recognized the smell, the sickly sweet odor she had noticed in Charlie's bedroom — chloroform — and a fresh shot of adrenaline tore through her.

Lashing out with her arms and legs, she tried to twist her face away from the cloth, but the man held her firmly. No longer standing, she felt herself being lifted and carried, then tossed into the back of the van.

She landed hard, her head banging on the wooden floor. The beefy man climbed in behind her. He slapped a piece of duct tape over her mouth, used another piece to bind her wrists in front of her.

She knew what was happening even as her limbs refused to function and her muscles went limp. She was only vaguely conscious of a familiar voice coming from inside the van as the other man rounded the vehicle and climbed into the driver's seat.

"I'm sorry," Jonathan said, sounding on the verge of tears. "They made me do it. You'll be okay. Just do . . . do what they tell you."

Her eyes slid closed. She thought of Dirk, remembered she had called his cell and left him a message. He'd find her. She'd told him she was meeting Jonathan. Dirk would know Jonathan was involved in her disappearance and he would go after him.

And God curse her ex-husband's black soul, Meg didn't dare imagine what Dirk would do when he found him.

Dirk left M-Jazz's luxury lakeside home late that morning, confident the protection detail he had arranged would keep the rapper safe for the next few days. Dee Montoya and one of the other guys who worked security for BOSS, Inc. had agreed to travel with M on his upcoming tour.

From the rapper's house, he drove straight to the office. Sadie had called before his meeting — thank Jesus — and said she was back at work. She'd assured him she hadn't forgotten her promise to look deeper into Jonathan Hollander.

Since then, knowing it would only slow her down, he'd forced himself not to phone her again. He glanced at his heavy black wristwatch as he pulled into the parking lot. He'd waited long enough.

Pushing through the back door, he climbed the stairs and strode down the hall to her office, tossing a wave at Ian, who sat at his desk pounding away on his computer keyboard.

His boss waved back and Dirk continued down the hall.

Sadie looked up as he reached her door. The worried frown on her face put him on alert.

"Glad you're here," Sadie said. "I phoned, but the call went to voice mail."

"I was working with a client. For the money I charge, I figured the guy deserved my full attention. I turned it off. Guess I forgot to turn it back on."

He did that now, but from the look on Sadie's face, what she had to say was more important than checking his messages.

"What've you got?" he asked, sitting down in the chair next to her desk.

"You wanted to know about Hollander. I've got enough to fill a book."

"Let's hear it."

"First, he doesn't have a troubled past, no sealed juvie records, nothing like that. His folks put him through Harvard, made sure he had the best of everything, made sure he ran with just the right crowd."

"Yeah, I found out that much from his Facebook page."

"What you didn't find out was the guy has big money troubles. His folks owned Hollander Steel. They lost everything in the late nineties, filed for bankruptcy in 2002."

"I read that on the Net. According to Meg, her dad didn't care about Jonathan's lack of family money. He had plenty of bullshit charm and the Hollander name."

"So that's old news. Well, get ready, because this isn't." She shoved her reading glasses up on her nose as she studied the computer screen. "A few years back, Hollander opened an offshore account in the Caymans and started dumping in money. I've got no idea where it came from, but it went in and out fairly quickly, most of it into the stock market."

"How much are we talking about?"

"A little over two million. I was able to follow some of his transactions. He lost almost all of it. There were no new deposits for a while, then six months ago the account in the Caymans gets another big hit, this time three million in a single lump sum. And guess what? That money gets drawn out, too."

"What'd he do with it?"

"I'm just guessing, but I think he may have paid back the original debt or whatever it was and invested what was left. The guy needs a good broker because those stocks went in the toilet, too."

"So he's broke."

"That's right. And if the second batch of money was borrowed, he owes someone at least three million bucks."

"Plus interest."

"Not much way around it these days."

The facts came sharply into focus. "So Jonathan Hollander had every reason to arrange the kidnapping of his son," Dirk said.

"Ten million in ransom. Money enough to pay back what he owed and plenty left over for him." Sadie pulled her reading glasses off her nose and tossed him a look. "This is your man. No doubt in my mind."

Dirk's hand fisted. No doubt in his mind either. "I've got to call Meg. Hollander still needs money, right?"

"Yup."

He pulled out his cell, saw that one of the messages he had missed had come from her. She never phoned while he was working so he listened anxiously to the call.

"Hey, babe, hope you're having a good day," she said.

He smiled at the warmth in her voice and the endearment she had never used before.

"I know how you are about Jonathan, so I wanted to let you know I'm meeting him for coffee."

His stomach tightened.

"We're going to the Starbucks on East Madison. Lots of people, so you don't have to worry. He wants to talk about Charlie. He's still Charlie's dad, you know, so I feel like I need to go. I'll see you tonight." The call ended.

Dirk frantically hit the Send button, returning the call, but her phone went to voice mail. He hit Redial, same thing.

"I gotta go." Slamming out of Sadie's office, he streaked down the hall, down the stairs, and out to the parking lot. Jerking open the car door, he jammed in behind the wheel and started the engine.

All the way to East Madison Street, he dialed Meg's phone. But he never got an answer.

Jesus God, he never got an answer.

CHAPTER THIRTY

Dirk found Meg's car at Starbucks, but there was no sign of her. He phoned Sadie and asked her to ping the location of Meg's cell phone, but Sadie said the phone was turned off. The closest she could get was a cell tower near Starbucks. Since then, nothing.

None of the Starbucks employees or customers had seen a woman who fit Meg's description — hard to miss with all that flaming red hair. One of the baristas remembered seeing a white van in the lot, but no one had caught a plate number. The barista remembered the van had blocked her view out the window for a while, then it was gone. No one saw anything out of the ordinary around the time the van had been parked outside.

He phoned Rose Wills, just to make sure Meg hadn't somehow returned back home. Rose said Meg had mentioned she had a couple of errands to run, had mentioned meeting Jonathan, and talked about an appointment with the leasing agent at Rainier Square. The agent had phoned half an hour earlier looking for Meg. The agent said she never showed up.

"It isn't like her to miss an appointment," Rose said. "I hope nothing's wrong."

Dirk worked to keep his voice even. "I'll keep looking till I find her, Rose. Can you stay late if she isn't back by the time you usually leave?"

"Of course. You don't even have to ask. You'll call, won't you? Once you know she's okay?"

"I'll call, Rose. I promise."

Next he headed for Seattle State Bank, where he asked to speak to Jonathan Hollander. His secretary said he'd been in early that morning but had left an hour or so after he got there and was taking the afternoon off.

Dirk had a file on Hollander that included his home address. He headed for Hollander's house. By the time he got there, with traffic jams and running down information, three hours had passed and Meg still hadn't answered her phone. His gut was churning, telling him Jonathan had lured Meg into some kind of trap. The guy was desperate for money. Clearly this was a second ransom attempt.

Dirk itched to call the FBI, but he needed more than an empty car in the Starbucks lot and a cheerful message from Meg on his cell phone.

He needed to talk to Hollander.

He knocked on the front door, pounded with his fist. No one answered. He had to find him. Every instinct told him Hollander knew exactly where to find Meg.

He hated waiting. He'd never been a patient man.

At the moment he had no choice.

Parking the Viper out of sight around the corner, he phoned Sadie one more time, told her where he was, and asked her to ping Meg's cell again. Sadie got the same result.

Running out of options, he phoned Agent Ron Nolan and laid it out for him.

"Meg's gone missing," Dirk said. "I think she's been kidnapped. She was supposed to meet her ex-husband for coffee, but I found her car abandoned in the lot. She had an appointment with her leasing agent this afternoon, but she never showed up."

"How do you know she isn't off shopping with one of her girlfriends?"

"Hollander's the man behind her son's abduction, or at least he's deeply involved.

He's got big-time money problems. You'll have to find a way to come up with that information yourself, but off the record, he's millions in debt. The first kidnapping failed; now he's got Meg. I figure we'll get another ransom note, maybe as soon as today."

"You sure about this?"

If he was wrong, he'd look like a fool. "I'm sure."

"All right. I'll locate him and have him brought in for questioning. For now that's the best I can do."

Questioning. Where Hollander would lawyer up and say nothing.

Not good enough, buddy, he thought, but said, "Thanks, Ron, keep me posted." Dirk hung up and climbed out of the Viper. Clipping his Browning nine mil onto his belt behind his back, he pulled his leather jacket on to cover it, grabbed his tool bag from behind the seat, and started for the house.

Hollander didn't know Dirk was on to him. Odds were he'd play this the same way he had before. Go on with his life as if he knew nothing. Not about Charlie's kidnapping, not about Meg's disappearance, or the ransom demand when it came.

A phone call to his cell would only tip him off. Dirk was betting that sooner or later he'd come home. When he did, Dirk would be waiting.

He made his way to the side gate, then slipped quietly around back. Manicured lawns, a covered terrace, a flower garden perfectly tended. Nice digs. Expensive digs. Hollander had been raised with money. He had expensive tastes.

Dirk took a look at the alarm keypad next to the back door. Wireless. He knew the system. He used a program on his iPhone to jam the signal, then worked his lock-pick tools in the door and let himself in to the house.

No sign of Hollander inside. No car in the garage. The house was immaculately clean, the interior professionally decorated, with a contemporary sofa in the living room, a pair of wingback chairs, and dark wood furniture. The only room that seemed to have had any use at all was the study, which, besides the desk, had a comfortable brown leather couch and a huge flat-screen TV.

He searched every drawer in the study. Nothing.

Dirk prowled down the hall to the master bedroom. He smiled grimly at the mirror over the big round bed. Mr. Casanova. Jesus, no wonder Meg had divorced him.

He searched the dresser drawers, scoffed.

Silk underwear. Figured. A throw rug covered the carpet in front of the chair. Seemed a little out of place so he went over and picked it up. The carpet underneath had recently been scrubbed, leaving a faint pale stain.

He prowled a little more. He wasn't sure how much longer he could pace through the silent rooms without going stir-crazy. He called Meg's number again, but still got no answer, called Sadie, who said the phone was still offline.

He was about to give up and go back to the office, try another approach, when the sound of the garage door opening put him on alert. He took a position behind the door in the kitchen that led to the laundry room and garage.

When Hollander walked in, Dirk recognized him — barely — from his photos on the Internet. Six feet tall, black hair, gray three-piece suit, good-looking in an over-the-top, *GQ* sort of way. But his hair badly needed combing and his expensive suit was wrinkled and covered with dirt.

The suit and hair were incongruous with the house and everything Dirk knew about the man. From the looks of him, wherever he'd been, he wasn't sipping cocktails at the country club.

Dirk felt a wave of fury so strong his hands balled into shaking fists. He waited out of sight behind the door until Hollander flipped on a light in the kitchen, then quietly stepped up behind him.

"Where is she?"

Jonathan shrieked and whirled to face him. "Who . . . who are you? How did you get into my house?"

"Tell me where you've taken Meg and I'll leave. You don't, I'm probably going to wind up killing you."

The color leached out of Hollander's face. He was older than Meg, forty to her not quite thirty, and his age had begun to show. "I don't know what you're talking about."

Dirk caught him by the front of his starched white shirt and lifted him up on his toes. "You're going to tell me. All of it. Where she is. Who took her. How many men are holding her. How much ransom they want for her release. What is it? Fifteen million this time? Twenty? You're going to answer every one of my questions — that I guarantee."

"You're . . . you're Reynolds."

"That's right. Now start talking."

Jonathan shook his head. "Meg didn't show up for our meeting. I don't know why. I was busy. I didn't wait long. I don't know what happened to her."

Dirk grabbed him around the throat and forced him to walk backward into the living room, then shoved him down hard in one of the wingback chairs. Crossing the room, Dirk pulled the drapes, flipped a switch that turned on a couple of lamps, then returned to where Hollander sat in white-faced silence.

"I know about the money you borrowed. I know you lost it in the stock market. Millions. That's why you kidnapped Charlie. You were willing to sacrifice your own son to get the money you needed."

"That's not true! I would never harm my son!"

"Where. Is. Meg?"

Jonathan started shaking.

Dirk pulled out the little derringer he kept in his jeans pocket and pressed it beneath Hollander's chin. "You want to die, Jonathan? Because it won't bother my conscience a lick to kill a little pissant like you."

Hollander jerked away. "You won't kill me. You think I know where to find Meg. If you kill me, you'll . . . you'll never find out."

A fresh rush of fury rolled through him. He wanted to grab Hollander by the throat and squeeze till his eyes bugged out.

But the bastard was right. Dirk pocketed

the pistol, took a steadying breath, and told himself to stay calm. He needed information, needed Hollander alive. He reminded himself to take it slow, bide his time.

Then he thought of Meg, of what might be happening to her — and lost it, drew back his fist, and punched Hollander square in the face. Jonathan's head snapped back and blood spurted from between his split lips. Jonathan whimpered.

"You're a real pretty boy, Hollander. You want to stay that way, you've got two choices. You can tell me what I want to know or I can knock every tooth out of your goddamned head, one by one, till you've got nothing left but bloody gums." Dirk drew back his fist.

Tears filled Jonathan's eyes. "Don't hurt me, I'm begging you. If I could tell you, I would. If I do, they'll kill me. They already cut off my toes!"

Luke's voice rumbled from behind him. He must have talked to Sadie. Dirk hadn't heard him come in.

"You don't tell us what we want to know, you won't have to worry about your toes." The soft *whoosh* of an eight-inch serrated blade sliding out of the sheath tied to Luke's thigh made Hollander cringe. "I'll cut off your fucking head."

Holding up the blade, Luke took an ominous step closer to the chair.

"Wait! I'll tell you! I'll tell you everything. Just . . . just don't hurt me again."

As Luke sheathed his blade, Dirk felt an unexpected wave of pity for the man whose life had been nothing but a string of bad decisions. He wasn't sure how far he would have gone if Hollander hadn't caved. Fortunately he didn't have to make that decision.

Luke, on the other hand . . .

Then again, with Luke, just the threat seemed to work.

"Where is she?" Dirk asked.

"She's on a plane out of the country. On her way to Argentina. I don't know where."

Dirk glanced at Luke, who looked as poleaxed as Dirk felt. "What the hell are you talking about?"

"Otto Gertsman. I owed him six million dollars. I couldn't pay him. Gertsman wanted Meg so we made a deal."

"For chrissake, you sold Meg for six million dollars?"

Next to him, Luke's features turned grim. "How much ransom is he expecting to get?"

"There is no ransom. Meg for the six million. That was the deal."

Dirk sat down hard on the sofa, his head dropping into his hands.

"Where in Argentina did Gertsman take her?" Luke asked with soft menace, clearly not feeling the least trace of pity for the guy and wiping away what little Dirk had once felt.

"Gertsman's company is based in Buenos Aires. That's all I know."

Dirk took a calming breath and shoved up off the sofa. "What about The Fixer? How are you and Raymond Neville connected?"

"I don't know anyone by that name."

"But you know someone who works for Gertsman, right? Medium height, athletic build? Maybe changed his appearance a couple of times since the two of you met?"

Jonathan looked sick. "Thomas Moore. Thomas Calvin. I don't know who he really is. He's Gertsman's man. He set up both kidnappings. I don't know anyone else who was involved."

"When did you see him last?"

"This morning. He flew out with Meg on a jet taking off from Boeing Field. I don't know any of the details."

Dirk pulled out his cell and sent a call to Sadie, put it on speaker so Luke could hear. "We need info on a guy named Otto Gertsman. Hollander set Meg up, but Gertsman's the man behind the kidnapping. His company's based in Buenos Aires." He glanced at

Hollander. "What's the name?"

"OGAR International." *Otto Gertsman Argentina,* Dirk figured.

"You get that?" he asked Sadie.

"I got it. So I guess you didn't kill him," Sadie said dryly.

Dirk almost smiled. "It was a close thing, but no. Dig deep, sweetness. Luke's here. We've got a couple of things to take care of; then we're heading out."

"You got it."

Dirk hung up the phone. His next call went to FBI Agent Ron Nolan. "I'm with Hollander, Ron, at his house. He set Meg up. She's on a jet to South America. Raymond Neville's trip to Argentina was a diversion. He came back, set up the second abduction. Now he's on the plane with Meg. Guy behind the kidnapping is a man named Otto Gertsman. Buenos Aires. You know anything about him?"

Silence fell on the other end of the line. "We need to talk," Nolan said. "I'll have my men pick Hollander up at the house and bring him in. Where are you headed from there?"

"Back to the office. I've got some things I need to do."

"I'll meet you there. We'll talk about Gertsman when I get there."

Unease filtered through him. "We need to keep Hollander's arrest on the down low until we get Meg back."

"That won't be a problem. See you there," Nolan said and hung up the phone.

CHAPTER THIRTY-ONE

A rough jolt shivered through her body and Meg slowly opened her eyes. For a moment she couldn't figure out where she was. Her mind felt sluggish and her head was pounding. There was a kink in her neck. She had to concentrate to force her limbs to move. Was she sick? Maybe she was in the hospital.

Then her gaze lit on the man on the wide leather seat across from her. Well dressed in navy slacks and a yellow button-down shirt, an expensive pair of shoes. Dolce & Gabbana, she thought vaguely, somewhere in the depths of her mind. Black hair, dark eyes, early forties. She didn't recognize the man and yet she felt a spike of fear just looking at his face.

She bit back a cry as it all came rushing back. Being drugged and abducted, seeing Jonathan when she'd been tossed in the back of a van. She dimly remembered being half-carried up the metal stairs into a sleek private jet, remembered the two rough-looking men who had guided her into a seat.

They'd said something to the pilot or copilot, something about her being afraid to fly. Drugs were mentioned, and alcohol. She'd been buckled into the seat, a blanket tucked around her.

She faintly recalled the jet roaring down the runway, surging into the air, but she hadn't been able to keep her eyes open for long.

She opened them now, realized the plane had hit a patch of rough air. She took a deep breath and tried to summon enough energy to sit up, but the black-haired man reached over and pressed a white rag over her nose and mouth. She tried to struggle, fought not to breathe in the sickly sweet smell, then the drug kicked in and she slipped once more into the dark depths of unconsciousness.

The office was buzzing with activity by the time Dirk walked in. Sadie had promised to talk to Ian, to phone Nick and Ethan and bring them up to speed. Montoya was working with M-Jazz, but a couple of other BOSS, Inc. contractors had agreed to cover if more help was needed.

Ian and Nick were sitting at the long

mahogany table in the conference room as Dirk strode through the open door. Luke had beaten him there — no surprise because he always drove too fast and, in his battered old Bronco, rarely got stopped. Sitting at the table across from Nick, Luke glanced up as Dirk walked in, then went back to work on his laptop.

Ethan walked in a few seconds later, spread open a rolled-up map of South America, then opened one of Argentina on top.

"I've got topos on the way," Ethan said. "Guy from the print shop is bringing them over as soon as they're ready." They could open a digital map on the computer and project it on the wall, but Ethan was old school. He liked to be able to mark things up and refer back to them.

"We're waiting for Sadie," Ian said. Brodie rose from his chair to study the maps spread out in front of him. "She should be down any minute."

Dirk glanced at the men in the conference room, the best men he knew. A tightness crawled into his chest. He should have known his friends would be on board, already hard at work to set a plan in motion.

He was bringing Meg back, hell or high

water. None of them seemed to doubt that. Be a lot easier now, with his friends there to back him up.

He shoved down the unwanted emotion. No time for that now. He moved to the head of the table to gain the men's attention.

"I spoke to Agent Nolan at the FBI," he started. "I'm hoping the feds'll be able to call in some international help on this, get Meg off the plane as soon as it touches the ground."

"Been my experience," Luke drawled, "in a situation like this, the feds are about as worthless as a roll of wet toilet paper."

A chuckle went around the room.

"I guess we'll find out soon enough," Dirk said. "Nolan's on his way to the office."

Luke ran a hand over his sun-streaked, brown hair. "Meantime, why don't we go over what we know so far?"

Dirk sat down at the head of the table. Whatever happened, this was his operation and everyone knew it, accepted it. "According to the barista at Starbucks, the van was in the parking lot around eleven a.m. We'll use that as the baseline for when Meg disappeared."

"Any way to get a line on the vehicle?" Nick asked.

Dirk shook his head. "Not even a partial

plate number. Got to be about a thousand white vans in Seattle."

"They would have had to drug her or knock her out," Luke said. "From what I know of the lady, it's the only way they could have gotten her inside."

The tightness returned to Dirk's chest. Meg would have fought them with every ounce of her strength. She had a little boy to think of. She wanted to be there to watch him grow up.

"They used chloroform on her kid," he said. "Probably immobilized her the same way. Hollander says they had a private jet waiting at Boeing Field to fly her out of the country. He didn't know if it was Gertsman's or a charter."

"A private jet's no problem for Otto Gertsman," Sadie said as she walked into the room, the wrinkles in her face more pronounced, curly platinum hair a little mussed. "Guy's got a small fleet of them. Gertsman's one of the richest men in South America and half the rest of the world."

She carried her laptop over to the conference table, the worry in her pale blue eyes kicking Dirk's nerves up another notch. Sadie sat down in one of the black leather chairs, opened her computer, and went to work.

A forty-eight-inch flat panel monitor hung on the wall at the opposite end of the table. In seconds a photo of Otto Gertsman appeared on the screen.

"Fifty years old," Sadie started. "Six foot three, gray-blond hair, and blue eyes. Born to German parents in an Argentine town called Villa La Angostura. It's in the Neuquén Province in the alpine region on the slopes of the Andes. It's an area heavily settled by Germans."

"Neuquén Province," Ethan repeated. Grabbing a yellow Sharpie, he located and circled the area on the map.

"A lot of Nazis fled to the region after the Second World War," Sadie continued, "including Herman Gertsman, Otto's grandfather. Grandpa Gertsman left Germany right before the war ended. He made no bones about being a Nazi; in fact he was proud of it."

"How did Gertsman get his money?" Nick asked.

"Inherited a lot of it. Good ol' gramps looted a fortune from the Poles, the Russians, the Jews, and anybody else who crossed his path. 'Course there's no proof of that. When Grandpa died, his son, Wilhelm, became a very rich man. He began to build a business empire. Wilhelm died and

404

left his money to Otto, who continued the tradition. Today OGAR International has interests in energy, steel metallurgy, airlines, shipping, petrochemicals, and automotive parts."

"My guess," Dirk said, "Otto also continued his family's association with the Nazi movement. That's his connection to Mad Max Bremmer, one of the men involved in the original kidnapping, a neo-Nazi born in the same region."

"Good guess," Sadie said. "Bariloche's less than sixty miles from Villa La Angostura."

"Hollander told us Gertsman's planning to take Meg to his compound," Dirk said, adding information he and Luke had pumped out of Jonathan before the feds had arrived to haul his ass away. "Any idea where it is?"

Sadie made a low sound of disgust. "Unfortunately the guy owns five palatial homes in Argentina alone. Got one near Nice in the south of France, got one in Macao. He's got property all over the world. He could be taking her anywhere."

Dirk's stomach knotted. "Christ." When were they going to catch a break? He raked back his too-long hair, reminding himself of the haircut he had intended to get that day.

He had wanted to look good for Meg.

The knot in his stomach went tighter.

"Take it easy, bro," Luke said, reading the tension vibrating between his shoulders. "We're just getting started." Luke grinned. "If it was too easy, it wouldn't be any fun."

Dirk whipped a look at his friend. Luke was trying to lighten the moment, give him the boost he needed. A faint smile flickered across his lips. "Yeah, what was I thinking?"

Ethan shoved back his chair, hoisting his heavily muscled frame up from the seat. "I've got a friend at Sea-Tac who owes me a favor. Odds are he'll know someone in the office at Boeing Field. The pilot had to file a flight plan. Maybe we can get the tail numbers off the plane, see where it's scheduled to land." Ethan pulled his cell phone out of his pocket and headed out the door to make the call.

As he disappeared from sight, a sandy-haired man appeared in the doorway: FBI Special Agent Ron Nolan. "Looks like a war room in here."

With Gertsman's photo still up on the screen, maps spread open on the table, iPads, and smartphones, it kind of did.

"Close enough," Dirk said. He shook Nolan's hand and Ian did the same. The men farther away gave him a nod. "I hope you're here to tell me you have a line on the plane and know where it's going, and men at your disposal to meet the jet when it lands."

Nolan pushed out a soft breath of air. "Unfortunately meeting the plane isn't going to happen."

"Told you," Luke grumbled.

"Do you at least know where it's headed?" Dirk asked.

"We're working on it. We should have the information very soon."

Ethan walked back in just then. "The plane was a chartered G4, tail number N108EC. The flight plan calls for a refueling stop at Juan Santamaria International Airport in Costa Rica. From there it's going to El Tepual International Airport in Chile. Looks like that's the final destination. The pilot is planning to fly the plane back to Seattle from there."

"Chile?" Dirk walked over to where Sadie was working her laptop. "What the hell's in Chile?"

Her fingers ran over the keyboard. Her head came up as she pointed to the info on the big screen on the wall. "You see that?" A Google map of the area pinpointed with a red balloon.

"Yeah, I see it. So what?"

"That's El Tepual Airport in Chile." She zoomed the map a little to the east. "And right there on the other side of the Andes — that's Bariloche."

A grim smile touched Dirk's lips. "Alpine region. He's taking her home. He's meeting the charter and picking her up in one of his own planes, flying her back to Bariloche or somewhere close by. He must have a place in the area. Good work — both of you."

"Let's see if we can find out exactly where he's headed." Sadie started pounding on the keyboard again.

Ron Nolan moved closer to the table, slid a glance past each of the men. "Whatever you're planning, it isn't going to happen." Sadie stopped typing. "At least not today or anytime for at least the next week."

"What the hell are you talking about?" Dirk shot Nolan a glare. "You need to put boots on the ground, get men to that airport before the plane arrives."

"Not gonna happen. Here's the deal. Interpol is all over Gertsman. According to them, the guy's involved in all kinds of criminal activities from drug smuggling to gun running. They want him bad. They've got a man deep undercover and they're within days — a week to ten at most — before they have everything in place to take

408

him down."

Anger vibrated through every muscle in Dirk's body. "And in the meantime what's going to happen to Meg? Gertsman didn't take her all the way to Argentina so they could have a nice little chat over afternoon tea. She's an internationally famous model. He wants her — just like any other red-blooded male. You don't think he's ruthless enough to take what he wants without her permission?"

"I know you're worried," Nolan tried to soothe. "But Meg's a big girl. She was a lingerie model, for God's sake. She knows how to handle men. All she has to do is placate the guy for a few days, give Interpol a little time."

Luke made a disgusted sound in his throat and Dirk moved into Nolan's space. "She's a mother, you bastard — not some fucking whore!"

Nolan backed a little away. "You need to take it easy, Dirk. You're not thinking clearly. You're too emotionally involved because you think she's yours. Isn't that right?"

Did Meg belong to him? Did she? Who was he kidding? She'd been his since the moment she'd invited him into her bed.

"She's mine, Nolan, and I protect what

belongs to me."

"Not this time, Reynolds. You're going to wait. If you try to interfere with the investigation, you're going to jail." He turned. "Same goes for the rest of you. You need to step back, let the authorities do their jobs." His voice softened. "Interpol knows what's going on. They're doing everything in their power to bring Megan home. And so are we."

A heavy silence hung over the room.

Dirk's jaw was clenched too tight to speak.

Agent Nolan turned and walked out of the conference room. No one said a word till they heard the back door leading to the parking lot close firmly behind him.

CHAPTER THIRTY-TWO

"Time to go to work," Luke said, breaking the silence, continuing as if the agent had never been in the room. "Before I got here, I put a call in to Morgan Flynn, my buddy in South America. Gave him a sitrep and asked him to be ready to handle the details should we have to go in and do the extract ourselves."

"Special Agent Nolan has just made that plan a go," Ethan said darkly.

"Flynn's currently in Uruguay, but he's done plenty of work in Argentina. He'll have access to whatever tactical gear and weaponry we need, and he's ready to go in with us once we get down there. I told him I'd get back to him as soon as things got under way."

Dirk nodded. Taking action eased the pressure between his shoulder blades. Luke had been right all along. He'd been a fool to think there'd be an easy way to bring

Meg home.

Nick spoke up just then. "I've been doing some checking." He looked down at the iPad on the table in front of him. "It's 2,972 nautical miles from Seattle to Costa Rica, a little less than nine hours flying time. Meg went missing from Starbucks at around eleven. That means the plane should be arriving at the airport in Costa Rica, our time, around eight p.m."

Dirk checked his watch. It was already a quarter till eight. "Without international help, we can't do jack to stop them from leaving Costa Rica."

"I figure they'll refuel and head out," Nick said. "It's another nine hours to El Tepual. This time they change planes, load Meg onto one of Gertsman's jets, and head for Bariloche. There's an airport there big enough to handle a business jet so that's likely the final destination. It's not that far from Chile, only a little over a hundred miles, but they have to get over some kickass mountains."

"That's eighteen hours total flying time," Luke said. "Plus the drive from Starbucks to Boeing Field, loading and takeoff, refueling stops and plane changes. With the five-hour time change, that puts them in Bariloche at eleven hundred tomorrow morning."

"Eleven a.m.," Dirk repeated. "Unless there's some delay or they run into inclement weather."

Ethan glanced at the men at the table. "That's six a.m. our time. It's gonna be a late night, boys. We'd better call our significant others."

Luke rose from his chair. "Since I'm currently and with any luck at all will remain without a significant other, I'll call Flynn, bring him up to speed, and get him started on lining up the gear and weapons we're going to need."

A noise sounded in the doorway. "Which, from what I've just overheard, is going to necessitate chartering a jet — among various and sundry other expenses."

Dirk turned toward the familiar deep voice. "Mr. O'Brien."

"Edwin will do. I wish you had phoned me. Instead, after I tried calling Meg's cell for the past few hours and never got an answer, I rang the house and spoke to Mrs. Wills. I could tell she was upset. She said you were looking for Meg, too. I had a feeling I'd find you here."

"I didn't want to call until I knew what was going on."

"And now you do," said the tall man with

the graying red hair.

"Unfortunately yes." He turned to the other men at the table. "This is Edwin O'Brien, Meg's dad." He made the introductions. "The lady behind the laptop is Sadie Gunderson. The blond guy is Ian Brodie, my boss. The man over there with the black hair and blue eyes, that's Nick Brodie, and the big guy, that's Nick's cousin, Ethan. You already know Luke."

Edwin gave a respectful nod toward the men. "I assume you're all here to help Dirk find Meg."

"That's right," Ian said.

"Whether you know it or not, you'll benefit from my assistance as well. Let me start by saying the undertaking you are about to embark upon will not be a cheap endeavor. Fortunately I have money to burn and I want my daughter returned safely home."

Dirk felt a rush of relief, followed by one of respect for Meg's dad.

Dirk reached over and pulled out a chair, inviting him to join them. "Sit down and I'll fill you in."

While the men left to refill their coffee mugs and call their women, Dirk sat down with Edwin O'Brien and told him Meg had been taken to Argentina. He told O'Brien he had spoken to the FBI and wouldn't be getting any help from them or anyone else, not while they were in the middle of an investigation involving the man who had abducted her, Otto Gertsman.

He told O'Brien about Jonathan Hollander and watched the blood drain from the older man's face.

"Jonathan was also involved in Charlie's kidnapping," Dirk said. "I'm not sure how he got tied up with Gertsman in the first place, but apparently Hollander owed him money. That's what set all this in motion."

O'Brien's big, freckled hand unconsciously fisted. "He's going to pay. I can promise you that."

"At the moment, Hollander is the least of our problems." Dirk ended the discussion by telling Meg's dad that his participation in the mission might wind up landing him in jail.

O'Brien seemed unfazed. "I want my daughter brought back — at any cost. Charlie needs her. Her mother and I need her."

"I need her, too," Dirk said softly.

For the first time since he'd entered the room, O'Brien seemed to relax. "Then I guess I don't have anything to worry about."

Dirk didn't tell the man he had everything to worry about.

All of them did. But the solution had gotten easier the moment Edwin O'Brien and his unlimited checkbook had walked into the conference room.

"By the way," O'Brien said to Dirk before the others returned, "my wife called my cell as I drove over. Apparently she suspected something was wrong. She asked me to tell her straight out what was going on. I told her Meg was missing, and that I was on my way to talk to you. She's picking Charlie up as we speak. He'll be staying with us for the duration. When you talk to Meg, you can tell her that she doesn't have to worry about her son. He's in good hands with his grandparents."

Dirk breathed a sigh of relief. He'd been worried about Meg's little boy, too. "That's good news. I figured we could count on you to watch out for Charlie, but I was hoping it wouldn't come to that."

"Unfortunately it has. I'll let Patsy know. I promised I wouldn't keep any more secrets from her."

Dirk nodded. He looked into strong features and pale blue eyes that reminded him of Meg. "I'll bring her home, Mr. O. I swear it. I won't come back until I find her."

O'Brien fixed a steady gaze on Dirk. "I shouldn't have interfered with the two of you the first time. I didn't come out and say it, but Meg knew I wouldn't approve. I was wrong about you. I hope it works out this time. You're everything a man could want in a son."

Dirk swallowed. He'd never had a real dad, not a man like Edwin O'Brien. Meg was lucky. "Thank you."

Dirk turned as the men filed back into the conference room carrying cups of fresh coffee. The guy from the print shop had arrived with the topo maps, which Ethan also spread open on the table.

Sadie returned to the room carrying her laptop, setting it back down on the shiny mahogany surface. Apparently she had never stopped working.

She looked up and caught Dirk's eye. "Gertsman's plane isn't landing in Bariloche," she calmly announced.

Dirk inwardly groaned. He prayed they weren't back to square one. "Then where the hell's he taking her?"

"Oh, he's headed home, just like you figured. But Otto doesn't need a public airport to land his fancy jet. He owns a hundred-and-eighty-thousand acres due east of Bariloche. Twenty by thirty miles of high desert country. Plenty of room for the seven-thousand-foot airstrip he built."

Nick whistled.

Sadie brought up photos of the arid landscape on the flat-panel screen, sagebrush and cactus that looked like parts of the American southwest.

"So he's got some kind of compound out in the desert?" Dirk asked, his mind already running scenarios of the best way to get Meg out.

"That's where his plane's landing. Otto owns another twelve-thousand acres up in the mountains a couple of hours away. His family estate's near Villa La Angostura, where he was born."

Sadie clicked up another series of photos. Rugged, snow-capped peaks, dense pine forests, and raging rivers, majestic beauty that seemed to have no end. Gorgeous to look at — and a real bitch to maneuver in and out of when it was completely unfamiliar terrain.

"Estancia Adelina," she continued. "That's what Gertsman calls it. Named after his mother. Otto entertains at the estate on occasion, but only his most intimate friends. I couldn't find out much about the house and grounds. Satellite picture shows it's big." The screen lit with a Google photo of the estate and the mountainous area around it.

"Main house has to be fifteen, twenty thousand square feet," Luke said.

"Those outbuildings look a lot like barracks," Nick said darkly, studying the white-walled, multiwindowed images on the screen.

Sadie flipped to another shot that showed the property around the house, surrounded by what could only be a high, protective wall. "Otto enjoys his privacy to the point of paranoia."

Dirk studied the screen. "The photos are great, but they're just a start. We need to know as much as we can about the region and the people before we go in. We can work on the plane, but even then, we'll have to recon the area once we get boots on the ground."

Sadie brought up photos of San Carlos de Bariloche, the town's full name. "Population eleven thousand. Big ski resort in the winter. Pretty fancy place, kinda the Aspen of Argentina. In the summer the tourists come for the lake it sits on. Got white sand beaches, bikini babes, fancy restaurants, chocolate shops —"

"Too bad we aren't going on vacation instead of going to war," Nick grumbled, getting a chuckle out of the group.

"One thing we know," Dirk said, "it's a

long haul to Argentina. We definitely need a jet. Ethan, you've chartered for some of your clients. Can you line something up?"

"I'll take care of it." O'Brien rose from his chair. "The G4 carrying Meg has a range of a little over forty-three hundred nautical miles. That's why it had to stop and refuel. A G6 can handle up to seven thousand nautical. It can fly straight through, no refueling necessary. And you can land right there in Bariloche. That'll help make up a little time. I know who to call. Let me get things rolling." O'Brien headed out the door.

"I need to update Flynn," Luke said, rising and also leaving the room.

While the men were gone, Dirk and the others tossed out possible strategies, but nothing could be locked in place.

"The trouble is we won't have the info we need until we get there," Dirk said.

"We'll just have to do the best we can," said Nick.

A few minutes later Luke walked back into the room. "I talked to Flynn. The good news is he knows a guy who knows a guy, baggage handler at the Bariloche airport. We'll be able to bring our personal weapons."

"How's that going to work?" Nick asked. "How do we get them through customs without winding up in jail?"

"We go in as American tourists," Luke said. "Just there to hike and fish and enjoy the lake and the sun. We wear our civvies, take our carry-on luggage with us, but leave our gear bags on the plane. Flynn's contact unloads them and takes them to a previously designated location. His services don't come cheap, but Flynn's pretty sure he can be trusted."

Dirk scoffed. "Unfortunately at this point *pretty sure* is about as good as we're gonna get."

"I can communicate with Flynn from the plane," Luke said. "Montevideo's only about a three-and-a-half-hour flight from Bariloche. He'll be there way before we are. We'll stay in contact, work out more of the details on the plane. I keep my weapons and a go-bag in the Bronco. I can be wheels up in fifteen minutes."

Dirk nodded. "Now that I know we can bring our own gear, I need a few things from my apartment." Yeah, like his AR-15 assault rifle, his S&W .45, tactical vest, survival gear, and extra ammunition.

"I need to collect my stuff, too," Nick said. "I'll go by my house, then meet up with you at the airport."

"Hold it." Dirk's gaze slid to Nick. "You're

out of this, Brodie. You've got a wife and a brand-new baby. You're staying right here."

"Bullshit." Nick's brilliant blue eyes flashed with determination. "I'm going."

Dirk ignored him. "Ian and Ethan, same goes. You're family men. Plus, this is going to be a military operation. You guys were great cops, but you're civilians. Luke and I know the drill. For us it's second nature."

"I'm a Ranger," Nick argued. "You need me. The two of you won't be enough."

"Morgan Flynn's going in with us," Luke said. "We were deployed together. The guy was one of the best operators I've ever worked with. He'll recruit whatever men we need."

"I can't just sit here and do nothing," Nick grumbled. "If it was Samantha —"

"I know," Dirk said softly. "Doesn't change the way things are."

"What about ground operations?" Nick persisted. "I could fly down with you, set up a base camp, handle communications, help you coordinate from Bariloche."

Dirk shot a glance at Luke, who ran it through his mind and started nodding. "Might not be a bad idea."

Ethan weighed in, his gaze swinging from Luke to Dirk. "From what Sadie says, the town's a big-time tourist destination. Nick should be safe enough there."

"All right," Dirk finally agreed. "You want in, Brodie, you're in. You're our man on the ground, but you stay in Bariloche."

Nick just grinned. Dirk figured that grin would be a thing of the past once Samantha got hold of him.

"The bad news is until Edwin gets a jet lined up, we can't go anywhere." Dirk glanced toward the door in time to see O'Brien striding back into the conference room.

"That, gentlemen, will no longer be a problem. Burton-Reasoner Industries has a G6 set to pick you up at Boeing Field. Should be gassed and ready to depart by eleven p.m." He dropped a brown leather satchel on the table. "Bank courier just arrived. I took care of it during the break. You'll find expense money in the bag. If you need more, just let me know and I'll have it wired to Bariloche."

Dirk released a breath of relief. Things were moving forward. They'd be no more than twelve, fourteen hours behind the jet that carried Meg. Trouble was they wouldn't be able to go in until they had more information, then had a plan laid out.

Surely Meg would know he'd be coming for her. Surely she could stall Otto Gertsman until he had time to get there. He clamped onto the thought like a dying man clinging to his last breath of air.

"Eleven p.m.," he repeated. "We'll head out now, collect our gear, and meet up at the airport. We do some groundwork on the plane, lay out a preliminary plan, and coordinate with Flynn on the way. We'll gather more intel once we get there, then make changes and fine-tune the mission."

Dirk shoved up from his chair. "All right, men, let's roll."

CHAPTER THIRTY-THREE

Meg awoke groggy and disoriented, every muscle in her body limp with exhaustion. Her head pounded and nausea churned in her stomach. Nothing around her looked familiar. She smoothed a hand over the pale peach satin comforter spread over the big king-size bed where she lay, her mind a jumble of disconnected thoughts.

A trickle of memory came creeping in. She remembered arriving on a plane, a sleek white jet that landed in the middle of nowhere, remembered the sun shining down on an arid landscape stretching for miles around her.

She frowned. She seemed to recall a car traveling over a winding road, but she didn't remember how she got to this bedroom, or how long she had been there.

Her gaze swung to bright light outside her window. Ignoring a bout of nausea, she forced herself to slide out of the four-poster bed and cross the room. Late afternoon, she would guess by the angle of the sun shining down on the reflecting pool in the middle of a formal garden.

Ignoring the headache pounding behind her eyes, Meg studied the landscape, no longer arid desert but tall, forested mountains. From what she could see of it, the house itself was a white colonial mansion, two tall stories with a flat roof and a long wing off each side. There was a swimming pool and a cabana.

There was also a high wall around the perimeter that looked as if it completely encircled the property. Her pulse kicked up when she spotted armed men in towers and patrolling the top of the wall, soldiers dressed in tan uniforms, automatic weapons slung across their chests.

Fear snaked down her spine. Where was she? How had she gotten there? Wherever she was, she was a prisoner, not a guest.

Her mind cleared a little more and she realized she no longer wore the skinny jeans and knee-high boots she'd had on when she'd left her house that morning.

She rubbed her aching temple. No, not that morning. She remembered going to Starbucks, remembered the white van parked outside. Dear God, she remembered being drugged and dragged inside the vehicle. Her pulse raced, pounded so hard her head spun. *Focus! Think!* She was in trouble. She had to concentrate, had to keep her wits about her.

She studied the position of the sun, remembered the long plane ride and drive up the mountain. The abduction had to have happened yesterday morning. She was missing at least an entire day.

Her chest clamped down. *Breathe!* She dragged in a lungful of air, turned away from the window, and looked down at the elegant satin nightgown falling gracefully over her hips to the floor. It was expensive lingerie in her favorite shade of peach, the sort she would have modeled for La Belle.

Except the sheer, ridiculously low-cut beige-lace bodice that barely covered her nipples would never have been allowed on national TV. Who had undressed her? Who had chosen the revealing nightgown and helped her put it on?

She struggled to recall, couldn't come up with the faintest memory. What had happened to her that she had forgotten? Dear God, she had to find out what was going on.

More memories jelled. She remembered the sickly sweet smell of the white rag pressed over her mouth and nose, the same as the chloroform that had lingered in Charlie's bedroom. She'd been unconscious. For God's sake, anything could have occurred.

Her fear inched up until her palms were sweating and her mouth felt dry. Whoever had removed her clothes, she prayed it wasn't the men who had abducted her. They were rough men, crude and brutal. Surely she would know if she had been molested — or worse.

She examined the peach satin gown. Neither of her abductors had the style and class to purchase such a lavish and elegant garment. Nor likely have the money to own a house with a bedroom fit for a queen.

She turned to survey her surroundings. Twelve-foot white molded ceilings, polished hardwood floors, thick-pile, cream-and-peach Aubusson carpet. Heavy peach silk draperies hung at the windows and a fireplace with a sienna marble mantel rested against one wall.

Who owned the house? Was it the person who had undressed her? She shivered at the thought, then clamped down on her fear. Better to stay calm, not imagine the worst.

Her mind moved backward once more and a bitter memory surfaced of the van in the lot outside Starbucks, of Jonathan being inside the van.

Dirk had been right. Her ex-husband must have been involved in Charlie's abduction. Jonathan had tried to ransom his own son for ten million dollars. When his plan had failed miserably, he'd had Meg kidnapped instead. How much was the ransom this time? Fifteen million? Twenty?

In an odd way the thought was comforting. Her dad would pay the money, no matter how much it was. Her dad would pay and she would go home. Then again, they'd planned to kill little Charlie. Perhaps no amount of money would be enough to keep her alive.

Her throat tightened as she thought of her little boy. Dear God, was Charlie all right? He'd been home with Mrs. Wills. She had to believe he was still there, that she and Dirk would make sure he was okay.

Her eyes burned and her vision blurred as Dirk's strong, handsome features rose in her mind, his sexy tattoo and hard-muscled body. So much between them remained unresolved. She wished she had told him she loved him.

She remembered the way he had saved her son, the way he was always there when she needed him, and hope stirred. She had left Dirk a message, mentioned she was meeting Jonathan. Dirk would figure out where she had been taken and he would come after her.

She knew it without the slightest doubt.

Dirk would come. All she had to do was survive until he got there.

Wiping away the wetness on her cheeks, she forced back her fear and noticed the huge bouquet of long-stemmed peach-colored roses rising out of a sculpted Lalique crystal vase. What kind of kidnappers treated their victim like royalty?

Anger began to replace her fear. Who the hell had the nerve to bring her here and hold her against her will? Dammit, where was she?

An hour passed. Meg considered banging on the door, but she wasn't ready to face her captors, at least not in a nightgown that left her nearly naked.

She glanced up at the sound of a determined knock and her pulse leaped. The door opened and a blond girl walked in. Early twenties, slightly pudgy, plain except for the pale hair pulled into a single long braid and her pretty blue eyes. She was wearing an old-fashioned maid's uniform, a white blouse and a black skirt with a white ruffled apron tied around her waist.

"My name is Gretchen. I am here to assist you with whatever you may need." A faint German accent ran through the fluent English the girl was speaking.

"Are you . . . are you the one who undressed me when I arrived?" Meg asked hopefully.

"Yes," she said, but it sounded more like *yah*. "I will be your maid for the length of your stay."

"Exactly how long will that be?" Meg asked, anger creeping into her voice.

The girl ignored the question.

"At least tell me where I am. I would very much like to know."

A hint of smugness tipped the corners of Gretchen's lips. "All your questions will be answered soon enough." There was no humility in the reply. This was no humble servant; more like a watchdog the kidnappers were using to keep tabs on her.

"I want to speak to whoever is in charge. The man who owns this house, perhaps. And I need some clothes — something that actually covers my body."

Gretchen walked over and opened the door to a huge walk-in closet. Dresses, skirts, tops, pants, jeans, long gowns, belts, purses, and shoes lined the walls. Meg knew

431

clothes. These were all extravagantly expensive designer fashions.

"I was sent to find out if you are feeling well enough to join your host for supper," Gretchen said. "I can see that you are."

The girl walked into the closet. In seconds she reappeared with a long, backless white silk gown. A Valentino label flashed as the girl draped the garment over the foot of the bed and placed a pair of white, ankle-strapped Gucci heels on the floor.

A chill swept down Meg's spine. She could tell at a glance the clothes were exactly her size.

"I'm sure you will wish to shower and refresh yourself before you dress for supper," Gretchen said. "You will find everything you need, including makeup, in the bathroom. Supper will be served in the dining room at seven. Someone will come to escort you."

Gretchen turned and walked out the door, which closed with an ominous click behind her. Meg ran over and turned the antique brass knob, but the heavy door was solidly bolted from the opposite side.

Meg crossed the room and sank down on the bed. Wherever she was, she was far from her family and friends. Far from Dirk and little Charlie. She thought of her little boy yesterday morning, remembered standing in the kitchen as Charlie came pounding down the stairs.

Meg had grinned down at him. "Slow down, cutie. You're gonna fall and break your head bone."

Charlie laughed his sweet little boy laugh and Meg scooped him up in her arms. Carrying him into the kitchen, she'd set him down on the table, his legs dangling off the edge.

"When is Dirk coming?" Charlie asked.

"He's working right now, but he'll be over later for supper."

"Can we go for ice cream in the Wiper?"

"After we eat maybe we can. Dirk's usually up for ice cream."

Charlie grinned. "Dirk's just like me." He tapped a small fist against his chest. "I like when Dirk stays at night. I don't have bad dreams."

Meg's heart squeezed. She kissed Charlie's silky red hair. "Neither do I, sweetheart."

When the little boy squirmed to get down, Meg set him back on his feet and he raced for the stairs. Charlie wanted a real father more than anything in the world, and he was falling for Dirk.

Meg had already fallen hard.

Now as she stood in the opulent bedroom

suite, her heart aching for the men she loved, she prayed yesterday morning wouldn't be the last time she would ever see them.

Flying at forty-five thousand feet, the Burton-Reasoner jet, an impressive Gulf-stream G650 that had to be worth at least fifty mil, winged its way southeast from Seattle. The interior, with its wide, butter-cream leather chairs, sofas, and polished burlwood tables, was configured so the passengers could conduct business while traveling in elegant comfort and style.

The bar and galley were fully stocked. There was a captain and cocaptain and a second crew to spell the men on the long, straight-through flight.

Dirk and Nick sat across from each other at the table while Luke leaned back on the sofa, his laptop on his knees. The plane was equipped with Wi-Fi, making it easy to dig around on the Internet as the trip progressed.

"Let's go over what we've come up with so far," Dirk said, ending the tap of fingers pounding away on keyboards. He shot a glance at Luke, the only one who had been to South America before.

"I know a little about Argentina," Luke said.

Translation: I was deployed down there doing the stuff of nightmares, but I'm not at liberty to talk about it.

"Been there a couple of times," he said, "but not the alpine region. As you know by now, in a way we got lucky. The seasons are reversed down there. Right now, it's summer. Gets hot in places, but that close to the Andes, heat won't be a problem. Be mid-seventies in the daytime and cool at night."

"You speak Spanish," Dirk said. "That's a big help." Luke had a gift for languages. It was one of the reasons he'd been such a valuable operator.

"It's beautiful," Luke said. "But in a lot of ways, still a third-world country. Lots of social problems, economic trouble, political turmoil, pockets of poverty, lots of corruption and crime."

"The corruption might work in our favor," Dirk said. "Payoffs can get things done when trying to plow through a mountain of red tape doesn't do jack shit."

"Plenty of cash in that bag Edwin handed us," Nick said. "Turns out some of it's in high-denomination pesos, which saves us a lot of trouble. It's about ten pesos to the

435

buck right now."

"Guy's no dummy," Dirk said.

Luke's penetrating blue eyes fixed on his face. "O'Brien's no dummy and neither is his daughter. Meg'll know we're coming. She'll figure a way to keep herself safe until we can get there."

Dirk swallowed past the knot in his throat. "Gertsman went to a lot of trouble to get Meg down there. Whatever he wants, he'll take it, one way or another."

"Jonathan said Otto was obsessed with her," Luke said. "I don't think he'll hurt her. Not right away. Not as long as she plays it cool."

Dirk glanced away. "She's got a little boy. She'll do whatever it takes to stay alive."

"That's right," Luke said softly. "And she's got you. She knows you'll love her no matter what happens down there."

His chest clamped down. His gaze fixed on Luke. "You think she knows that?" It was true. His friends could see it. But he wasn't sure Meg knew.

"Yeah, I do," Luke said a little gruffly.

Nick's features hardened. "We're bringing her back so you don't need to worry. We'll get there before anything bad happens to her."

Dirk managed to nod, grateful these men

had his back. "So . . . how hard you think it's going to be to get her out of there? I went back into Google Maps. In those satellite images, the place looks like a fortress. No way to tell how many men he's got guarding the compound."

Luke shrugged. "Might be nothing to it, just a quick snatch and grab. Might be Gertsman doesn't figure anyone will try to go in head-on. He might think he got away clean, that no one even knows he's the one who took her."

Nick leaned forward. "Even if Hollander talks, Gertsman might figure her family will go to the Argentine authorities, try to persuade them to get involved — which, with a man as powerful as Gertsman, they'd likely refuse to do."

"Or they'd drag their feet so long it wouldn't matter," Luke added. "*Mordida* rules, like in most of South America."

"There's always a chance the estate will only have a handful of security people around," Nick finished.

Dirk cocked an eyebrow at two of his best friends. "Is that what either of you actually believes?"

Both men glanced away.

"I didn't think so."

"Okay, so it won't be a cakewalk," Luke

said. "We never really thought it would be, right? We've got a basic plan. Let's lay out plans B and C and hope one of them will actually work."

CHAPTER THIRTY-FOUR

Wearing the Gucci heels and long white silk gown, her back and shoulders mostly bare, Meg took a calming breath and walked over to answer the knock on her door. Not that she could actually open it.

"Come in."

When the lock turned and the door swung open, a man, impeccably dressed in a navy-blue suit and a pair of highly polished, blunt-toed, black designer shoes, stood on the other side of the threshold.

"Good evening. I hope you're well rested."

Meg blinked at the perfect European English. She didn't recognize the man with the buzz-cut brown hair and blue eyes who stood in front of her, and yet she did.

"I remember you. You had black hair and dark eyes, but you're the man on the plane."

"Very observant, Ms. O'Brien. Most people are far less so."

Anger rolled through her. "You're Raymond Neville." The man with unlimited disguises. The man who had almost killed her and Charlie. She remembered Agent Nolan had called him The Fixer. Neville — who had ruthlessly murdered Mickey Degan. She wanted to run out of the room, out of the house, but she shoved down her fear and stood her ground.

"You change your appearance like you change your dirty shorts, but nothing can mask the evil in your eyes."

Neville's expression never changed. "I didn't realize your detective boyfriend was quite so efficient. My mistake."

"You tried to murder me. You tried to kill my son."

"In order to succeed in any endeavor, one must be flexible. I needed to get away. I knew your friend Reynolds wouldn't let you drown — or at least I imagined he would do his best not to let that happen. As it turned out, he managed the feat remarkably well."

She remembered her fear as she had watched her little boy being tossed into the lake, and a fresh round of anger rolled through her, making her mouth feel tight.

Neville's gaze remained on her face. "If you're determined to blame someone, blame yourself for getting Reynolds involved in the first place. If your father had simply paid the ransom, you wouldn't be here now."

She bit back a furious retort. Already she had given Neville too much information. Now he knew Dirk had discovered his identity. It was dangerous to reveal anything that might be used against her.

He offered his arm. "Time for supper. We wouldn't want to keep your host waiting."

"Who is he?"

"I believe he would rather introduce himself."

She wanted to refuse the arm Neville offered, but she had decided to cooperate. Dirk would find her. He just needed time. She would do whatever it took to make certain he got it.

They walked out of the bedroom suite into a marble-floored hallway, then descended a sweeping marble staircase into an entry beneath a massive crystal chandelier.

Neville led her past an elaborate two-story library, past several elegant salons, all furnished impeccably with plush sofas, silk draperies, and eighteenth-century antiques.

Making their way over polished wood floors, they walked through a set of double doors that slid out of sight into the walls, into a magnificent dining room with a long mahogany table, a dozen high-backed chairs along each side. A pair of crystal chandeliers glittered overhead and silver candelabra ran the length of the table.

At the far end, a large man with silver-blond hair shoved back his chair and rose to greet her. Every bit of six-three, he had very pale blue eyes and an equally pale complexion. Early fifties, she thought, once powerfully built but beginning to succumb to his proclivity for the finer things. A little too much alcohol and gourmet food, she imagined.

Neville released her arm and stepped back a few paces as the man approached. "Ms. O'Brien, it is a pleasure to meet you at last." He graced her with a smile and a very refined bow. A trace of the same German she had heard in Gretchen's voice marked his words.

"My name is Otto Gertsman. I am your admirer of several years and also your host for what I hope will be a very pleasant stay."

Anger burned through her. He had ruthlessly kidnapped her, had tried to kidnap her son. She clamped down on her temper, arched a russet eyebrow instead. "I'm your guest, then, not your prisoner?"

His smile widened. It was warm and a little too friendly. She could detect an edge, though he was doing his best not to show it.

"Ultimately that is for you to decide, my dear. For now why don't we enjoy our supper and afterward I will give you a tour of my home."

Time, she reminded herself with a steadying breath. She needed time. She accepted his arm and let him guide her to the end of the table, where he pulled out a chair and seated her to his right. From the corner of her eye, she saw Neville back away, turn, and disappear out of the dining room.

She returned her attention to her host. For now she would think of him that way, as her host instead of her captor. Dirk would find her, she repeated firmly. Somehow he would make the connection between Neville and Gertsman and track her to wherever she had been taken.

The big German took the chair next to her at the end of the table, made a show of pulling his napkin out of its silver ring and spreading it across his lap. Meg did the same.

An ornate silver ice bucket sat on a stand next to the table. Gertsman wrapped a big hand around the neck of a bottle of chilled champagne and lifted it out of the bucket. Dom Perignon. Nothing but the best for her *host.* She wanted to reach over and slap his face.

Instead she waited as he filled a Baccarat crystal flute and set it on the table in front of her, filled one for himself, then lifted his glass in a toast.

"To meeting you at last."

Meg looked at the bubbling pale liquid in her glass and her stomach roiled. "I'll drink your toast, but only if you give me your word there is nothing in the flute but champagne." No drugs, nothing that would make her as helpless as she had been before.

He lowered his glass. "You were brought here for a number of reasons. Only one has to do with you and me and what may transpire in our future. You have my word that subterfuge will have no part in anything that happens between us from now on."

She took a deep breath. For whatever reason she believed him. Perhaps raping an unconscious woman wasn't enough of a challenge.

Time, she repeated, deciding to make that her mantra. More desperate for a drink than she could ever recall, Meg lifted her champagne flute and clinked it against the one Otto Gertsman held in a thick, pale hand. The ring of expensive crystal and Gertsman's lascivious smile sent an icy shiver down her spine.

With no fuel stops and pushing the twin jet engines, the pilot set the G6 down, local time, a little before eight o'clock p.m. The aircraft rolled the length of the Bariloche runway, turned, and taxied back to the executive terminal. In the distance mountains rose up, the near hills barren, then climbing steeply to forested terrain, to far distant peaks still white with snow.

In a pair of khaki cargo pants, a short-sleeve, blue-flowered Tommy Bahama shirt, and low-topped leather hiking boots, Dirk descended the metal stairs to the tarmac. Luke followed in khaki shorts, a yellow tank, his yellow-and-black sneakers, and a flat-brimmed Panama hat. Nick's tourist look involved a cheap camera slung around his neck.

The evening summer air was cool, but it wasn't dark yet. Single file, Dirk led the men toward a fat little black-haired, mustached man who waddled toward him.

Hector Fernandez was a local who worked as a tour guide, along with various and sundry odd jobs that paid the bills for him and his family. Flynn's contact had brought him aboard to help them get through customs and acquaint them with the area.

According to Luke, Flynn had already arrived in Bariloche and started setting up a base camp. He'd rented a Chery Tiggo, an Argentine SUV, and a cabin off National Route 231, the road to Villa La Angostura and Estancia Adelina. Apparently the man was as efficient as Luke had said.

"Welcome to Bariloche, *amigos.*" Hector flashed a toothy white smile.

Dirk shook the little man's hand and the men introduced themselves. Hector must have been a regular at the airport, must have known whose palms to grease, because in minutes they were through customs, out of the terminal, and walking across the parking lot. Hector tossed their carry-ons into the trunk of a slightly battered Renault, cars still manufactured in Argentina, and they all climbed aboard.

"Please excuse the poor English," Hector said, then went on to give them background info on the town in a mix of Spanish and heavily accented English that was relatively easy to understand.

The village was perched on the south shore of Nahuel Huapi Lake, a combination of modern four-to-eight-story apartments, offices, and hotels that rose up the side of the hill. In other sections, the buildings were stone and wood and looked as if they belonged in Austria or Switzerland.

City squares and clock towers, streets lined with restaurants, souvenir stores, and chocolate shops. With the car windows down, the aroma of coffee and chocolate pervaded the air. Somewhere down the block Dirk could hear the sound of an accordion playing a lively polka.

Since Luke was fluent in Spanish he sat up front with the driver, but the men spoke English as much as possible. As they drove the streets, Hector pulled over in front of a locals' joint called La Salamandra and ran in to get a bag of empanadas, a kind of deep-fried meat-and-cheese–filled pastry. Hector ate them with a tea called maté, while the guys washed theirs down with ice-cold Cokes.

None of them had slept much on the plane and they were hungry and exhausted. The food gave them a badly needed boost.

Another few minutes into the ride and Luke ordered the little man to pull the car over to the side of the road.

"All right, Hector, you've fed us and shown us all the tourist spots. Now before it gets too dark to see, show us the rest."

Hector's chubby hands tightened around the steering wheel. "Señor, I do not think that is such a good idea."

447

A lengthy conversation ensued in Spanish before the little man, with a sigh of resignation, turned a corner and headed up the mountain.

Sometimes plans B and C turned into plan D. They had to be aware of their options.

"Bariloche is really two cities," Luke explained. "You've just seen the lower part, a rich tourist town on a beautiful lake surrounded by snow-capped mountains. The upper city is where the poor people live. No paved roads, no gas, no sewage, no hospital or public transportation."

As they drove up the hill, small houses of wood and scrap metal lined the road. "The only heat they've got is wood," Luke said. "Every year people die from carbon monoxide poisoning from fires in makeshift stoves or trash cans."

"I thought you'd never been here," Dirk said.

Luke just shrugged, which could have meant yes or no.

They drove the town, getting a look at the dark-skinned people who prowled the streets, a mix of Argentines and Chilean and Bolivian immigrants.

The sun was setting, reminding them of the time change. "We've seen enough to get a feel for what's going on," Luke said to Hector. "Take us to the cabin."

Hector nodded, seemed relieved to be back on familiar ground. From the upper city, they headed back to the village, drove past the airport and turned onto Route 237, then north on 231 along the lake toward Villa La Angostura.

Thirty miles out of town, the driver made a turn onto a lane winding into the mountains. Another few miles and he pulled into the gravel driveway of a small log house and parked between a silver SUV — the Chery — and a mud-covered, four-door Jeep.

The cabin was made of log and stone with a wide wooden deck out front. A massive, dark-haired man in jeans and an olive drab T-shirt stretched over a heavily muscled chest walked out on the porch.

"That's Flynn," Luke said, cracking open his door and stepping out of the car.

Dirk and Nick also climbed out. Hector rounded the vehicle, opened the trunk, and set their carry-on bags on the ground.

"Señor Luke, you have my phone number, *si*?"

"I've got it," Luke said. "We'll call if we need you again."

Hector took the money Nick handed him.

"*Gracias,* señor," the rotund driver said.

"Remember," Dirk warned, "we were never here."

"*Sí, sí.*" He waved a chubby hand above his head. "*Vaya con Dios,* señores." Hector climbed back into the Renault and drove away.

"You think Fernandez will keep his mouth shut?" Dirk asked Luke, thinking of the men's earlier conversation in Spanish.

"He was well paid. He's got a family and he wants them safe. Long as he isn't in any danger, he won't say a word."

As they climbed the stairs to the deck, Morgan Flynn walked over to introduce himself. They all shook hands, then another man walked out of the log house into the fading evening light.

"Emil Ramos," Flynn said, tipping his head toward the other man. "Emil was raised in the area, still has contacts here. He's the guy who's been making all the arrangements."

Dirk shook Ramos's hand. He was of average height, slender build, dark-skinned, with thick, black hair cut short. If he'd been handling the prep, so far he'd done a good job.

"Your gear from the plane should have arrived by now," Ramos said with only a trace of an accent. "There is a farm just down the road. That is the drop location. I will make the pickup and return."

Dirk nodded. "Sounds good."

Ramos sauntered off toward the muddy Jeep — apparently they were everywhere — climbed in, fired the engine, and disappeared out of sight behind the pine trees lining the driveway.

"There's something besides our weapons we're going to need," Flynn said, still standing on the wooden deck in front of the cabin.

"Yeah, what's that?" Dirk asked.

"A chopper. If you've got the money, Ramos has a helo lined up and ready to go."

"Who's gonna fly it?"

"One phone call and I'll have the pilot on his way. Name's Brandon Elliott. Army Night Stalker. They don't get any better than that."

"What's he doing down here?"

"Got in a beef with his commanding officer. Long story. Left the army and wound up down here working as a merc. You want me to make the call or not?"

Dirk had been hoping for this. It was the option he favored. They had to get Meg out of the mountains, and the harsh terrain would make it harder than hell to travel on foot. The chopper could have them back at the airport in a tenth of the time it would take to navigate the curvy mountain roads.

"Make it happen," Dirk said.

Flynn just nodded. The guy was massive. At least six-five, solid muscle, and too damned good-looking. Dirk silently vowed to keep him far away from Meg.

Meg. His chest clamped down. He couldn't think of Meg, not now, couldn't let his fear for her get in the way of the focus he needed to get her away from Gertsman and safely back home.

"Let's go inside," he suggested. "See where we stand and figure our next move."

CHAPTER THIRTY-FIVE

The evening dragged on. Meg did her best to finish at least some of the lavish meal of European culinary delights Gertsman's staff served. Delicacies like oysters and Beluga caviar, a creamy chilled vichyssoise, a succulent local dish of sausage and peppers, fresh halibut in lobster sauce, and a magnificent chateaubriand, each course paired with a fine French wine.

Gertsman beamed as dessert was carried in on a silver tray by one of three tuxedo-clad waiters.

"Schwarzwälder Kirschtorte," he said as the waiter set gold-rimmed porcelain dishes on the table in front of them. "Cherry Black Forest cake. One of my favorites."

Meg thought of the mountains outside her bedroom window, thought of Gretchen and the once-blond, blue-eyed man next to her at the table. Maybe she was in Germany. She took a drink of Gewürztraminer, the sweet dessert wine the waiter had poured for this course, sucked up her courage, and very casually asked, "So your lovely home is in Germany?"

Gertsman merely smiled. "I'm afraid not, my dear. You are not in the homeland. You are in Argentina. You must recall your visit to Buenos Aires some years back. You mentioned in *La Nación* how much you were enjoying the country."

Her head spun. The Buenos Aires newspaper had interviewed her during a modeling shoot for La Belle. Of all the places she could have imagined, South America had never entered her head.

Dear God, how would anyone ever find her? Beneath the table, she curled her fingers around the napkin in her lap and squeezed as hard as she could to control her skyrocketing fear.

"I remember," she said, surprised to sound so calm when the voices in her head were screaming. "What little of the country I saw was beautiful. However, as we both know, I was quite unprepared for a second visit."

"And yet you are here."

She squeezed hard on the napkin. "I have a son, Mr. Gertsman. I have responsibilities. Surely a man of your intellect understands that I must return to Seattle."

Gertsman's soft features hardened, the pale eyes gone as cold and as unwavering as a snake in pursuit of its prey.

"There are circumstances of which you are unaware. For the time being you will remain here." Leaving his dessert untouched, he shoved up from his chair. "From now on you will address me as Herr Gertsman or Otto. Do you understand?"

She'd made him angry. She remembered Raymond Neville's cold-blooded murder of Mickey Degan. She could only imagine what a man of Gertsman's obvious power would do if she pushed him too far.

She reined herself in. "As you wish, Herr Gertsman." She smiled. "Otto." Setting her napkin aside, she lifted the skirt of her long, white silk gown out of the way and also rose from her chair. "Perhaps we could finish our dessert later, after you show me your magnificent home."

Gertsman's thick shoulders relaxed. "It would be my great honor . . . Megan."

Her mouth went dry. She could feel those chilling blue eyes sliding over her in a slimy caress. Clearly this man wanted her. How far would he go to have her? How far was she willing to go to appease him?

Meg blinked to hold back tears and pasted

on a smile she prayed looked at least somewhat sincere. Taking Otto Gertsman's arm,
she let him guide her out of the dining
room.

The men sat around a low wooden table in
front of the sofa in the little log cabin. The
furniture was simple, a couch and chairs, all
of it pine, handmade from the tall trees
climbing the mountains behind the house.
There was a bathroom, one small bedroom,
a kitchen with an eating area, and a living
room. An old wood-burning stove sat in the
corner.

Dirk's gaze ran over the array of muni-
tions on the table and lying on the floor: a
short-barreled tactical shotgun, a Beretta 9
mil, an HK A1 carbine, flash grenades, and
extra ammunition.

Nick, who was staying at the cabin with
Emil, wore only his Glock .45, while Dirk,
Luke, and Flynn wore their tactical gear,
carried night vision goggles and binoculars.
Their faces were blackened with greasepaint, each carried a radio, and Dirk also
carried the satphone.

They'd run through tonight's surveillance
mission at least three times. Everyone knew
which position to take and what his job was.

Dirk checked the load in his Browning,

the S&W .45 that was his backup weapon, then grabbed his AR-15 from where it leaned against the wall and slung it over his shoulder.

Dirk studied the men, all totally focused on the mission. "Okay, let's get this done."

Dirk led them outside into the dim light of a quarter moon. Intermittent cloud cover drifted overhead, providing shadows that would help keep them from being spotted. Tonight they would recon the compound, bring the info back, and fine-tune the mission. Tomorrow night they'd go in and bring out Meg.

Dirk's jaw tightened as he climbed into the front passenger seat. He didn't want to wait till tomorrow. He wanted Meg out of there — now. But they couldn't just go in balls to the wall, not with so many unknowns and Meg's safety to consider.

Flynn slid in behind the wheel, driving the route he had traveled earlier that day. Luke sat in back. It was ten miles farther up the road to the turnoff south of Villa La Angostura. Another five miles to Estancia Adelina.

Flynn spotted the road up ahead and turned the vehicle sharply to the right. The man had done his homework, piling up a ton of info in the short time he had been in

Bariloche. The SUV climbed a steep, winding lane into the mountains. Four miles in, Flynn pulled off the road and parked out of sight in a copse of trees.

On foot and traveling through the forest, it took awhile to reach the compound, or at least the high, white-stucco wall around it. Keeping well out of sight, they fanned out and took up positions on the hillsides around the enclosure, climbing until each man had a vantage point high enough to see inside.

The place looked surprisingly familiar, Dirk thought, recalling the photos he'd studied in Seattle and on the long plane ride to Bariloche. A massive colonial with gardens and fountains, swimming pool and cabana, all elegant and welcoming.

Unlike the two outbuildings, which, as they had feared, were barracks housing Gertsman's private army, men who patrolled the walls and guarded each of the four corner towers.

Beneath the moon sliding in and out of the clouds, foot soldiers patrolled outside the walls as well. Through his night vision goggles, Dirk tracked their movements.

His radio crackled to life. "Looks like plan B," Luke's voice said calmly.

"Roger that," Dirk said.

"Copy," said Flynn.

Plan B wasn't good news. The place was even more heavily fortified than they had figured. Getting in would be nearly impossible.

Unless they took down a couple of guards and dressed in their uniforms. Gertsman's soldiers moved easily in and out through the gates in the walled fortress around the main house.

Watching from their positions on the hillsides, they counted the number of armed men, timed their movements, their shift changes, noted that only a single guard stood at the rear and front doors of the house itself.

Dirk smiled grimly. Gertsman figured he was safe inside his walled fortress. He wasn't worried about those walls being breached.

If luck was on their side, tomorrow night the man would be in for a big surprise.

Though Meg had pleaded a headache shortly after supper — which wasn't a lie — Gertsman insisted on showing her his opulent home and expansive grounds.

The formal gardens, with their perfectly manicured hedges and rows of blooming flowers, were magnificent. As they strolled

459

beside a Roman fountain, Otto pointed out ancient Greek statues. Meg bit her tongue to keep from saying they belonged in a museum, not locked out of sight on some billionaire's secluded estate.

Instead she forced herself to concentrate on the conversation even as her gaze kept straying to the soldiers in the guard towers and those on top of the walls.

Dear God, even if Dirk figured out where she was, how would he get inside? How would they get back out? If he found out where she had been taken, he would surely come, and if he was caught, he would be killed.

Tears burned her eyes. She fought not to cry and shoved the emotion away. As the evening wore on, Gertsman showed her his collection of Fabergé eggs and his Stradivarius violin, showed her magnificent Flemish tapestries, and an ancient Qing dynasty vase worth millions.

"Tomorrow I will show you my art collection. I am sure you will recognize many of the artists. They are all quite renowned."

Exhausted as she was, Meg managed to keep her smile in place.

It slipped away as Gertsman walked her upstairs to her extravagant suite. "It was a lovely evening, my dear. I look forward to many more. In time, if things go well between us, perhaps we'll find a way for your little boy to pay a visit now and then."

A faint sound escaped her throat. *Oh, dear God!* Just the thought of Charlie being exposed to a man like Otto Gertsman made the bile rise in her throat. Before she could form any kind of reply, Gertsman leaned forward and pressed a chaste kiss on her trembling lips.

"I realize we need a little time to get to know each other. Tomorrow we'll enjoy the day together, starting with breakfast on the terrace. There's a movie theater downstairs. I have quite a collection of films. We'll watch one after supper."

She managed to nod.

Gertsman's smile slowly shifted and something hot slid into his eyes. "I'll expect to be invited into your bedroom tomorrow night, my dear Megan. You have tomorrow to prepare yourself."

Fear coagulated into a hard ball in the pit of her stomach. Meg swayed a little on her feet.

Otto took her trembling hand and pressed the back against his thick lips. "Sleep well, my dear. I look forward to seeing you in the morning."

Otto opened her door and Meg forced her

461

frozen limbs to move, carry her inside. The door closed solidly behind her and the bolt slid into place.

Long seconds passed. Her eyes burned. She swallowed against the tightness in her throat. For the first time since she had been abducted, Meg gave in to the painful sobs she had locked away, and the flood of tears tracked hotly down her cheeks.

Their recon mission accomplished, Morgan Flynn drove up in front of the cabin just as the satphone started ringing. Dirk pulled the phone out of his pack.

"Reynolds."

"Ron Nolan. I've been trying to reach you. Gertsman knows you're in Bariloche. He's put his men on alert and he's moving Meg in the morning. No idea where."

"How the hell did you get this number? How did you even know we were in Argentina?"

"Until I got the call from Interpol, I didn't. Not for sure. I had a hunch you and that crazy bastard Brodie wouldn't listen to reason. I got your number from Ian."

Working to hang on to his temper, Dirk put the satphone on speaker so the men could hear. "Go on," he said.

"After I left your office, I gave Interpol a

heads-up, told them you might get in the middle of things. I'm FBI, Dirk. I didn't have a choice. The good news is they decided to treat this as a black operation. As far as Interpol is concerned, they don't know anything about your beef with Gertsman. They don't know you from Adam and have no idea why you're in Argentina. The bad news is you get in any kind of trouble, there's no going to the American consulate or anybody else. You're on your own, start to finish."

"Yeah, I got that the first time. So how did Gertsman find out?"

"He's got connections all over the region. Hell, all over the country. The G6 stirred somebody's interest. Whoever it was must have followed up, found out you flew in from Seattle, managed to get a look at your passport info. According to Interpol's inside man, Gertsman just got the tip twenty minutes ago."

Dirk rubbed a hand over the bristles on his cheek. Exhaustion mixed with frustration added to his fear for Meg. "Anything else I should know?"

"I'm afraid there is. Turns out, according to Interpol, the women Gertsman brings to his most heavily guarded compound have a habit of disappearing."

Dirk's whole body tightened.

"If you're going to move, it had better be soon. Good luck, my friend." Nolan hung up the phone.

For several seconds Dirk didn't stir. They still sat in the car, Luke in the seat behind him.

"So Gertsman's moving Meg tomorrow," Dirk finally said. "Or he's making her dead."

Luke swore foully.

"We've got to go in tonight," Dirk said.

Flynn shook his head. "We aren't ready. We need more time."

"We don't have any more fucking time!" Dirk felt Luke's hand on his shoulder, steadying him. He took a calming breath. "Look, we worked things out on the way back down the mountain. We're as ready now as we will be tomorrow night. All we need is the chopper." His gaze locked on Flynn. "Is there a chance you can get Elliott lined up to do an early extract?"

"I don't know. He was planning to do a flyover tomorrow, locate a satisfactory pickup site."

"He can do it using satphotos and night vision gear," Luke said. "If he's a Night Stalker, that won't be anything new to him."

Flynn started nodding. "All right, let's see if we can get Elliott on board." He opened

464

his door and stepped out of the SUV. Dirk and Luke followed.

"Let's bring Nick and Emil up to speed," Dirk said as they strode toward the cabin door.

Flynn pulled out his cell. "In the meantime I'll make that call."

Thirty minutes later, the situation still fluid, they were working on plan C. Elliott was on his way. At a cruising speed of 150 miles an hour, it wouldn't take long for the helo to reach the extraction point.

If Elliott could find one. Dirk had to trust that he would.

They had decided to move the jet out of Bariloche. Gertsman had people there. He could have soldiers waiting when they returned to the plane.

The G6 would make the short, just over one-hundred-mile flight to El Tepual Airport in Chile. They'd be a helluva lot safer in another country.

The bad news was the helo would have to fly them out over the Andes, snow-covered monsters even in the summer. The pilot would have to navigate the passes. Weather could be a factor, as well as the capabilities of the helicopter itself.

And moving up the time line left them a

man short. The guy Flynn had lined up to go in with them couldn't make it on time. Nick insisted on filling the position, though Dirk was against it. They were almost ready to leave when Dirk turned to Luke, the man who was more a brother than a friend.

"Before we head out, there's one more thing. I need you in command of this mission, Luke. You're the senior operator here. You're the man for the job." Luke was Delta, the best of the best. "Will you do it?"

Something flashed in his friend's brilliant blue eyes. Then quiet purpose settled over his features. Dirk felt the rightness of his decision, and calm control replaced the nerves he'd been fighting.

Luke gave a faint nod of his head, took a breath, and turned to the others. "At the moment, plan C is definitely our best option. If the situation changes, you'll hear from me. There is one thing: Nick, you need to be on that jet."

Determination flashed in Nick's eyes. He shook his dark head. "No way. You're a man short. You need me to go in with you."

"We need someone on the ground who knows where we are and what we're doing. If plan C turns into a goat fuck, you're our only chance of getting the hell out of here."

When Nick looked like he might argue,

Luke's features hardened. "You're on the plane, Nick. Emil can take you to the airport. It isn't a suggestion, it's an order."

There wasn't a man in the room who would go against the steel in Luke's voice. Nick gave a resigned nod of his head.

"Move out," Luke said, and they were gone.

An hour later, Gertsman's army had three men down and Flynn was positioned in a sniper's nest well hidden up the mountain.

Dirk tugged down the officer's cap he wore with the tan uniform he had removed from one of the guards. He flicked a glance at Luke, who also wore a tan soldier's uniform. Luke gave the go sign.

It was time to breach the walls.

Chapter Thirty-Six

A faint noise roused her from a deep, exhausted slumber. Meg's eyes slowly opened as awareness slipped through her. Her gaze shot to the door. Had Gertsman decided not to wait? Was that the reason Gretchen had insisted she change out of the long, white evening dress into the peach satin nightgown she had worn before?

Her eyes strained into the darkness, lit dimly by thin rays of moonlight slanting in through the window. She heard the sound again, closer this time, and fear crawled through her. She jerked upright just as a hand clamped over her mouth.

"It's Dirk. Don't scream." The soft whisper of his deep male voice had her eyes filling with tears.

She nodded and his hand fell away. Meg came up on her knees and threw her arms around his neck. Dirk's hold tightened fiercely around her.

"I knew you'd find me," she said, wiping away the wetness on her cheeks. "I knew you'd come. But I . . . I still can't believe you're really here."

His gaze ran over her face. Then he pulled her even closer and his mouth crushed down in a brief hard kiss. "I'm here, baby. We're going home."

Meg blinked up at him. "Is Charlie —"

"He's okay. He's with your parents."

"How did you get in? There're soldiers everywhere." Then she saw he was wearing a tan uniform like the ones she had seen on the soldiers patrolling the grounds. It was a ridiculous time to think how good he looked in it.

"Luke disabled the security system on the house. He's downstairs. We need to get going." He tossed a bundle of clothes on the bed.

"What's that?"

"He was smaller than I am. They might actually fit you. You need to hurry."

She looked down, saw it was another tan uniform, didn't let herself think what he must have done to get it. Instead she hurriedly peeled off the nightgown, leaving her momentarily naked. She ignored the faint growl in Dirk's throat as his hazel eyes ran over her, darker now and intense.

She dragged on the tan uniform pants and stuck her arms into the sleeves of the tunic, fastened the brass buttons up the front, covering her bare breasts.

Dirk picked up the peach satin nightgown, his hand tightening around it in a fist. "If he hurt you, I'm going to kill him."

Meg went up on her toes and pressed a kiss on his hard mouth. "You got here in time. He was coming to my room tomorrow night."

The muscles in his body relaxed. "It wouldn't have mattered — I want you to know that. But I'm glad you're okay."

She kissed him quickly, then finished dressing. The pants were tight in the hips, but the length was okay. The tunic wasn't made to fit her curves, but it would cover her and keep her warm. She pulled on the socks, still warm, making her a little queasy, jammed her feet into the worn leather boots, which were too big for her narrow feet. She tightly tied the laces.

Dirk settled a round, billed military cap on her head. She'd noticed Gertsman's soldiers wearing them.

"Put your hair up underneath."

She did so quickly, twisting the bright strands into a knot and stuffing them inside the cap, still a little afraid this was only a dream. She told herself Dirk was really there, that somehow he was going to get her out of the house, away from Otto Gertsman.

He tugged down the bill of his own cap, settling it a little lower on his forehead. He needed a haircut, she thought, and actually smiled as she noticed the soft, dark strands curling at the nape of his neck beneath the rim of the cap.

"You ready, baby?"

She nodded. "What's the plan?"

"We go out together, turn left, and head for the servants' stairs. I'll lead you to them. We'll end up down in the kitchen. There was no one there when we came in. Luke'll be waiting for us."

He gave her a final quick kiss, pulled his weapon from the holster strapped to his thigh, and urged her toward the door.

They had only taken a couple of steps when the door burst open and the overhead light went on. A group of armed men stood in the doorway. Raymond Neville pointed a gun straight at Dirk's heart. Otto Gertsman stood behind two uniformed soldiers, who also brandished semiautomatic pistols.

Her head spun. For a moment she thought she might faint. Dirk eased her a little behind him, his pistol raised, the barrel directed at Gertsman. Meg clamped down on her fear even as her heart batted wildly inside her chest.

"Well, Mr. Reynolds," Gertsman said, "I was told you had figured out where our dear Megan had been taken and were on your way to engage in a daring rescue. You made good time indeed. I'm quite impressed. You realize your appearance in my house will cost several of my men their lives."

"It wasn't their fault," Dirk said, his pistol held steady. "It was yours for taking something that didn't belong to you."

Otto's pale blue eyes shifted to Meg. "I believe you will soon discover that Ms. O'Brien is my property now, to do with as I please."

She felt Dirk stiffen.

Otto tipped his head toward Neville in silent command but spoke to Dirk. "It would be quite uncivilized and extremely messy to kill you and the lady in such a beautiful suite of rooms, but sometimes sacrifices must be made. If you wish her to live, put down your weapon."

Dirk's gaze ran over Gertsman as he assessed the situation, seemed to conclude that Gertsman wasn't lying. He was too meticulous to kill them inside his precious home. Or maybe he just enjoyed taking his time, toying with his prey.

Whatever the reason, with Luke some-where in the house, they still had a chance to escape.

Dirk bent and carefully rested his weapon on the floor.

"Now the other one," Neville said. Dirk dragged a second pistol from behind his back and also set it down on the floor. "Kick them away."

Dirk shoved them aside with his boot. Neville caught Meg's arm. She made a little sound as he jerked her away from Dirk.

"Shall we go?" Otto said mildly.

The soldiers shoved Dirk forward out into the hall, their pistols leveled at his back. Meg could feel Neville's gun barrel pressing into her side as he urged her along the cor-ridor behind them. Gertsman also walked beside her. All of them knew Dirk wouldn't act as long as she was in the line of fire.

Dirk's hands were free, though. *Big mis-take,* Meg thought. He was a Ranger. He could probably kill a man ten different ways with those strong hands.

When they reached the top of the sweep-ing staircase, Gertsman caught her arm and turned her to face him.

"You, my dear, look surprisingly fetching in that uniform. I feel myself becoming aroused at the prospect of stripping you out of it and having you on your knees in front of me wearing just the hat."

The growl returned to Dirk's throat.

"There is an interesting room downstairs," Gertsman continued. "Completely sound-proof and filled with all sorts of interesting . . . objects. Once Mr. Reynolds has been disposed of, I shall enjoy demonstrating how some of them work."

Meg whimpered. Her legs were shaking as she descended the sweeping marble staircase. She knew Dirk was biding his time, waiting for the right moment. She reminded herself that Luke was somewhere near. If he had been killed, Gertsman wouldn't have been able to resist gloating.

She had to stay alert, be ready for anything that might happen.

"Keep moving," Neville said when they reached the first floor, urging them down a second set of stairs to the lower level of the house. She caught a glimpse of the theater Otto had mentioned as they walked past, then on down the corridor; one of the men pulled open a heavy steel door and took a step back, allowing her to walk inside.

Meg's lips thinned at the Nazi flag hanging on the wall at the back of the room. There were glass cases filled with German war memorabilia, pistols and rifles, knives and helmets, black SS uniforms with red-and-black swastikas on the sleeves. There were photos of Adolf Hitler, several posed with the same man.

Whoever it was looked a good deal like Otto. Someone in his family, perhaps his father, or more likely his grandfather.

"I was hoping one day to be able to share all of this with you," Otto said expansively, glancing around at his prized possessions. "But that is impossible now."

He pointed to another glass case, this one filled with wooden clubs and leather whips, things that might have been used by the guards in the prison camps. "Of course there are some other items we may still enjoy."

A sick feeling swept over her as she re-alized Otto still used the items in the cases, got a sexual thrill out of whatever he did with them.

Oh, God.

Gertsman turned to Neville and the small group clustered in the doorway.

"Get rid of Reynolds. The woman will stay here with me. I have plans for her. When I'm finished, you may do with her as you wish."

Dirk's gaze flashed to Meg. *I'm coming*

back, those hard hazel eyes said. Neville shoved him forward, farther down the passage. The other two soldiers fell in behind him and Neville and the men disappeared.

The sound of the heavy steel door closing her in rang like the blade of a guillotine falling. Saying a prayer for Dirk and one for herself, Meg took a breath for courage and turned to face Otto Gertsman.

Dirk kept walking, his boots echoing on the cement floor. Raymond Neville, his hair short-cropped and brown today, along with the soldiers, one a tall blond, the other a big Argentine with very black hair, herded him toward a door at the end of the corridor.

The door appeared to be an outside entrance to the basement. They were taking him out of the house, a neater, cleaner way to dispose of him. Dirk walked in front, the two soldiers and Neville a few paces behind, all with their guns aimed at his back. Neville kept his pistol steady. The man was a professional. Once they were outside, he'd pull the trigger, and he wouldn't miss.

"Open the door," Neville instructed.

The two armed men moved past Dirk toward the exit. *Fatal mistake,* Dirk thought as his arm snaked out, wrapped around the

476

blond soldier's neck, twisted hard, and threw him off balance. At the same time Dirk grabbed the man's pistol, aimed, and fired a quick double tap into Raymond Neville's chest.

One down, two to go.

Dropping low and whirling, he aimed at the third soldier, realized he was going to be an instant too late. The echo of a shot rang out, but he felt no pain. Instead a blossom of scarlet appeared on the soldier's tan uniform in the center of his chest.

"Interpol," the blond man said, his small caliber backup weapon still smoking. "Helmut Mueller. We must go." Interpol's inside man. Dirk was damned glad to see him.

"I owe you big-time, Mueller." Both of them turned and began moving quietly back down the hall. Scooping up Neville's pistol along the way, Dirk checked the load, a full thirteen rounds in the Browning Hi-Power, a weapon made in Belgium and favored by British Special Forces. The gun felt good in his hands.

He returned the SIG he'd taken from Mueller as they moved in silent rhythm along the hall. With the echo of shots still ringing in his head, he expected Gertsman's army to descend on them any moment. He glanced at the blond man, who seemed to be reading his thoughts.

"Soundproof," Helmut said. "The whole floor."

Dirk felt a jolt of satisfaction. He smiled grimly and kept moving. A door opened up on his right. Dirk swung his weapon two-handed toward the threat, relaxed as Luke appeared, his custom Beretta aimed at Mueller's head.

"Don't shoot him," Dirk said. "He's Interpol. He's with us."

"Helmut Mueller," the man said.

"Luke Brodie. Glad you decided to join the party."

Dirk kept moving toward Meg, fury burning hot in his blood. He had to reach her, had to get her away from Gertsman. Luke caught up with him just as he reached the heavy steel door, reached out, and solidly gripped his shoulder.

"Slow and easy," Luke said. "Take a deep breath."

Luke was right. If he went in hot, he might get Meg killed. He was glad he'd put Luke in charge.

Pistol wrapped in both hands, he positioned himself on one side of the door. Luke and Helmut took the other. Dirk turned the knob, was relieved to find the door unlocked, and shoved it open.

He went in low while Luke went in high, both of them sweeping the room with the barrels of their semiautos. Dirk stopped dead cold when he spotted Meg standing off to one side, naked to the waist, her pretty breasts quivering, her hat still on. Her hands shook as they gripped Gertsman's pistol, aimed squarely at the big German's balls.

Dirk felt a slow smile spreading over his face.

Luke grinned. "That's my girl."

Shoving the Browning into the holster strapped to his thigh, Dirk strode toward Meg, grabbing her tunic off the floor along the way.

"Easy," he said, taking Otto's Walther P38 from her shaking hands and shoving it into the back of his tan uniform pants.

He pulled Meg into arms. "I've got you, baby. You're okay." He held her hard against him, felt her shaking. "You did great, honey. You're amazing."

"Yeah, Otto . . ." Luke strolled over to where Otto stood with his hands in the air. "You fucked with the wrong woman this time. You're lucky she didn't pull the trigger."

Gertsman's face turned a livid shade of red.

Meg buried her face in Dirk's chest. He caught a faint sob as she fought to hold back tears. "I th-thought they killed you."

Draping the tunic around her, he gestured toward the blond Interpol agent. "Neville's dead. That's Helmut Mueller. He's Interpol. He took out one of the bad guys."

Meg dragged in a shaky breath and nodded, turned away from the others to put on the tunic.

Helmut came forward, his weapon aimed at Gertsman. "I need to call this in to my people."

"You!" Otto spat at Mueller's feet. "Your family served mine for years. I thought I could trust you."

"Your family paid well and my family had to eat. They hated what your family stood for."

Gertsman's cold eyes shifted to Dirk. "You will never get out of here alive. My men have their orders. They will shoot you on sight. You will be dead before you reach the wall."

"He's right," Helmut said. "Unless he calls off his men, there is no way you can get out of here alive."

"Then I might as well just shoot him now," Luke drawled, raising his pistol.

"Better idea," Dirk said. "We take him

hostage. Walk right out of here with Gertsman in front of us."

The corner of Luke's mouth edged up. "Yeah, that was my backup plan. Good call." Luke shoved his semiauto into the big German's back. "All right, Otto, keep your hands over your head and let's go. I want to see you goose stepping out that door."

Otto didn't move. Dirk walked up and stuck his pistol beneath the German's fleshy chin. "You walk out now, we let you live. Helmut takes you into custody and one of your fancy lawyers has a chance of getting you out. You don't —" Dirk nudged the barrel a little deeper. "You're a dead man."

One look at Dirk's face and Gertsman knew he meant every word. Otto lifted his arms a little higher, turned, and started walking.

CHAPTER THIRTY-SEVEN

"Stay close," Dirk said. But Meg was already so close the leg of her borrowed uniform brushed against his thigh as they reached the back door and walked out into the yard.

Luke stopped at the edge of the terrace. The clouds had parted and the moon was out, offering plenty of light to see the enemy. More than enough for the soldiers to see Gertsman leading the procession across the yard.

"Hören Sie Menschen! Legen Sie Ihre Waffen auf dem Boden!" Helmut's voice rang with authority, telling the men to put their weapons on the ground. Luke repeated the order in Spanish.

A few complied, most just held steady. Luke and Helmut told the men Herr Gertsman was their prisoner. That the soldiers must let them pass or Gertsman would be killed.

The men grumbled between themselves

even as Luke pushed Gertsman forward. Dirk kept Meg close beside him. Helmut took the rear position, walking backward, providing some small degree of cover. Gertsman's hands remained above his head, Luke's pistol pressing into his spine.

The top of the wall was lined with armed soldiers, assault rifles slung across their chests, their fingers on the triggers. There were men outside the walls and half a dozen in the courtyard between them and the gate. Luke kept forcing Gertsman forward. If the man gave the slightest resistance, they would all be cut to pieces.

Dirk kept walking, Neville's pistol in hand, Gertsman's Walther riding in the small of his back. They were through the gate, outside the compound heading up the hill toward the forest, moving steadily forward.

Perspiration ran between Dirk's shoulder blades. He knew where on the hillside to look for Morgan Flynn, knew where the man had set up his sniper's nest. He was there, covering their movements, probably praying, same as Dirk, that Gertsman would just keep walking.

They had almost made it to the cover of the trees when Gertsman made his move. He pretended to stumble, pitched forward, and started shouting for his men to fire. Chaos erupted.

Men grabbed their rifles and pistols and started firing. Dirk laid down a line of fire, shoved Meg to the ground and followed her down, then both of them crawled toward the trees. Fired from his position on the hill, rounds from Flynn's big M40 .338 slammed into one target after another.

With Meg under cover behind a thick-trunked tree, Dirk continued firing, wounding a man to his left and downing one to his right as the soldiers tried to flank him. Flynn held his position, providing cover as they moved up the hill.

Luke grabbed a downed man's AK and slid in behind a granite boulder. Helmut was twenty yards farther up the hill behind a tree, laying down a steady stream of gunfire. Dirk turned to see Otto Gertsman below them, racing back toward the gate, a dead soldier's pistol in his hand.

Dirk fired his last bullet, tossed the Browning aside, and pulled the Walther, laid down a trail of bullets, kicking up dirt next to Otto's feet. The German slammed into one of his own men, dragged him in front as a shield, and started firing back.

The M40 on the hill sent a deadly bullet flying. The heavy slug tore through the soldier's chest and all the way through Otto Gertsman.

"We're half a click from the LZ," Luke said into his radio, speaking to Brandon Elliott, the chopper pilot. "We've got ten, maybe twelve men searching the forest behind us. They aren't far away."

"Roger that," said the pilot. "I'm ready. All you got to do is get here."

"Copy that." Luke tipped his head toward the top of the hill, urging the others to move. They didn't have far to go. The trick was to get there without being spotted.

Luke looked down at Meg, who walked next to Dirk, still wearing the tan uniform he had taken off one of Gertsman's men, though her hat was long gone, exposing her fiery hair. Luke and Dirk had stripped down to the camos they'd had on underneath.

"How you holdin' up, darlin'?" Luke asked.

She managed to smile. "You two got me this far. I'll make it the rest of the way."

"Good girl." Luke started walking. If Meg couldn't keep up, Dirk would carry her. So far she was hanging in, though the terrain was worse than rugged, a steep climb through heavy brush and fallen tree limbs. Tall pine forests cut by rushing streams and

485

big granite boulders surrounded them.

The night was gone, the sun coming up, turning the horizon a grayish pink and adding to the difficulty of staying out of sight.

"I hear it," Dirk said.

Luke caught the whine of the chopper engine seeping through the quiet woods. "We're almost there."

A minute later they stepped into the clearing, little more than a bare level spot fifty yards wide in a patch of wooded hillside. Elliott had to be damned good to set the big Sikorsky down at night without the rotors colliding with the branches of the trees.

They ran for the chopper, just the three of them. Helmut had peeled off as soon as they were away from the compound, disappearing silently into the woods. He knew the area, had contacts. He had a meet set with Interpol in Bariloche. What was left of Otto Gertsman's criminal empire was finished. Helmut Mueller had collected enough data to make sure of that.

Morgan Flynn stayed with them till they reached the LZ.

"If you ever need a place to light," Luke said above the roar of the engine and the whir of the blades, "plenty of work in Seattle."

Flynn smiled. "Thanks, but I've still got

places to go and people to see."

Dirk helped Meg into the chopper, turned, and shook Flynn's big hand. "We couldn't have made it without you."

Dirk followed Meg inside, strapping himself in beside her, while Luke strapped into the copilot's seat and pulled on a helmet. He caught Flynn's wave as the big man disappeared into the trees.

The engines revved and the chopper lifted away. Elliott made it look easy as he navigated the hostile mountain wind currents and guided the forty-foot blades through the tiny opening, into the early morning sky.

They were almost clear when a shout echoed from the tree line and gunfire erupted. Men spilled into the clearing, firing their weapons into the air.

"Fuck!" Luke grabbed the AK-47 assault rifle he'd confiscated during the firefight and laid down a burst into the soldiers below, sending them running for cover. Bullets dinged off the fuselage.

Dirk fired a steady stream as Elliott pulled back on the collective and the chopper shot higher into the air. It didn't take long before the clearing was far behind and they were heading for the tall mountains in the next range over.

Now all they had to do was navigate the

dangerous peaks and valleys of the treacherous Andes and hope nothing else went wrong.

Meg sat in the middle of the rear seat, strapped in next to Dirk. She needed to feel his powerful, hard-muscled body close beside her, needed to feel safe and protected.

With the roar of the engines and the *whop, whop, whop* of the rotors, it was too noisy to speak. But every once in a while she felt the squeeze of his hand holding hers or the brush of his lips against her hair.

There was so much she wanted to say. She prayed he was ready to hear it. But first they needed to reach the company jet waiting for them at the airport in Chile.

Meg closed her eyes as exhaustion rolled through her. Climbing the mountainous terrain to reach the landing site, combined with the fear of being recaptured or shot, had her muscles shaking with fatigue and her nerves stretched to the breaking point.

Wearing boots several sizes too big had rubbed blisters on her feet and the rough material of the uniform chafed her bare breasts beneath the tunic.

She felt Dirk's reassuring hand squeeze. It didn't matter how awful she felt. She was safe from Otto Gertsman. Charlie was safe and she was on her way home.

She leaned her head against Dirk's shoulder. The helicopter was flying through rugged, icy mountain passes instead of trying to top the chain of peaks that climbed more than twenty thousand feet into the sky.

The pilot she had met as she climbed aboard the chopper, Brandon Elliott, had managed to spirit them away from Gertsman's men. Now, as the chopper headed west, he seemed more than capable of navigating the Andes' jagged, snow-capped peaks.

The roar of the engine began to lull her. They were on their way home, on their way back to safety. Meg had just drifted to sleep when something changed inside the cabin. She roused herself to listen, realized the whine of the engine was different. A clattering had started, interfering with the rhythmic roar of the motor.

Dirk leaned forward, said something to Luke, who was wearing a helmet and able to communicate with the pilot. Whatever Luke said put the tension back in Dirk's shoulders.

He turned toward her, shouted loudly enough for her to hear. "Chopper took a hit when we lifted off. Elliott's looking for a place to set down."

Her stomach instantly knotted. Outside the window, nothing but snow and rocky, craggy peaks. Meg started shaking. So did the helicopter.

"No . . ." she whispered. *No! No! No!* Not when they were so close! Hadn't she been through enough? Hadn't all of them?

The sound changed again. The whining shifted to a strained, higher octave, followed by the grating of disintegrating metal. She looked past Dirk through the glass bubble, down at the white expanse of ground below them, closer now than it had been a few minutes ago.

"We're over the summit!" Dirk yelled. "We've crossed the border into Chile."

If he thought that would make her feel better, he was wrong. The mountains didn't end at the border. Where in God's name were they going to land?

The helicopter made a hard left turn, broke free of the sheer rock walls around it, shuddered, then seemed to fall out of the sky. Meg bit back a scream.

"We'll autorotate down. Just hold on!" Dirk tugged her seat belt tighter. Alarms were sounding, lights in the cockpit flashing all sorts of warnings. Dirk pushed her head toward her knees and wrapped her arms around the back of her neck, then took the same position himself.

Trembling all over, Meg slanted a look toward the window, saw the ground rushing up, heard what sounded like a piece of metal tearing free, felt the helicopter plummet, shudder again, then tip sideways, fall the last few feet, and plunge into the snow.

A jarring blow slammed her backward, then forward again. The rotors tore off. Sharp pieces of metal crashed into the laminated glass, slicing, ripping the helicopter to pieces. Meg didn't realize she was screaming until the chopper finally shuddered to a halt. She gasped for air, her head reeling. She heard the click of a seat belt and felt Dirk leaning over her, checking her for injuries.

"Are you hurt, baby? Tell me where."

She clamped down on her fear, tried to control her shaking. "I-I'm okay."

His hands ran over her a couple more times. He wiped a trace of blood off her cheek. "You've got a few nicks. I don't think it's anything serious. We're down, baby. We're okay." He was bleeding in a few places, too, trickles of red running down from his temple.

"What . . . what about Luke and the pilot?"

Dirk was already leaning over the seat, shutting down alarms and powering off systems, checking the other two men.

"They've got injuries. We need to get them out of here in case the fuel ignites."

"Oh, God."

Dirk caught her shoulder. "We're down. We're okay. All of us are going to make it out of here. Yeah?"

Meg took a shuddering breath and nodded. "I'll help you get them out."

Working together, they dragged out the pilot, who was unconscious. Meg pulled off Elliott's helmet while Dirk made sure he was breathing properly and checked for broken bones. Easing the man out of the plane, Dirk did a fireman's carry, hauling him far enough away to be safe if the chopper caught fire.

Meg made her way over to Luke. The door had been ripped away, making it easier to reach him. His eyes were closed and he was groaning.

"It's Meg. I'm right here, Luke." She removed his helmet. "Can you hear me?"

His eyes slowly cracked open and fixed like blue lasers on her face. "I hear you. . . . I think I'm okay." He moved, hissed in pain. "Well, mostly okay. Dirk?"

"He's helping the pilot. How badly are

you injured?"

He shifted a little, ground his teeth. "Broken collarbone, I think. My ankle hurts. I hope to hell it's not broken."

"Can you get out? Lean on me and I'll help you."

Luke flashed a pain-filled attempt at a smile. "Dirk hit the jackpot when he found you, darlin'." Raising his good arm, he draped it over her shoulder, leaned on her to hoist himself out of the chopper.

When he tried to stand, his ankle gave way. "Son of a bitch."

Dirk hurried over and took her place, draping Luke's good arm over his shoulder, helping him hop around the chopper, over to where the pilot lay on the snow.

For the first time Meg noticed the hand Dirk pressed against his side as he helped Luke lie down next to Elliott. "You're hurt. How bad is it?"

"Bruised a couple of ribs. Hurts like hell, but I'll live."

He reached up and wiped a trickle of blood from her forehead just below her hairline. "We're all pretty well banged up. Elliott's in and out of consciousness. He had a split in the back of his helmet where something hit him in the head. Looks like a bad concussion." He looked back at the chopper. "I need to check the radio, see if it's working, and get the survival gear."

Meg nodded. She wanted to just sit down on the snow and weep. Instead she pitched in to help Dirk salvage as much of the gear as possible, stripping the helicopter of everything they might be able to use.

"According to Luke," Dirk said as they worked, "Elliott got off a distress signal before we went down. The bad news is he didn't get a response, so there's no way to know if anyone heard it."

She turned to survey their surroundings. Above them, a ridge of jagged, snow-covered peaks ran as far as she could see. Below them, there was a line where snow had melted, revealing the bare ground underneath. Farther down the mountain the forest began. At least it was summer. She couldn't begin to imagine how brutal the place would be in the winter.

Meg shivered against an icy gust of wind and wondered how far it was to any sort of civilization.

CHAPTER THIRTY-EIGHT

Dirk began pulling gear out of the bags he had taken from the chopper. His ribs were aching, but he didn't think they were broken. The cut on his head could use a few stitches, but they'd found a first aid kit in the helo and Meg had helped him construct a butterfly bandage that would have to do. He'd have a scar, but he had plenty of those already.

"We've got a couple of one-man tents and a pair of sleeping bags," he told Meg. "Water and a couple of MREs — that's meals ready to eat. They're not too bad in a pinch. Elliott had a GPS and batteries in his gear bag. Looks like he carries a Glock nine mil. We've got plenty of weapons. Might be able to hunt up some food if we run out. I found blankets and a big canvas tarp in the helo."

He went back again to the old Sikorsky Elliott had been flying, scrounged around, brought back a handful of water bottles and a few more MREs.

Dirk walked over to Luke. They had immobilized his shoulder and packed ice around his ankle; best they could do for now.

"The radios are down," Dirk said. "No help there. The satphone took a hit. Case is smashed. It won't send, so we can't call anyone."

"Leave it on. It might be transmitting a signal. Maybe someone will pick it up."

Meg walked up just then. "Nick went to Chile on the jet. He's going to know something happened to us when we don't make it to the airport."

"Unfortunately he'll start looking in Argentina," Luke said. "He'll figure something went wrong with the op."

"We can't wait for someone to find us," Dirk said. "Not with Elliott's head injury and being low on supplies. We need to get the camp set up. Put up the tents and get everyone ready for the cold tonight. Elliott wisely chose to dump the chopper in the snow. Judging from the angle that blade sheared off, he probably saved our lives."

"Yeah, that was some flying," Luke said. "Amazing we didn't end up crashing into the side of the mountain."

Meg shuddered. Dirk shot a warning glance at Luke and put an arm around her shoulders. Meg didn't need to be reminded how close she had come to dying — again.

"Unfortunately we're going to freeze our asses off if the wind comes up," Dirk said. A flurry of snow whipped off the ground, proving his point.

He studied the terrain beyond the snow line, where the ground was ruthlessly steep and covered with dense forests and heavy vegetation.

"According to my GPS," he said, "we're only about fifteen miles from a road. If Luke and Elliott weren't injured, we could walk the hell out of here."

Luke sat up a little straighter. "Are you kidding? I just need to make myself a crutch and I'm good to go."

Meg rolled her eyes and Dirk grinned. "You need to stay here, keep Meg and Elliott safe. I'll head out for help. You can hold the fort till I get back."

Luke raised a dark eyebrow. "So you trust me with your woman?"

Dirk grinned. "After seeing what she did to Gertsman and you not being a hundred percent — yeah."

Luke laughed. It was a good sound, one that promised everything would be okay.

"Let's get this place tricked out," Dirk said. "Then I'm out of here."

By noon Dirk was ready to leave the camp. Elliott was conscious, with a pounding headache and fighting nausea. Without his helmet he was a good-looking, dark-haired man, powerfully built, with dark eyes, a strong jaw, and a cleft in his chin. Meg had used the snow to make an ice pack for the back of his head.

They'd used broken pieces and parts and cut up upholstery from the chopper to immobilize Luke's shoulder and get his arm in a makeshift sling. He downed a handful of aspirin from the first aid kit with a swig of water, then insisted Dirk make him a crutch out of a long strip of heavy aluminum he found.

Dirk figured a way to pad one end with chunks of foam rubber, and though Luke's shoulder must have been hurting like a bitch, he was hobbling around the camp as if the funny-looking crutch was attached to him.

They put up a lean-to against the relentless sun beating down on the glaring snow, and managed to locate a couple of pairs of sunglasses. Dirk shoved Elliott's wrap-around shades over his eyes and walked over to pitch the tents and get the sleeping bags ready. There wasn't much they could use for a signal fire, but he did the best he could, then soaked the debris with fuel dripping out of the chopper.

He strapped on a backpack he'd loaded with his GPS, a water bottle, and some energy bars. He'd run out of bullets for the Walther so he was carrying Elliott's Glock. His palm-sized .22 rode in his front pocket.

Gertsman's men had missed it. The little gun had been part of his escape plan as he'd walked down the hall with Neville, a desperate plan at best. Thanks to Helmut Mueller, he hadn't had to try it.

He was ready to head out when Meg walked up to him. "I wish I could go with you."

"You aren't dressed for it, baby. Those boots have to be killing you, and the truth is, you'd just slow me down."

She pressed her lips together and he could see she was fighting not to cry. "I know." She looked into his face. "I need to tell you something. You don't have to say it back. I just . . . I love you. I —"

"Jesus, Meg, you picked a piss poor time for this." Dragging her into his arms, he kissed her long and deep, ending the conversation. "I've got things I need to say to you, too, but not here. Not now. Not until we're out of here and safe. Yeah?"

"I just . . . I wanted you to know."

"Dammit, I love you, too. I wish we were somewhere else. Somewhere romantic so I could say it right."

She smiled, leaned up, and very softly kissed him. "You saved my life. There's nothing more romantic than that."

"Yeah?"

She smiled. "Yeah."

"We still have a lot to discuss."

"I know." She kissed him sweetly. "Please be safe. I don't want to lose you again."

Dirk started to tell her not to worry, that nothing could keep him from coming back. He'd spent weeks in the mountains of Afghanistan. The Andes were higher, just as harsh and remote, but he knew what he was doing. He had to get Meg safely home to her son. That was reason enough for him to return.

A distant sound caught his attention. It was the distinctive whopping of a chopper. Hope surged through him. He looked up to see a helicopter coming straight toward them. Dirk threw his hands in the air and started waving. Meg was jumping up and down, waving her arms and shouting.

"Light the fire!" Dirk shouted across the

camp, but Luke was already crouching down on the snow, setting the fire ablaze.

"They see us!" Meg shouted. "They're circling!"

Dirk watched the big red search and rescue B-429 hover, then sink lower, finally settle itself gently on the snow. When the heavy doors slid open, Nick Brodie jumped down from inside, followed by a two-man medical team who headed straight to where Elliott lay on the snow.

"Man, am I glad to see you," Dirk said as Nick walked toward them.

"Not as glad as I am to see you." Nick leaned in and clasped his shoulders in a solid man hug.

Meg hugged Nick, and Luke hobbled over to join them. "Good to see your ugly face, cuz. How the hell did you find us?"

Nick smiled. "The satphone. Sadie's been keeping track of our movements all along. When the signal stopped just over the border on this side of the Andes and you didn't show up at the airport, I figured you were in trouble. Sadie charted your last location and I called search and rescue at Puerto Montt. It's one of Chile's SAR bases, only seventeen miles from the airport at El Tepual."

"So as usual Luke was right," Dirk said.

"I'm damned glad you were on the jet instead of with us on the chopper."

Nick smiled at Luke. "Yeah, and I'm sure he'll never let us hear the end of it."

Luke just grinned.

It didn't take long for the rescue operations people to have Brandon Elliott secured and aboard, then Luke. Meg refused to go, determined to stay till the helicopter returned to bring Dirk and Nick out of the makeshift camp, along with what they could gather of their gear.

By the time the second group had reached the El Tepual airport, Luke had been patched up, Elliott had been admitted to a nearby hospital, and Interpol had phoned, clearing their way through customs. They owed Helmut Mueller again.

Once aboard the G6, Dirk settled next to Meg. He reached for her hand and held on tight, and Meg snuggled against him. She fell asleep on his shoulder before the jet surged up off the tarmac.

CHAPTER THIRTY-NINE

Meg paced the floor of her living room. It had been five in the morning Seattle time when the jet set down at Boeing Field, sixteen hours after leaving Chile.

Ron Nolan and two other FBI agents were waiting, along with an agent from the Department of Justice, the branch of U.S. law enforcement that worked with Interpol. The agents swept everyone on the plane directly into intimidating black SUVs with dark-tinted windows and drove them to FBI headquarters.

Meg had been separated from the men and questioned for hours, then released into the care of her dad, who drove her back to his house. She'd worried about Dirk, Luke, and Nick all the way.

Her mom and Charlie were waiting, hugging her and making her cry again, this time with joy. She sat on their living room sofa with Charlie on her lap, keeping him close, which for once he didn't seem to mind. Wisely, her parents hadn't told him about his mother's kidnapping or anything about where she was. He was just having a nice little visit with his grandparents, which Charlie had loved.

Though she had been missing for several days, there'd been nothing on the news, nothing in the papers. Interpol was still working the Gertsman case and they were determined no information would be leaked before they were ready.

Jonathan remained in custody. Apparently the international nature of the crime made him a flight risk. He wouldn't be getting out on bail.

After lunch, still tired though she'd slept for hours on the plane, she'd let her dad drive her and Charlie back home. She had phoned Mrs. Wills and told her that she was safely returned, but asked her housekeeper not to come over until the next day.

Meg needed time to unwind, as well as time with her son. And she was worried about what was happening with Dirk, Luke, and Nick.

Would the FBI arrest them? Her father had said the bureau had threatened retribution if they got involved in the kidnapping case. A rescue mission to Argentina definitely qualified as that. Her dad had a team of lawyers on standby in case the worst happened.

Meg glanced at the clock on the fireplace mantel in the living room for at least the hundredth time. The afternoon was ticking away, a cloudy, stormy day that matched her mood. Rain was predicted. She could hear the wind whipping the branches against the window.

"Time for your nap, sweetheart," Meg said, lifting her son into her arms and holding him close.

"Where's Dirk?"

"He'll be over later." Meg prayed that was true, that he wouldn't be in jail. She carried Charlie upstairs and put him in his youth bed, and he snuggled into his pillow.

For hours he'd been chattering about how much fun he'd had with Grandma and Grandpa, oblivious to how close his mom had come to dying.

He yawned and closed his eyes and she leaned over and kissed him. "Sleep tight, sweetie." Since her arrival at her parents' house, her little boy had worn himself out regaling her with tales of getting pizza, going for ice cream, and playing on the merry-go-round at the park. He was sound asleep in seconds.

Meg wandered back downstairs, feeling lost without her cell phone, which was somewhere in the white van the FBI was still trying to locate, along with the men who'd abducted her.

She wished Dirk would call. There was a landline in the kitchen. Twice she had almost phoned his cell, but she didn't think it was a good idea to call him while he was being questioned at FBI headquarters.

She meandered aimlessly around the kitchen, then heard the sound of footsteps coming up on the porch. *Let it be Dirk,* she thought, *not the FBI with more questions.*

Hurrying toward the door, she paused to look out the front window, saw Dirk's orange Viper parked at the curb, and her heart jerked. Quickly opening the door, she didn't wait for him to come inside, just threw her arms around his neck and hung on hard.

His hold tightened around her. "Hey, baby."

She eased back a little. "I was so worried. I was afraid they would arrest you."

His arms still around her, Dirk walked her backward into the house and closed the door. "The investigation's still ongoing. They didn't want the news media breaking the story. They'll probably have more questions, but Interpol vouched for us and it looks like we're all in the clear."

A sigh whispered out. "Thank God."

Dirk glanced around. "Where's Charlie?"

"I just put him down for his nap."

"He okay?"

She smiled. "He had a great visit with his grandpa and grandma. That's all he talked about. It wore him out."

"Good, then he'll be asleep for a while." Something hot came into his eyes. "I know we have a lot to discuss, but it's going to have to wait." He slid a hand behind her neck, tipped her head back, and very thoroughly kissed her.

"I almost lost you, baby. When I found out you'd been kidnapped, I went a little crazy. I forced myself to focus, to keep what might be happening to you locked out of my head. But it was nearly impossible to do. After everything that's happened, I need to be inside you. I need to feel you deep."

Meg's throat tightened. She didn't wait, just leaned up and kissed him. In Argentina she'd thought she might never see him again. "I need you, too."

Sliding his hands into her hair, he took her mouth in a fiery kiss, cupped the back of her head to hold her in place, and just kept kissing her. She could feel him rock hard against her. She understood his need, felt it, too.

They had almost died. She needed Dirk to make her feel alive again.

Dirk took the kiss deeper, hotter, stronger, lifted her a little and wrapped her legs around his waist; then he carried her into the family room. The backyard was fenced so no one could see them. Before she'd been a little shy about making love in there, but today she didn't care.

By the time Dirk set her on her feet next to the big overstuffed sofa, she was on fire for him. Meg framed his face in her hands and kissed him, felt the roughness of his sexy horseshoe mustache, reached for his long-sleeve T-shirt and pulled it off over his head.

Muscles rippled across his carved, powerful chest. His eyes were hot and dark as he reached for her, a man on a mission. In seconds he had her sweater and bra off. Meg toed off her sneakers while Dirk tugged down her skinny jeans and panties and tossed them away. She reached for the zipper on his faded jeans, but he beat her to it, buzzing it down, then sliding his jeans down far enough to free his erection.

Meg's insides flushed with heat. His big hands gripped her waist as he sat down on the sofa and pulled her down to straddle him.

"Your ribs," she worried.

"Doesn't matter," he said and fastened his mouth on one of her swaying breasts. She could feel the rasp of his whiskers against her skin and pleasure speared through her, slid out through her limbs.

Meg braced her hands on his wide, hard shoulders as damp heat settled in her core. When she pressed her mouth against the head of the dragon climbing up the side of his neck, a shudder moved through him. She loved his maleness, the way he could make her body respond with nothing more than a kiss. She loved everything about him.

"I can't wait," he said. "Not this time." He was trying to dig out a condom when she stopped him.

"I got a birth control shot in the hospital. We don't need it."

Heat glittered in his eyes. He lifted her a little and plunged, burying himself deep. With a groan that turned into a sigh, he pulled her mouth back to his and kissed her, softly this time, the sweetest, most achingly tender kiss she had ever known.

"I love you," he said. "So damn much."

He claimed her mouth again, sending all thought out of her head. Gripping her hips,

Dirk took her, driving hard, thrusting deep. Pleasure burned through her, grew hotter, fiercer. She climaxed hard, then came again.

She was his, he was telling her with his powerful body. She belonged to him.

And that was exactly what Meg wanted.

Naked at last and snuggled together on the sofa, Dirk kissed the top of Meg's head.

"So pretty," he said, toying with her breasts. They were plump and round, just the right size to fill his hands. "I almost shot Gertsman myself just for looking at them."

He could feel her smile. "You're making me want to jump you again," she said. "Unfortunately we have to get dressed. Charlie might wake up and come downstairs."

"I know."

She sat up and turned to face him. "That's what it's like when you have a child."

It was time for their talk, he figured. Time to get everything out in the open. They put their clothes back on, then sat back down on the sofa. He'd showered before coming over but hadn't taken the time to shave or get the haircut he so badly needed. Hell, he needed another eight solid hours of sleep, but this was more important.

"The truth is I don't know squat about

kids, Meg. I don't know if I can be the kind of dad Charlie deserves."

She reached over and caught his hand, laced her fingers through his. "Charlie loves you already. I love you, and you're the best man I know. I couldn't want a better father for my son." She squeezed his hand. "But it isn't always easy. It takes a lot of work to raise a child."

She was asking if he was willing to take on the job. Charlie was a good kid. With a little help, he'd grow up to be a good man. "I never had a real dad, not the kind who gave a damn about me. I'd do my best for Charlie."

Meg's eyes glistened. "I know you would."

Dirk got up from the sofa and began to pace. He wanted Megan O'Brien more than he'd ever wanted anything in his life. But not unless he was sure it would work for both of them.

"What about my job, Meg? I work security. You saw firsthand what that means."

She stood up, too. "Yes, I did. It means that you help people. What I saw firsthand was how good you are at what you do. Your work is important. You saved me and women Gertsman would have harmed in the future. I wouldn't want you to change who you are."

His eyes found hers. They had a lot going for them, but they were still far different people. He needed to be sure she understood. "Even if that's true, we've still got a problem."

"Which is . . . ?"

"I remember when you were on tour, Meg, the way you looked in those fancy designer dresses. You're opening a fashion boutique. Your father's a member of the country club. You'll be going to elegant parties, mingling with the elite. I wear jeans, Meg, not Armani suits."

She looked up at him and the love in her eyes made his chest feel tight. "Would you wear one if I asked you to? I mean, if it were something special I had to attend? I remember how hot you looked in that tuxedo you wore in New Orleans. Would you dress up for me if I asked you?"

Dirk couldn't stop a grin. *She thought he looked hot in a tux?* "When you put it that way, hell, yeah. Baby, I'd do just about anything for you."

Meg threw her arms around his neck. "I love you so much. We're going to have so much fun."

Dirk pulled her closer. "So . . . you gonna marry me?"

Meg leaned up and kissed him so thoroughly his blood began to pound. "I thought you'd never ask."

Dirk figured he could take that as a yes.

EPILOGUE

Meg had the table set and was finishing the spaghetti dinner she had cooked as she waited for Dirk and Charlie to get home. Dirk had gone for one of his rare haircuts, had taken Charlie for a trim as well.

The kitchen smelled of simmering ground beef, onions, and tomato sauce. She would slide the garlic bread into the oven as soon as her men got home. Val Brodie — she and Ethan had gotten married last month — had been teaching Meg to cook, and she thought she'd been doing a pretty fair job. Dirk and Charlie seemed to appreciate her efforts, and it wasn't really as hard as she'd imagined.

Even after opening She, her sportswear boutique — work she was loving — she had time to cook at least three meals a week. It turned out Dirk wasn't a half-bad cook himself so they traded back and forth as much as they could.

He was just about finished rebuilding his house at the lake. They'd decided to keep it, use it on weekends or just for a getaway spot when their jobs got too hectic.

A lot had happened since the kidnappings. Brandon Elliott had been released from the hospital in El Tepual just a few days after he was admitted. He was somewhere in South America with Morgan Flynn, off on another adventure.

Jonathan was in prison. He'd been charged with bank embezzlement, conspiracy to kidnap, accessory to murder, and half a dozen other crimes. He'd come up with information that had helped the FBI apprehend the two men in the van, then pled guilty to lesser charges. But he'd still be in prison for years.

Gertsman's criminal empire had crumbled; dozens of his cronies had been jailed in Argentina. Interpol had found plenty of evidence at the compound; Helmut Mueller had done his job. The place really was a fortress. In one of the outbuildings, they'd even found old canisters of deadly sarin nerve gas, originally invented by the Germans.

Meg shivered at the ugly memories of the time she had spent there. If it hadn't been for Dirk . . .

She broke off the thought at the sound of a car driving up in front of the house. Wiping her hands on the apron she wore over her jeans, she started toward the front door.

It swung open before she got there. Dirk ducked his head, Charlie on his shoulders, and walked into the entry.

"Hey, baby, sorry we're late."

"That's okay, but —" At the mischievous grin on his face, unease slid through her. "All right, what have you done?"

Charlie started wiggling. "Dirk sold the Wiper!" he shouted, grinning. "We got us a new car!"

"Oh, no." Disappointment trickled through her. She tried not to pout. "How could you sell the Viper? I loved that car."

"I know, baby, but it wasn't much good for a family." He set Charlie on his feet, reached out, and grabbed her hand. "Come on. The one I bought is a lot more practical."

Her lips refused to curve. "My car's practical enough. I liked the Viper."

Dirk just laughed and tugged her forward, out the door onto the porch. She gasped at the gorgeous metallic-blue, four-door Porsche parked at the curb.

"Four hundred twenty horses, honey. Zero

to sixty in less than six seconds. Tops out at nearly a hundred seventy miles an hour." He grinned. "Gets good mileage, too."

Meg started laughing.

"What?"

"I should have known you weren't ready for a station wagon."

Dirk grinned. "I got a good price for the Viper and a great deal on the Porsche. It's last year's model, but it's real low mileage."

Meg turned away from the car and looked up at him. "I love you, Dirk Reynolds."

"Me, too," Charlie said.

Dirk lifted the little boy and settled him against his shoulder as if he'd been a father for years. He caught hold of Meg's hand. "After we got our hair cut, Charlie and I had a talk. He thinks we've waited long enough. He wants us to get married."

Tears burned behind her eyes. Dirk hadn't brought up the subject since that day in the family room. "That's what Charlie wants. What do *you* want, Dirk?"

"I want to marry you more than anything in the world."

Her eyes welled. The sexiest man on the planet wanted her to marry him. The best man she knew. There was a time happiness had seemed so far out of reach. Meg looked at the two men she loved most in the world.

"I want to marry you, too," she said.
Dirk and Charlie high-fived each other.